KT-416-872

'The master of the Victorian detective novel turns to a modern whodunit; and a terrific job he makes of it'
The Times

'No one has done this kind of thing better since Dorothy L. Sayers. A must for crime buffs'   *Mail on Sunday*

'A consummate story-teller'   Colin Dexter, *The Oldie*

'A comedy of bad manners, full of oddball characters and wacky events develops into a perfectly realised murder mystery'   *The Wall Street Journal*

'A bravura performance from a veteran showman: slyly paced, marbled with surprise and, in the end, strangely affecting'   *New York Times Book Review*

'A marvellous achievement – masterfully plotted and totally absorbing'   *Deadly Pleasures*

'Peter Diamond may be my favourite fictional police detective – perky, dogged and very clever'   *Scotsman*

'Diamond is forever'   *The Sunday Times*

Novels by Peter Lovesey

Peter
LOVESEY
THE
REAPER

sphere

SPHERE

First published in Great Britain in 2000 by Little, Brown
Published in paperback in 2001 by Time Warner
This edition published in 2014 by Sphere

Copyright © 2000 by Peter Lovesey

The moral right of the author has been asserted.

*All characters and events in this publication, other than
those clearly in the public domain, are fictitious
and any resemblance to real persons,
living or dead, is purely coincidental.*

All rights reserved.
No part of this publication may be reproduced,
stored in a retrieval system, or transmitted, in any
form or by any means, without the prior
permission in writing of the publisher, nor be
otherwise circulated in any form of binding or
cover other than that in which it is published and
without a similar condition including this
condition being imposed on the subsequent purchaser.

A CIP catalogue record for this book
is available from the British Library.

ISBN 978-0-7515-5359-8

Typeset in New Baskerville by Palimpsest Book Production Ltd,
Falkirk, Stirlingshire
Printed and bound in Great Britain by Clays Ltd, St Ives plc

Papers used by Sphere are from well-managed forests
and other responsible sources.

MIX
Paper from
responsible sources
FSC
www.fsc.org   FSC® C104740

Sphere
An imprint of
Little, Brown Book Group
100 Victoria Embankment
London EC4Y 0DY

An Hachette UK Company
www.hachette.co.uk

www.littlebrown.co.uk

Vouchsafe O Lord, to keep us this day without being found out.

Samuel Butler

1

'May God forgive you.'
'You don't mean that, Bishop. You want me to roast in hell. I can see it in your eyes.'

The bishop muttered, 'That's what you deserve. You're the worst case I've come across. A wicked young man.'

'You have evidence?'

'In the car. A dossier this size.' Actually the shape the bishop made with his hands looked rather like a blessing.

'Then it's a fair cop.'

The young rector was taking it well – too well, flippantly even. He sat serenely on his swivel chair in his comfortable office in Foxford Rectory, his Wiltshire home. The bishop's summing-up was true. The Reverend Otis Joy was young, still in his twenties, and wicked. The afternoon sun through the leaded windows cast black bars over him, yet he managed to look benign, thanks to a generous mouth with laughter lines at the edges, a fine, straight nose and deep-set eyes of that pale yellowish brown that is disarmingly called hazel. A sharp intelligence lurked there.

The bishop, on the other side of the desk, did not appreciate what was going on. If you knew Marcus Glastonbury, you would not expect him to appreciate anything out of the ordinary. At the last General Synod, towards the end of his specially dull speech on improving communication in the Church, a pigeon that had crept through a window of Church House had fluttered down and perched on the microphone. Bishop Marcus was the only one who hadn't laughed.

'Speaking of cops . . . ?' Joy raised his eyebrows.

The bishop didn't follow him.

'. . . are they involved?'

'Oh.' A shake of the big, bald, consecrated head.

'Thank God for that.' Joy watched the bishop wince. 'Or would you rather we left the big fella out of it?'

The bishop drew in a sharp, shocked breath as if he had been struck. He was in danger of being undermined. 'I have not consulted anyone . . . yet.'

'Not even in prayer? He knows, anyway. No use pretending he doesn't.'

'It's a crime by any definition, secular or temporal,' said the bishop. 'There's no escaping that, which is why I'm here.'

'To do a deal?'

That suggestion was not received well. It drew forth a sound remarkably like a growl.

Joy leaned back, letting the chair rotate a little, and studied his accuser. He'd never seen old man Glastonbury dressed like this, in an ordinary blue shirt, striped tie and crumpled linen suit, perfect, he thought, for importuning in the park. It was supposed to make the bish less conspicuous, of course. This was the Church under cover, about to trade with the devil, disagreeable as it must be. The gleaming blue BMW had crunched onto his gravel drive without warning. A knock on the door and not a word of greeting when it was opened. Glastonbury had stood there with a bulging briefcase under one arm, which he handed to Joy to carry inside. No friendly handshake. No response to the usual courtesies. When a bishop refuses a whisky, watch out.

The bishop made an effort to seize the initiative again. 'Not to beat about the bush, you're an embezzler. You have systematically robbed the Church of funds. It's a criminal matter that ought to be reported.'

'But won't,' murmured Joy.

There was a shocked pause. 'I don't think I heard correctly.'

'You did.'

'I don't have to take such insolence from a parish priest. I'm looking for some sign of contrition.'

'Like grovel, grovel?'

'I can't believe what I'm hearing. I was told you were a first-class priest, popular, hard-working, a most able preacher who fills the church most Sundays.'

'The people fill the church, my lord.'

'Your previous parish, St Saviour's, has the highest opinion of you.'

'This is about St Saviour's?'

'Yes.'

'Who blew the whistle, then?'

'I did.'

'You?'

Bishop Glastonbury tilted his head in a superior way and for a moment it caught the light and shone as if he were freshly anointed. His vanity was well known in the diocese. 'I take an interest in all my parishes. After you left, and the new vicar arrived, there was a spectacular improvement in the St Saviour's income.'

'That's a matter for rejoicing.'

'It increased by something like forty per cent.'

'A miracle.'

A cold stare. 'But there was no obvious reason. The

church membership actually dropped away after you left. I make it my business to study the parish returns at the Diocesan Board of Finance, so it came to my attention. They're all on my computer at Glastonbury. Any departure from the norm stands out. I sent for the bank statements. I looked at the books. What I discovered shocked me more than I can say. I was forced to the conclusion that—'

'I had my fingers in the till?'

'The collection plate.'

'Get real, my lord.'

The bishop twitched again.

Joy told him, 'I'm not such a dumbo as to help myself to twenty quid's worth of small change.'

'I was speaking figuratively. If it *had* been the collection plate you were robbing, the parish would have got onto you before this. I had to dig deep to find the discrepancies.'

'And you did?'

'Eventually. The bogus bank accounts. Two roof funds, set up with different banks.'

'Ah.' Joy raised a hand like a footballer acknowledging a professional foul.

'The so-called parish rooms account.'

'That, too.' He lifted the other hand.

'I put up one hypothesis after another to explain the unthinkable, a priest who systematically robs his own church. It was so monstrous that I confided in no one else. You can't share suspicions like that until you're absolutely sure.'

'Dead right, my lord.'

'So this is a private visit. As far as my staff are concerned, I have an afternoon off. That's why I'm dressed informally. I wanted to put the charge to you in person. I hope to hear that it's a misunderstanding.'

'But that would be a lie.'

The logic escaped the bishop. 'Consider your position. You're one of the best regarded young priests in the diocese. Don't you have anything to say in mitigation?'

'Before you pronounce judgement?'

'Before we talk about the next step.'

'Ah – the next step.' Joy's eyes glittered. 'What are you after? Your cut?'

Shock, extreme shock, set Marcus Glastonbury's mouth agape like one of the gargoyles on the roof of his cathedral. 'That's abominable.' He looked about him as if for support from the shelves of religious books, the palm crosses pinned to the notice board, the gilt-framed print of *The Light of the World* and the solid glass paperweight of St Paul's Cathedral. 'Have you no shame?'

'I find it gets in the way. What do you expect – wailing and gnashing of teeth?'

The bishop made a huge effort to get control of his features again. 'You realise, of course, that it's over. You can't continue in the Church.'

'This church? St Bartholomew's? They haven't complained, have they?'

'The Church of England. You're finished, Joy. You must resign the priesthood.'

'Resign?' The young man made it sound like a foreign word.

The bishop played it down a little. 'We'll find some form of words. A nervous breakdown, some unspecified illness. There are ways it can be handled.'

'I'm not the first, then?'

'And you must make good the money you took. What did you do with it?'

'Blew it.'

'But on what?'

Otis Joy rotated the chair and looked out of the window

at the bishop's beautiful car. 'On the trappings of success. Monstrous, isn't it, the cost of keeping up appearances?'

Marcus Glastonbury's voice piped up in outrage, 'I won't let you get away with this.'

'Vengeance is mine, saith the lord bishop.'

It crossed Joy's mind that he might have done himself more good by quoting from the Sermon on the Mount on the subject of mercy, but he doubted if it would make much impression on this bishop. Instead he was compelled to embark on another strategy. He turned the chair to face the front again, pointing a thumb over his shoulder at the BMW parked on his drive. 'The Church does all right. It can afford to write off a few grand. It's a major player in the property market, owns big chunks of London.'

'That's deplorable.'

'How right you are. And it pays peanuts to the clergy.'

'That isn't what I meant. It's deplorable that a priest should characterise the church in such a way.'

'Face facts, Bishop. Lambeth Palace doesn't want a major scandal.'

'Is that a threat?'

'It's why you're here. You see, I don't intend to hang up my dog-collar, not for you or anyone. They call this a living, which means for ever. Or till you find me another just as suitable.'

'But you're morally corrupt. How can you possibly continue as a priest?'

'I won't be the only one.'

Their two minds were not in tune, nor ever likely to be.

The bishop became more practical. 'If you can't pay back the money immediately, we can make an arrangement, so much a month.'

'And I continue here?'

'Absolutely not. You're unfit for the ministry. I've offered you a discreet way out and you must take it. We'll use your PC.'

Otis Joy played the words over in his mind. The parish council? The local bobby?

With the air of a man who has just scored the winner, his visitor pointed to Joy's own personal computer on the table against the wall. 'You will sign a letter of resignation.'

'A computer-literate bishop, for all that's wonderful.'

Now the bishop picked up the briefcase and took out a laptop, like a service engineer preparing the invoice. He placed it on the desk in front of him, opened it and started tapping the keys.

Joy asked, 'Is this resignation letter already on disk?'

'In draft form. It doesn't go into details. You and I know the reasons behind this and there's no need for the rest of the diocese to rake over the embers. There.' He passed the laptop across the desk.

'I'm impressed,' said Joy. 'Do they issue these to all bishops?'

'Read it, man.'

Appropriately the little screen was heavenly blue. The words were less attractive.

I, Otis Joy, Rector of St Bartholomew's Church, Foxford, beg leave to resign from Holy Orders with immediate effect. This is for personal reasons. It is final and irrevocable.

'Bit terminal.'

'Do you agree the wording?' demanded the bishop, obviously feeling he had the upper hand now. 'We'll download onto your machine and do a print-out for you to sign.'

'Right now?'

'If they're compatible.'

'More than you and me. Don't I get time to think about it?'

'I shan't leave without your resignation. And I want a written undertaking to repay the Church the sum you embezzled, which I estimate at not less than fifteen thousand pounds.'

'Is that on the machine as well?'

'No. We'll do this first.'

'OK.' Joy handed the laptop back to the bishop. 'You'll need paper for the printer.' He opened a drawer, took out a sheet of headed notepaper and handed it across.

This sudden act of capitulation was greeted with a nod that was part satisfaction, part triumph. The high-tech bishop crossed the room and sat at the rector's modest machine. He connected his laptop, switched on and touched several keys.

'I must see this.' Joy got up and came around the desk and stood at the bishop's shoulder.

The text of the letter appeared on the screen.

The bishop touched more keys and fed in the sheet of paper. The printer hummed and brought forth the resignation.

'There.' He took a silver Montblanc fountain pen from his pocket and unscrewed the top. 'Sign.'

The pen was not required. Unseen by the bishop, Otis Joy had snatched up St Paul's Cathedral. He swung it with tremendous force at the back of the big, bald head.

The impact of solid glass against bone was irresistible. Marcus Glastonbury was killed by the first blow. He got two more to be certain.

After a wedding rehearsal in the church – but before rigor mortis set in – Joy returned to the rectory, his pastoral duties over for the day. He felt as shaky as anyone does with a dead bishop waiting for disposal, but he was in control. He trusted himself not to panic. In fact he was experiencing quite a surge of adrenalin at the challenge of the things to be done. A clergyman's life is more structured than lay people ever appreciate, and there is quiet satisfaction at coping with whatever life throws at you and still conducting services on time. He confined himself to a quick supper of pilchards on toast, a banana and a can of beer, whilst thinking over the fine points of his arrangements. He had a plan. When you live with the prospect of someone like Marcus Glastonbury knocking on your door, you think through the options you have. He was a keen student of criminology.

For example, he knew about forensic science. He knew better than to leave traces on his clothes. The blood-spotted stock and dog-collar he'd been wearing that afternoon were already in a plastic sack awaiting disposal.

Before doing anything else about the late Marcus Glastonbury, he went upstairs and stripped completely. As if he was well used to going naked, he padded downstairs to the kitchen, put on rubber gloves, and went to the office to check the scene. The body still lay where it had fallen in front of the computer table. The head wound had seeped badly. Otis Joy was not a man for profanities, but this could only be described as a bloody mess. The old Wilton rug he had inherited from the previous incumbent would definitely have to go.

He knelt beside the dead bishop, not in prayer, but to remove anything that might link him with the killing. An entry in a diary, or a scrap of paper with the rectory address would be a gift to the plod. Through his job the rector had a privileged relationship with death, so he didn't flinch as he went through the bishop's pockets and made a small heap on the desk. Car keys and a pocket bible.

A wallet thick with banknotes and plastic. The high life: American Express, Mastercard, Visa, the Vintage Wine Club. What was it St Paul wrote in his First Epistle to Timothy? 'A bishop then must be blameless . . . sober, of good behaviour . . . not given to wine . . . not greedy of filthy lucre.' Maybe the filthy lucre was meant for charity. Maybe flying saucers have landed. He found the diary, noted that there was no entry for this day, and put it back. He put the cap on the Montblanc pen and replaced it in an inside pocket. Replaced two twenty pound notes and everything except the car keys, one of the credit cards and the bible.

Then the doorbell rang.

The clergy are used to unexpected callers, but Joy had suffered one already. This was inconvenient. He was tempted to ignore it. Then he remembered his car was standing on the drive, unlocked, advertising that he was at home. He had taken the precaution of backing it out of the garage, and putting the bishop's BMW out of sight in there.

Suppose someone was dying and wanted a last Sacrament. He hoped not, for both their sakes. Standing up, he remembered he was naked and looked round for something to cover himself.

The bell rang again.

He fetched an apron from the kitchen and, like Adam, tied it around his waist.

He opened the front door a fraction, just enough to peer round, with only his head and one bare shoulder showing.

'Oh, great timing!' There was an embarrassed laugh from one of his younger parishioners, Mrs Rachel Jansen, blond, slender, unthreatening – if any caller can be called unthreatening when there's a corpse back there on the office floor.

He told her, 'I'm on a messy job. You'll have to excuse me.'

She said, 'I can easily call back when you're decent, Rector. I mean—'

She had turned quite red.

'No,' he said with more force than either of them expected. 'It's all right. I'm wearing something.' He opened the door wider to prove it.

The sight of the young rector in yellow rubber gloves and a striped apron did not lessen Rachel Jansen's embarrassment.

He smiled at her. 'Saves my kit.'

She nodded several times, humouring him. She seemed unable to speak.

'What can I do for you?'

She took a step away, raising her hand dismissively. She found her voice again, and it was nervous. 'Really. Don't trouble.'

'Out with it, Mrs Jansen.'

She was trying to find an exit line.

'Fire away,' insisted Joy.

The words came in a rush. 'The day before yesterday I put a white plastic sack through your letterbox. Help the Aged. Old clothes. Isn't that it behind you at the bottom of the stairs?'

He glanced over his shoulder, taking care not to present his back view. It was the Help the Aged sack and it contained his bloodstained clothes.

'If you look,' said Rachel Jansen, 'it's printed on the side.'

'I'm sure you're right.' He was trying to give the impression of calm. 'Hang on. I meant to put in something else.' He took two steps backwards as if Mrs Jansen was the Queen, snatched up the sack, backed further to the

kitchen and tipped everything out and grabbed two perfectly good shirts he had washed the day before and left
on hangers to dry over the boiler. He stuffed them into
the sack and returned to the door. 'Hope these will do.'

She thanked him and left, still pink at what she had
seen, or almost seen.

He closed the door and said aloud, 'Joy, my boy, you
don't come closer than that.'

The next phase of the plan was to remove the body from
the office. The bishop was no lightweight. Joy hauled him
to the centre of the Wilton and dragged rug and corpse
across the polished floor, through the hall and kitchen
to the back door of the garage. Opened the boot of the
BMW, took a grip under the arms, lifted the torso to a
sitting position, braced like a weightlifter, made a supreme
effort and heaved the upper body high enough to flop over
the storage space. With the main weight in position, raising
the legs was easier. He persuaded them in and threw the
rug over the corpse and brought down the lid. It was good
to have the thing out of sight.

Work remained to be done: office work, he told himself
with a smile. He fetched a bucket, filled it with hot water
and detergent and used an old-fashioned scrubbing-brush
on the bloodstains.

The floor looked better after repeated scrubbings. No
doubt a scene-of-crime team would find plenty to interest
them, but he had no intention of letting such people into
his office.

He took a shower, changed into a sweatshirt and jeans
and passed a salutary half-hour studying the dossier from
the car. The bishop had gone to some trouble assembling
all this evidence of malpractice. Five years of bank statements and photocopies of the St Saviour's parish accounts,
with copious marginal notes in red and more pages of

calculations. Copies of his (under)statement of income to the Church Commissioners, ensuring that he got the maximum stipend. Grisly reading. The only good thing about it was that apparently no one else had seen it.

He tore each sheet into small pieces and made a fire in the grate in the dining room. Whilst the evidence was turning to ashes, he fetched the bishop's laptop from the office and got to know the controls. The resignation letter wanted some modification now. He deleted his name and substituted the bishop's. Then he made more adjustments. The wording on the screen now read:

> *I, Marcus Glastonbury, Bishop, profoundly regret the embarrassment my actions must cause the diocese and the Church. I can see no alternative.*

After reading it through, he added the words *Pray for me.*

He opened the bishop's briefcase and looked for stationery. He found a sheaf of notepaper headed with the address *The Bishop's Palace, Glastonbury*, and printed the note. As a final touch he opened the pocket bible, looked up the parable of the prodigal son, underlined the phrase '. . . hath devoured thy living with harlots . . .' and slotted the white ribbon marker in place.

After midnight, he returned to the garage and took his Moulton fold-up bike – with the characteristic small wheels and Hydrolastic suspension – from its hook on the wall. A Wiltshire product, his farewell gift from a grateful congregation at St Saviour's, that little bike was going to come in useful tonight. He stowed it on the back seat of the BMW. He put on gloves, started up and drove out into Rectory Lane. Small risk of being seen; less of being recognised. People noticed the dog-collar before they looked at anything else. Without it, he could drive through the village in broad daylight and they would look straight through him.

The young rector's leisure-time reading in forensic science provided him with the useful knowledge that when a body is moved after death the post mortem signs are not so reliable as pathologists once supposed. Hypostasis, the gravitational effect of blood cells, was once believed to show how the body was lying immediately after death, but more recent studies showed that secondary gravitation could take place. When a body was moved to a new position, the hypostasis relocated as well after a further few hours.

He drove ten miles into Somerset around the town of Frome and out on the Shepton Mallet Road, the A361, stopping at the all-night filling-station. But not for petrol. As the bishop himself had remarked, Otis Joy was a wicked young man. He bought a copy of *Men Only,* and studied it for a time. Then he took it to a payphone and used the bishop's Visa card to call one of the sex lines advertised in the back pages. 'Madam Swish, able with a cane' seemed a neat match for a bishop. He let the recording run on for a good ten minutes before hanging up. If the police were any good at their job, they would check the credit card statement when it came in. Marcus Glastonbury alive at 12.40 a.m. Alive and kinky.

At Nunney, he left the main road for the country lanes, into an area he had once walked. The site he had in mind was a disused quarry, one of several around the village of Egford where the local stone was mined. This one had been left with a massive face of rock where the exposed carboniferous limestone could be seen tilted and folded under the more even Jurassic strata.

It was pleasingly quiet out here. A fox crossed the lane, turning confidently to look at the car. Small, white moths swooped into the beam of the headlamps. He spotted the sign ahead saying *Quarry: Strictly No Admittance.* Pulled up and got out to pull the chain off the gatepost. Drove in and along a track rutted by heavy lorries. Up a steep incline to the highest point of the hill overlooking the excavation.

This was it, then. He stopped and got out. There wasn't enough moonlight to see much, and certainly not the length of the drop. It didn't matter. He knew he was standing at the top of a sheer cliff at least a hundred feet high. He got in again and backed the car close to the edge, switched off, got out, opened the boot, pulled back the Wilton rug. He didn't enjoy sliding his hands under the torso and drawing it towards him in a macabre embrace. He hauled the thing out: awkward, back-straining work. With an extra effort he succeeded in taking the weight on his shoulder and staggering to the edge, where he first let the corpse flop on the ground for fear of falling over himself.

He stood for a time, recovering his strength.

Crucial things remained to be done. He replaced the credit cards in the pocket of the bishop's jacket. Rolled up the bloodstained rug. Removed his trusty little bike from the BMW and snapped it into shape. Moved the car away from the edge and parked it a few yards back with the doors unlocked and the keys in the ignition. The suicide note, the bible and *Men Only* would tell their own story on the passenger seat.

One last effort, then.

He bent down to roll the body over the edge, into the quarry. Grappled with the slack, solid bulk, sickening to the touch, and got a surge of relief when it tipped over. There was the satisfying sound of shifting rubble as it struck something far below. Then silence.

This might have seemed the right moment to offer up a

prayer, if not for the bishop, then for himself. Not so. He was more concerned about things on earth. With a leafy branch he swept away his footmarks.

He rubbed his hands, got on his bike and rode off with the bloodstained rug. It ended up two miles away, face down and weighted with stones in the River Frome, where it was soon invisible under a layer of mud.

Then he cycled home.

2

Chocolate cakes were in heavy demand at the Foxford Church fete, held in the rectory garden. The devil's food, Black Forest, death by chocolate, brownies, chocolate fudge and chocolate orange sold in the first hectic ten minutes, before anyone bought coffee or lemon. Apple cake was almost as popular. In fact, anything with fresh fruit in it, cheesecake, pies and tarts included, sold easily. Rich fruit cakes, being more of a winter treat, were slower to go, but they found customers in the first hour.

Rachel Jansen was assisting. She would have been better on the garden stall, because she knew as much about plants as anyone in the village, but a local nurseryman had an arrangement with the organisers and sold his own produce, giving a percentage to the fete profits. The honour of running the cake stall went to Cynthia Haydenhall, the Chair of the Women's Institute, who behaved as if she had cooked them all herself. Rachel enjoyed Cynthia's company in the way she enjoyed rum truffles and Bette Midler: in small delicious amounts. Cyn was fun and the source of wonderful gossip, and she liked to dominate. Her improbably black hair was scraped back, bunched and fixed with Spanish combs, suggesting that when things went quiet she might climb on the trestle table, clap her hands and perform a noisy flamenco over the cakes. There was no chance of people ignoring her.

She had made it clear at the beginning that she would run the show, price the cakes, sell them and keep things tidy. To be fair, the system worked. They reached the point when the only cakes left were a slab of Madeira as solid as cheese, some weary-looking coconut pyramids and Miss Cumberbatch's toffee crispies, steadily congealing into a solid mass attracting wasps.

'Should we cover these?' Rachel suggested to Cynthia, knowing it was unwise to do anything without asking.

'The toffee dreadfuls? I don't know what with, amigo. We've only got this roll of kitchen towel, and that will stick to them.'

'They won't be saleable if we let the wasps crawl all over them.'

'It's an open question if they ever were saleable. Is Miss Cumberbatch still here?'

'Over by the bottle stall, with her brother.'

'Right.' With that decision made, Cynthia dipped below the table for a cake tin. 'In here, while madam has her back turned. I'll dispose of them later.'

'We can do the same with the others. They're never going to sell now.'

Rachel should have known better than to make two suggestions in the space of a minute.

'Oh, yes they will,' Cynthia informed her. 'The rector hasn't been round yet. Last year at the end of the fete he bought everything off the stall just so that no one's feelings were hurt.'

They looked across the lawn to where the Reverend Otis Joy was trying the coconut shy. On this warm afternoon not many had bothered with it. His throw missed the coconuts by a mile, perhaps on purpose. The rector wasn't supposed to win things.

'So he gets the cakes nobody wants,' Rachel said. 'Poor

guy. He deserves better. We should have saved something he can eat.'

'We don't know what his taste is.'

'I bet he likes chocolate. Devil's food cake. All men go for that.'

Cynthia vibrated her lips at the idea. 'You can't offer devil's food to a bible-basher.'

'He'd see the joke. He's got a sense of humour.'

'In spades,' Cynthia agreed. 'He could tour the clubs with his sermons.'

'As a stand-up?'

Their eyes met and each of them stifled a giggle.

'And he's so relaxed about everything.'

'Not a bad looker, either,' said Cynthia.

'Generous, too. He'd give you the shirt off his back,' said Rachel, her thoughts returning, as they had more than once, to the afternoon when she'd called for the Help the Aged sack. The rector in his apron was sharp in her memory. The crop of silky dark hair across his chest had been a revelation.

'That's what Christianity is all about,' said Cynthia.

'Oh?'

'It's his job. Thinking of others.'

'But it's easy to be generous if you can afford it,' Rachel pointed out. 'Vicars don't earn much.'

'Don't you worry about him,' said Cynthia. 'He lives rent free in the largest house in the village. He's always smartly dressed. I expect he has a private income, on top of his stipend.'

'Is that possible?'

'Of course it is. Family money. Stocks and shares. Property. He could be better off than we are.'

Rachel thought back to the two shirts in the Help the Aged bag, not frayed at the cuffs and not a button missing.

Cynthia returned to the subject of the cakes. 'Leave out the coconut pyramids, anyway,' she summed up. 'They're edible. Not everyone's choice, that's obvious, but Otis can well afford them. We'll spare him the Madeira. It could sink the *QE2*, by the look of it.'

The way the 'Otis' tripped casually from Cynthia's tongue was noted, as she intended. Every woman in the parish was on tenterhooks to see who would make a play for the rector. Cynthia wasn't on first-name terms. Who did she think she was kidding? As a divorced woman living alone she might consider herself a catch, but she was at least eight years older than he was, if not ten.

Rachel, at twenty-eight, was about his age, and trapped in a childless marriage with Gary, forty-two, pot-bellied and trying to beat hair loss by training his side bits across the top.

As for the rector, the word from his previous parish was that he had been married to a pretty French woman, who had died quite suddenly.

Tragic. He deserved a second chance at matrimony. But not with Cynthia, surely.

And now he had taken his three throws and missed, and was striding across the lawn towards them. He'd taken off his blazer for the coconut shy and swung it over one shoulder. In his sunglasses and straw hat, he could have passed for a youthful Harrison Ford.

He stretched out his hands. 'This is where the action is. I couldn't get near until now. Tell me, ladies, is it you, or the cakes?'

'Well, the cakes have all gone, but we're still here,' said Cynthia, beaming and entirely missing the point.

'Am I too late, then? No, I see you have some of my all-time favourites – marguerites.'

'Coconut pyramids, actually.' Cynthia couldn't resist correcting him.

'Whatever. I'll take them. And the damage, Mrs Haydenhall?'

Rachel heard and savoured that little touch of formality.

'You can have them for thirty pence,' said Cynthia.

'No special price for the clergy,' said the rector. 'I'll pay full whack.'

'Twenty-five, then,' Rachel said at once.

He thought a moment, then laughed, and looked at Cynthia. 'You weren't *over*-charging me?'

'It was worth a try,' said Rachel. She was careful not to look at Cynthia. 'In a good cause.'

When the rector had moved on, bag of cakes in hand, to the next stall, Cynthia said to Rachel, 'What a strange thing to say. It made me look quite foolish.'

There was an unkind answer to that, but Rachel held herself in check. 'Just a bit of fun, Cyn. He knew what was going on. They're human, you know.'

Cynthia turned her head like a hen and looked in the opposite direction.

Rachel nudged her in the ribs. 'I saw him eyeing up *your* coconut pyramids.'

She swung around, her spirits restored. 'Go on – you didn't!'

'He fancies you something rotten.'

'The rector?' Cynthia's eyes shone. 'He ought to be ashamed of himself.'

Not far away, someone else was discussing the rector. Owen Cumberbatch had recently come to live with his sister in Foxford. Tub-shaped and triple-chinned from many years' consumption of pub food and beer, Owen had been a publican all his adult life, steadily drinking the profits. When the brewery retired him, he no longer had a home, so he appealed to his family for help, and his youngest sister, being single and in possession of a good house, was the family's choice for fall guy. Owen was already well known in Foxford as a man eager to impress, claiming friendship with Peter O'Toole, Denis Thatcher, Placido Domingo, Tiger Woods and the late John Lennon, and the names were always prefaced with 'my old chum'. To be fair, he usually had some intriguing inside knowledge of his chums to confide, just enough to create uncertainty.

Pausing by the bottle stall, he was telling Bill Armistead, the organiser of the Neighbourhood Watch scheme, outrageous things about the rector's career as a serial killer. 'Oh, yes, he's clever with it, but there's no denying he did away with several in his last parish, including his wife and the sexton. I lived in the next town, you see, so I saw what was going on.'

'I didn't know sextons still existed,' said Armistead, sidestepping the main issue. He didn't want to be caught discussing such slanderous nonsense.

'There's one less at St Saviour's, Old Morden, I can tell you that,' said Owen with a smile.

'What do they do exactly?'

'Sextons? Look after the building and the churchyard, dig the graves and toll the bell, of course. This one was an awkward cuss, I heard. He disappeared one night. He's on the missing persons' list to this day, but no one's going to find him. Only Otis Joy knows where he is, and he won't tell.'

Armistead looked about him. Nobody was close enough to listen. 'What would a man of God be doing, knocking people off? I can't believe a priest would kill people.'

'That's the clever part. No one suspects him.'

'Except you.'

'Except me, yes. It's an ideal situation for a serial killer when you think about it. A position of trust. Nobody expects the priest to slip them poison in the communion wine.'

'Now that's ridiculous.'

'There you go. You don't believe he'd do it, so he'd get away with it.'

'You've got a fertile imagination, Owen, but you want to be careful. If he's really in the murdering line, he'll top you one of these days for spreading stories like this.'

Owen took that as a compliment. 'I'll watch out for him, then, be on my guard day and night.'

At last came the time when the raffle was drawn, the bottles of sweet sherry, the knitted dolls, the cheap chocolates and the baskets of fruit claimed, and they could dismantle the stalls. The cakes had raised over eighty pounds. Cynthia strutted across to hand the money to Stanley Burrows, the parish treasurer, confident that *her* stall had raised more than any other.

Rachel was left to deal with the trestle table. She didn't mind. It was a relief to do something her own way. And even better when someone behind her said, 'You can't lift this on your own.'

She knew the voice. A little *frisson* of excitement fizzed through her.

Together, she and the rector carried the table across to the church hall and stacked it with the others. 'How about a cuppa in the rectory?' he offered.

Blushing, she said, 'That's kind, but—'

'It's open house. Other people are coming.'

'Oh. In that case . . .'

'And I won't be serving coconut pyramids.'

She laughed. 'Saving them all for yourself?'

'Don't ask.'

'But the whole point about the pyramids is that they were built to last, weren't they?'

'Not these.'

The great and good of the parish gathered in the rectory and Rachel was disturbed to find that through some oversight Cynthia had been left out. It couldn't have been deliberate. She went outside to look for her, but she had definitely gone. She would have wanted to be there, and should have been.

Returning, she went into the kitchen to help, not from altruism, but to get a sight of how the rector lived. The kitchen was huge, old-fashioned and spotless.

Two full kettles were slowly coming to the boil. He was alone in there unwrapping biscuits, trying inexpertly to loosen the paper at the top.

'Careful,' she said, and some little demon made her add, 'You may need your apron.'

His eyes flashed and he was quick to respond, 'I only put it on to answer the door.'

She showed him how to cut the packet with a knife. She arranged the biscuits on a plate and offered to carry them in.

'Great idea – but not till I pour the tea. The Potter children.'

'Are they keen on biscuits?'

'Anything. On the last Sunday school outing, Kenny Potter ate three people's picnic lunches and was sick before we got to Weymouth.'

'Watch out, then,' said Rachel. 'I saw him with his sisters going through the hamburgers this afternoon, followed by candy floss.'

He pulled a face. 'Pink alert.'

She laughed. 'So how can I be useful?'

He gave that a moment's thought and said mysteriously, 'By not being useful. Take a seat. Relax.' He went on to explain, 'You've been hard at it all afternoon. This is my chance to thank you.'

'And all the others,' she pointed out.

'And all the others,' he repeated in a downbeat tone that Rachel took as a compliment.

Since this seemed to be getting personal, she said, 'But you've been on duty like the rest of us.'

'So I have,' he said. 'Let's forget the others and clear off to the pub.' He aimed two fingers, pistol-style, at his head. 'Joke. Shouldn't have said that, you a married woman, and me . . . I think we're coming to the boil, don't you?' He took a large blue teapot to the kettle and warmed it in the approved fashion before tossing in several teabags. 'And if anyone mentions coffee, pretend you didn't hear.'

Rachel carried in the first tray. This wasn't her imagination. The rector was getting frisky. If that was what the church fete did to him, what was he like after a couple of beers?

She didn't find out that evening, though she stayed long enough for a glass of the elderflower wine he had bought from the bottle stall. With a couple of other people she helped stack up plates beside the deep, old-fashioned sink that had been there since the forties. The rector was insisting that he would do his own washing-up later.

'He could do with a dishwasher,' one of the women commented.

Nobody spoke, but there were smiles all round.

Gary wasn't in when she got back, and it was too late to do anything useful in the garden, so she made herself a sandwich and settled down to watch Jack Nicholson in *The Witches of Eastwick*. Men with devilry appealed to her, at least on screen. There wasn't much of the devil in Gary these days. On Saturday evenings he was with his jazz circle, a pathetic crowd of middle-aged blokes in black T-shirts and sandals who drank real ale and listened to records of players of fifty years ago they referred to familiarly as Dizzie, Bird and Bix. The sight of them stretching their necks to bob their bald heads like wading birds was not pretty. Upstairs Gary had a tenor saxophone he had been trying to master ever since his schooldays. She found out about it only after they married.

And why did they marry? There *had* been a spark of something when Gary had come to paint the outside of her parents' house and posted a note through her bedroom window suggesting a date. She'd always had a wild streak in her own character, so she didn't hesitate. He was in better shape in those days, with dark, sleeked-back hair. He knew which clothes to wear, took her to discos, to parties, to London. Helped her learn her lines for the plays she was in. Talked about what they would do with their lives, the foreign countries they would visit on their world tour. Made love to her under the stars on the beach at Weymouth, inside the tower on top of Glastonbury Tor, on a punt (carefully) on the river at Oxford, in a first-class compartment on the last train home from Paddington and in a hot-air balloon over Bristol, drunk on champagne, while the other passengers pretended to admire the view from the opposite side. He took risks then. He would have done it between the aisles in Sainsbury's if she had asked. Never mentioned the heart murmur he was supposed to have had since childhood. She heard about that much later. That murmur was his excuse to avoid all strenuous work. 'Can't take risks,' he'd say. So the garden was Rachel's responsibility. Fortunately she didn't mind. Plants in their infinite variety fascinated her. Without knowing their botanical names she had a passion for flowers and a sound knowledge of the best way to care for them. And, it has to be said, they gave her the excuse to get out of the house when Gary was home.

'Can't take risks.' These days the biggest risk Gary took was stepping out of doors without his baseball cap. Didn't want the wind blowing that streak of hair off his scalp.

She told him once that the Walkman he used to listen to jazz was rubbing on his scalp, making him bald. Mean. He was sensitive about hair loss, but she was sick to the back teeth of hearing the tinny sound. He believed her for a while and took to wearing the headband under his chin, which made no difference to her frustration and just made him look more ridiculous than ever, with his silly spit of hair linking up to form an oval around his head, like a slipped halo.

There had been other boyfriends before Gary. She attracted them, knew how to perform the balancing act between sex and her reputation. She liked men, needed someone to share with. Yet by nature she was not a liberated woman. Oh, she was willing to have a career, make a contribution, but basically what she craved above everything was marriage and children. Chances had gone by. Men more attractive than Gary – men she had slept with – had found other partners and taken jobs in places she would have adored to live in, one in San Francisco and another Paris. Even Aberdeen, where her second lover ended up working for an oil company, would have been an improvement on Foxford, Wiltshire – or Wilts, as she thought of it.

No use moaning, she often told herself these days. Get on with life. The marriage was childless and barren of romance, so she put her energy into her part-time job, three days at the health centre as a receptionist; the garden, which she'd cultivated as a traditional cottage garden, with shrub roses, laburnum, foxgloves and herbs; and amateur dramatics, always a passion; plus her charity work and her support of the church. It was her Christian sense of duty that made divorce too awful to contemplate. True, she had erred and strayed in her youth, but she took the solemn vows of Holy Matrimony seriously. She had not been with another man since her wedding day.

Gary came in around eleven-thirty, after she had rewound Jack Nicholson and was watching some inane Saturday night programme aimed at the teenage audience. He wasn't a smoker, but some of his friends were and she could smell the cigarette fumes clinging to his clothes. He peeled a banana and flopped into a chair, the baseball cap still on. 'How'd it go?'

'The fete, you mean?' she jogged his memory. He wouldn't recall how she was spending her day. 'Top result. With weather like that, it couldn't miss. We were really busy on the cake stall.'

'Did you bring one home?'

She shook her head. 'It isn't the thing.'

'What isn't?'

'For the people in charge to put cakes aside for their own use.'

'Very high-minded. What happened to the ones you didn't sell?'

'Everything went. If you really want cake, I can cook one tomorrow.'

'Don't bother. You'll be at church tomorrow.'

'Not all day. There's time.'

Gary shook his head. 'So how did he shape up?'

'Who?'

'The new sky pilot.'

'Have some respect, Gary. He's the rector. And he isn't all that new. He's been here since last year.'

'A bit flash isn't he? Wears red socks.'

'I hadn't noticed the socks,' she said casually and untruthfully. 'Who cares what colour his socks are if he does his job well? He stayed all afternoon.'

Gary laughed. 'He couldn't very well bog off, could he? What time did it end?'

'Five, or thereabouts.' She chose not to speak of her invitation to the rectory afterwards. Instead she said, 'He made a good speech to open the fete. He said the word "fete" came from "feast". He'd found a parish magazine from the nineteen thirties with a correction notice about a day of prayer and feasting in support of the Congo mission. It should have read prayer and fasting. He's always got a funny story.'

Gary said without smiling, 'Must be the way he tells them. What are they saying about the bishop, then?'

'The bishop?'

'Yours, isn't he? Glastonbury? It was on the local news tonight. Took a jump, didn't he?'

'The *bishop*?'

'They found him at the bottom of some quarry and his BMW at the top.'

'Oh, that's awful! You're serious? Dead?'

'He made sure of that. The drop looked like Beachy Head. What made him do that, for Christ's sake?'

'I can't believe it. He confirmed me.'

'P'raps he was on something. Thought he could fly with the angels.'

Gary's tasteless humour left her cold. 'Poor man.'

They stared at the screen for a while, locked in their own thoughts. Rachel eventually suggested coffee.

'Don't bother.' He reached for the remote control and turned down the sound, the unfailing sign that he wanted to say something momentous, however casual he tried to make it sound. 'I was talking to the lads. I don't know who mentioned it. Gordon, maybe. There's a travel agent in Frome offering three weeks in New Orleans for nine hundred quid. That's everything. Flight, hotel.'

'In America?'

'That's where New Orleans is.'

'You're thinking of going?'

'It's the jazz capital of the world. Buddy Bolden, Jelly Roll Morton, King Oliver.'

'And you'd like to go?' she pressed him. She would have preferred New York or San Francisco, but she would cheerfully settle for New Orleans, strolling the sunny streets in shorts, eating Cajun food in the French Quarter or on one of those Mississippi paddle boats. It would be the nearest thing to the world tour they had promised each other all those years ago. 'When?'

'It has to be soon. The offer only lasts through September.'

'I'm game,' she said. 'We can afford it, can't we?'

Looking uncomfortable, Gary ran his stubby fingers under the neck of the T-shirt and eased it off his skin. 'It's a trip for the guys.'

'What?'

'If I go, it's for the music.'

She sat forward. 'I'm not included? Is that what you're saying?'

'Nothing is fixed yet.'

'I'm going to bed.'

She left him in front of the screen, trying to look as if there was something of interest going on. Upstairs, in the privacy of the shower, she tasted her tears, and mouthed the word 'bastard' repeatedly, hating him for his selfishness and herself for letting it get to her. Was this what twelve years of marriage added up to, putting up with life in this poxy village, living decently, staying faithful to a boring, unattractive nerd who ignored her except when he wanted 'a ride', as he crudely called it? She felt a visceral rage at the humiliation, the discovery that she hadn't even entered his plans.

Well, she wouldn't demean herself by begging to go with him. Even if he saw how wounded she was, changed his mind and condescended to let her join him, she would refuse.

In their kingsize bed she lay so close to the edge of the mattress that she could feel the beading under her knee. She heard the selfish sonofabitch come upstairs, take off his things, go to the bathroom. Next, his bare feet crossing the carpet and finally the springs moving as he got into bed. She breathed evenly, feigning sleep. If he reached for her as he usually did on a Saturday, she would take her pillow and sleep in the spare room.

He had the sense to leave her alone.

3

Everyone in Foxford knew about the bishop's death before Otis Joy announced it in Morning Service, but something had to be said. As usual, the young rector found the right words. 'It appears he took his own life,' he said on a note of shocked disbelief that spoke for everyone in the congregation. 'If so, that's specially difficult to understand, but I don't think we should try without knowing all the facts. God moves in mysterious ways. Marcus Glastonbury was an able, honest and caring bishop, strong in his leadership of the diocese. Some of you knew him personally, as I did. A great loss. I'm sure there will be a memorial service in due course and some of us will be there. For the present, let us remember all he did to encourage this, our church, as we pray for him.'

This, their church, was Saxon in origin and there was a legend about its building that showed how the conflict between good and evil was strong in the minds of the early Christians. The first site proposed had been half a mile away, at a place where the 'old religion' had been practised. The foundations were put down and the building began, but by night the Devil was supposed to have come and removed some of the stones to their present site. The builders persevered, and so did the powers of darkness until a decision was taken to give way and build at this end of the village. If the legend had any truth in it, and the Devil chose the site, you would think people would be wary of some devilment lurking in the walls. Not, it seemed, in the modern age.

All that remained of the Saxon church were some stones built into the tower at the west end. The present St Bartholomew's was a nineteenth-century reconstruction with a short, recessed spire. Inside were traces of medieval carving: an early thirteenth-century arch in the north porch and a window with motifs of around 1320. The Victorian restorer had done a good job. The interior was simple, light and welcoming. The timbers of the hammerbeam roof gave a feeling of solidity.

This century's contribution was mainly in the fabrics sewn and woven by the women of Foxford: the embroidered altar-cloth with a floral design; the dossal, or hanging back-panel for the altar, representing the Annunciation; the lectern fall with crucifix in padded gold kid; the individual kneelers, memorials to past worshippers; and the priest's vestments, including a magnificent cope handworked in combinations of metallic threads, kid-leather, beads and stitches. Usually it came out for weddings, baptisms and the great festivals of Christmas, Whitsun and Easter. Otis Joy was modest in his choice of vestments the rest of the year.

William Cowper's hymn 'Sometimes a light surprises' was an inspired choice to follow the prayer for the bishop, a perfect link to happier matters. The fete had raised the record sum of £520. Standing in the aisle with one hand resting on a pew-end, the rector said, 'You know, we in the Church are sometimes uncomfortable about money-raising. Money is the root of all evil. Does anyone know who said that?'

'St Timothy,' spoke up one of the Bible Class.

'Sorry, George, but no. I think it was the Andrews Sisters.

Anyone remember the song? You're not going to own up, are you? "Money is the root of all evil, take it away, take it away, take it away." What Timothy said was, "The *love* of money is the root of all evil." Not quite the same thing, is it? Now you won't catch me challenging the teaching of the Bible. But I don't think our church fete had anything to do with the love of money. Let's face it, this was the *giving* of money, your money, as well as your talent, your time, your cakes and your runner beans, all for the upkeep of the Lord's house. So let's rejoice in our five hundred and twenty pounds. Speaking for the church, I thank you warmly.' He paused and smiled and looked as grateful as if the profit from the fete were his birthday present, turning to let his gaze take in everyone in the crowded church. 'The sellers of tickets, the buyers of tickets, the stall-holders, the generous folk who cooked and knitted and gave things to stock those stalls, the brass band, the fortune-teller and the humble donkey. Teamwork. Brilliant. There's another text I like, and I won't ask where it's from, because I can't remember myself, but I know how it goes: "A feast is made for laughter, and wine maketh merry: but money answereth all things." Which brings us tidily to hymn three-seven-seven, "Let us, with a gladsome mind, Praise the Lord, for he is kind".'

Rachel, in her place to the left of the aisle, six rows back, praised the Lord whilst noticing how the rector, lustily leading the singing, had caught the sun at the fete. It had picked out and reddened the angles of his face – the broad forehead, the interesting cheekbones, the ridge of his nose and the point of his chin, making him look more ruggedly attractive in his robes than any member of the clergy ought to appear. She – it must be said – was singing the words of the hymn without taking in the meaning. And during the sermon, with Otis Joy's dark head and the top of his surplice showing above the pulpit, she tried mentally dressing him in a variety of uniforms, as you would in those children's books with sections you put together in different combinations. Cowboy, soldier, policeman, pilot, boxer, bridegroom.

All too soon they were singing the last hymn and he said the Grace and made his way up the aisle to the door, passing so close to Rachel as she knelt in prayer that she felt the movement of air from his cassock.

The pews creaked with the weight of people resuming their seats to dip their heads in a last, silent prayer. These days the church was filled for Morning Service. Two extra rows had to be provided with stacking chairs from the church hall. No other rector in living memory had achieved such support except for the Christmas Midnight Service.

The organ started up again to the tune of 'For all the saints' and the movement towards the door began. Rachel filed out behind two old ladies in black straw hats who always sat behind her and sang half a bar after everyone else. When their turn came to shake the rector's hand, they congratulated him on his sermon, but he didn't appear to hear. He was already in eye contact with Rachel.

'I didn't thank you.'

'Thank me?'

'For your help.'

'You just thanked us all, beautifully.'

'At the rectory last evening.'

'It was nothing, really,' she said, enjoying the touch of his hand. 'We all joined in.'

'But you did more than your share.'

She shook her head modestly and was starting to move on when he added, 'Look, there's something else, if you don't mind waiting a few minutes. Would you?'

She managed to say, 'Of course.' Her voice piped up in a way she didn't intend, but he had surprised her. Puzzled and a little light-headed, she stepped forward into the sunshine and stood on the turf to one side of the path to let the others pass. Her friend Cynthia Haydenhall emerged in a pink two-piece and a matching hat that she held with a gloved hand in case the wind blew.

'I've seen the figures. We came out top – and that's official,' she told Rachel. 'The cake stall took more than anyone else.'

'Great,' said Rachel, trying to sound as if it mattered.

'It isn't just the effort on the day. It's chivvying people to do the baking. I do no end of work on the phone in the week before. And knocking on doors.'

'I know.'

'Shocking about the bishop, isn't it?'

'Dreadful.'

'There's more to it than they said in the *Sunday Times* this morning, you can be sure of that.'

'Is there?'

'The gutter press will be full of it.'

'I haven't heard anything.'

'Bishops don't jump into quarries without a reason.'

'I suppose not.'

The triumph of the cake-stall team over all opposition had strengthened the bond between them, Cynthia was certain. 'Are you waiting for someone, poppet, or shall we walk together?'

Rachel said the rector had asked her to wait.

Cynthia gave the hat such a tug that it slipped askew and had to be put back with two hands. 'Oh.'

'Can't think what it's about,' Rachel said disarmingly. 'Is Christian Aid week coming up soon?'

'He doesn't organise the collectors. I do.'

Rachel cursed herself for forgetting that Cynthia was the one woman who couldn't be fooled by that piece of sophistry.

'Maybe I left something behind yesterday. I'm hopeless like that. Always have been.'

'I didn't see anything of yours when we left.'

'Neither did I. It's a mystery.'

'In that case I'll leave you to find out,' said Cynthia, all her chumminess used up.

'Right, then,' Rachel said inadequately.

People were still emerging from the church in numbers, so she moved aside to encourage Cynthia to move on quickly. If she had not been so keen to get rid of her crotchety friend, she might have taken more care. She took a bold step back, forgetting this was a churchyard. Her heel nudged awkwardly against the raised edge of an ancient gravestone. She lost her balance and tipped backwards.

Her bottom took the main impact, a hard landing on a stone slab that would leave bruises for a week, but the real pain was mental, acute embarrassment at exposing legs, tights and knickers – oh, yes, the full show – to the faithful of Foxford as they emerged from church enriched with pious thoughts. Struggling to restore decency, she hauled herself to a sitting position and tugged at her skirt. Already she was surrounded by Good Samaritans.

Cynthia had swung around and said, 'My God – what happened to you?'

'I'm fine, fine,' she insisted before she knew if she was, or not. 'I tripped, that's all. So silly.'

And now the advice came from all sides.

'Take a few deep breaths.'

'Try putting your head between your knees.'

'Don't get up yet. You'll feel faint.' She couldn't. She

was fully hemmed in. Seated on a grimy old gravestone, wishing she was anywhere but here.

'Would a drink of water help?'

'Do you want smelling-salts, dear?' (from one of the two old ladies who sat behind her). 'I always have them with me in church. It gets so close sometimes.'

'Was it a faint?'

'No, I'm perfectly all right. Really.'

Then: 'May I? Excuse me. What's happened here?'

The voice of the rector himself, trying to find a way through the crush.

Someone made room for him and he crouched beside her with a hand on her shoulder. 'Rachel! What's up . . . ? Are you hurt?'

'I don't think so. I'd like to get up.'

Cynthia said, 'She'll be all right, Otis. She says she's fine.'

He asked them to make room. She was shivering as if it was winter.

She tried to get up. Rested her right hand on the slab and cried out with pain the moment she put pressure on it.

'You *are* hurt,' said the rector. 'Here, let me help.'

She managed to get to her feet with his support. In any other situation, Otis Joy's arm firmly around her back would have been bliss, but she was in no state to appreciate it. All those anxious faces did not help.

'You OK, Rachel?' he asked, still with his hands on her shoulders as if she might lose her balance.

She hadn't noticed until that moment of pain. She just felt numb at several points of her anatomy, including the arm. She said she was sure she'd be all right. Without thinking, she tried to brush the back of her skirt, now covered in the yellow stuff that grew on the stone. A stab of pain travelled up her arm.

'It could be broken,' said the rector. 'Let me see.'

He held the arm lightly and asked her to move her fingers. There must have been people qualified in first aid or nursing among the bystanders, but this was church territory and he was taking charge and no one had better interfere, not even Cynthia.

Rachel didn't want a fuss, yet couldn't hide the discomfort. The rector said she ought to get the arm X-rayed and meanwhile they had better immobilise it. As if it was the most natural thing in the world, he pulled his surplice over his head and improvised a sling for her.

The one good thing to come out of this mishap was that Otis Joy insisted he and no one else would take her to hospital. In no time at all she was seated beside him in his rattling old Cortina being driven to Bath.

'I should have offered you some aspirin,' he said. 'Idiot. I've got some in the vestry for emergencies.'

She said the pain had virtually gone now that the arm was supported.

'Are you right-handed?'

She said she was.

'Isn't it always the way?'

'It's my garden that bothers me. It'll be a wilderness in no time.'

'Won't your husband take a turn out there?'

She smiled. 'You don't know him. He's flying to America, anyway.'

In Accident and Emergency she was seen almost at once and then sent to another section for the X-ray. Otis Joy got up to go with her.

'There's no need for you to wait,' she said. 'I'll be all right now.'

He refused to leave her.

'I could be here for hours,' she said when they were seated in the radiography department.

'All the more reason for me to stay. After all, it was my fault.'

'Why?'

'If I hadn't asked you to wait, this wouldn't have happened.'

'No, it was my own stupidity,' she repeated. 'I stepped off the path without looking.'

'It's in a dangerous place, that grave, so close to the church door. You're not the first to trip over it. I've a good mind to have the slab levelled flush with the turf.'

'You couldn't do that. What would the relatives say?'

'They've long since gone. It belonged to one of the previous rectors, the Reverend Waldo Wallace.'

'Now that you mention it, I've seen the name before.'

'The incumbent for over fifty years, until about eighteen eighty,' he said. 'And much loved by the parish. He brewed his own beer and supplied the pub. Believe it or not, tithes were still being paid in those days. Each year at harvest time, good old Waldo gave a tithe dinner at the rectory, a jolly for the whole village.'

'With beer?'

'His home brew. It was a real bender. And a midnight firework display. Said he waited all year to hear the ladies crying "Ooh!" and "Ah!" as the rockets went up.'

She giggled. 'You made that up.'

'No, Waldo said it. Pre-Freud and quite innocent, I'm sure. He never married.'

She didn't know what to say.

'Anyway,' Otis Joy added smoothly, 'he wouldn't have wished this on you.'

She said Waldo Wallace sounded a sweetie.

'Oh, sure. But on the other hand,' he said, 'we all get

our kicks some way. If Waldo liked to hear the ladies going "Ooh!" and "Ah!", maybe he had something to do with you tripping over his grave.'

'All he heard from me was "Ouch!" I hope I said nothing worse.'

'He must have heard some ripe Anglo-Saxon in his time. We clergymen do, you know.'

'Not from a woman, surely? Waldo was never married, you said.'

'He would have had a housekeeper, and I bet she dropped a plate occasionally and said something stronger than "Oh, my word".'

Rachel was called for the X-ray. There would be a further wait while they processed it and showed it to a doctor. She was feeling guilty about taking so much of the rector's time on a Sunday.

'Don't you have Evening Service soon?' she asked when she returned to the waiting area.

He looked at his watch. 'Oceans of time.'

'It must be hard, trying to find space for your own life.'

'This *is* my own life,' he said. 'I don't think of it as a job. True, there are fixed points in the week, services, PCC meetings, choir practice, and so on, but I make time for other things when I feel the need. Wouldn't be much use to anyone if I never relaxed.'

'So what do you do?'

'In my spare time? Fresh air and exercise. I like to get out. Music.'

'What sort? Classical?'

'Catatonia.'

'You're kidding?'

'There's some very good bands about these days.'

'I'm surprised.'

'I grew up with pop. Didn't you?'

'I thought you were going to say Mozart.'

'Can't fault him, but I hear a lot of solemn music in church. Give me something with a heavy beat and grunge guitars.'

'My husband thinks it's cool to listen to jazz, Benny Goodman and stuff. To me it's more dated than Beethoven.' She felt a small stab of conscience for knocking Gary (not to say Beethoven), but it didn't trouble her much because she also felt the hurt of the proposed New Orleans trip. 'His jazz crowd like warm beer and late nights.'

He grinned. 'Thick, floppy sweaters.'

'Old jeans and sandals. And cigarettes. Not many women go for jazz, unless they sing with a band.'

'How does a jazz musician wind up with a million pounds?' he asked suddenly.

'I don't know.'

'By starting off with two million.'

She was called to see an orthopaedic specialist. The X-ray showed she had a fracture above the wrist, a common injury known as a Colles' fracture, the doctor explained. The lower end of the radius had broken off and displaced backwards. There was damage to a ligament, but this was normal. It would require some manipulation.

Forty minutes later, she came back with her forearm encased in gleaming white plaster. 'What do you think?'

'I think you should get straight on the phone to your lawyers,' he said. 'Sue the Church of England. Take them to the cleaners. They're not short of a few bob.'

'You'll get the sack, talking like that,' she told him, speaking with a freedom she wouldn't have dared to employ an hour ago.

'I'm a disgrace.'

On the drive back to Foxford, she said, 'You've been so kind. I don't deserve such treatment.'

'Why not?'

'Well, I'm surprised you talk to me at all after that time I knocked at your door and you were only half-dressed.'

'Less than half,' he said, and she thought, Oh my God, why did I bring this up?

But he was amazingly untroubled. 'It reminds me of the vicar who called on one of his parishioners and got no answer, so he took out his visiting card and wrote on the back, *Revelation, 3, 20.* When the lady checked the verse she found: "Behold I stand at the door and knock: if any man hear my voice and open the door, I will come into him, and will sup with him, and he with me." On the following Sunday the lady in question dropped a card of her own into the collection plate. It read: *Genesis, 3, 10.* And when the vicar checked, he found: "I heard thy voice in the garden and I was afraid because I was naked; and I hid myself."'

Relaxed again, Rachel said, 'Well, after that, I'd better make it clear I can't offer you supper, but I hope you'll come in for coffee when we reach my house.'

He wouldn't this time, he said, and she understood why, considering it was his busiest day.

'One day in the week?' she said, and boldly added, 'After all, we do have some unfinished business.'

'What's that?'

'Whatever it was you asked me to wait and see you about after church.'

'Oh,' he said. 'Slipped my mind. Just an idea. In view of the accident, it may have to wait.'

Next morning she received a spray of pink, yellow and white carnations. The message inside read, 'Sorry about the break. Get well soon. Love Waldo.'

'Who the hell is Waldo?' demanded Gary.

She was tempted to say he was someone she'd fallen

for, but Gary wouldn't see the humour in it. Already he was suffering hardships because she couldn't use the arm properly to make breakfast. Any sympathy had been short-lived. So she explained whose grave she had fallen over and said the flowers were obviously a joke.

'Bloody expensive joke,' said Gary. 'Some people have more money than sense.'

4

The treasurer of the Parish Church Council was Stanley Burrows, a retired headmaster. He had taken early retirement at fifty-six, when Warminster reorganised its education system and created a Sixth Form College (a disaster, in Stanley's eyes). He was now approaching his seventy-fifth birthday. Overweight and inclined to wheeze after getting off his knees in church, Stanley was a sober, honest and God-fearing man, treasurer to the last three rectors. Each year he reminded the PCC of his age and suggested a younger person might be willing to take over, but no one else did anything about it. The feeling in the parish was that while Stanley was up to the job he should continue. Why not, when the accounts were always up to date and never questioned by the auditor? The diocesan quota was paid by standing order. The verger, the cleaner and the organist received their cheques. The rector was given his expenses. Stanley had an excellent relationship with Joy, who urged him not even to dream of giving up.

'But it doesn't give me the satisfaction it used to,' Stanley confided this year. 'It's more and more difficult to achieve a balance, I find.'

'That will be the quota,' said Joy. 'Between ourselves, Stanley, I think the diocese will undermine everything if they go on pushing up the figure as they do. They don't understand the problems of running a parish year in, year out.'

'Precisely what I found in education,' said Stanley, helped onto his favourite hobby-horse. 'The people at County Hall had no conception what it was like to be head of a school with out-of-date textbooks and temporary buildings. All the money went to that damned great folly up the road, if you'll forgive my language.'

'The Sixth Form College?'

'The Ivory Tower, I call it.'

'Still, if that's the way our masters want to spend the money . . .'

'The men in suits,' Stanley said with contempt, regardless that he was never seen in anything else.

'We can only carry on as usual. It's the same with the church. We must trust that the Lord will provide. And the coffee mornings.'

'There's a limit to those, Rector. You can't put on more than one a month. People won't come.'

'We have the income from the fete,' the rector reminded him. 'Beat all records this year.'

'We couldn't get by without that. I was going to mention that some extra came in late as usual. The unsold secondhand books were offered to a dealer and raised twenty-five pounds, and thirty-eight more came in from door-to-door sales for the raffle. It's cash in hand that we can put into your contingency fund.'

'You think so?'

Stanley nodded emphatically. 'It's the best thing that happened to this parish for years, that little account with the Halifax. I mean, if all these extras showed as income in the accounts, our quota would be sky high.'

'You're happy to continue with this unofficial arrangement?'

'More than happy. It's our salvation, Rector.'

The word 'salvation' was a little strong for a man of the

cloth. 'A safety net, anyway. But I think we should keep it confidential.'

'Absolutely. We don't want the new bishop to hear of it when he's appointed. He'll only raise the quota.'

'There's no need for anyone to hear of it.'

'Specially the bishop.'

'We don't need to personalise it, Stanley. You and I know that the board of finance does the sums and recommends the figure to the synod.'

'Sorry. I shouldn't let it get to me.'

'But you're right in principle. They don't need to know every detail. We pay our share to the diocese, Stanley.'

'And on time. Do you know, I've heard of churches – no names, no pack-drill – who wait until the end of the year before stomping up. It's unfair on the rest of us, because that money could have been accruing interest for the diocese and bringing down our quota.'

'In theory, anyway.'

'Well, it wouldn't have to rise so steeply.'

'And are you still adding all the columns yourself, without using a calculator?'

Stanley was proud of his mental arithmetic. 'It keeps the brain ticking over, Rector. The day they allowed the damned things into the classroom was a disaster. But if ever you find a discrepancy in my figures, I'll be happy to hand over. Some day it's going to happen. The brain cells don't replace themselves.'

'I don't see any sign of yours failing,' Otis Joy was quick to assure him.

'That's a relief.'

'Truth to tell, Stanley, most of the clergy are duffers with money, and I'm no exception. Finance doesn't excite me in the least. I know it's part of a priest's job and can't be shirked these days. In fact, it seems increasingly to dominate parish business. So it's specially helpful that you manage our accounts so well.'

Those words acted like a blessing. Stanley left the rectory in a glow of self-esteem, firmly resolved to continue as treasurer for at least another year. The more he saw of this young rector, the more he liked him.

Otis Joy, too, was quietly satisfied. He had been fortunate with treasurers at the two churches he had served as priest. Retired men, both of them, committed Christians, anxious to co-operate fully in the mundane business of financing church activities. How can a rector effectively carry out God's work if he is worried over money?

Take the matter of expenses. No priest wants to be a charge on the parish. Treasurers always feel embarrassment at being asked by the rector for petty cash. He is their minister, their spiritual father, so it can be uncomfortable dealing with his claims for car and public transport expenses, telephone, postage, stationery, secretarial assistance, office equipment, maintenance of robes, fees for visiting clergy and – a major item for an active priest – hospitality at the rectory. Fortunately his main income, his stipend, is not the business of the parish treasurer.

Otis Joy's solution to the thorny subject of expenses was the contingency fund, a building society account entirely at the disposal of the rector. It was fed by injections of cash. A church takes in most of its income in the form of cash. Collections at services are the prime source, but each fund-raising event brings in packets of coins and notes: fetes, coffee mornings, jumble sales, choral concerts, safari suppers, skittles, barbecues and social evenings. There are boxes in church for visitors to contribute a few pence to the upkeep, to buy candles, postcards and guide-sheets. Cash, cash, cash. Everything is bagged up and counted, but there are always late payments, niggling amounts that add to the work of the treasurer. The remedy was to siphon all the extras – with the treasurer's connivance – into the rector's contingency fund. This money didn't go through the books, so it simplified the accounting. More importantly, it reduced the total amount showing as parish income, and discouraged the DBF from increasing the quota.

Weddings, baptisms and funerals were another source of funds. The parochial fees were displayed on the board in the church porch, and it was convenient (the rector always explained to the families) to have them paid in banknotes, rather than cheques. He received the money in person, on the day, and paid the organist, bell-ringers and choir. The residue was his personal fee and that of the parish church council. It went into the contingency fund.

In return, he didn't pester the treasurer with frequent requests for petty cash. They had an understanding that he would draw a token amount, a nice, round figure – enough to keep the accounting simple, satisfy the auditors and everyone at the Annual General Meeting.

A happy arrangement for all concerned.

Later in the week at a confirmation class held in his office at the rectory, someone asked him about hell.

The question came from one of the adult candidates, a ginger-haired chartered accountant with freckles and a dour expression whose only charm was his name, which sounded like a seaside resort. Burton Sands had come late to the faith, but he was not a typical born-again Christian. He had chosen the Church of England after carefully investigating its claims and obligations. He'd picked it as a superior form of unit trust, a low-risk investment that might pay decent dividends in the long term.

'Hell?' said Otis Joy, as if it were a foreign word.

'Yes.'

'We give it a low profile. It's a concept we're not too comfortable with in the modern church, but I'll say this' – he smiled and tried to duck out with a quip – 'you won't find it in the travel brochures.'

'Yes, but do you believe in it?' Sands pressed him.

John Neary, a plain-speaking countryman, said, 'It's where you go if you arse about, isn't it?'

Ann Porter, the only woman in the group, sanitised the remark with, 'If you err and stray like lost sheep.'

'We all do, of course,' the rector admitted. 'The Bible tells us that all have sinned and come short of the glory of God, so—'

'See you down there, Rector,' said Neary.

Everyone except Sands smiled, and the atmosphere improved. In some ways Neary was the saving of this group, the opposite pole to Sands. He watched football, and fiddled with his car and kept a few beehives in the back garden.

Joy tried to strike a more positive note. 'Happily, there's redemption. When you're confirmed, you repent of your sins and renounce evil.'

'So will I go to hell if I'm not confirmed?' Sands asked.

'Snap out of it, Burton. Be positive. Lead the Christian life and you may enter the Kingdom of Heaven.'

'But if we don't,' persisted Sands with his interest in the other side of the balance sheet, 'if we sin and break the Ten Commandments and forget to say our prayers, what then?'

Neary yawned and said, 'Let's face it. It's impossible to keep the Ten Commandments. Everyone breaks the old thou shalt nots.'

'All of them?' chipped in Ann Porter. 'Speak for yourself.'

'No, I'd rather hear it from you, love,' Neary was quick to respond. 'You must have broken some. Which ones?'

She reddened. 'I'm not going into that.'

There were children of twelve and thirteen in the class, looking interested. 'We don't have to make this personal,' the rector cautioned.

'What she means,' Neary continued to bait Ann Porter, 'is that she has a clean sheet on number six. She hasn't murdered anyone.'

'Not yet – but I might, and soon,' murmured Ann.

'I guess we're all in the clear when it comes to that one,' Neary blithely carried on. 'Murder, I mean.'

There was a pause.

'Well, don't all shout at once,' said Neary.

'I'm still waiting for someone to answer my question,' said Sands like a dog with a bone. 'What exactly is hell?'

All eyes were on the rector, who for his own reasons had gone quiet. It was Neary who offered a partial reply. 'The Bible talks about hell fire, so we know it's hot.'

'Oh yes?' said Ann Porter, glad of the chance to get back at him. 'With little red demons prodding you with tridents?'

Otis Joy made a serious effort to get back on track. 'It may not be the same for everyone. We may all have our personal hells.'

'Like a Barry Manilow concert?' said Neary.

'For all eternity,' said Ann.

'Do you have to reduce everything to a joke?' said Sands. 'You talk about personal hells, Rector. What's yours?'

'Mine?' Joy blinked, startled to be asked. Confirmation classes were not his favourite duty. You could bank on getting some bumptious candidate like this one, wanting to challenge theology. 'Losing my job is the worst thing I can possibly imagine.'

'But that happens all the time, people being made redundant.'

'Not to the clergy,' said Neary. 'That's a job for life. It's even called a living, isn't it, Rector?'

There was a day in the week, generally Tuesday, when Joy was free of parish duties. He arranged his diary to preserve that one clear spot, and got in his ancient car and drove out of the village early in the morning and was not seen all day. The lights in the rectory did not come on until late. He never spoke of what he did, and nobody had the cheek to ask.

Theories abounded, however. It was put about at first that he was a betting man and went to the races. Later, that he bought and sold antiques, or books, or postage stamps. There was a strong rumour that he visited a mentally handicapped brother in a residential home in Bath. Another, more earthy, that he had a mistress, a married woman living on the south coast.

Stanley Burrows said, 'What does it matter as long as he carries out his duties here? It's none of our business. He doesn't demand to know how we spend every minute, so what right have we to poke our noses into his private life?'

'He is our rector,' Cynthia Haydenhall said at the bring-and-buy coffee morning Otis Joy had asked to be excused from. 'We expect him to be above reproach.' She had become cooler towards Joy since he left her out of his tea party after the fete.

'There's no reason to think he's doing anything to be ashamed of,' said Stanley.

Over by the door, Owen Cumberbatch rolled his eyes as if to suggest that the complacency of these people was beyond belief.

His sister, whose inescapable toffee crispies were being offered around, was quick to say, before Owen opened his mouth, 'I think our rector is the best thing that ever happened to Foxford. We've had some dull old sticks at the rectory in recent years. He treats the job as if he enjoys every minute. It's infectious. That's why the church is full on Sundays.'

Mr Prior, the eighty-year-old sidesman, came in on the end of the conversation. 'What's that? Who's infectious?'

'Our rector, according to Miss Cumberbatch,' said Cynthia unhelpfully.

'Is that where he is today – having treatment?' asked Mr Prior.

So another rumour was hatched.

Between the raffle, the sale and the fifty-pence entrance fee, seventy pounds was raised for the church. At the end of the morning, Stanley took it home in a brown paper bag.

He was in for a shock. A burglar had entered his cottage while he was out. Ninety-two pounds was stolen, together with a video-recorder, a Waterford rose-bowl – the last memento of his grandparents – his ivory chess-set and the silver clock he had been given by the school on the day he retired.

George Mitchell, the local policeman, came eventually. He asked to see the place where the break-in had happened and Stanley had to admit that he never locked his back door. Living in the village, he'd thought he was safe. People in villages trust each other. So the thief had just opened the door and walked in. PC Mitchell clicked his tongue and shook his head. He told Stanley he had better not mention to the insurance people that the house was left open. Stanley said he didn't see why it should become an insurance claim if the police did their job and the property was recovered. PC Mitchell shook his head and told him to get real and said theft was the most commonly reported offence. The chance of catching anyone was about one in a hundred. They didn't have the manpower to hunt down petty thieves. Stanley was outraged. He pointed out that it must have been a local person who knew about the bring-and-buy sale and had chosen a time when the cottage was empty. PC Mitchell agreed and said someone would take fingerprints, but if he were in Stanley's shoes he would file that insurance claim.

Stanley didn't tell the police or anyone else that the stolen cash was church money waiting to be banked. He should have paid it in the previous day, only it had been a fine afternoon and he'd mown the lawn instead. Now he was conscience-stricken.

As soon as PC Mitchell left, Stanley drove to the bank in Glastonbury and drew a hundred in cash from his personal account. So as not to make the transaction obvious, he passed the next twenty minutes sitting on a bench looking at the Abbey ruins. Then he returned to the bank, picked a different teller and paid ninety-two pounds of his own money into the church account together with the seventy raised at the bring-and-buy. No one would find out he had been so careless. But he decided after all he would no longer continue as treasurer.

He called at the rectory the same evening. Unfortunately Otis Joy had still not returned from his day out.

The local policeman may have treated the incident lightly, but the rest of Foxford did not. Burglaries were rare in the village. The last had been three years ago, when a series of garages were raided at night, and a number of power tools taken. Professional thieves were responsible that time, the local CID had decided. A spate of similar crimes had been going on in Wiltshire villages all through the summer. A gang operating out of Bristol was suspected. Amateur or professional, the outcome was the same. No arrest.

Nobody doubted that Stanley's burglary was a local job. It was common knowledge that he lived alone and had some nice things in his cottage. And the whole village knew he never missed a church social event.

Cynthia Haydenhall was convinced unemployed youths were to blame. She said in the shop next morning that if she were the police she would raid three houses on the council estate and she could guarantee she would recover Stanley's property. 'We all know who these petty thieves are. You see them hanging about the street looking for trouble. In times past we had a village constable who dealt with them. My gran told me about an incident during the war when they had bins in the street for collecting waste food for pigs. Pig-bins, they were called. Someone was tipping up the bins at night, looking for scraps, or something, and making a disgusting mess. The village bobby lay in wait and caught one of the local youths in the act. Grabbed him by the collar and marched him straight to his parents' house, woke them up and ordered the father to thrash his son's bare backside in front of the entire family, little sisters as well.'

'It sounds a bit extreme,' said the shopkeeper, Davy Todd. 'He was probably hungry. It weren't as if he was robbing anyone.'

'It taught him a valuable lesson,' Cynthia said in a way that defied anyone to argue. 'I often think of it.'

Davy Todd made no comment.

'It didn't do much good,' an old woman piped up from behind the greetings cards. 'If that's Bobby Hughes you're speaking of, he's done three stretches since for robbery with violence. He's coming up to seventy and he's never learned.'

'Some folk think we should bring back the stocks,' said Davy Todd. 'Not to mention the ducking-stool.'

Cynthia took this as personal and left.

Stanley found the rector at home when he called at lunchtime.

Otis Joy invited him in and put a supportive arm around his shoulders. 'I heard what happened yesterday. Devastating. What's the world coming to?'

He went to a cupboard in his office and poured a couple of whiskies.

Stanley wasn't there for small talk. He stated his decision. 'The burglary is a great shock. I'm afraid it's altered everything, Rector. My confidence has gone. Someone younger must take over.'

Joy was unprepared for this. 'Don't say that, Stanley. We can't let them win.'

'It's brought me to my senses. Stupid old buffer, thinking I can do the job until I pass away. I'm a security risk at my age.'

Joy leaned forward, concerned, without any show of alarm. 'You didn't lose any church money?'

'No, it was all my own,' Stanley said, sending up a prayer to be forgiven.

'Because if you did, I'll gladly make it up from the contingency fund. That's what it's for.'

A shake of the head from Stanley.

'In fact, I'd like to help you anyway,' Joy decently offered. 'How much did you lose?'

Stanley blinked, shocked by the suggestion. 'That's church money. I'm not here for help, Rector. I just want to tender my resignation.'

'This minute?' Now Joy's voice had a suggestion of panic. He took a slug of whisky.

They talked on for some time, with Stanley resisting every appeal to reconsider.

'Well, I'll have to think,' said the young rector, 'and, er . . .'

'Pray?'

'Good thought. Yes, pray. Coming out of the blue like this, it's a shock, a real facer. We're going to need time to find the right man or woman. That won't be easy.'

'There are plenty of able people,' Stanley pointed out. 'All you want is someone with a grasp of elementary accounting and a commitment to the church. I can say from experience, it's commonsense stuff.'

'That may be so, but the choice is crucial. The whole thing will have to go through the PCC.' Otis Joy rolled his eyes upwards. 'And then there's the problem of handing over.'

'There's no problem.'

'I can't agree. If we *do* appoint someone else, they'll need to learn our ways of doing things.'

'What do you mean, Rector?'

Otis Joy cleared his throat. 'How we deal with my petty cash claims, for instance. You and I have an understanding, but a new treasurer may be uncomfortable with it.'

'The Building Society account?'

'The contingency fund, yes.'

'I'm sure whoever takes over will see the sense in it. A slight diversion from the norm, but good for the church, our church, anyway. I'll explain it fully when I hand over the books. I believe in giving it to them straight, and I'm sure you agree.'

Joy didn't agree at all. The prospect of a new treasurer was alarming enough, and Stanley giving it to them straight would be calamitous. He was deeply perturbed. He could see everything unravelling. 'It's not so simple.'

'Why?' said Stanley.

'We don't know who they might appoint. It could be someone who doesn't appreciate the advantages of the fund.'

Stanley shook his head. 'Why shouldn't they? If they can't allow a man of the church some discretion what's the world coming to? I'm very clear about this, Rector. It doesn't matter a bean who takes over. I'm honour bound to show him the accounts in full, including your statements from the building society.'

'I don't keep them.'

'You don't?' Stanley blinked and stared.

'Have I committed a *faux pas*? I told you I'm hopeless with money.'

Stanley had turned a deep shade of pink. 'I expect it's all right. No doubt it's all on computer somewhere. The new treasurer must have chapter and verse on everything we've done. You do see that?'

'In time, yes, but . . .'

'No, Rector. Forgive me, but this is an accounting matter. The handover is when you open the books and explain everything.'

'But this doesn't have to be an overnight thing. We'll need a transition. A few months of working together.'

'No. My mind is made up. A clean break. I'm through with the job. It's better for the new person to start without me looking over his shoulder.'

Most people can be charmed, persuaded or threatened out of an unwise decision. There are just a few who are totally intractable.

'Even so,' said Joy, realising he'd lost this one.

'Look at it this way,' said Stanley. 'If I dropped dead tomorrow, you'd be forced to appoint someone else.'

Otis Joy sighed heavily. 'And I thought we had years

ahead of us.' He took Stanley's glass to the cupboard and refilled it.

Stanley died in bed that night.

5

He was not found for two days. People came to the cottage, got no answer and went away. The paperboy unthinkingly pushed the previous morning's *Daily Telegraph* through the letterbox to make way for the next one. The meter reader from SWEB made a note that this quarter would be another estimated reading. Bill Armistead, local organiser of Neighbourhood Watch, calling to offer sympathy about the break-in, assumed Stanley was having a lie-in. Even the police knocked at the door to check details of the stolen property and went away without doing anything.

The irony of all this was that the back door remained unlocked. Anyone could have walked in.

Finally the publican at the Foxford Arms remarked that Stanley hadn't been in for his usual for a couple of lunchtimes and Peggy Winner, who lived opposite, said she'd noticed his bedroom curtains had remained drawn. The publican said someone had better get over to the cottage and see if the old boy was all right.

Bill Armistead went around to the back door and walked in. Upstairs he found Stanley Burrows dead in bed. The doctor, when he came, confirmed that death must have been at least thirty-six hours earlier because the effect of rigor mortis had already come and gone.

The circumstances of Stanley's passing horrified everyone.

It was assumed that the trauma of being burgled had brought on a heart attack, and for a time a lynch mentality took over. If the burglar had been identified for sure he would not have lasted long in the village. As it was, a number of youths came under strong suspicion and were treated with contempt by everyone who had known Stanley. Two of them were drop-outs from the new Sixth Form College, a point that would not have escaped the old headmaster.

The death was reported to the coroner, who ordered a post mortem. The analytical findings demonstrated that Stanley had died from the effects of amylobarbitone, a sedative, mixed with whisky. An inquest was arranged.

Suicide, then? This was even more shocking than the heart attack theory. No note was found, but it is common knowledge that you don't take barbiturates and alcohol together unless you want to do away with yourself. The idea of the heartbroken old man alone in his cottage mixing his fatal cocktail moved people to tears. They had known Stanley was in a state of shock after the burglary. They hadn't realised it amounted to black despair.

On Sunday, Otis Joy referred to the tragedy in church. 'Stanley Burrows was a loyal member of this congregation for over thirty years. He served on the parish council as our treasurer, a very able treasurer. Stanley was a staunch friend to me, but of course most of you knew him much longer than I did, as your headmaster, or the headmaster of your children. His passing is hard for us to bear – the more so because of the tragic circumstances. I'm not going to speculate on what happened, and I urge you all – everyone in the village – to be restrained in your reaction. Stanley was a gentleman in every sense of the word. He, of all people, wouldn't wish this to lead to thoughts of revenge. He taught the virtues of civilised behaviour. Let us remember that as we pray for his immortal soul.'

In his pew towards the back, Owen Cumberbatch exhaled loudly and impatiently. His sister, beside him, gave him a sharp dig in the ribs.

To end the service, the rector chose a hymn Stanley had often sung in school assemblies, 'Lord dismiss us with thy blessing', and hands were dipping into pockets and bags for Kleenex long before the 'Amen' was reached.

To Rachel, in her usual pew, the rector's words had been specially touching. He had this gift of striking exactly the right note for the occasion. On her way out of church she almost complimented him, and then decided it was inappropriate. Instead she smiled and put out her left hand (her right was still in plaster) and found herself holding two of his fingers and giving them a squeeze. He smiled in a restrained way. 'I hope it's mending nicely.'

'I expect so,' she said.

'How long do you have to wear this?'

'Another four itching weeks.'

'I've always said the best cure for an itch is to scratch it. Try a knitting needle.'

'Well, it's not all bad,' she managed to put in. 'I got some lovely flowers out of it.'

'Mind how you go, then. Watch out for Waldo's grave.'

She was tempted to ask if he'd remembered what it was he wanted to see her about on the day of the accident, but that might have seemed pushy. She moved on.

By the lychgate she overheard a snatch of conversation she found mystifying. Bill Armistead was saying to Davy Todd, who kept the shop, '. . . out of order, totally out of order and told him so.'

'Silly old bugger,' said Todd.

'It's daft. He couldn't hold down a job like his, telling

folk how to behave, praying and preaching, if he were up to things like that.'

'Nobody could. What would be the point?'

'Mind, they do go off the rails, some of them.'

'Yes, a bit of how's your father, drinking, gambling, but this is way beyond that. No, it's bullshit. Got to be. If he believes that, he wants his head testing.'

Rachel edged around them and walked up the street. She couldn't believe anyone had been spreading malicious stories about Otis, and didn't want to find out.

The senior churchwarden, Geoff Elliott, spoke to the rector after everyone else had gone. 'It may seem indecently soon to be speaking of this, but we'll need a new treasurer now.'

'Spot on, Geoff,' said Joy. 'The sooner the better.'

'We churchwardens can act in a temporary capacity, but we need someone to take on the job properly. For the sake of continuity, he ought to come from within the PCC, as Stanley did.'

'Is that a problem?'

Elliott cleared his throat. 'I've, er, sounded out the others and nobody is too confident of taking it on. You need someone good at figure work. We have the power to co-opt, of course.'

'And you have someone in mind?'

'That young fellow Sands is a chartered accountant, I understand.'

'Burton Sands?' said the rector, unable to disguise his horror. 'He's in my confirmation class. He isn't confirmed yet.'

'He will be, won't he?'

'Well, as it isn't by selection, yes. I wouldn't have thought of him for treasurer myself.'

'He's a regular church-goer. A serious young man. Very stable, I would think. And we can be sure he understands how to draw up a balance sheet.'

'I don't doubt that.'

You solve one problem and another rears its head. Joy could not in his wildest dreams imagine himself disclosing the existence of the contingency fund to Burton Sands. Neither did he wish to operate extra accounts without the treasurer's knowledge. That had been the problem in the last parish, ending with the visit from the bishop. Far better to find someone co-operative, like Stanley. What a crying shame Stanley had ruled himself out.

'Is there a problem with Burton?' Elliott asked.

'I wouldn't put it so strongly. It's just a feeling I have that he may upset people. He's a prickly character. A parish treasurer needs tact. He'd be dealing with ordinary folk who get things in a muddle or forget to ask for receipts or hand in money later than they should. I don't know how Burton would measure up.'

'Well, of course we need someone you can work with, Rector.'

'I can work with anyone, but . . . Let me think about this before we ask him. There may be someone we've overlooked.'

'He's the only accountant in the congregation.'

'But Stanley wasn't an accountant. As he remarked to me once, almost anyone could do the job. It's commonsense stuff.'

'But a lot easier if you're a trained accountant,' said Elliott stubbornly. 'In the meantime, Norman Gregor and I will plug the gap.'

'Top stuff,' said Joy, and added optimistically, 'Who knows? Maybe you'll find it's a doddle.'

'It's only until we get someone permanent,' Elliott

stressed. 'We're thinking of days rather than weeks. And we can't do much without the account books.'

'Take them over as soon as you want. It's just a matter of collecting them from Stanley's cottage.'

'The books aren't there, Rector. The police have them.'

Joy's face twitched into stark horror. '*The police?*'

'You know PC Mitchell – George, from the cottage with the willow growing in the front. He also acts as the coroner's officer. He took possession of the books. I think it's to make sure they're in order, just in case something worried Stanley enough to make him suicidal.'

Joy shook his head. 'If anything made him suicidal, it was the burglary.'

'They have to do the job properly.'

'George Mitchell should have come to me.'

Eliott's face coloured deeply. 'My fault, Rector. He explained to me what he was doing and I ought to have mentioned it to you before this.'

One of Otis Joy's strengths was speed of action. Burton Sands as treasurer? No way.

There had to be a better candidate, someone more approachable, more co-operative and who saw the sense in not rocking the boat. Numerate, of course, but they didn't need to be a maths professor. The rector's candidate. No parish council would dare veto the rector's choice.

But who?

None of those deadbeats on the PCC wanted the responsibility. The nominee had to come from the congregation at large. A number of treasurer-like faces came to mind as Joy mentally scanned the line-up he saw every Sunday from his pulpit. There was no shortage of people who had worked in offices and probably on committees as well. Unfortunately not one of them struck him as suitable.

He couldn't predict how they would react to the contingency fund.

Stanley – God rest his soul – had never asked to see a statement from the building society. Even Stanley might have been perturbed to know that the deposits were never less than a hundred pounds a week and the withdrawals about the same. A steady sixty from the hire of the church hall for bingo, bridge, boy scouts, table-tennis and line-dancing. Thirty to fifty for a wedding, baptism or funeral. Extra from the coffee mornings, the fete, the safari suppers and whatever. Bits and bobs from the 'upkeep of the church' boxes and the sale of pamphlets. It all came in the form of notes and coins that went straight into the building society. You don't want loose change lying about the rectory or you run the risk of theft, as Stanley Burrows had discovered.

The right choice was crucial.

Who can find a virtuous woman? states the Book of Proverbs, *for her price is far above rubies.* Finding the right treasurer was about as difficult. And now that Joy thought about it, a woman was not a bad idea, virtuous or not.

The coroner's officer in his police uniform called at the rectory about four in the afternoon. A civilised time. It was a golden September day and Otis Joy brought tea and cake into the garden. Not coconut pyramids, but a fine three-layer chocolate cake, a gift to the rector (with twenty-four pounds and a few pence in extra takings) from the recent coffee morning.

'It's about Stanley, of course?' he said striking the right note between chirpiness and respect for the dead.

'Only a few questions, Rector.' PC George Mitchell was a Wiltshireman through and through, in his fifties now, calm, slow of speech, with a faint smile that rarely left him. The rector had long since learned to respect the intelligence behind soft West Country accents. 'He was quite well known to you, I expect?'

'As one of the Church Council? Naturally.'

'Treasurer.'

'And a good one. He held the office for many years, didn't he? Long before I came.'

'A demanding job, would you say?'

Otis Joy smiled and pointed to the piece of cake on PC Mitchell's plate.

Mitchell took a moment to see the point, then let his mouth relax into the start of a smile.

'It never depressed him, so far as I know,' said Joy. 'Is that what you're wondering?'

'The books appear to be in order. Up to date.'

'They would be. Stanley was methodical, as a treasurer should be.' He signalled a shift in tone by putting down his cup and saucer. 'Nobody informed me you were taking away the church accounts. I have to say I take a dim view of that.'

'I was acting for the coroner,' said PC Mitchell without apologising. 'We don't upset people for the sake of it, but when all's said and done, we have the job to do and the power to carry it out.'

'When will we get them back?'

'Today, if you like. We've finished with them.'

'Barking up the wrong tree, then?'

'We bark up all the trees, Rector.'

A wasp was hovering over Otis Joy's cake. 'The cause of Stanley's death is obvious, isn't it?'

'Not so much as you'd think. He didn't leave a note. That's unusual, him being so methodical.'

'Surely the burglary . . .'

'In my job, you learn not to make assumptions. I just

assemble the facts for the coroner. When did you last see Stanley?'

The wasp had settled on the cake. It wouldn't move, even when a paper napkin was waved over it. 'Now you're asking. I'm hopeless at remembering.'

'But I expect you keep a diary. You'd need to, with all the things you have to do.'

'Good thought. Did Stanley keep one?' Joy suggested as a diversion.

'None that we found.' PC Mitchell leaned across and flicked the wasp off Joy's piece of cake with his fingernail, killing it outright. 'I'd like to see yours.'

'I could fetch it if you like.' The offer was half-hearted. Mitchell gave a nod.

'But I can't let you take it away. I depend on it.'

There was no reaction from the coroner's officer.

In the security of his study, Otis Joy turned to the relevant page of the diary. He was ninety-nine per cent sure he hadn't made a note of Stanley's visit on the day of his death. Stanley had not made an appointment. He had come at lunchtime, fretting over the burglary. The chance of anyone having seen him was slight. Mercifully the rectory was not overlooked. It stood at the end of a lane behind the church.

As he thought, there was no record of the visit in the diary.

Back in the garden, George Mitchell had finished his slice of cake, and was biting into a plum he had picked.

'It's just an appointments book,' Joy explained. 'Baptisms, weddings and funerals and the odd Parish Council meeting.'

Mitchell licked his sticky fingers and wiped them on a paper napkin before handling the diary.

'This is the ninth, the day of the burglary.'

'Is it? I wouldn't remember.'

'You had a day off by the looks of things.'

'That's right. I'm busy on the Sabbath, you see. I take my day off some time in the week.'

'What do you do? Potter about the house?'

'No, I need to get out of the village. There are interruptions if I stay in.'

'So you wouldn't have had a visit from Stanley?'

'I wasn't here.'

'You're certain?'

Otis Joy hesitated. Did Mitchell have some information? 'I told you I went out for the day. What's this about?'

Mitchell turned over the page and looked at the innocuous entries for the 10th: a visit to the church school for scripture lesson; two home calls on recently bereaved families; a wedding preparation meeting; an ecumenical meeting with the Methodist and Catholic clergy at Warminster.

'It's about money,' Mitchell said, and Otis Joy twitched.

'Damned flies,' he said, rubbing his face.

'On the day of the burglary, Mr Burrows visited the bank and took out a hundred pounds in cash from his personal account. When he was found, he had less than twenty in his wallet.'

'Wasn't some cash stolen from the cottage?'

'Ninety-two pounds. But that was in the morning. He drew out this money in the afternoon.'

'And spent about eighty apparently,' said the rector, trying to sound uninterested. 'Perhaps he had a bill to pay.'

'According to the parish account book, he paid a hundred and sixty-two pounds into the church account the same afternoon. Seventy of that was the takings from the bring-and-buy morning. I think the other ninety-two was his own money.'

'Why?'

'I think he was too ashamed to tell anyone it was church money that was stolen in the burglary.'

Joy frowned. 'He didn't say anything to me about it.'

'He wouldn't, would he?' said George. 'You didn't see him to speak to.'

'I mean he could easily have phoned.' The rector sighed heavily. 'But you must be right, George. This puts everything in a different light.'

'How do you mean, sir?'

Otis Joy's brain was in overdrive. 'Knowing Stanley as I do, it would be a body blow to lose church money through carelessness. Devastating. The cash must have been lying around in the house. Usually he banked everything at the first opportunity. He'd take this as a personal failure. I don't like to think of the torment the poor man suffered.'

George Mitchell was saying nothing.

'So,' the rector summed up, 'you've got your explanation. Poor Stanley. He made up the money from his own savings rather than let anyone know. And even then he couldn't live with the shame of it.'

This plausible theory seemed to find favour. George nodded, wiped his forehead and replaced his police cap.

'George, you must come here again when you're off duty,' said Joy. 'Do you play chess, by any chance?'

'Not my game, sir.'

'Well, I wouldn't challenge you to Cluedo. With your police training, you must be red hot. Scrabble?'

'I get the tiles out with my wife once in a while.'

'Let's indulge, then. How about Monday evening?'

George looked bemused by the prospect of Scrabble with the rector. 'All right, sir. Monday evening it is.'

'Shall we say seven-thirty? And do call me Otis. Everyone does.'

6

Stanley had a bigger send-off than any departing Foxford soul in years. People were standing at the back of the church. There just wasn't room for the extra chairs from the church hall. Former pupils and teaching colleagues came from miles around. The school choir filled the front pews and the singing was glorious.

The Reverend Joy was equal to the occasion. He was in his element that morning, telling the mourners it had become the custom to treat funerals as the celebration of a life and that Stanley's life was worthy of more than that – of a fanfare – regardless of the tragic circumstances of his passing.

He told an enchanting story to illustrate Stanley's devotion to the church: 'Sometimes at the end of a service, when we look at the offerings on the collection plate we find a foreign coin – put there by mistake, I'm sure, along with the occasional button.'

He waited for some murmured amusement, and got it.

'And you can't get anything back for foreign coins, unfortunately. The exchange bureaux refuse to accept them, so what do we do with them? For years, and long before my time as rector, they were put in an old tin that once held toffees. This troubled Stanley, this money earning nothing for the church. So when he went on holiday to Spain last year – I think it was his first foreign holiday – he said he would take the half-dozen or so peseta coins with him. I said yes, we'd be glad to get shot of them and perhaps he would like to chip in a few English coins in their place. But no, Stanley's idea wasn't to spend the money. He meant to find a Spanish church that kept *their* foreign coins and do an exchange. A lovely thought, typical of Stanley's thoroughness.

'I think he must have spent most of his time on the Costa del Sol calling at churches instead of relaxing in the sun. Eventually he found a priest who produced a wooden box containing foreign coins, some of them English. They did their little deal, and Stanley returned with six coins of the realm. I congratulated him. He said yes, it was progress, but unfortunately the coins had been kept a long time. They were pennies of the old sort, no longer legal tender. However, he hoped we might be able to sell them. They went into the toffee tin.

'Not to be beaten, he got in touch with a coin dealer, who offered to come and look at them. Pennies of certain years when not many were minted can be worth quite a bit of money, we discovered. Our hopes were raised. But the pennies from Spain turned out to be common ones and the dealer wasn't willing to make an offer. Then – of all things – the dealer took an interest in the toffee tin. It was at least fifty years old, he said, and people collected old tins, so he gave us a fiver for it. Five pounds for a rusty old tin! Truly the Lord works in mysterious ways. So now we keep the pennies with all the foreign coins in a plastic Tupperware box and whenever I see it I think of Stanley's broad smile when his efforts finally paid off.'

After the service, the coffin was taken to a local crematorium where the close family took leave of Stanley at the short committal conducted by Otis Joy. A younger brother from Leicester said a day that could have been an ordeal had been made uplifting by the rector's sensitive handling.

Back at the cottage, Stanley's family had got in a few salad things, some cooked meats and cheeses. And there was wine. It didn't amount to anything so riotous as a wake, but everyone was welcomed and the mood was relaxed and positive.

Stanley's brother Edward brought the rector a cup of tea and said, 'I was wondering if by any chance you're from Market Harborough. There are quite a few Joys there.'

'I'm sure there are. No, I've been asked before. No connection. I'm not sure where my family originated. Father travelled all over Europe. He was an acrobat.'

'What – with a circus?'

'You name one – he was in it.'

'And did you learn circus skills?'

'Am I one of the Joys of Spring? Not really. My parents died when I was seven. I could juggle a bit, once.'

'Don't you keep it up?'

The rector laughed. 'Not much call for juggling in the Church of England. As for walking the tightrope . . .'

'Well, you need confidence to stand up and preach a sermon, I'm sure.'

'True. But I have off days. Then I'm tempted to wake everyone up by walking up the aisle on my hands.'

He moved into another room, spotted Rachel, and went over.

She was coping quite well one-handed, drinking tea, until he approached. The hand with the cup jerked and some slopped onto the carpet.

'Clumsy,' she said, annoyed with herself. 'Will it stain?'

'It won't trouble Stanley if it does.'

The ends of her mouth curved. 'True.'

'I was about to ask how you're coping.'

'Quite well until a moment ago.'

'Back at work yet?'

'Yes. They make allowances.'

He looked about him to make sure no one else was listening. 'Ever done any simple accounting?'

Rachel pricked up her eyebrows in a look of mild alarm. 'I leave all that to my husband.'

'But you know the principles, I'm sure. Double entry book-keeping, that sort of thing?'

'We had a few lessons at school. I don't think I shone, exactly. Why?'

He shrugged. 'A wild guess. You have this aura of efficiency. I can picture you whipping out a calculator when you go shopping.'

She was laughing. 'An aura of efficiency! I've had some things said about me, but that's a first.'

'Sorry,' he said. 'I guess that's the last thing a lady wishes to hear. I'm not very tactful, am I? I tell the prettiest woman in the village she's efficient.'

She flushed scarlet. 'That's a first as well.'

He pointed to his collar. 'With this on, Rachel, I can speak the truth without fear or favour. You know more about figure-work than you let on.'

He moved off to another group. Rachel remained where she was, dazed and disbelieving.

Nearby, Owen Cumberbatch had cornered Peggy Winner and was airing a sensational theory. Poor old Stanley Burrows hadn't taken his own life. He was the rector's latest murder victim.

'Owen,' Peggy said, 'you do come out with the silliest nonsense. They were on the best of terms.'

'Until something went wrong,' said Owen, never at a loss. 'Stanley must have found something out about the previous killings.'

'Keep your voice down, for God's sake,' she told him. 'You're a disgrace, putting this kind of thing about.'

'I believe in speaking the truth, however uncomfortable it is,' Owen insisted.

'Like your nights out with your old chum Laurence Olivier. What sort of chumps do you think we are, Owen? You chance your arm all the time, just to get attention. We might have believed you the first time, some of us, but there are limits, you know.'

'I've no need of attention. I'm pointing out facts that ought to be obvious.'

'Facts? A load of apple sauce, and that's putting it politely. If you've got information, take it to the police.'

'I might.'

'I think you're jealous, just because he's popular with the ladies.'

'My dear, I don't need to be jealous of anyone in that department. I've had my moments, and still would, given encouragement. But you put your finger on it when you speak of popularity. He's the golden boy. You've heard that expression "He could get away with murder"? Well, a certain gentleman has and does, and I'm the only one who sees it, apparently.'

The inquest on Stanley Burrows found that he committed suicide. It was confirmed that he died of an overdose of amylobarbitone mixed with whisky. The burglary was thought to have so unhinged him that he took his own life. 'I can think of no case that better illustrates that familiar phrase "while the balance of his mind was disturbed",' commented the coroner. 'Here was a retired man living an orderly life in a quiet village whose peace of mind was cruelly shattered by someone entering his house and stealing his property. Not only his personal property, but ninety-two pounds that belonged to the church. Mr Burrows was treasurer to the Parish Council and the money had been in his house ready to be taken to the bank. One of his last acts was to make good the loss from his own savings, but clearly he still felt he had let down the church. Whoever was responsible will have this on his conscience. It is a distressing end to a good life.'

The only matter unexplained was how the amylobarbitone came into Stanley's possession. His GP stated that he had never prescribed this or any other sedative for Stanley. The drug was not much used these days. 'It is not of over-riding importance,' the coroner stated. 'There is no question that the deceased had taken the drug, or that there was a supply of capsules in the cottage. One was found on the kitchen floor, and the empty whisky bottle was discovered on the table. That is established. We may speculate how he acquired them, allowing that amylobarbitone is rather outmoded. People don't often throw old medicines away when they have no further use for them. Sometimes we have to turn out someone's medicine cabinet after their death. I've done it more than once, and if I wanted some sleeping tablets without going to my doctor to ask for them, I could have kept them. It may be as simple as that. Or, more simple still, they may have been prescribed for Mr Burrows years ago, when he was under the stress of full-time teaching, before he became a patient of his present doctor. The salient point is that he swallowed the tablets and a generous amount of whisky. As an intelligent man, he would have known it was a deadly combination.'

Joy was not called to give evidence. No one knew Stanley had called at the rectory on the evening of his death. And no one knew the rector stocked almost as many varieties of sleeping pill as the average pharmacy. His years of visiting the sick, the dead and the bereaved had given him good opportunities.

The jury returned a verdict of suicide.

On the same evening PC George Mitchell called at the rectory for a game of Scrabble and told Joy how the inquest had turned out. They were having some close matches, and George usually won. He was better at spotting the squares that tripled the points.

Before Gary left for New Orleans with his jazz cronies, he told Rachel her broken wrist wasn't going to stop him going.

She said with dignity, 'Why should it? I can manage.'

'I'm just telling you I don't feel guilty. You'd like me to feel a total shit, but I don't.'

'Come off it, Gary. I didn't break the wrist on purpose.'

'Just an act of God, was it?'

'What?'

'An act of God. It happened in the churchyard under the rector's nose. God arranged it. There's got to be some dividend from all the Sundays you've spent in church.'

'Drop it, Gary.'

'God could have put the mockers on my trip, couldn't he? I'd have to be a right bastard to leave you here with a broken arm. Well, maybe I am. You take all the sympathy that's going. Wallow in it. I'll send you a postcard.'

'I can't wait.'

He left for Heathrow Airport the same evening.

Rachel opened a bottle of wine to celebrate and picked up her copy of *There Goes the Bride,* in which she was cast as Miriam in the Frome Troupers' October production. She was halfway through her first glass when the doorbell rang. She said, 'Heavens above!' – and had a premonition that Otis Joy was there. She dashed to the mirror and scraped her hair into place and freshened up her lipstick.

When she got to the door, Cynthia Haydenhall was standing there, all dressed up for a visit. The disappointment must have been screamingly obvious because Cynthia said, 'Were you expecting someone else, then?'

'No. I was sitting with my feet up, having a glass of wine.'

'Where's Gary?'

Cynthia was unstoppable when rooting out information.

'On his way to New Orleans for the jazz. He left twenty minutes ago.'

'Oh? How long for?'

'Three weeks.'

'And you didn't go?'

'It's a sad old lads' thing.'

'You don't mind if I come in, then? I've heard something that will make your hair stand on end.'

With a build-up like that, it was impossible to send her away.

Seated in Gary's armchair, with a glass of Merlot in her hand, Cynthia explained, 'I know someone who knows someone who works for the Church, in the diocesan office. She says – this is Gospel truth, Rachel – Marcus Glastonbury, the bishop who killed himself, was into SM.'

'What's that?' said Rachel, thinking it must be shorthand for spirit messages, or some form of worship regarded with suspicion by the church establishment.

'Come on, amigo. We're grown-ups. What do you think it is? Sado-masochism.'

Rachel was speechless, eyes popping.

'Isn't it shocking?' Cynthia launched into her hot gossip. 'He liked to have his backside whacked by women in black corsets. The night he killed himself he was on the phone to some creature who called herself Madam Swish, "able with a cane".'

Now Rachel couldn't stop herself from giggling. 'Say that again.'

Cynthia repeated it, shaking with laughter. 'It isn't funny at all really. I bet he didn't tell her what he did for a living.'

'He wouldn't, would he? How do they know about this?'

'His credit card.'

'He used his credit card to make the phone call?'

'Those sex lines are expensive. You'd jolly soon run out of coins.'

'And they traced it back. The church people?' Rachel was smiling again, thinking of some pure-minded person in the diocesan office getting through to Madam Swish.

'No, the police. They found it on his bill from Visa. You see, his state of mind on the night he died has to be investigated. There's got to be an inquest. They reckon he was so ashamed after using the sex line that he killed himself.'

'Poor bloke.' She felt guilty now, for laughing.

'He'd marked his bible at some passage about harlots. It was found in the car with a porn mag.'

'That's awful.'

'Of course it won't get out,' Cynthia said. 'They're going to keep it confidential.'

Some chance, with you telling all and sundry, thought Rachel. 'Surely it will have to be made public at the inquest?'

Cynthia was at her most irritating now, airing her supposed inside knowledge. 'There's no need for that. In a case like this, the police tell the coroner ahead of time and he agrees to take certain bits of the evidence as read.

It won't affect the verdict. There's enough to show that he meant to commit suicide. I mean, you don't drive your car into a quarry and park it at the top by accident.'

'But they have to show he was depressed.'

'That's no problem usually. Bishops are under a lot of stress. Someone will say he was overworked and worried about his health, or the state of the world. It's the best way to handle a sensitive case like this.'

'Maybe,' said Rachel, not entirely convinced.

'For the sake of the Church.'

'And his family, I reckon. Did he have a wife?'

'No, but there are two sisters in their seventies. They wouldn't want the sordid details in the papers.'

The facts were clear. Little else of substance needed saying, but Cynthia plainly didn't want to leave it.

'Of course, you know why some men want to be humiliated like that, don't you? I've heard the excuse that it goes back to the public school system, canings, and so on, but it goes much deeper than that. It's all about guilt. They're men with troubled consciences. Their minds are filled with lustful thoughts about women, and they feel so guilty that the only remedy is a good thrashing. It's the natural thing, really – for men of that sort, anyway. I don't think women are like that at all. Suffering is built into our lives, our monthly cycles, childbirth. Guys don't have any of that. They need punishing.'

'You sound as if you wouldn't mind dishing some out,' ventured Rachel, as the wine talked.

Cynthia smiled and took another sip, becoming skittish. 'Why not, if they're attractive men? I could name a few bottoms I wouldn't mind beating.'

'Bishops?'

'God, no. They'd be flabby and covered in pimples.'

'Who, then? Name them. You said you would.' Rachel

could be just as shameless as Cynthia at stoking up the
girl-talk.

'I said I *could*. I didn't say I would.'

'Go on,' she coaxed her.

Cynthia hid most of her face behind the wineglass.
'Michael Owen, Leonardo DiCaprio, Johnny Depp.'

'I thought you were talking about people we *know*.'

'I couldn't.'

'Couldn't do it or couldn't say?'

'You've made me all flustered now.'

'Never. Attractive men, you said. Are there any in
Foxford?'

'Several. All I'm willing to say is that they're under thirty
and not at all like the bishop.' Cynthia reached for the
bottle and filled her glass again. 'My idea is that they
deserve a good beating and have to report to me and
bend over my laundry basket for me to administer six of
the best. And I make it sting.'

'Wow!' said Rachel. The detail of the laundry basket gave
Cynthia's whimsy unexpected substance. This was a full-
blown fantasy. 'So what have they done to deserve this?'

'Oh, passed me in their car without offering me a lift.
Or ignored me in the village shop.'

'You're very severe.'

Cynthia smirked. 'Only on the ones I secretly fancy. If
I'm feeling lenient I wait for a second offence. It's only in
my head, so it doesn't really hurt anyone.'

Rachel was imagining some innocent bloke accepting
an invitation to a meal in Cynthia's cottage.

'The other day, after the church fete, when you didn't
get invited back to the rectory did you . . . ?'

'Take it out on the rector? You bet I did. He got a right
seeing-to.'

'Oh, Cynthia!'

'Well, it wasn't very nice of him, considering all the work I do for the church. You're going to tell me it wasn't deliberate, just an oversight, and perhaps it was, but he ought to have thought of me first – well, among the first.'

'Hey,' said Rachel, 'do you think he knows about the bishop? Would they tell him?'

'I'm sure he doesn't. The clergy are the last people they would tell. It might undermine their respect for bishops in general.'

'Or give them ideas.'

'I don't think Otis is in any danger of going the way of the bishop,' said Cynthia. 'I hope not, anyway.'

Yes, ducky, thought Rachel, it would ruin your steamy little fantasy if he enjoyed being whacked.

Soon after, with no sign of another bottle being opened, Cynthia got up and left, no doubt to startle someone else with her privileged information.

7

B ad news for the confirmation class. Their service was postponed because of the death of the bishop. Immediately Burton Sands demanded to know why another bishop couldn't take over. The church was an inefficient organisation if it couldn't cope with a sudden death. There were over a hundred diocesan and suffragen bishops in the country and surely one of them could step in.

This bloke is a pain, thought Otis Joy before answering patiently, 'In theory you're right, Burton. There's nothing to stop us inviting another bishop, but this is our diocese, and we think it's rather special, like a family. It wouldn't be the same without our own bishop.'

'But our own bishop died last week. The one who confirms us is going to be a stranger, whoever he is.'

'Or she,' chipped in Ann Porter.

'There's no such thing as a woman bishop in the C of E,' said Neary.

'So what's the delay?' asked Sands, not wanting to get into *that* debate.

'These things can't be rushed,' said Joy. 'All kinds of consultation has to take place.'

'And praying,' John Neary helpfully reminded him.

'Praying as well, yes.'

'Would you go for it?' Ann Porter asked.

'Go for . . . ?'

'Bishop.'

'Me?' Joy laughed. 'I'm just a baby. They won't take anyone under thirty. That's official. What's more, you have to be of good character.'

'Is that a problem in your case?'

'Major problem, yes. The dean and chapter wouldn't want a serial sinner like me.'

There were smiles all round the class. He was a breath of fresh air, this rector.

Sands chipped in now. He was interested in the age barrier. 'If you're the right man it shouldn't matter how old you are. Big business has the vision to promote young people to top positions, so why shouldn't the Church?'

'Interesting question, and if I wanted someone to fight my corner I'd choose you, Burton, but I'm happy as I am. Bishoping is boring. I steer clear of things that don't excite me much, like committees. I like what I do.'

'Is it really exciting, being Rector of Foxford?' Ann asked.

'I wouldn't change it for the world.'

This was scheduled as the last of the confirmation classes, but Joy suggested he called another one in the week before the service, whenever that might be, just to remind everyone how it went.

At the end, Sands lingered after the others, wishing to say something, his entire body language confrontational. 'You'll be wanting a new treasurer for the PCC.'

'Yes.'

'Responsible job.'

'Very.'

'Someone asked me if I'd be willing to put myself forward. I don't suppose it matters that I'm not confirmed yet.'

Joy was quick to say, 'That's no problem, Burton. You're in the pipeline, so to speak.'

'Right.'

'The only hiccup is that I've already spoken to someone else.'

The brown eyes narrowed. 'Who's that?'

'I'd rather not say until they make their decision.'

'But I'm a chartered accountant.'

'I know. Isn't it crazy, us overlooking you? Maybe at some future time.'

'Are you saying you don't want me?'

'Not at all. I didn't know you were up for it, that's all.'

'It's up to you, is it?'

'No, the PCC appoints the treasurer. Obviously I'm in a tricky position since I've talked to someone else already. Didn't expect you to come forward. It's not a plum accounting job.'

'I want to do it. What happens? Do we have an election, or what?'

'You're set on this?'

Sands nodded.

Dead set, Otis Joy thought grimly. 'You'd better speak to someone else on the council like Geoff Elliott.'

'I already did. He's the one who asked me.'

Difficult. 'Did he? I see. No problem, then.'

Sands was still unwilling to leave it. 'As a candidate for the job, I'd like to look at the books.'

'The annual statement? That gets published at the end of April. Anyone can have a copy.'

'I said the books. The account books.'

'What for?'

'To see what really goes on. The statement you're talking about is just a summary. Tells you what they want you to know.'

Joy made light of it. '"What really goes on"? I hope you're not suggesting I eat the communion wafers on the quiet.'

'It's a reasonable request, isn't it?'

'Sounds reasonable to me, yes, but we don't even know for sure if there's more than one person applying for the post.'

'I am. That's the point.' His freckled face had become ominously pink.

'OK, Burton, I'll talk to the PCC. See what the form is.'

Burton Sands had no conception of the risk he was running. Joy watched him leave the rectory, rather as the hangman watches a condemned man in the exercise yard, taking stock. He looked at his watch. It was after eight, not too late to make a phone call to his first choice for treasurer.

Rachel, alone in her cottage, thought this might be Gary to say he'd arrived safely in New Orleans. Over there it was still afternoon.

In US style she gave a cheery, 'Hi.'

'Hi, there.' Definitely not Gary. 'That *is* Rachel?'

'Yes.'

'Otis here. The rector.'

'Oh. I was expecting a call from my husband. He's in America.'

'Sorry to disappoint you.'

Disappoint me? You're joking, she thought.

'I can call again at a better time,' he added.

'No, don't. Gary's got all night to get through – if he remembers. Knowing him, he won't.'

'You're alone, then? I was hoping to come round and talk about something.'

'That's all right.'

'It's getting late. There's never a right time, is there?'

'Now's fine by me.'

'Ten minutes, then?'

'I'll get the kettle on.'

Or should I have offered to open a bottle, her wilder self suggested when she'd put down the phone. Wow! Alone with Otis after dark. What would Cynthia say to this?

Cynthia. Panic seized her. What if the rector had got wind that gossip was being spread about the bishop and was trying to put a stop to it? Cringe!

Bloody Cynthia. To be lumped with her as a village blabbermouth was horrible.

She barely had time to freshen her face when the doorbell chimed.

He was in one of those grey shirts with a little strip of dog-collar across his throat. Formal, by his standards. She was so fearful of what he would say that she avoided eye contact.

'Tea or coffee, Rector?'

'How kind. Whatever.'

The perfect cue for the wine bottle, but she chickened out. Merlot didn't fit the butter-wouldn't-melt image she had to project.

He came through to the kitchen, insisting she shouldn't make the tea alone. She'd forgotten about her fractured arm. For a few minutes they talked about Gary's trip. You would think she'd been to New Orleans herself the way she listed its attractions while busying herself with the cups and saucers, desperate to put off the moment when he came to the point.

Then he managed to get in with: 'You won't mind me saying this, Rachel. I feel I know you better than many other women in the village.'

She felt the hairs rise on her unplastered arm.

He went on: 'I guess it's because we've shared in a couple of awkward moments, like the evening you caught me starkers except for an apron.'

'And my pratfall in the churchyard, which was worse,' she said before he could.

'I wasn't there when you fell over,' he gallantly said. 'When I arrived you were sitting on Waldo's grave with everyone around you. What I'm trying to say is that your calmness under fire is impressive. Cake stalls at the fete, door-to-door collections, a broken wrist – you take it all in your stride.'

'No use getting in a flap,' she said, wondering how this linked up with gossip about the bishop.

'Exactly. Thing is, I'm on the lookout for someone with a sure touch and a calm temperament.'

No reprimand, then.

Her face must have lit up, because he said, 'You'll do it?'

'What?'

'The job of parish treasurer. I started to mention it the other day when I asked if you had any experience of book-keeping.'

Reeling at how mistaken she had been, she succeeded in saying, 'But I told you I don't have any.'

'This is kids' stuff, Rachel. You don't need a degree in accountancy, just a steady personality. Stanley Burrows had it. He was no mathematician. Couldn't even use a calculator. I'd rather have someone like you than a busybody who throws a spanner in the works every time we need a ten-pound float for a Sunday School outing.'

She let him fill the teapot, wondering what had got into his head. Was she deluding herself, or did he fancy her like crazy?

'I might be willing to give it a go if someone could help

me at the beginning,' she said after a moment. 'There's no one I can ask, with Stanley gone.'

'Ask me. I'll spend as long as you wish going over the books.' His golden-brown eyes glittered encouragement and that sexy voice of his made it sound like a come-on.

'Thanks.'

He carried the tray into the living room.

There, he spotted her copy of the play and asked about her acting, bombarding her with questions that sounded as if he really wanted to know. It was like being on a first date, and she basked in his interest, telling him everything, from the walk-on as a maid in an Ayckbourn comedy with the Frome Troupers to her great week as Portia in the prize-winning production at the Merlin. She made him laugh about the battles over the choice of play, of how transparent people are when pushing their choice – the would-be St Joans being pressed reluctantly into bimbo parts in bedroom farces.

'How I sympathise,' he said. 'It must be hellish for actors having to go downmarket. You know the story of Julie Andrews. I can't say how true it is, but she's supposed to have gone around wearing a badge that said "Mary Poppins is a Junkie".'

Rachel had relaxed enough to laugh at that.

'All these egos fighting it out,' he said. 'This is fascinating stuff. I want to see the next show. October, you said. I'll be there. Front stalls. And I want to hear all the backstage goss, whose lines are cut and who demands a better costume. It's always a lot more fun than the play itself.'

'From a safe distance,' she said, 'but not if you're in the thick of it.'

'You can tell me. I can keep a secret better than most.'

She smiled. 'OK.'

'I haven't kept up with the stage since I was ordained.

It's a pity, but there isn't time for everything. And we do get a certain amount of theatre in church. Dressing-up, for one thing. And making an entrance.'

'Speaking lines.'

'And trying to hold an audience.'

'Singing.'

'Not my strong point, Rachel. The Sung Eucharist is an ordeal for me, and worse, I'm sure, for the congregation. Thank heaven there's no dancing in the C of E – not in the churches I've known, anyway.'

'Like Hare Krishna?'

'Or whirling Dervishes. I'm not a pretty mover.'

In this self-mocking mood, he seemed open to the kind of question Rachel put next. 'What led you to become a priest? Was it a calling?'

'In a way it was. A Road to Damascus thing. I was raised as a Catholic. Went to a Jesuit school. When I was in my early teens I went to a C of E wedding at a church tucked away in the country and heard the vicar conducting the service in the simple, lovely words of the sixteen sixty-two Prayer Book – "Those whom God hath joined together let no man put asunder" – and I thought, magic! This is what I must do. My future was decided that morning. Of course it was a hard slog in theological college learning the doctrine, but I never wanted anything else.'

'Even though the words have been modernised?'

'They changed them a long time before I was ordained. I understand the reason and I don't knock it. As you know I still make a point of using the traditional liturgy one Sunday each month. Some people come specially for that service. I never see them otherwise.'

She ventured into another personal area. 'You've got the ideal name for the work you do.'

'My name?' He smiled. 'I've taken some stick for it, but

people remember it, which isn't a bad thing. I can tell you a story of how it came about, but I can't guarantee it's true. The midwife at my birth was a West Indian called Miss Pushmore.'

'No!'

'Really. People *do* get names that fit their jobs. And the story goes that at the critical moment Miss Pushmore cried out, "O, 'tis joy, it's a boy!" – but I don't believe that one. And I don't believe the other story either.'

'What's that?'

'That my parents didn't realise what they were doing when they named me. It's more likely, isn't it, that they were feeling playful when they were going through the possible names, and had a laugh about Otis and then decided it sounded rather good and took it seriously?'

'You never asked them?'

'They died when I was this high.'

'Oh.'

'At seven, I was shipped off to a children's home in Ireland. The nuns didn't call us by our names much. It was a case of "You, boy. Hold out your hand."'

'I'm sorry.'

'Don't be. It paid off in the end. Learned my Bible from the nuns. Served me in good stead.'

'Otis is distinguished. I like it,' Rachel told him, wanting to hear more about his personal history, but not by probing.

'Then feel free to use it. I've already dropped into the habit of calling you Rachel.' He looked at the clock on the wall. 'I should be off. Thanks so much for the tea. And, more importantly, for agreeing to let me put you up for treasurer.'

'If you're sure you want me.'

'That's why I'm here. Between you and me, I wouldn't

say anything about your inexperience to other people in the village. Let them think you're confident you can handle it with ease.' He picked up the tray and carried it through to the kitchen.

She followed. 'Does it have to be confirmed by the Parish Council?'

'Yes, and there may be another name bandied about, but you have my support, which ought to swing it.'

She was alarmed by that. 'Someone else is up for it?'

He put down the tray, turned and reached out, placing both hands on her upper arms. 'My dear, you don't have to do a thing. It's pure formality. The PCC has to have a couple of names to consider so that it doesn't look like a fix.'

She felt his fingers squeeze her slightly and convey something extra.

'Trust me?'

She nodded.

'Say it. Say, "Otis, I trust you."'

She repeated the words.

'Good. The next time I call, it will be to congratulate you.'

He let go of her, went to the front door and opened it. 'I hope you get your phone call.'

She didn't understand.

'Your husband.'

'Oh.'

She watched him go.

Gary didn't call that evening, but she wasn't bothered. Her thoughts were all on this amazing conversation, on the way he'd held her, looked into her eyes, spoken to her.

'*Trust me?*'

She finished the wine, shaking her head at intervals. She was mature, married, sexually experienced, yet she felt like a teenager with a crush on some unattainable man. She could still feel his touch on her arms. Why would he single her out for this job she had no aptitude for unless he fancied her? '*I'm happy to spend as long as you wish going over the books.*' So was it just an excuse to spend time with her? And what did he want – companionship? Or, God forgive her, a relationship?

He'd been married, if the stories were true, and tragically his wife had died. He was young, living alone, probably desperately lonely, sexually frustrated. Priests are not without the same needs and desires as other men. He could easily be telling himself he needed some female company, a friendship, someone to relax with. And more? Surely he couldn't be planning an adulterous affair with her? That would be against the faith he preached.

Fleetingly, sinfully, she cast him in the role of her lover, gripped by such desire for her that he broke his vows or promises, or whatever priests are supposed to live by, and made passionate love to her while Gary was away. It was graphic and easy to picture, this image of him naked as she'd almost seen him once, only this time he was here with her, in this cottage, in her own bed, tender, adoring, passionate and vigorous.

She stood up, hot from her fantasy.

Ridiculous.

She was an adult, a member of the church, a wife. She'd agreed to take on a job for the church, and that was all. He'd recognised her qualities, her calmness under pressure, and seen that she was the right person to manage the accounts. That was reality.

Yet in bed that night she imagined the other thing and heard him saying 'Trust me?' so clearly that his head could have been on the pillow beside her.

'Otis,' she said. 'Otis Joy.'

8

S candals about the clergy usually break in the Sunday press just before the faithful go to worship. The story headed BISHOP'S LEAP OF SHAME was no exception. The village shop had sold out of the *News of the World* by nine-thirty, and the sense of shock had turned to a quirkish mood of high spirits and even some amusement by the eleven o'clock service. Bishops have always been figures of fun – from a distance. The Reverend Joy had never shirked an issue yet, so how would he deal with the Bend Over Bishop and Madam Swish's telephone service?

He was on form. 'Flagellation,' he opened his sermon, and the pews creaked with the clenching of buttocks. 'We Christians know plenty about it, or should. "Of the Jews five times received I forty stripes save one," St Paul tells us. "Thrice was I beaten with rods." Our Lord himself was scourged.'

No one was amused any more.

'Through all the ages, saints, monks, nuns and penitents have punished themselves, or been punished with whips, canes and birches. It was thought to be cleansing, a penance. So how does a penance become a perversion? When it turns you on. If it's about penitence, okay. If you enjoy it, no, no. Then it's masochism.'

The shocking word carried up the old stone walls and sounded off the roof. Joy paused, and lowered his voice.

'The papers tell us – and we all believe the papers, don't we? – that Marcus, our bishop, indulged in flagellation. How? On the phone, using a credit card. His actions harmed nobody. And afterwards he was found dead. End of story. Pretty depressing stuff. You wouldn't think so, reading the papers – and, in case you're wondering, I saw them too. They play up every salacious detail, as they always do when the clergy are caught out. Yes, we expect our bishops to be of good character. Marcus strayed from the path, if this report is true. Who has not done a foolish, humiliating thing at some time in his life? I don't mind telling you I have. I try to lead the good life, and sometimes I fail. Let's take a moment now to think about our own moments of weakness and shame.' He paused.

No one even cleared his throat.

'And now imagine the worst of all scenarios: not just that your sin is trumpeted to the entire nation, but that all the good things you did in your life are downgraded by this act. Now hear the word of the Lord. "He that is without sin among you, let him cast first a stone."'

It was a chastened congregation that filed out into the sunshine.

Monday's Scrabble evening with George Mitchell had to be put off. The Parochial Church Council met at the rectory to appoint the new treasurer. It was the first full attendance in a long time. After the usual opening prayer, Otis Joy said, 'A problem, ladies and gentlemen. Two names have been put forward, one from Geoff Elliott, the other from me. If I vacate the chair, as I wish to in this case, Geoff, your vice-chairman, should take over, but . . .' He smiled.

Norman Gregor, the churchwarden who farmed the fields below the village, took over the chair. He invited Elliott to speak first, and a fine case he made for Burton

Sands. 'This young man is extremely keen to take up the post and there's no question as to his competence, accountancy being his profession. He's a regular attender at services. True, he hasn't been confirmed yet, but he's been attending the rector's confirmation group, and I don't see that anyone could object if we invited him to become our treasurer. A more able and committed candidate would be hard to find.'

Gregor said with a twinkle in his eye, 'But the rector believes he has found one. Over to you, Rector.'

The meeting was treated to a *tour de force* in the art of persuasion. Like a beaten man Joy sighed and spread his hands. 'These decisions are tough, aren't they? You've heard the case for Burton. Who could top it? Rachel Jansen isn't an accountant. She's less keen than Burton to take the job. Less confident. I had to sell the idea to her. So what are her qualifications? Like Burton, she's in church every Sunday. She's active in charity work and well known in the village for house-to-house collections and the support she gives to all our social events. A calm, intelligent woman unlikely to ruffle feathers.'

'Why isn't she on the PCC already?' someone interrupted.

'Fair point. Rachel is one of those people who don't push themselves forward. She's not pushy. I've discovered in my short career in the church that it's worth making the effort to persuade such people to get involved. The reason we're having this discussion is that none of you wants to be treasurer. We're forced to look outside the PCC. Now that Rachel and I have talked, she'd like to be considered for the post.'

'You fancy yourself as a talent-spotter, Rector,' commented Peggy Winner, the third churchwarden.

'I just believe she could do the job.'

The chairman said with a smile, 'Let's have the sub-text, Rector. What's your objection to Mr Sands?'

'No objection at all. I know Burton well from the confirmation group. You have to admire his persistence. He's a stickler for detail.'

'Isn't that what you want in a treasurer?'

'Yes, it's essential.'

Peggy said, 'It's a question of how it's done, isn't it? Maybe the rector thinks Burton doesn't have the delicate touch a woman has.'

'That's unfair,' said Elliott.

'The rector didn't say it,' the chairman pointed out, 'and I don't think he's finished yet.'

Joy nodded. 'I wouldn't suggest we give the job to Rachel because she's a woman. After all, our last treasurer was a man and he was a model of tact. You only had to watch Stanley being gently diplomatic when some old dear got her sums wrong.'

'But we don't want a doormat for treasurer,' Elliott couldn't resist pointing out.

'Rachel is no doormat, Geoff,' said Joy.

'I wasn't speaking personally.'

'Right.' He played his trump card. 'There's just one thing I would add. Whoever takes on the post automatically becomes a member of this council. I may be speaking out of turn, but I think we'll find meetings going on rather longer if Burton is here than they do at present. He likes the sound of his voice and he's strong on points of order.'

'Oh, Christ,' said Gregor and spoke for so many others that the blasphemy passed without comment.

There were looks all round the table. No question: the rector had won the day. There wasn't even a vote. Elliott withdrew his nomination and Rachel was appointed as the new treasurer.

The meeting ended in just under the half-hour. 'If Sands had been here, we'd have been discussing it till midnight,' Norman Gregor said to Peggy Winner as they lingered outside on the drive.

'What was it about?' she said.

Norman's shaggy eyebrows popped up at the question.

'What's the rector up to?' Peggy said. 'What's the hidden agenda here?'

'I'm not with you, Peg.'

'Rachel's a sweet woman, but who'd think about her for parish treasurer?'

'The rector did.'

'Yes, and we all backed his choice because he's the top banana. I was expecting him to tell us she took a degree in maths or worked in a bank or something. No experience. Nothing. He's got his doubts about Burton Sands. Fine. Pick someone else, but why pick Rachel?'

'Maybe it's for her sake.'

'Why?'

'To get her involved more.'

Peggy was scornful of that theory. 'She's involved. More involved than most of us. She goes round the houses collecting for this and that. She's always in the thick of it when we have a fete or a safari supper or carol-singing. And she's into acting, for heaven's sake. She was in that thing about the women's Turkish bath, *Steaming*. She doesn't need bringing out.'

'What do you think, then?'

A grin spread over Peggy's face. 'Not for me to say.' But it was transparently clear what she meant.

'She's married,' said Norman.

Peggy nodded, still grinning.

'And him a man of God?' said Norman. 'You must have it wrong.'

'He was hitched before. He knows what it is to be with a woman.'

'But not someone else's wife. That's against the Commandments. You want to be careful what you say, Peggy. The rector's a much respected man here and Rachel's not that sort of woman at all, what I've seen of her.'

'He took her off to the hospital in his car the day she broke her arm.'

'So he should have, too. It happened on his patch. If you want my opinion, Peggy, you read too many of those Jackie Collins books.'

'I didn't say they were up to things . . . yet.'

'Oh, come on!'

Peggy laughed. 'We'll see.'

'I hope not,' Norman said. 'He's a breath of fresh air to this village. I'd hate to see him caught with his pants down.' He opened his car and tossed his briefcase inside. 'Would you like a lift, or would that be *my* reputation down the plughole?'

Otis phoned Rachel with the news. As he'd expected, she was still uncomfortable with the idea. He told her the decision had been so clear it hadn't even been put to the vote. She was ideally suited to be treasurer, he insisted, and it was nice that the PCC had shown such confidence.

He said he wasn't able to visit her that evening to congratulate her personally as he had one more pastoral call to make.

Disappointed, she didn't want to appear selfish, wanting a share of his time when he was so committed to his work in the parish. She knew from things she heard at work that he spent hours comforting the sick, the bereaved and the lonely.

'How about some time Wednesday evening?' he suggested, and her spirit soared. 'I can't manage tomorrow. It's my free day and I won't be around.'

'Somewhere nice?' she asked on impulse, knowing it was none of her business, but giving him the chance, if he wished, to take her into his confidence. Instantly she knew she sounded like a chattering schoolgirl angling for a date.

'Not specially,' he said. 'Is Wednesday possible? It isn't just about congratulating you. We should start to look at the books.'

'Wednesday is fine . . . Otis.'

'Excellent.'

They fixed a time of seven-thirty.

Immediately she put the phone down it rang again.

'So, big spender, when are you off to the Bahamas?'

Cynthia, being waggish.

'With the church money, you mean?' said Rachel. 'No chance. I'll be lucky if I get to Weymouth with the Sunday school.'

'Congratulations anyway, darling. I just heard. How refreshing to have a woman write the cheques. I was rooting for you, of course. We didn't want that tepid little teabag taking over. He thought he was home and dry, no contest, him being a chartered accountant.' Hoots of laughter came down the phone. 'He won't have the faintest notion how it happened. How did it happen?'

'I've no idea, Cyn. I wasn't there.'

'And no one's told you? Hasn't the rector been on yet to give you the news?'

'Yes. A few minutes ago.'

'I should think so, too. Is he coming round to share a bottle of bubbly with you?'

'No, Cynthia,' she said, not liking the drift of this. 'There isn't any cause for celebration. It's just a job I was asked to take on.'

'Yes, but he put you up for it. He should stand you a drink, at the very least. You'll see him later, I expect?'

Questions, questions, questions.

'No. He's busy.'

'Tomorrow? Oh. Forgot. That's his day off. He'll be away before breakfast and back about midnight. Where *does* he go every Tuesday?'

'I haven't the faintest idea. Cyn, who else was up for treasurer?'

'Didn't anyone tell you? Sourpuss. The one who never smiles. He would have been a real damper on the parish council.'

'Yes, but who? Did you say he's an accountant?'

Cynthia laughed. 'A *chartered* accountant, my dear. He goes off every day in his pinstripe suit to Warminster clutching his little briefcase with his tuna sandwiches inside.'

Now she knew who Cynthia meant. 'Burton Sands. And they chose me? I don't understand it.'

'Otis wanted you, that's obvious. He'd rather deal with you than a pain in the arse like Burton, and who wouldn't? Good thing you're happily married, ducky, or tongues might wag.'

'For pity's sake, Cynthia.'

'How is Gary? Has he phoned you from America?'

Cynthia didn't let up.

'Not yet. It's difficult with the time difference and everything. I'm sure he's having a good time.'

'Not too good, I hope.'

When she came off the phone, Rachel shook her head and sighed, but less over Cynthia than the remarkable decision of the PCC.

She made herself tea, trying to understand how Otis could have swung the decision her way. He could charm the birds off the trees, she knew, but she couldn't imagine how he persuaded anyone she would make a better treasurer than Burton Sands. Yet it had been so obvious, he'd said, that it hadn't even been put to the vote.

Wednesday evening, then. What would she put on? The suits she wore to church each Sunday simply would not do. In her own home she ought to strike a less formal note, not the sweater and jeans she was wearing right now, but something that set a relaxed mood, for him, as well as herself. A dress, she decided, and nothing too tartish. She had a dark green frock she had bought in Kensington last time she had been to London, with sweet little fabric-covered buttons to the neck and a full skirt. Gary had liked it. No – she thought the minute Gary sprang to mind – I won't wear that old thing. I'll go to Bath tomorrow and look round the shops. Treat myself to something really special. A drop-dead dress, as they say in America. Well, a stunner, at least.

Then there was the food. He wouldn't expect a full meal at that stage of the evening, but she had to offer something. Sweet or savoury? A warm dish would be best. She was brilliant at individual soufflés that always rose and spilled over the top, but they needed whisking, and it might be difficult dashing between the Magimix and the account books. The food ought to be ready-cooked and warmed up with the minimum of fuss. Quiche, or pizza. Quiche, she thought, for the rector. Better still, some of those extra-special cocktail snacks from the delicatessen in Bath. She'd get them at the same time as she got the dress. And if she served cocktail snacks, she had to have a bottle of wine.

A bit OTT?

Not for Otis. Hang the expense. She'd get a vintage red and see if it went to his head.

Early the next morning while most of Foxford was sleeping, Otis Joy drove out of the village in his old Cortina and headed south, humming 'All things bright and beautiful'. Along the quiet Wiltshire roads rabbits were nibbling at the verges. Freshly drilled wheatfields testified to autumn, yet still it felt like summer. The sun was showing above the downs and the sky was so clear that he could see the fading of the moon. He was wearing jeans and a check shirt. No dog-collar on his day off.

As usual he took the A350 through Warminster and down into Dorset by way of Shaftesbury. He was at Blandford Forum by eight. There, he left the main road and drove into the town and stopped for breakfast at a small café that was open from seven-thirty and known to a few locals and early-morning travellers.

He went in and sat at his favourite table by the window, with a good view down the street. They even had the morning papers.

The woman who took the orders and did the cooking as well at this time of day came out of the kitchen holding a menu, saw who it was, smiled and said, 'Well, you won't be needing this. Your usual, is it?'

'Of course,' said Joy.

She smiled. 'Lovely morning. And how are you, Mr Beggarstaff?'

9

She felt terrific in the dress. She had found it in Northumberland Passage, in a shop she didn't know existed. Calf-length and loose-fitting, raw silk in a colour they called bronze, with hints of scarlet in the weave, it wasn't drop-dead, but it oozed style. Which wasn't wasted on Otis Joy. He made no comment when he arrived, yet the glint in those deep-set eyes said enough.

Rachel thought it a pity he hadn't left the clerical collar at home this evening. True, it was only the token strip of white above a pale grey shirt. Otherwise he was casual, but smart, in a dark green jacket and cream trousers fashionably loose in the fit.

He was holding a carton stacked high with account books.

She suggested they did the business part first and he looked mildly surprised as if he couldn't think what the other part was. She told him she had some nibbles to warm up for later and he gave her another glance.

The business part.

She had a coffee table ready for him to spread out the books and she'd placed it in front of the sofa. She would sit beside him and make nothing of it. No other arrangement would work. The sofa was a four-seater that dominated the room, so it wouldn't be a squeeze. The only problem was the enormous soft cushions that threatened to suck you in like a swamp as they took your weight. She let him find out for himself. He sank in some way and then struggled against it and managed to perch precariously on the edge. Without fuss Rachel took her position next to him.

He busied himself leaning over the box to lift out the contents, and they made a daunting collection. When everything was on the table he picked up the main account book, a huge leather-bound volume as big as the lectern Bible in church, and opened it. 'Here we go, then. You see how simple it is? The income – that's the money from the offertory, renting out the church hall, fund-raising events and all the rest – goes on this side, and we have the debits on the left, here, with columns for the diocesan quota, petty cash, postage, printing, station-ery, insurance, wafers and wine for the eucharist and so forth.'

'They're beautifully kept,' she remarked.

'Stanley was a tidy writer.'

'My figures are going to look crude after his.'

'Doesn't matter as long as they add up. Have you got a calculator? Stanley never bothered with one. A bit old-fashioned. Like the elderly civil servant at the Treasury who advised every government since the war.'

He'd lost her momentarily, laying the ground for one of his funny stories.

'Brilliant man. Genius with figures. He could analyse a balance sheet quicker than any computer. Only whenever he was asked for advice he'd first of all go to the safe in his office, unlock it and take out a scrap of paper and look at it. Then he'd fold it and put it back and close the safe before summing up the state of the nation's finances. On the day he died, the people he worked with rushed to the safe and took out the piece of paper. It said, "Debits on the left, credits on the right."'

She gave a polite smile. The joke wasn't one of his better ones.

He said, 'If you'd like a calculator, get one on expenses.'

'I'm sure we've got one. I might have to charge the church for some new batteries.'

'Fine. Enter it in the petty cash book. Now look at these regular payments. They're covered by standing orders at the bank.'

She studied the columns of figures, trying to focus, and thinking, God, I've got him on my sofa close enough to . . . and we're talking about standing orders. 'Your own expenses don't amount to much.'

'True.' He didn't elaborate.

We're mature, sexually experienced adults sitting here like virgins on a first date because he's in holy orders and I'm married. Pulling a clergyman must be the ultimate challenge. God, she thought, I must keep that wild streak of mine in check.

'Have we cracked it?' he asked.

'Mm?'

'Is it clear to you?'

'So far. I won't make too much of a mess of it, I hope. What else do I need to know?'

'One step at a time.'

'If you don't mind, I'd like to get the full picture.' Just a hint that he was patronising her.

'Sure.' He smoothed his hands along the tops of his thighs. He was unusually tense and it distracted from the things he was saying. 'No pressure at all until early next year. We work to the calendar year, so in January we make sure everything is in shape and hand the books, receipts and so on to the auditors. The audited accounts are ready for the February meeting of the PCC.'

'And I must be ready for questions.'

'Possibly, but I doubt it. The whole thing went through on the nod last time. And after they approve them, we present them to the Annual Parochial Church Meeting.'

'That's all?'

'There are some statistical returns for the diocese that we don't need to bother with at this stage. I'll give you all the help I can.'

'Thanks.'

They looked at the petty cash book and the box file containing the vouchers and invoices. It was all immaculately sorted in transparent folders. At one stage the chequebook fell on the floor and they both reached for it and their hands touched.

Electric.

She handed the chequebook to him and he returned it to the file without actually looking at her.

'Happy so far?'

She nodded. 'Except for one thing.'

He said with a note of caution, 'Yes?'

'I'm puzzled why you put me up for this when Burton Sands is a professional accountant.'

He continued to rearrange the books. 'The PCC made the decision, Rachel.'

'At your suggestion.'

'Well, that's true.' Now he turned to her, and their faces were tantalisingly close. His hazel eyes locked with hers, slipped away and then returned. 'I wanted you for this. I know you'll do it well. The others simply agreed with me.'

'Why me?' she pressed him.

He turned aside, clearly reluctant to say more. 'This job doesn't really require a professional. What matters is how it's handled. The right touch.'

She wished she had waited until after the wine to ask

that question. She might have got the answer she was fishing for.

She said the eats should be ready and he said he hadn't expected anything, but he sprang up and offered to help with the carrying.

'*Wine*?' he said when she gave him the tray with the glasses.

'You do drink red, I hope? I thought you must, so I opened it before you came.'

'An act of faith.'

'You do drink it?'

'When I get the chance.'

The savouries smelt delicious. She took them from the oven and followed him in from the kitchen and reclaimed her place beside him on the sofa.

He was sitting further back, slightly more relaxed. 'Let's drink to your success.'

'Yours,' she said. 'You talked them into it.'

'Ours, then.' They touched glasses and drank. 'Hey, this is a cut above, isn't it? What are we drinking?'

'Chateauneuf du Pape, ninety-six.'

'Papist? Doubly wicked.' He reached for a filo-wrapped bite. 'You shouldn't have.'

'It's a treat for me. Gary's a beer drinker. I don't buy wine normally. One or two glasses and I get bosky.'

'*Bosky.* That's an old-fashioned word.'

Old-fashioned situation, she thought, a man and a woman sharing a sofa, sitting up primly like this. 'I expect you're very level-headed.'

'I wish. I'm not a regular drinker either. Can't afford it. There's a cellar in the rectory where Waldo Wallace made his beer, but now it just has cobwebs and old copies of the *Church Times.*'

'It must be difficult being a priest. At certain times, I mean.'

He gave the wrong answer. Totally off message. 'Not at all. I wouldn't change it for the world. It's a real high being a front man for God.'

'Yes, but there must be times . . .'

'You can't compare it with ordinary jobs, Rachel. I could earn more cleaning windows, yes, but what I do is immensely satisfying. Even if you put aside the spiritual highs, I have the status, the dressing up, the preaching, the sense of being needed. I get invitations all the time. I can't say I always strike lucky as I have tonight – your hospitality, I mean – but I meet people, lovely people.'

'They can't all be lovely. There must be some you'd rather not spend time with.'

'Not many.' His eyes flashed. 'And if I play my cards right, I can get the PCC to outvote them.'

She had another try to get him off this topic. 'Being good all the time must be a strain. Everyone knows who you are.'

He laughed. 'I'm not good *all* the time. Good at covering up. That's the first thing you learn.'

She smiled back, doing all she could to fan this faint spark. 'I expect your sins are very tame compared with other people's.'

'Don't count on it. But I never talk about them. Bad public relations. May I have another of these? They're yummy.'

'And a drop more wine?'

'Only if you join me.'

'I'll fetch the bottle.'

'No. Let me.' He was definitely lightening up.

When he sat down again he was closer to her. Their faces almost touched when he turned to speak. 'There's one more thing I'd like to mention.'

'Yes?'

'About the books.'

The bloody books. She couldn't believe it. 'Oh, I thought we'd—'

He talked across her, as if he hadn't a clue what she was leading up to, or trying to. 'An arrangement I had with Stanley that I hope you'll go along with. It's to do with the quota we pay to the diocese. Did I tell you about the quota?'

'I know what it is.'

'A large chunk of our income, that's what it is, Rachel, and they've hiked it up in recent years. I don't mind shelling out what I think is fair, but small country parishes like ours pay way over the odds.'

'Shame.' Flippant she may have sounded, sarcastic even, but she didn't need church politics at this stage of the evening.

'That's putting it mildly.' He missed her reaction completely. 'And the more successful you are in fund-raising, the more they penalise you. So I talked it over with Stanley and we opened a new account called the contingency fund. I use it for my expenses – which is why they're so modest.'

'The *what* fund?'

'Contingency. A sort of hedge against the unexpected.'

'I didn't notice it in the books,' she said, beginning to pay attention.

'No, you wouldn't. That's the point. It's separate from the bank stuff. A building society account.'

'And it doesn't go through the books?'

'Exactly.'

'Is it legal?'

'All above board, yes. It's in my name. They tax the interest at source.'

'But if it's church money . . .'

'It goes on church expenses.'

She wasn't at all sure about this. 'But where does the money come from?'

'Extras. There are always dribs and drabs that come in late after something like the fete. Instead of inflating our bank account I put them into the contingency fund.'

She was alerted to something irregular now. 'There must be a statement to show how much is in there.'

'Among these things? No. We don't want the diocese making waves and putting up the quota, do we?'

'Is that certain to happen?'

'Certain as the Creed. Some churches have been forced to close because they can't pay their way. People have worshipped in St Bartholomew's for a thousand years. We can't let it go just because in the twenty-first century the Diocesan Board of Finance is too grasping.' It was a passionate speech. Not the one Rachel had hoped to hear, but strong in emotion.

She was uneasy. She didn't like the sound of this contingency fund. She would be treasurer, and treasurers carried the can.

She must have sighed, or perhaps her face gave too much away, because he placed his hand over hers. 'Rachel, you see the point of this, don't you?'

She turned to look at him, responding to his touch.

Those amazing eyes of his were wide in anticipation, melting her.

She nodded, telling herself sometimes you have to go with the flow. 'Yes, I see.'

And now their faces were so close that it seemed the most natural thing for their lips to meet lightly, as if to seal an understanding, and so they did.

The hell with the contingency fund.

As they drew apart she grabbed the back of his neck
with her good arm, pulled him towards her again and
kissed him with passion, pressing her lips hard against
his. He responded by leaning towards her, pushing her
firmly back into the corner of the sofa. Their mouths
relaxed and found a better position. His fingertips were
on her face, stroking her cheek, a light, sensuous touch
that thrilled her. Then the fingers moved across her neck
and over her breast.

This is it, she thought. I'm seducing a priest. I'll pay for
this on Judgement Day and I don't give a toss.

There was a crash. Not the gates of Heaven being
slammed. Just his leg or hers nudging the coffee table
and knocking over the wine bottle.

He drew back and looked behind him.

'Oh, no!'

He sat right up and so did she.

The bottle was on the floor, on its side. He grabbed
it up. A large stain was spreading over the mushroom-
coloured carpet.

She said automatically, 'Oh, Jesus!' Then, 'It's all right.'
It wasn't. She ran out to the kitchen and fetched a sponge
and warm water.

When she came back he was trying to clean splashes
off the account books with a handkerchief. She knelt and
rubbed at the carpet with her one good hand. The stain
was the size of a saucer.

'I think I'm only making it worse.'

'Want me to try? There must be something you use for
wine stains. Salt?'

She shook her head, attacking the stain past the point
when she was making any difference. She was putting off
the moment when they faced each other again. They'd
messed up in every sense.

He suggested she let the stain dry and use a commercial stain-remover. He'd stopped trying to clean up the books.

'They're not too bad,' he said. 'It can't be helped. I'm really sorry about the carpet.'

'My own fault,' said Rachel. 'Made a right idiot of myself.'

'Don't say that. Don't say anything. Let's have a pact. No blame, no regrets, no thoughts of what might have been, right?'

That would be impossible, but she murmured something.

'Above all, no talking about it to anyone else.'

'Agreed.'

He said, 'I've got to go. You understand why?'

'Mm.'

He smiled faintly. 'Potent wine.'

'Yes.'

'It doesn't mean we can't work on the books again. In fact we must. You're going to need help. I'll just have to stick to the one glass in future.'

'Me, too.'

She went to the door with him. Before leaving, he put his hand lightly on her forearm and said, 'Thanks.'

She watched him to the gate and up the street. From first to last it had been a cringe-making mistake. And when she closed the door and went back inside, and saw the great box of account books and the stain on the floor, she made a sound deep in her throat that was nothing less than a howl.

10

New Orleans had been paradise. Gary was back, red-faced and triumphant, keen to talk about his great adventure, but in a way that put Rachel down. 'You've never heard anything like it and never will. Jeez, those long, hot nights in Preservation Hall and the Palm Court Jazz Café. We were cutting it up until dawn usually.'

'Which was why you didn't get to the phone.'

'I called you.'

'Once in three weeks.'

'Sure, honey.' He'd taken on some outdated Americanisms that irritated her even more. 'By the time I was waking up most days, around two in the afternoon, I needed to eat, and when I got to thinking of calling home it was always too bloody late over here, with the time difference, so I didn't disturb you. There wasn't much I could tell you anyway. It's a blur, but, man, what a blur.'

The Southern cooking – even in the inexpensive places Gary and his friends had patronised – had suited him better than he expected. Glaring at the pork chop and two veg Rachel served up, he talked with relish about delicacies she could only imagine, gumbo and po-boys, black-eyed beans and jambalaya.

He was so high from the trip that he didn't notice the wine stain on the living room carpet. Rachel had tried glycerine and a carpet shampoo and got some of the colour out. It was still an eyesore. She'd brushed in talcum powder and made a small difference, but not enough.

He said, 'I can't think why I left it so late in my life to make a trip like this one. You can keep your holidays in Budleigh Salterton. I'll be jetting to the jazz spots in future.'

The cosmopolitan Gary was a new infliction. Practically every statement he made about America downgraded England – and, by association, herself.

Later the same evening he said he wasn't feeling so good.

Rachel said it was probably the jet-lag.

'I don't think so.'

'How do you know? You've never been on a jet before.'

'Neither have you. I've got this pain across the chest. Can't shift it.'

'Could be something to do with the way you were sitting in the plane.'

'Hope it's not my heart.' He'd always insisted he had a heart murmur, whatever that was. Just an excuse for not helping with the garden, Rachel always thought.

'If you're worried, let's call the doctor.'

He didn't want the doctor, but after another hour of groaning and self-pity he thought better of it and let her phone. Old Dr Perkins was on duty that evening and he was at the cottage inside twenty minutes. After pressing the stethoscope to Gary's chest, he said that the beat was a little irregular, but nothing to be alarmed about. 'You say you've just had a long flight from the United States – and some over-indulgence there, am I right? It's a big effort for the body, bigger than we appreciate, flying for hours and then having to adjust to another time. This may well be a touch of angina.'

'Angina? At my age?' Gary was horrified.

'What are you – mid forties?'

'Only forty-two,' Gary said, and the hurt at the doctor's over-estimate sounded in his voice.

'It's better than a full blown heart attack, I can assure you. If you're sensible, it needn't hamper you unduly. Some of my patients have had angina for years and lived well into their eighties.' He produced a nitroglycerin tablet for Gary to chew and told him it should relieve the pain rapidly. It would still be necessary to have some tests on the heart function and he would arrange a hospital appointment.

The tablet worked, and Gary was still asleep when Rachel left in the morning for her appointment with the orthopaedic surgeon.

The bliss! It had been worth an 8.30 hospital appointment to be released from that horrid, heavy, grease-stained plaster. Now she was in the front garden making up for lost time, attacking some of the most vigorous weeds. Festoons of bindweed had taken over while she'd been unable to work out there, and when she tugged it away in satisfying armfuls she revealed other horrors, ground elder, couch grass, creeping buttercups and sticky groundsel. Some wild flowers she was willing to tolerate in a cottage garden. Harebells, columbines, the pink foxgloves, the purple monkshood and the dog rose hedge coexisted with the expensive plants she had bought from nurseries. The majority of the weeds had to go. Just about everything needed attention. If it wasn't overgrown, it was ailing. But she enjoyed being out there.

Cynthia Haydenhall rode unsteadily up the village street on her bike with bulging carriers dangling from both handlebars and a pair of marrows in the wire basket between them. She spotted Rachel and came to a rasping halt and jumped off the saddle. A couple of onions fell out of one of the bags and rolled across the road. Rachel stepped out of her garden to retrieve them.

'You're a bit overloaded, aren't you?'

'Harvest supper on Saturday. It's all left to the WI as usual.'

'I'd forgotten.'

'You're coming, I hope?'

Rachel hesitated. 'I'm not sure. I may give it a miss this year.'

'You can't do that. It's for church funds. Now you're the treasurer, it's a must.'

'It doesn't mean I have to turn up to every event.'

'You always have.' Quick on the uptake, as usual, Cynthia peered at her friend. 'Something upset you, did it?'

'I'm fine. Just busy.'

'Tell you what, darling. If you come, I'll reserve the seat next to Otis for you.'

Rachel felt the blood rush to her face. 'No, don't.'

'You're a big wheel on the PCC now. You're entitled to sit beside the rector.'

'You sit beside him.'

'Be like that,' said Cynthia. 'Last time we spoke you'd have given your eye teeth for an offer like that. What's up? Is Gary back from the States?'

Rachel glanced up at the curtains, still across the bedroom window. 'He is, as it happens, but that's got nothing to do with the harvest supper. You know he never comes to anything like that.'

'He's smelt a rat, has he? Bad luck.'

'What do you mean?'

'Your fling with Otis.'

For a moment she was flustered, and it showed. How on earth had Cynthia found out? She made a show of denying it. 'Cynthia! Leave off, will you? There's no fling, as you put it.'

'Joking,' said Cynthia.

'People will get the wrong idea.'

'He picked you for treasurer.'

That was all she meant, thank God. 'Because no one else wanted the job.' Purely to divert Cynthia from the subject of Otis, she said, 'I wouldn't mind helping out in the kitchen.'

Cynthia assessed the offer. 'No, I can't upset my team. Daphne, Joan and Dot do the cooking every year. Besides, you're not WI.'

'They'd be glad of some help. They all know me.'

'You want some credit for helping out.' Satisfied that she understood what this was all about, Cynthia unbent. 'I suppose I can stretch a point and find you a job if it's the only way we'll get you to come.'

It was agreed that Rachel would help with the preparation and serving. Cynthia eased back onto the saddle and wobbled to her next engagement.

On the same September morning Peggy Winner was shopping in Warminster and decided to treat herself to a coffee in Rosie's, a teashop located in a whitewashed cellar below the high street. Peggy had a special affection for the place. Years ago, under different management, it had been Chinn's Celebrated Chophouse, perfect for intimate trysts with the tall Mauritian evening-class teacher she had for conversational French and much more. Alain had long since returned to his own country and surely forgotten all about suppers in Warminster, but Peggy still felt a sense of adventure going down the steps and through the stone passageway, if only for an innocent coffee and scone.

The interior was divided into three. You came first to the cooking area where you could inspect the cakes on offer, and, dipping your head to avoid the beam, progressed to the two rooms where the tables were. Peggy usually went right through to the back where it was quieter.

This morning someone was at the table she thought of as her own. Silly to be like that, only she was. She stared at the young man as if he was something she had trodden in, and then did a double-take. It was Burton Sands, from the village, in his business pinstripe and drinking black coffee. Their eyes met and she couldn't very well sit at another table. Blast him, she thought.

'You don't mind?'

He shrugged and shook his head. She might as well have been a stranger, and it seemed she was to him.

Peggy had enough charm for both of them and decided to help him out. 'Funny, two Foxford people meeting down here. I'm Peggy Winner. I decided to reward myself for doing the shopping. It's so snug, isn't it? What's your excuse?'

'I work here.'

'What as?'

'I'm a chartered accountant. We have an office over the road, above the newsagents.'

'Yes, of course, you were up for treasurer. I'm on the parish council.'

'I know,' said Sands without animation.

The waitress came for Peggy's order. She asked if the scone could be warmed.

'I feel like a traitor when I use the supermarket instead of the village shop,' Peggy said, to be conversational. 'I suppose we're all guilty of that, and one of these days we'll lose our shop.'

'Why wasn't I chosen?'

He wasn't willing to talk about the village shop. 'That's not for me to say,' Peggy guardedly said.

'I was better qualified.'

'In book-keeping, you mean? True, but there are other considerations.'

'Such as?'

The intensity of the young man put Peggy off her stroke. Before she knew it, she was giving him the inside information she had meant to keep to herself. 'Mrs Jansen was the rector's candidate. That has to count for something. After all, he has to work with her.'

'She's treasurer to the parish, not to him,' Sands pointed out.

'Yes, but in practice . . .'

'You don't want someone who's in the rector's pocket. You want an independent treasurer.'

'I'm sure she isn't in his pocket, as you put it.' In his trousers, maybe, Peggy thought in passing. 'And I'm confident she'll do the job conscientiously.'

Burton Sands took a sip of coffee and flicked his tongue around his lips. 'Someone hinted to me that she got the job because the rector fancies her.'

Peggy laughed as if she hadn't heard a whisper of the rumour. She believed it, but she had to be discreet. 'Even if it was true, which I doubt, it wouldn't be the first time a woman got the job for her good looks. How can anyone tell?'

'He's a man of God. He's not supposed to look at women in that way.'

'Oh, come on, Burton,' said Peggy impulsively. 'Lighten up. Vicars are only human.'

'If she was given the job because the rector lusts after her, then it's little short of deplorable.'

'You sound like the Old Testament. I didn't say that was why she got the job. Don't put words in my mouth.'

'Especially as she's married.'

'You'd better watch what you say.'

'I don't mind speaking out if it's the truth.'

'But is it?'

He looked into the dark dregs of his coffee as if the answer was there. 'I'll find out. When I start on something I always see it through. Always.'

She could believe him. He looked obsessive. If by some mischance this man got together with Owen Cumberbatch, the result would be explosive.

He pushed the cup to one side and said, 'I'm going back to the office now.'

She made some polite and untrue remark about the pleasure of being with him. He didn't reply.

After he'd gone she had some anxious moments going over what she'd said and wondering if he would spread it around. When her coffee and scone were served, she finished them and hardly noticed.

When Gary finally discovered the stain on the carpet and said, 'What happened here, for Christ's sake?' Rachel gave him most of the truth, explaining about her new responsibility as treasurer to the PCC and how the rector had wanted to show her the account books and she had felt obliged to offer refreshment in the shape of wine and finger food.

'You what?' he said with a glare. America hadn't mellowed him at all.

'He wanted to go over the figures. You can't do that in ten minutes. I had to offer something and it was a choice of coffee or wine. I decided wine was easier. Coffee's such a performance and you can't serve instant to a guest.'

'So you bought a posh wine and knocked the bottle over. Clumsy cow.'

Blocking out the insult, she went into her prepared bit. 'That's it. So embarrassing, too. I could have died! Most of the stain has gone as you see. There's just this tidemark at the edge. We can buy a small rug and cover it.'

'Not out of my money, we won't.'

'Have you got another suggestion?'

'Work some bloody overtime and pay for a new carpet. How come you got lumbered as treasurer anyway, dozy bitch? You're crap with figures – you know you are.'

Let it pass, she told herself, though she felt the crude words like a series of body blows. He wants me to react. 'I don't do much for the church. It was hard to say no. He took so much trouble when I broke my arm, driving me to hospital and everything.'

'Don't do much for the church? You're there every Sunday putting our hard-earned in the plate. Isn't that enough?'

'Most of them do a lot more. The choir, the flower rota, bell-ringing, helping with Sunday school. I've never done any of that.'

'You rattle a box for Christian Aid.'

'That's nothing. Some people have prayer meetings in their homes every week.'

His eyebrows shot up. 'Don't even think about it, right?'

She could have mentioned that his jazz friends came and played their music when she was trying to watch the gardening programmes, but she didn't want a row. He was working up to something and he could get violent. She'd been pushed around before; not blows, exactly, but strong, frightening pushes.

He actually started a new conversation. 'Speaking of the vicar—'

'Rector.'

'His name is Otis Joy, right?'

'So?'

'Bloody stupid name.'

'If you say so.'

'But memorable. There can't be more than one pillock with a name like that – or so I thought. Now listen to this. There were these Canadians staying in our hotel. Good blokes. Three of them, from Toronto. We had a few Buds with them, got talking, as you do. I don't know how we got around to funny names, but we did. My old doctor, Screech, and that dentist of yours called Root.'

'Stumps. His name was Stumps.'

'I thought it was Root. Well, I told them it was, and it seemed hilarious when we were half-pissed, as we were. Then one of these Canadians said he once knew a guy called Otis Joy who was training to be a priest. He went through school with him.'

She was amazed. 'You're kidding.'

'Straight up. Otis Joy.'

'It can't be our rector. He's not Canadian.'

'Didn't say he was. It's just coincidence, the name.'

'What age would he have been?'

'How would I know?'

'The man who spoke to you. If he went to school with this Otis Joy they must have been about the same age.'

Gary thought for a moment. 'Younger than me. More like your age. Pushing thirty.'

'That's another coincidence, then, the age. Otis can't be any older than I am. A Canadian, you say?'

'If they were at school together in Toronto he must have been.'

'Did you tell him you knew a priest with the same name?'

'No, it would have spoilt his story, wouldn't it? I mentioned it to the lads later on. They reckoned Otis is a more common name over there.'

'Is it?'

'No idea. There was Otis Redding, the soul singer.'

'I've heard of him.'

'You have? Big deal. He only sold about a billion records.'

She was silent, pained by his sarcasm.

He said presently, 'Are you going to tell your precious rector?'

'I don't know.'

'I might, when I see him next,' he said. 'Just because he wears his collar round the wrong way people don't like to go up to him in the street. I don't bloody mind. I'd like to see his face when I tell him. Probably thinks he's unique.'

She called his bluff: said he was welcome to come and talk to the rector at the harvest supper on Saturday. 'There won't be black-eyed beans, but it should be warm food. I offered to help with the cooking.'

'You're going overboard on the good works, aren't you?' he said. 'What is it with this vicar? Don't tell me you've got the hots for him.'

She said, with a force that gave too much away, 'It's nothing to do with him. The WI organise it.'

'You're not WI.'

'I was asked to help.'

'And he'll be there. You said he would.'

'Of course, but only as a guest.'

'Admit it. You fancy him.'

'That's absurd, Gary. I'll be working in the kitchen, preparing the food. I won't even see him.'

He stepped towards her and pressed the flat of his

hand against her chest. The push was a light one, but frightening. 'Lying cow.'

'Don't do that.'

'I'll do as I like. You'll feel the back of my hand if you've been up to anything, you slag.' He pushed her again, harder. 'Getting in wine like that. It's bloody obvious what you had in mind.'

'No, Gary.'

'It's a come-on, isn't it? The old man's in America, so come and screw the arse off me. I tell you, Rachel, if that randy preacher got inside your knickers while I was away, I'll give him such a hiding he won't be able to hobble into his pulpit again. Ever. And after I finish with him, I'll sort you out.'

Her voice shook. 'Will you listen to me, Gary? You couldn't be more wrong.'

'No? You want to see your face when you say that.' He stabbed his finger towards her several times. 'You're lying, woman, and it shows. I said I'd beat the shit out of Otis sodding Joy, and your red face just bought him a month's worth of hospital food.'

'Don't. Don't be so stupid.'

He leered at her. 'We'll see if his reverence tells the truth or not. You're really wetting yourself now, aren't you?'

'Please, Gary.'

He mimicked her. 'Please, Gary.'

'What can I say? If you don't want me to go to the harvest supper, I won't.'

'Do what you bloody like.'

'Please don't talk to the rector. It's going to make fools of us. It's so humiliating.'

He walked away from her. 'And you can fix me some supper the night you go out. A curry,' he said. 'And I mean a curry worthy of the name, with some flavour to it. After what I had in New Orleans, the shit that passes for food in this country is bloody tasteless.'

She had one ready in the freezer, thank the Lord. And if he wanted extra flavour, he could have it.

She didn't bring up the subject of Otis again, hoping Gary would reflect on the stupidity of accusing a clergyman of immorality. She wasn't all that confident. His time in America had made him even more confrontational. He swore at the paper boy when he left the gate unlatched. And late on Friday evening he opened the bedroom window to shout at some youths who were making a noise in the street.

On Saturday, he went up the street to the village shop to pay the paper bill. Rachel watched him from the front garden, where she had gone to prune some of the roses. He was in what he called his weekend togs, a disgusting old green pullover and jeans, and of course the greasy flat cap that disguised his baldness.

Then, to her horror, she spotted Otis striding towards the shop from the other end of the village. *Please God, no,* she thought.

Was it her imagination, or was there a sudden change in Gary's style of walking? He put one foot in front of the other in a more sinister, purposeful way, and she knew, just knew, he fancied himself as a gun-slinger in a western. He'd taken his hands from his pockets and was swinging his arms in a pathetic parody of John Wayne.

She watched in torment, gripping the pruning shears, openly staring, willing Otis to stop and talk to someone else, or call at one of the cottages, or think of something he'd forgotten and turn back.

But Gary marched right up and confronted him near the door of the shop, and Rachel's stomach clenched and her mouth went dry. The two men talked earnestly, it seemed to her, and for longer than a polite exchange. She wasn't close enough to see Otis's reaction, and didn't really wish to. In despair, she turned away and deadheaded more of the roses.

Gary looked smug when he returned. He'd treated himself to a bottle of whisky and he opened it straight away and slumped in front of the television with his feet over the arms of her favourite chair. He said nothing to Rachel about what had passed between Otis and himself and she was too afraid to enquire, in case it started a fight.

She made ham sandwiches for his lunch. She didn't want to eat. Trying to sound normal, she reminded him that she had to go early in the afternoon to help cook the harvest supper. She told him she'd defrosted the curry and put it in the oven on the timer, to be ready whenever he wanted it during the evening. He didn't thank her.

'I'll have it when I get back.'

'You're going out?'

'Only up to the rectory. Unfinished business.' He hadn't looked away from the TV screen.

Rachel froze.

11

A casserole – or beef stew – was the traditional meal for the harvest supper. Traditional since the WI had been in charge, anyway. Probably in the days of Waldo Wallace's tithe dinners, more ambitious dishes were served. The advantage of a casserole was that it could be cooked hours ahead of time and kept simmering in a large stewpot that had once been used for the school dinners. The team of Daphne, Dot and Joan, with help from Rachel, worked through Saturday afternoon. Into that pot went diced beef, floured and lightly fried, then a real harvest crop of vegetables: onions, carrots, turnips, parsnips, peppers, aubergines, chopped celery and potatoes. Pearl barley was tossed in with favourite flavourings from bayleaves to garlic. And of course beer and water. No other cooking was required. Bread rolls were put out on the tables with jugs of cider and lemonade and there were packets of crisps for the children.

It might seem from this that Foxford's entire harvest went into the pot, but no. The hall was decorated with produce from the fields and gardens: some old-fashioned sheaves of corn made up for the occasion; overgrown marrows and pumpkins nobody would eat; baskets laden high with apples and pears; tomatoes, eggs and the harvest loaves with their plaited designs. All this would be moved to the church at the end of the evening and rearranged for

the Sunday morning's Harvest Festival service, along with
the tins of grapefruit and baked beans that were always
donated, reminders that 'all good gifts around us' were
sent from heaven above, even if some were packaged by
Tesco's.

Rachel busied herself cutting vegetables, saying little,
wondering if Otis would have changed his mind about
coming.

The evening was supposed to start at seven, but most of the
tables were full a quarter of an hour before. The appetising
smell drifting downwind from the church hall must have
had something to do with it.

A cynical observer might have said that tonight was
the pagan part of the harvest celebration, reaching right
back to pre-Christian feasts. No hymns or prayers. No
reminder of the holy, aweful Reaper with the fan of
judgement winnowing 'the chaff into the furnace that
flameth evermore'. Just the Warminster Folk Group with
country songs and dances. The local cider ensured a
boisterous atmosphere.

Cynthia came into the kitchen like the lady of the manor
visiting the skivvies. She'd squeezed herself into a black
glittery dress with thin shoulderstraps and a rollercoaster
of a plunge.

'The casserole smells divine, darlings. You've done
brilliantly, as I knew you would. I can't wait to try it, but
I'll have to be patient, for Otis's sake. He's a little late.
Unusual for him.' She came over to Rachel. 'You look pale,
dear. If you want to sit down, the others will understand.'
In a lower voice, she added, 'You *did* say I could partner
him this evening. I'll behave myself. Promise.'

Cynthia's intentions were the least of Rachel's worries.
She hoped Otis would stay away, but not to thwart her

friend. She hadn't spoken to him since that blighted evening in her cottage, and now she wondered when she ever would. In church she'd twice managed to slip past him after morning service while he was in conversation with someone else. The fiasco on the sofa and the spilt wine had been galling enough and now Gary playing the jealous husband was just too much.

The truth of it was that Otis still obsessed her. She knew he had been aroused by her and they had been tantalisingly close to making love. The possibility was there, and she desired it, dreamed of it, wicked as it was. Now Gary was back from America and breathing fire, she ought to dismiss Otis from her thoughts. She couldn't, and she wouldn't, so she had to suffer mental torment.

Cynthia went off to look for him.

'I think we should start serving,' suggested Dot. 'We can't keep everybody waiting for the rector's sake.'

Thankful for something to do, Rachel ladled the steaming casserole into bowls and handed them across. In her apron and with her hair wrapped in a scarf, she was clearly not there to socialise. There were several mentions of her arm being freshly out of plaster, and she smiled and nodded, but it was obvious to anyone that she didn't have time to talk.

Then, God help her, Otis arrived in the hall. Cynthia pounced, leading him by the elbow to a reserved seat at the far end of the room where the folk musicians were playing. When he was settled, she put her handbag on the seat beside him and went off to collect his food as well as her own. Mercifully Rachel was spared having to speak to him.

In his cream-coloured summer jacket, he was looking relaxed and attractive and evidently telling more of his jokes, because every so often the whole table burst into laughter.

Rachel ladled a spoonful for herself and went into the poky kitchen to eat with the other helpers. One of them advised her to sit down. There was still the washing-up to come and it all had to be done by hand.

She was feeling relieved. She said, half-joking, there ought to be another team for the wash-up. Some men, for a change.

'Some hope,' said Daphne Beaton. 'They're all in their glad-rags, aren't they? We made the mistake of bringing our aprons.'

'I'd lend mine to anyone,' said Rachel.

'Even the rector?' said Daphne – and it wasn't meant to make Rachel blush, but it brought to mind that evening she'd called at the rectory and found Otis wearing nothing but an apron.

She managed to say in a calm voice, 'Him included. Specially him. No, to be fair, he washed up after the fete.'

'He's a sport,' said Daphne.

One of the others said, 'Wasted, isn't he, handsome young fellow like him, living alone in that rectory?'

'You want to help him out, Dot?'

'I wouldn't mind,' said little Dot, all of seventy-five, and toothless.

'More cider, love?' said Daphne, laughing.

From the hall came a timely chorus:

'Then fill up the jug boys, and let it go round,
Of drinks not the equal in England is found.
So pass round the jug, boys, and pull at it free,
There's nothing like cider, rough cider, for me.'

With the singing underway, it was time to start on the dishes. Some had already been stacked on the serving table. The four women set about collecting the rest and bringing them into the kitchen for the wash-up.

Rachel was running the water, wondering if it would get hot enough, when a voice at her shoulder said, 'I'll do that.'

A man.

She turned to see. That strange young man Burton Sands already had his jacket off and was rolling up his sleeves. Now that there actually was a man on hand to help, Rachel wasn't sure if she wanted one there. Not this one, anyway.

She said, 'You'll miss all the fun.'

Nice try, but there was no stopping him. 'It's no fun watching people you know make fools of themselves.'

'Your clothes will be ruined.'

Daphne, returning with a stack of dishes, said, 'Don't turn the man away, for God's sake. We'll find you an apron, Burton.'

So he was kitted out for washing-up duties and took over at the sink, with two of the four women wiping up and the others tidying. He worked solemnly and thoroughly, saying little, while the others chatted as freely as before, or almost.

The stacks of dishes were steadily reduced and in a surprisingly short time the kettle was on for tea. Burton said he didn't want one, yet showed no inclination to leave. Only when Rachel got up and rinsed her cup did the young man roll down his sleeves and reach for his jacket.

'Are you going back in there?' he asked her.

'No, I thought I'd slip away now. I didn't come for the party.'

'I'll go with you.'

Daphne, not missing anything, said, 'Ay-up.'

Solemn as ever, Burton said, 'What's that?'

'Now we know why you volunteered – so you could walk Rachel home.'

It was meant as part of the banter that had been going on for the last hour, but Burton's response made it seem intrusive. 'I want to ask her something. Do you mind?'

'No prizes for guessing what,' said Daphne, to hoots of laughter.

Rachel kept quiet. When the sexual innuendos start, you're better off saying nothing.

'He was only the washer-up, but he went home with the best dish.'

Then Daphne's friend Dot said, 'Leave off, Daph. We'd still be washing up if it wasn't for the help Burton and Rachel gave us.'

It all turned into a chorus of thanks.

And Rachel, much against her inclination, found herself walking up the street with Burton at her side.

He came to the point at once. Small-talk wasn't his style. 'How much experience of book-keeping have you got?'

This night, of all nights, she could do without being quizzed about the job she hadn't wanted in the first place. Not wanting an argument, she said, 'Enough – if you're talking about the church.'

'You've done it before?'

'A certain amount.' Not quite a lie. She'd learned the basics at school.

He said, 'I was wondering why you put up for treasurer.'

There was an easy answer. 'I think we all ought to help where we can, don't you?'

'I could have done it.'

'So I heard,' she answered. 'At the time, I didn't know you were interested.'

'It was your decision, was it? Nobody asked you.'

'The rector asked me. I don't expect he knew you were a candidate.' Why don't you let go? she thought. What's the point in pursuing this?

'He knew I wanted it. I told him myself. He said he'd already spoken to someone else – obviously you. He must think a lot of you.'

'That doesn't follow,' she said. 'He thought I could do the job, that's all.'

'If it were me, I'd do it on computer.'

'I'm sure you'd do it brilliantly, Burton, and I expect your turn will come.'

'Have you got a computer?'

'No.'

'The rector has. I've seen one in his study up at the rectory. He could let you use it.'

'Maybe, but I'd rather work from home.'

'It's easier on the computer.'

'It's easy, anyway, or I wouldn't have taken it on,' she said, irritated by his manner.

'Have you met the bank manager yet?'

'Look, I don't need you to tell me how to do the job, Burton. I'm sure it's kindly meant, but I happen to believe the most important part of being a treasurer isn't knowing how to add up columns or use a computer or talking to bank managers. It's to be independent of everyone, whether it's the rector or the other members of the PCC or someone like yourself with a professional training in accounts.'

They'd reached her cottage. She added, 'Thanks for your help with the washing up.' Then she put her key in the lock and went inside without looking back.

12

The reek of curry was overpowering. She went straight to the kitchen and carried the casserole dish to the toilet and flushed away what was left. Then returned and ran water over the dish, switched on the fan over the hob and opened all the windows. A few squirts of air freshener helped, but it would be hours before she could feel the house was her own place.

The television was blaring some police programme, and Gary wasn't watching. She could hear him clumping about upstairs.

She called up that she was back and about to put on a kettle.

If he answered, it was indistinct. She switched on and got out the mugs. Personally she fancied tea at this time of the evening. She turned down the volume on the television and switched to the news, and watched without taking much in while the water came to the boil.

She called upstairs again. 'Tea, or coffee?'

No answer.

'Gary.'

She thought she heard him vomiting. She knew if she went up there to see him she would just get sworn at.

She made the tea and left it to brew. Collected his dishes and cutlery from the other room and washed them.

Vomiting was an understatement, judging by the noise from the bathroom.

The tea would be too strong if she left it, so she poured herself one and turned up the television again to shut out Gary.

Before the news came to an end she heard the boards in the bedroom creak. Better face it now, she thought, and went up to him.

The bedroom smelt vile. He was groaning, curled in a foetal position on the bed, still in his clothes. 'God, I feel terrible. What was in that bloody curry?'

'The usual things. Can I get you something? Water?'

'Yeah. My mouth is on fire.'

By the time she'd fetched a jug and a glass from downstairs he was back in the bathroom, retching. This was shaping up to be some night, she thought.

When he came out, he could hardly walk straight. 'Feel giddy,' he said. 'L-legs won't hold me up.'

She took his arm and steered him to the bed. 'I'd better phone for the doctor.'

'Don't want a doctor.' He made a strange hissing sound that became the start of: ''s only a sodding curry. Where's that wa . . . wa . . . ?' He sat on the edge of the bed and gulped some down. 'Can't even swallow . . . Throat hurts. Bur . . . burning . . . right down . . . g-gullet.' The words had to be forced out. 'Pain in the gut . . . unbeliev—'

'Don't talk, then. Lie down and rest.'

'S-s-spinning round.'

'Sit up if you want, then.'

'Whatyersay? Can't hear you.'

'Sit up. I'll get an extra pillow.'

'Flaming hell.' He tried to get off the bed, and his legs folded under him. She grabbed him around the waist and helped him back, ramming a pillow behind him.

She removed his shoes. 'What were you drinking tonight – pure alcohol?'

He shook his head.

'Stay put, Gary. If you need to be sick, I'm getting a bucket.'

'Ri . . .'

Time to call the doctor, she thought, whatever he says. He was getting more incoherent by the minute.

When she went back with the bucket, he had tipped sideways off the pillow and seemed unable to get himself upright. She spoke to him and he mouthed words, but no sound came out.

She ran downstairs and phoned Dr Perkins at home. The old doctor – the only one in the practice she wanted for this – told her he was off duty and somebody else was on call for emergencies.

She wasn't going to settle for anyone else. Working at the health centre entitled her to this favour, surely. 'You saw him the other day, doctor. He's much worse than he was then. He's very ill indeed, and I'm worried, dreadfully worried. I've been out at the harvest supper and I came back and found him in a terrible way. I think it's some kind of stroke. He can't speak. Please come.'

He said he would.

She went back to Gary. He was lying as she had left him, taking noisy gasps of air, saying nothing. She tried tidying the mess of the bedclothes. She told him Dr Perkins was coming. It didn't seem to register.

She had no idea how long it was before the doorbell rang. Gary was a dreadful colour and had lost the power of speech altogether.

Dr Perkins got nothing coherent from him. He bent over him and listened to the breathing. Lifted one of his eyelids.

Tried the stethoscope, and seemed to take an age making up his mind.

'When you first got in, was he able to speak?'

'Yes, he was fully conscious.'

'Did he speak of a pain across the chest? Difficulty breathing?'

'A pain, yes. Severe pain.'

'Laboured breathing?'

'You can hear him, can't you?'

Dr Perkins nodded. 'I'm afraid it's the heart.'

'Angina?'

He shook his head. 'More serious this time. Help me sit him up.'

They propped him against the pillows at a better angle. The doctor rolled up Gary's sleeve and gave him an injection. That horrible, noisy breathing calmed a little. 'Stay with him, please. I'm going to use your phone.'

She sat by the bed, staring at her unconscious husband. His body twitched or convulsed a couple of times.

'I've called the ambulance,' the doctor said when he came back. He felt for a pulse. Used the stethoscope again.

Gary was silent, his eyes closed. He was ominously still.

Suddenly Dr Perkins thrust away the pillows and dragged Gary quite roughly to a flat position and began thrusting the heel of his palm against the lower sternum.

Cardiac massage.

Rachel couldn't bear to stay in there. 'I'll look out for the ambulance.'

She stood by the open front door waiting, looking along the lane for the flashing blue beacon. How long did they take to answer emergencies? After some time – and still no ambulance – she was aware of a hand on her arm. Dr Perkins drew her inside, away from the door.

'Is he . . . ?'

'Gone, I'm afraid.'

'Gone? Dead, you mean?'

'Cardiac failure. I tried all I could.'

'Oh, God. I can't believe this is happening.' She felt numb.

'Is there someone who can be with you? Someone I can call? A neighbour?'

She had a thought, and dismissed it. She couldn't ask for Otis at this time. She gave Cynthia's name.

He called Cynthia. He also made other calls, cancelling the ambulance and ringing the mortuary instead.

It was over, then, her marriage to Gary. She was a widow now.

Dr Perkins made her some fresh tea, heavily sweetened, and asked her questions about the onset of Gary's heart attack. She tried to recollect what had happened since she got back from the harvest supper. It all seemed remote in time already, as if it had happened to someone else. 'I came in about nine, because the news was coming on. He'd left the television on and he was upstairs, ill, being sick and complaining of pains.'

'In the chest?'

'Yes, but it seemed like indigestion. He'd eaten a curry and I thought that must have upset him. He was going to the bathroom a lot. I tried to do what I could for him, fetching water, and so on. His legs went at one point and then he was getting breathless.'

'Because of the pain,' said Dr Perkins more to himself than to Rachel.

'And he seemed to lose control of his speech. Well, you saw him. By the time you arrived, he couldn't speak at all.'

'Classic heart attack. You acted promptly,' he said. 'Nothing else you could have done.'

'The other day you said it was just angina and he could live to eighty or something.'

He adjusted his spectacles and peered at her in surprise. 'On balance, that looked the probable diagnosis. No point in alarming the patient until something more serious shows up in the tests.'

'So he *was* at risk.'

'Sadly, events have proved it so.' The elderly doctor was fidgeting with his fingers, clearly uncomfortable with the cross-examination. It was known at the health centre that he got things muddled occasionally, even if his bedside manner couldn't be faulted.

Still Rachel pressed him. 'There's no question that it was anything else but a heart attack?'

He was firm in response. 'That's what's going on the certificate as cause of death, my dear. I'm sorry. He was quite a young man, and unlucky, but there's no telling how long any of us will survive.' He said he would leave her some tablets to help her sleep that night, and a prescription for more.

She experienced the strangeness of being cocooned by shock. Tears wouldn't come. She heard things without really listening. Drank the tea without tasting it. Was distantly aware of men in dark suits coming to take Gary's body out of the cottage to an unmarked van.

Cynthia arrived and still Dr Perkins lingered. There were details he needed for the certificate, he said. 'When did I see him last?'

'Don't you remember? Tuesday, wasn't it? About the angina.'

'The angina?' he said uneasily. 'Well, with hindsight, it must have been more serious than angina.'

She and Cynthia exchanged a glance while Dr Perkins hastily finished the paperwork. He folded it, and sealed it in a brown envelope. 'You'll need that for the registrar. I'm also leaving a form with some details about all that. And now I must be going. I can't tell you how sorry I am.'

She thanked him for coming out.

His departure was the cue for a fresh pot of tea. She would be awash.

Dear old Cynthia was more than equal to the task of saying enough for both of them, wittering on about the harvest supper and what people had been wearing and what they'd said and how much had been raised for church funds as if no other thing had happened in the past three hours.

'What time is it?' Rachel asked suddenly.

'Gone midnight.'

'You'd better go now.'

'I'm not leaving you, poppet,' said Cynthia. 'If I leave, you come with me. There's a spare bed at my place.'

Rachel said she would rather remain in her own place.

'As you wish,' said Cynthia. 'I'll make up a bed for you here. You won't want to be upstairs on the bed where he . . . It's a wonderfully comfortable sofa, yours.'

She was persuaded to take one of the sleeping pills. From under her quilt on the sofa she was vaguely conscious of Cynthia unfolding one of the loungers from the sunroom. She knew nothing more until a fresh mug of tea was put into her hand next morning.

Cynthia was a staunch friend. Rachel was to discover in the coming days that people she thought she could rely on for support were somehow unable to bring themselves to speak to a bereaved woman, even crossing the street to avoid her. Not Cynthia. She insisted on clearing up the room where Gary had died, and the bathroom, scrubbing and polishing and tidying, eliminating every trace of the tragedy. She loaded the bedding into the washing machine and hung it out to dry and did the ironing. And she reminded Rachel of things she should do.

'Does he have parents or brothers and sisters?'

'A stepsister who lives in France. They didn't have much to do with each other.'

'We'd better contact her, just the same. Any close friends?'

'His jazz cronies, I suppose.'

'You'll need to inform them, but I think the first thing you have to do is fix the funeral. There's no point in calling these people twice. You want to tell them he's gone and give them the date of the funeral all in one.'

'All right.'

'We'll do it together. Did he want a Christian funeral?'

'I suppose so. He wasn't a church-goer, but I think he would.'

'He didn't leave a will?'

'I'm sure he didn't. He'd have mentioned it.'

'You need to speak to Otis. He's coming, anyway. I phoned him first thing this morning. We agreed on ten-thirty.'

Rachel felt a stab of annoyance that this had been fixed without any reference to her. A meeting with the rector was a necessary part of the process, she knew, but she ought to have been consulted.

She thanked Cynthia for all she had done, and said she would value some time to herself now.

'You mean you don't want me here when Otis comes to comfort you? No problem. I'm not short of things to do.'

Rachel hadn't the strength to smooth ruffled feathers.

Precisely on time, in his dark suit and with his face creased in sympathy, he stepped across the threshold with hands held wide and open. 'What an ordeal. My poor Rachel.'

She backed off, turning from him to close the cottage door. It would have been easy to step towards him for the embrace he was offering. This wasn't the moment. She didn't want sympathy from Otis. She wanted passion, and it would have to wait. So she received him formally, showed him into the front room and said, 'Why don't you sit there –' (with her back to the sofa and indicating an armchair) '– and I'll make some coffee.'

'Can I help?'

'No thanks, I need to be occupied.'

He didn't sit. She left the door to the kitchen open and he stood in the living room and talked. 'I believe Dr Perkins was with you when it happened?'

'Yes, I called him specially.'

'Is he your GP?'

'No. He was already treating Gary.'

'For his heart?'

'Angina, he first thought, but it was more serious, obviously.'

She spooned some instant coffee into two mugs and poured on the hot water.

From the other room, he said, 'This will be the medical certificate, in the envelope on the wall unit.'

'I suppose it is.'

'You'll need it for the registrar.'

'That's right.'

'Have you seen what he put as the cause of death?'

'It's not going to make any difference now,' she said without giving a straight answer. 'Gary's gone, and that's it.'

'You have a right to know, Rachel. Old Perkins could have put anything down. He's a touch absent-minded.'

'I think it's sealed.'

'But only just. Would you like me to open it and see what he put?'

'I don't know if we should.'

'Nobody said we shouldn't.'

'All right, but be careful,' she called from the kitchen, not wanting him to know she had looked inside the envelope already, and sealed it again.

She brought in the coffee.

'Coronary occlusion,' he told her. 'An occlusion is blockage of a coronary artery. A heart attack, in other words.'

'You're well up on the jargon.'

'It goes with the job. I'm often called when someone is not long for this world. Or just after. The good news is that he hasn't initialled the form on the back.'

'What would that mean?'

'Whenever there's anything iffy about the cause of death, the doctor says so on the certificate and initials the back, to show he's reported it to the coroner. This one couldn't be more straightforward. You take it to the registrar and get the death certificate. We can fix the funeral as early as you like. That's if Gary would have wanted a Christian service.'

'He would, I'm sure.'

'So?'

'The sooner the better.'

'It's Saturday now. Tuesday morning?'

'Isn't that your day off?'

He sacrificed his day off with a flap of the hand. 'Did Gary ever express any preference about burial or cremation?'

'Not really. He never thought about dying. You don't, do you, at our age? Black, or white?'

'A dash of milk, please. Most people choose cremation these days.'

'That's it, then.'

'Is anyone helping you with the arrangements?'

'Cynthia Haydenhall. She's a good friend, a great support. She'll come with me to the register office.'

'I found myself beside her at the harvest supper.' He made it sound like pure chance.

Rachel suppressed her first smile since Gary died.

'Full of the joys of life,' he said.

'That's Cynthia.' She sat across the room from him, in Gary's chair, as proper as a Victorian lady 'at home' with a guest.

'And on message. Not much in the village escapes your friend.'

It sounded very like a caution. She gave a smile that said she didn't need warning about Cynthia.

He changed tack. 'Oddly enough, I spoke to your husband only yesterday. First he came up to me in the street. He'd met someone with a similar name to mine.'

'No,' she corrected him. 'He met someone who knew someone called Otis Joy.'

'Was that it? I got muddled, then.'

'But you didn't mind?'

'Not in the least. It's one of those things. The laws of chance make it likely that someone, somewhere in the world, will share the name, and somebody I run into at some stage in my life will know of it.'

'The long arm of coincidence.'

'Right.' He looked into his coffee. 'Actually there was another matter Gary wanted to talk about.'

She blushed. 'You and me?'

'Well, yes. He was all fired up. Seemed to have the idea—'

'I know,' she broke in, acutely embarrassed. 'Gary was like that, quick to think the worst of me. Quite mistaken, couldn't have been more wrong. I tried to stop him speaking to you, but he would insist. He wasn't violent, was he?'

'No, no. I defused him. Invited him up to the rectory for a man-to-man chat, as they say. By the end of the afternoon, when he came, he'd calmed down a lot. It was civilised. He accepted a drink, listened to my version of events – everything I told him was the truth, by the way, though I didn't go into unnecessary detail – and went away with a better opinion of us both.'

It all sounded so simple, and she could believe it now.

'Thank you. I wish . . .' She didn't complete the sentence.

He made a dismissive gesture. 'By the way, Rachel, I can easily arrange for someone else to take over the books, at least for a time.'

For a moment she wasn't sure what he was talking about. 'Oh, the parish accounts. No, I can manage. Really. I'll be glad to have something to do.'

'I'll visit you anyway,' he said, clearing his throat. 'It's one of the duties of a priest to comfort the bereaved. If you need comfort, that is.'

'I do. Please come,' she said. 'I'm not sure about comfort. As you know, Gary and I weren't all that close as a couple. It's a matter of getting used to being alone, I suppose.'

'And we must talk about the funeral, choice of hymns, and so forth. We can do a simple committal at the crematorium if you wish.'

A simple committal. How boring. She looked down at her wedding ring and turned it, and the frivolous part of her character stirred. 'I had something else in mind. It's not very practical, but I'd love to give him the sort of send-off they do in New Orleans, with a procession and jazz musicians serenading the coffin along the street.'

'In Foxford?'

'It would be different.'

He was frowning. For once, this supremely confident man was unsure how to react. 'Are you sure you want that? I thought you had a low opinion of jazz.'

'It's Gary's funeral, not mine.'

'True.' He was still hesitant. 'It's an amazing thought. I just assumed you'd want something low-key.'

'Like I said, this is for Gary.' She wasn't being honest here. This was not just for Gary. She wanted it herself. It was inspired. She didn't want to be the main player at the funeral, with all eyes watching to see how distressed she was – or wasn't.

As if he sensed that she wouldn't be budged from this eccentric idea, he snapped his fingers and laughed. 'Hey, I love it! A procession to the Pearly Gates. He'd be so proud.' Then, as a sudden difficulty struck him, 'But can we find a band at such short notice?'

She brushed that small problem aside. 'His friends will do it, I'm sure. I think they used to jam together occasionally.'

It was evident that the lady's mind was made up and the best Otis Joy could do was bite the bullet. 'If I know anything about jazzmen, they take any chance to launch into a spot of Dixieland. They probably know other musicians, too. Let's do this in style.'

13

T here was a complication when Rachel went with Cynthia to register the death. Neither of them much liked the fussy little man who took them through the form, but that need not have mattered. When they'd supplied all the information, including things Rachel considered unnecessary, such as her own date of birth, he asked if she had decided about the method of disposal.

Cynthia glared at him as if he'd broken wind. 'That's a horrible way of putting it.'

He said, 'Madam, I know of no phrase that expresses the matter more tastefully.'

'You could say his last journey. "Have you decided anything about his last journey?"'

'It wouldn't do. People would think I was talking about the hearse.'

'There must be better words you could use. Let's face it, you're dealing with someone who has just lost her dear husband.'

'Personally,' he said, drawing himself up, 'it jars with me when people speak of losing their relatives, as if they expect them to turn up at a lost property office.'

'Leave it, Cyn,' said Rachel. Turning to the registrar, she said firmly, 'I've chosen cremation.'

'That was the deceased's wish?'

'He expressed no wish. That's my decision.'

He said, 'I only ask because there are certain formalities that your doctor may not have explained. Before a cremation can be authorised, a second doctor must examine the – er – remains.'

'Why?'

'The law requires it, Mrs Jansen. Just a safeguard. The doctor will visit the mortuary. It needn't concern you.'

'But it does concern me. We've supplied the death certificate. What's all this about?'

Cynthia, trying to be helpful, said, 'You can get one of Dr Perkins' partners from the health centre.'

'Not a partner,' the registrar corrected her. 'This must be an independent opinion from a medical practitioner of at least five years' standing. He must certify that he knows of no reasonable cause to suspect that the deceased died either a violent or an unnatural death, or a sudden death of which the cause is unknown.'

Cynthia said, 'He was being treated for heart disease, for heaven's sake.'

'That's the point of a second opinion. If there's any uncertainty, that doctor informs the coroner, and a post mortem is held.'

'I don't want that,' said Rachel impulsively. 'I hate the idea of it. We'll have him buried.'

'Don't let him sway you, love,' said Cynthia.

'I've decided.'

The registrar said, 'I should warn you that a burial is more expensive.'

'So be it. Gary has suffered enough. I want him laid to rest without any more doctors interfering.'

Otis, when she told him on the phone, sounded surprised.

'I just want to get on with the funeral,' she explained.

'No red tape. No second opinions. I know what doctors are like. It could have been referred to the coroner. This way, we can give him his send-off, as planned, on Tuesday.'

'Do you have a plot?'

'I beg your pardon?'

'A place in a cemetery.'

'*That* plot. Yes. At Haycombe. I wouldn't want him in Foxford churchyard.'

Jazz sessions can be found in most towns most weekends, but funeral gigs are something else. Foxford had seen nothing like it. Come to that, the whole of Wiltshire had seen nothing like it, and maybe the whole of England. From an early hour on Tuesday morning, people started claiming the prime positions along the village street. They stood about waiting, cheerful without being rowdy. Some sat or stood on the drystone walls and a few dropped cigarette packets and drink cans into village gardens, but no serious damage was done and the mood was respectful. The cars, minibuses and coaches were directed into one of Norman Gregor's fields at the approach to the village. Free, but compulsory parking, with a police barrier to enforce it.

In the two days since it was arranged, Gary's New Orleans-style send-off had caught the public imagination to such an extent that jazz bands were being bussed in from as far away as Brixton to join the procession. The story had been in the Sunday tabloids, on television and radio. Camera crews were setting up at all the obvious vantage points along the street and above it on scaffolding. The service would be relayed on loudspeakers because there was no way everyone could crowd into the church.

Rachel was caught off guard by all the interest. Having suggested the street procession herself, she could hardly call it off, but she had no idea that the jazz community would find it such a draw. The phone had gone so often over the weekend that she'd had to have her calls redirected to a public relations agency. They made it clear she was not available for interviews.

Others in the village were happy to talk, and Gary got a better press than he deserved, because no one wanted to be heard speaking ill of the dead. In death, a pig of a man had become not just a Very Important Person but a great lad, popular all round, who loved his jazz, liked his pint in the local and had a good word for everyone. Never gave a hint of his heart problem. To be cut down at forty-two was cruel.

The organisation of the music was taken over by a black trumpeter from Bristol who called himself King Gumbo and had a sixteen-strong band. In keeping with New Orleans tradition, the shuffling progress to the church was to be solemn and plaintive, a slow blues march. Other bands would take their cue from King Gumbo's beat. Later, after the cremation, there would be another procession through Foxford, when the mood of the music would become playful and irreverent.

Not everyone in the village thought all this was a good idea. One or two called it a freak show and worse, but the majority were willing to keep an open mind and joined in cheerfully. Otis Joy had announced the arrangements in church on Sunday, urging everyone to respect Gary's love of jazz, move to the rhythm and rejoice in the Lord.

The main assembly point was in front of the Foxford Arms (not yet open for business). King Gumbo, magnificent in black tails with gold satin lapels and epaulettes, top hat, white gloves and a huge gold-fringed Gumbo Jazz Band sash across his chest, marshalled the marchers as well as anyone can marshal jazz musicians. Five bands and several solo players – totalling seventy or more – drew up in formation across the street, brass instruments gleaming in the pale October sun.

Hats were removed in respect when someone spotted the hearse approaching the village along the lane. What wreaths covered the big black Daimler! The roof rack was a mass of colour and the coffin hardly visible for floral tributes shaped into trumpets, saxophones, tubas and drums. Rachel's wreath was a huge music stave made of white Arum lilies. She arrived with two of Gary's jazz friends and took her position behind the hearse. She was in a new black coat with artificial fur trimming and a black straw hat. When she saw the crowds she had a moment of panic and thought of going straight to the church, but having suggested the whole thing she had no choice except to join in.

A whistle blast from King Gumbo at the head of the procession alerted everyone. The Gumbo band drummer began a slow beat. Responding to a plaintive note from King Gumbo's muted trumpet, the saxes took up the touching blues melody 'Spider Crawl'. Trumpet and clarinet combined and spoke to each other between the twelve-bar chord sequence. Further back in the line, other bands blended in. Swaying, taking tiny flat-footed steps, the leaders of this extraordinary cortège took the first steps up Foxford's street towards the church. The hearse crawled behind them and after the hearse came Rachel, walking alone at the head of a column of mourners from the village.

The strains of 'Just a Closer Walk with Thee' took over. The crowd listened respectfully, many swaying to the music. Gary, everyone agreed, would have approved.

They took almost forty minutes to reach the church, only six hundred yards off. At regular intervals King Gumbo stopped and bobbed and swayed to the beat, and everyone was compelled to do the same. The hearse-driver quietly cursed and kept the engine running and thought about asking for a higher fee. But all along the route, the visitors enjoyed the music and the spectacle, following along and joining the end of the procession.

Otis Joy waited at the lychgate of St Bartholomew's to receive the coffin, dressed simply in black cassock. Behind him, the church was full except for the places reserved for the principal mourners and the Gumbo Jazz Band. 'I am the resurrection and the life . . .' he began, when the coffin was finally withdrawn from the hearse and borne towards him. Hundreds came to a halt, in the churchyard and a long way back along the street.

Inside the church, the coffin, with just Rachel's wreath resting on it, was lowered onto trestles. Rachel took her place in the front pew. She was the only family mourner, but she had Gary's jazz friends sitting beside her. They had helped choose the hymns, gospel numbers movingly sung by a choir that specialised in spirituals. That line of 'Swing Low, Sweet Chariot' – *coming for to carry me home* – had a poignancy she had never been aware of before. She pressed a Kleenex to the corner of her eye.

And Otis was equal to the occasion when the time came, finding noble things to say about a man who had not had a noble thought in his life. '"Behold, I show you a mystery,"' he began with a text from St Paul. '"We shall not all sleep, but we shall all be changed. In a moment, in the twinkling of an eye, at the last trump: for the trumpet shall sound and the dead shall be raised incorruptible, and we shall be changed."'

He spread his hands, his voice subdued. 'Never in its long history has our church echoed to such singing. Gary's devoted wife Rachel and his friends decided this was what he would have liked, and how right they were. He loved his jazz. It's a strong consolation in a time of great sadness that he managed to visit New Orleans shortly before his final heart attack. Gary was not specially religious by temperament, but he found spirituality in music, and he would rejoice that the music he loved has provided this marvellous send-off today. He was taken from us at only forty-two, gathered, very suddenly, on the evening of our harvest supper. He could have told you of great jazzmen who died young, like Bix Beiderbecke and Charlie Parker. I'm often asked for a reason why good men and women are sometimes taken from us prematurely. We have to accept it. In those words I spoke from the Prayer Book, "The Lord gave and the Lord hath taken away." Our thoughts now must be with Rachel. May she come through the grief of the present days and find peace. For Gary, there is peace already. Like Mr Valiant-for-Truth in *The Pilgrim's Progress*, "So he passed over, and the trumpets sounded for him on the other side." And today in our village they sounded for Gary on this side as well.'

After the service, the Gumbo Jazz Band serenaded the coffin with the 'Beale Street Blues', a number traditionally played in slow-drag tempo. Then the hearse was driven to Haycombe for the burial. Rachel had resisted all suggestions of using a plot in the village churchyard.

Inside the cemetery gates, the undertaker (who had been rather upstaged by King Gumbo) had his moment of attention, walking in front of the cortège wearing his top hat. Rachel and the jazz friends went to the graveside with Otis, who spoke the words of committal. Quietly, they took leave of Gary.

On their return to Foxford they were greeted with the enlivening blare of 'When the Saints Go Marching In' played lustily by King Gumbo and his lads. This was up-tempo time. The mutes were off, the top hats were back on and the music swelled. All the bands joined in, giving full vent to their playing, bobbing, stomping and swinging to the end of the street and back again, ending at the pub.

King Gumbo sank two glasses of beer in a short time and said, 'Man, oh man, that was some boogaloo.'

In Rachel's cottage, over cheese and wine, the real Foxford people, friends and neighbours, had come, as if to reclaim the occasion for the village. Long after the camera crews and jazz bands had gone, this was the community that would help the young widow adjust to her changed life. More humdrum than big drum, as Bill Armistead put it. The talk was subdued compared to the bedlam in the pub, but all agreed it had been a day to remember. 'And wasn't the rector wonderful, the things he said?' Peggy Winner enthused. 'I was so proud of him. He had me in floods of tears, and between ourselves I was never very fond of Gary.'

'That's a gift from God, being able to fit your words to the occasion like that,' said Geoff Elliott. 'Not that I recall what was said, but I found it moving at the time. Beautiful words, yes.'

'And not the same words he used at poor Stanley's funeral. Not the same at all.'

'Different man,' Elliott pointed out.

'Yes, but two funerals coming so soon, one after the other, it would be easy to repeat yourself.'

'No, no, Peg. He thinks it through. Next time someone goes, it will be different again. You'll see.'

'I hope no one else is going,' she said. 'Two in just over a month is more than we can afford to lose.'

'And that's not counting the bishop.'

'The bishop wasn't a Foxford man.'

'No, but he was our bishop. It's a connection. Rector remembered him in church, if you were there.'

'I was – and he said just the right thing in the circumstances.'

'In the circumstances, yes.' Geoff Elliott's eyes widened slightly at the memory of the bend-over bishop, so slightly that no one else noticed.

Two of the confirmation class were drinking orange squash and talking with approval about the service. 'Considering Gary wasn't a church-goer, it was wonderful,' Ann Porter remarked to Burton Sands. 'I said a prayer for him, hoping he gets to heaven.'

'If he wasn't a believer, he won't,' said Burton flatly. 'You know what the *Te Deum* tells us. "Thou didst open the Kingdom of Heaven to all believers."'

'We don't know what he believed,' Ann pointed out. 'Just because he didn't come to church every Sunday, it doesn't mean he was a heathen.'

'It's unlikely.'

'Well, I wouldn't count him out,' said Ann. 'As a matter of fact, he may have been on the point of joining the church. I saw him walk through the rectory gates on the day he died.'

'What, like a ghost?' said Burton.

'No, silly. Before he died. This was about five in the afternoon. He must have been calling on the rector, and it wouldn't surprise me if he'd seen the light.'

'You're guessing.'

'Maybe he had some kind of message from God that he hadn't got long to go.'

'Maybe,' Burton echoed, but with a heavy note of scepticism.

'We can't really ask Otis, but I'd give anything to know.'

Across the room, Cynthia Haydenhall was being helpful,

topping up people's glasses. 'She'll manage, I'm sure,' she confided to Mary Todd from the shop. 'She'll go through a period of grief, of course, but she's a survivor. She'll bounce back.' She checked where Rachel was, making sure she was too far away to hear. 'And they weren't as close as some couples are, if you understand me.'

'I'd noticed that.'

'She'll miss him, of course, but . . .'

'She's just a young thing,' said Mary Todd. 'She won't be alone for long, if I'm any judge.'

'Do you think so?'

'If she looks after herself, keeps her hair nice.'

'She's in the Frome Troupers. They're a lively lot. Not many men, though.'

'It's always the problem in amateur dramatics.'

'She was all set to star in *There Goes the Bride* on Friday. I suppose they'll have to find a replacement now.'

'Shame. She must have been looking forward to it, learning the part and all.'

'Well, you can't act in a farce the same week you bury your husband.'

The rector put his head around the door, and Cynthia shimmied through the crush to offer him a drink. He'd taken off his cassock and was wearing a dark suit. He said, rather curtly, she thought, that he wished to speak to Rachel first.

'I think she's handing out sausage rolls. She's bearing it very well.'

'Good.'

'Everyone agrees you excelled yourself in church, Otis. You gave a wonderful address.'

'Doing my job, Mrs Haydenhall. Where exactly is she? I don't see her.'

'In the kitchen, I expect.'

He went in search of her.

The party in the Foxford Arms continued past closing time and the last coach left Norman Gregor's field after midnight. Rachel heard it pass the cottage, music still being played and audible between the gear shifts. It would be a long time before she chose to listen to jazz again.

Alone now, she had nothing to do. The guests had insisted on washing and wiping every last teaspoon. Everything was put away. They had emptied the ashtrays and vacuumed the carpets. The place looked better than it had in weeks. The possibility hadn't occurred to them that she would have liked something to keep her busy.

Her brain was too active for sleep. It fairly fizzed with words said in the past twelve hours, things meant to cheer or console, most of them hopelessly wide of the mark. The only true comment – and it sounded tasteless, however it was put – was that Gary would have been happy with his own funeral. 'You could almost say he was a lucky man,' someone said. 'It softens the blow, doesn't it?' Another remarked, 'You did him proud, Rachel. You'll always be able to say you sent him off in style.'

She put on the kettle for a cup of tea, and went round checking that the doors were locked and bolted. She wasn't afraid to be alone. Just wanted the chance to come to terms with her changed life and get over the feeling of numbness that had gripped her since the moment of Gary's death.

She had to keep telling herself she was free.

Gary was gone, six feet under. Out of her life.

In the eyes of the village, she was not far short of a saint. Bravely she'd suppressed her own grief to arrange this spectacular funeral. She'd held back the tears all day.

She was no saint, and she didn't feel very brave.

In a curious way, she felt as if she was outside her own

body, looking at herself, trying to understand how she could have done what she had. The decision to do away with Gary had been made quickly, impulsively. There was none of that malice aforethought. Not much, anyway.

He had made the fatal mistake of asking for a strong curry and she'd had this sudden prospect of release like the clouds parting. An end to a gruesome marriage and a new life with Otis, the man she loved.

With astonishing clarity she'd seen how much she despised her husband and wanted to be rid of him. He was unattractive, oafish, selfish, messy, abusive, shabby, conceited, undersexed and old, old, old. His return from New Orleans had brought it home to her, literally. She couldn't bear to be close to him any longer. She knew the man she wanted, and she'd seen the unattached women of the village closing in on him. She knew how urgent it was to set herself free.

She also knew her plants and their properties. She had monkshood in the garden, a thriving clump that grew waist high and produced pretty purple flowers in May and June, and she knew of its reputation. In the medical centre where she worked, she'd checked the book they kept for emergencies: *The Dangerous Plants of Britain.*

Aconitum napellus, the source of aconitine, also known as monkshood, wolfsbane, leopard's bane, women's bane, blue rocket and devil's helmet, is without doubt the most poisonous plant in Britain. Every part of it, the flower, the leaves, the stems, the roots, is potentially deadly. As little as one fiftieth of a grain has been known to cause death, and one tenth is certain to prove fatal.

Significantly, though, only one case of murder by aconitine was listed, and that was from over a century before, a Dr

Lamson who had foolishly given himself away by buying the stuff from a chemist. Surely if the plant was so deadly and so common in gardens, it must have been used on other occasions. If so, it had not been detected in a hundred years.

Apparently Dr Thomas Stevenson, a leading Victorian toxicologist, was giving evidence in a murder case when he was asked if he knew of any poison that was undetectable. He answered, 'There is only one that I can recall and that is—' 'Stop!' cried the judge. 'The public must never hear of it.' That poison, Stevenson later disclosed in a lecture to medical students, was aconitine, the extract of aconite.

Rachel's decision to do away with Gary had been quickened by opportunity. He'd asked for a curry worthy of the name. So he got it.

The blue rocket.

She'd used the tubers of a rootstock of monkshood from the garden, chopping them like any root vegetable and adding them to the curry before she put it in to warm. The only difference from horse-radish root was that it slowly turned red when cut, rather than staying white. At first he wouldn't have been troubled by the tingling and burning sensation in the mouth characteristic of aconite. What else does one expect from a good, strong curry?

He'd gone through some of the symptoms before she got home from the harvest supper, yet it had still been a terrible test of her nerve watching him in dire pain losing his faculties while she tried to judge the exact moment to call Dr Perkins. Gary had to be alive when the doctor came, yet beyond medical help. She'd timed it right, thank God. The last symptoms of aconite poisoning, after hours of pains and nausea, are loss of speech, impairment of vision and convulsions – readily diagnosed as a heart attack. In fact, the cause of death is cardiac failure resulting from paralysis of the centres in the brain. Dr Perkins didn't know anything about aconite poisoning, but he could recognise a heart attack, and he was dealing with one by the time he was called to Gary. Poisoning didn't cross the old doctor's mind. Why should it have? You don't expect a poisoner to call the doctor to her victim.

But of course it had been necessary to have a physician attend him, make the diagnosis and, crucially, sign the certificate.

She had amazed herself by her self-control. Now it was all over she couldn't believe she had done it, murdered her own husband and watched him die. Was this really the woman who prayed in church each Sunday and went round the village collecting for Christian Aid? She dreaded her own symptoms now: the numbness wearing off and the full horror flooding in. There was going to be a reaction soon. Her personal hell.

She forced herself to concentrate on practicalities.

How will I live with what I have done?

A term of mourning – or what appeared as mourning – would follow. Respect was more accurate. Not respect for Gary, but for the conventions of village life. A widow didn't have to drape herself in black these days, but some show of solemnity was wanted, whatever her private feelings.

What a change in her life. No more fun with the Frome Troupers. All those weeks of learning her part and rehearsing *There Goes the Bride* had gone out of the window.

The months to come had to be endured. Low key. Smiles but no laughs. The one consolation would be the visits from Otis. The beauty of it was that he would come openly, in his capacity as priest, doing his duty, comforting the bereaved.

She craved his comfort.

And in time, maybe as soon as the spring of next year, she and Otis could begin to be seen together at village events. She didn't want to wait much longer just to satisfy decorum. This was her life ticking away. Why waste so much of it for fear of a few mean-minded gossips who would say she'd hardly seen one husband off before she was taking up with the rector? They'd say the same if she waited till the autumn, or the year after. Some people were like that. Their disapproval had to be faced.

She warmed the teapot and put in some dried camomile. Camomile tea is a great calmer. She'd harvested it from the garden a long time ago. Gary had never cared for it. He'd often told her he didn't trust her country remedies. She smiled at the memory.

While the camomile was infusing she switched her thoughts to Otis.

He had come looking for her as soon as he reached the cottage after the burial and she could recall their short conversation with total accuracy.

'Can't stay long, I'm afraid. Just want to say how bravely you coped today.'

'Everyone is helping me.'

'Yes, but none of us had any idea what a huge event it would turn out to be.'

'Don't I know it.'

'You're almost certain to feel a reaction later, and I'm going to help you through it. Count on me, Rachel. Call me any time. I'll come and see you anyway, but you may want to pick up the phone. Day or night, don't hesitate.'

'Thanks.'

His eyes locked with hers and she was certain they conveyed much more.

Here she was then, at almost one a.m., extremely tempted to call him, yet resisting. She didn't trust herself in this state. She might blurt out everything. She was going to have to button her lip. Of all things, she didn't want Otis finding out that she had committed murder.

So she drank the camomile tea and tried listening to the radio for a bit, thinking she'd get a sense of what else had happened in the world while she had been so preoccupied, bring some balance back into her thoughts. Much earlier, some of the television programmes would have reported the funeral, the perfect off-beat item to finish the newscast. 'And finally, a funeral with a difference. When the Wiltshire village of Foxford took leave of jazz enthusiast Gary Jansen earlier today, it did so in New Orleans style, and hundreds came to see it.'

She'd missed all that, and she wasn't sorry. The radio was more serious in tone – a dramatic fall in share prices, more evidence of global warming, a plane missing somewhere and a drugs find in a yacht off the south coast. The world moved on, and she was just an insignificant part of it, calmer now and ready – she hoped – for sleep.

14

Rachel spent the morning answering letters of condolence and the afternoon in the garden uprooting things. She was glad she had so much to do out there. The physical work shut out unwanted thoughts and she would get better sleep that night after all the digging. She had decided to clear the jungle around the pond and, as always, each job took longer than she expected. For obvious reasons, the monkshood had to go, but it was a struggle. The root system was well established and went deeper than she expected.

People came by as she worked and she noticed once again how many of them avoided saying anything – when normally at least a friendly 'hello' was exchanged. Bereavement had turned her into an untouchable. What did they think – that she would burst into tears?

There were no such inhibitions for Cynthia. 'Great idea, darling,' she said, parking her bike against the wall. 'Go for it, I say. Come and do mine when you've finished.'

Rachel straightened up and leaned on her spade. 'There's more than enough here to keep me going.'

'If you'd like to break off for a cuppa, I'm about to make one.'

'I'm in a disgusting state.'

'Don't worry. You can leave your wellies outside the door.'

Nice to be reminded she still belonged to the human race. To call on Cynthia was to lay yourself open to the third degree, but after the last few days there was little that was not public knowledge already. She hadn't often been inside the thatched cottage at the other end of the street. And she felt the need of company. She went indoors to wash and put on something presentable.

A gas-flame fire was going merrily in Primrose Cottage by the time she'd walked up the street. Cynthia liked the country life on her own convenient terms, so it was her repeated pestering of South West Gas that had persuaded them to lay on a supply for the village. Her cottage was as comfortable as any town house. The thatch was kept tidy with a wire mesh covering, and heaven help any wildlife that tried to make a home in it. The mullioned windows were double-glazed. Round the back was a satellite dish for one of the new wide-screen digital TV sets. She hadn't yet succeeded in bringing cable TV to Foxford, but no one put it past her.

She poured tea through a strainer into a porcelain cup. 'If that cushion troubles you, toss it out.'

Rachel tugged out the cushion awkwardly placed behind her and rearranged it. Embroidered on it was the slogan *Good Girls Go to Heaven.*

For a while they went over the detail of the funeral. Cynthia now regretted being inside the church because she hadn't seen the street procession. 'You caught the march-past *and* the service. You saw it all, did it all,' she told Rachel as if she was talking about a trip to Disneyland. 'You were *in* the march.'

'I had no choice.'

Cynthia smiled. 'True. We couldn't have swapped. I thought the place to be was inside the church, and I boobed. It wasn't. The story of my life. I've sat through funerals before, but I've never seen one of those death marches. Is that what they call them?'

'You must have seen it when we came back.'

'Yes, but by then the whole thing was too hyper for my liking. Carnival time. I wanted to see the slow, dignified stuff. Mind you, the service was lovely. Didn't Otis hit the spot?'

'You mean . . . ?'

'That bit about the trumpet sounding on the other side. Gave me goose pimples.'

'Brilliant, yes.'

Cynthia leaned back in her chair and grinned wickedly. 'I could play some good notes on his trumpet, given half a chance.'

Rachel didn't find that amusing.

Cynthia continued, 'He still has enemies in the village, you know. You wouldn't believe it, but he does.'

'Anyone with a fresh approach is going to upset some people. He upset you not long ago.'

'I don't remember that.'

'You've got a short memory. After the fete, when you didn't get invited back for a cup of tea,' Rachel reminded her. 'That was a laundry-basket offence, you told me.'

The colour flooded into Cynthia's cheeks. 'Lawdy! Did I? Well, I think the man is absolutely gorgeous. I could pleasure him at breakfast, lunch and tea, but it's unrequited passion up to now. He doesn't give me any encouragement at all. It's you he fancies.'

Now Rachel blushed. 'Oh, come on.'

'I can see it in the way he looks at you. His eyes follow you long after you've gone by. Now that you're a merry widow, he'll be on the case. Just see if he isn't. Listen, hand me that ruddy cushion. There isn't room in that chair for both of you.'

As she passed it across, Rachel read the message on the reverse: *Bad Girls Go Anywhere*. 'You say the daftest things, Cyn.'

'Want a bet? Has he been round to comfort you?'

'Of course not.'

'He will. It's his job, comforting widows.'

'He has more important things to do.'

'Nonsense. You're top priority. If I were you, I'd bake some cakes and have a bottle of vino ready. But he won't be round today. I was up early. Saw him drive past about six-thirty. He's taking the day off, I reckon. Generally it's Tuesday when he goes missing, but he had the funeral yesterday, so he took today instead. Where he goes in that old banger of his I couldn't tell you. But we've been over that before, haven't we? He's a man of mystery, our rector.'

'He's entitled to some life of his own. Who are these enemies you mentioned? Burton Sands, I suppose?'

'Him, yes. And Owen.'

'Owen who?'

'Miss Cumberbatch's brother.'

'The fat man? I don't think I've ever spoken to him.'

'Well, don't. He spreads the most hair-raising gossip about poor Otis being a serial murderer.'

Rachel spilled tea into her saucer. 'That's horrible.'

'Of course it's horrible and quite impossible, but Owen witters on about it to anyone daft enough to listen. He's a prize bullshitter, pardon my French. You mention a place and Owen Cumberbatch has been there. Name some famous person and he knows them personally. No, to be accurate, he usually names them first.'

'Why is he spreading lies about the rector?'

'Says he knew him in his previous parish. Where was it? St Saviour's at Old Mordern.'

'Where's that?'

'Near Chippenham, I think.'

'What's he got against Otis?'

'Apart from being a serial killer?' Cynthia shook with laughter. 'I wouldn't know, darling.'

They both laughed, since the notion of Otis killing anyone was so preposterous.

'Next he'll be claiming Otis murdered your Gary.'

Rachel caught her breath and felt a spasm through her body. 'He'd better not.' Her cheeks were burning and her heart pumped harder. To hear it suggested that Gary could have died of anything except natural causes was deeply alarming and had to be dealt with immediately. 'Listen, Cynthia. If anyone in this village – Owen or anyone else – spreads a vicious rumour like that, I'll sue them.'

'Otis would have to sue him, poppet,' Cynthia pointed out. 'It wouldn't be you he was defaming.'

In spite of aching all over from the gardening, Rachel couldn't get to sleep that night. Cynthia's casual linking of Gary's name with murder had devastated her. Where had the woman got such an idea? There was no reason for any suspicion about the death. Everything was watertight. Gary had been treated for a heart problem only days before he died. The doctor was satisfied, the medical certificate written, the death certificate collected, the curry disposed of, the monkshood eradicated and the corpse buried. She'd given Gary the best funeral anyone ever had in Foxford. She ought to be untouchable.

How infuriating, then, how bloody unfair, if rumours started just through Owen Cumberbatch's malicious gossip. No, get this straight, she thought. Owen hadn't said anything. It was Cynthia anticipating things that might conceivably enter Owen's head. It was Cynthia who had hit the button – good-hearted, ever-cheerful, yappy Cynthia. And this time she wasn't even trying to make mischief. She'd come out mindlessly with the truth – or at least a half-truth. Gary was a victim of murder.

Rumour was so insidious. Mud sticks. If this came to the ears of old Dr Perkins, he could start thinking back and questioning his diagnosis.

Am I panicking? she thought.

Maybe this was the reaction kicking in, the depression everyone was warning her about. The numbness of the first shock was passing, and she was becoming prey to her own nerves.

She mustn't let it get to her. She'd done everything right up to now. All she had to do was hold her nerve and make sure Cynthia held her tongue.

She sat up, put on the light and took one of the sleeping pills Dr Perkins had prescribed for her. Sensibly, she forced her thoughts onto another track: her future life with Otis after they married. Some drastic updating would be necessary in the rectory and she hoped Otis was generous with money – one aspect of his character she knew nothing about. Starting with the kitchen, which was hopelessly old-fashioned, she began planning the changes she would make.

When she finally drifted into sleep, she had totally reorganised the kitchen and was mulling over colour schemes for the main reception room.

At lunchtime the next day a stranger walked into the Three Golden Cups in the North Wiltshire village of Old Mordern and asked for a lemonade. The five or six local men in the bar turned and stared. Sometimes a driver would ask for low-alcohol lager or a shandy, but lemonade, for a man, was pretty unusual. Yet this stranger had the look of a lemonade drinker: a humourless, freckled face, a rigid don't-even-ask stance and carroty hair out of the nineteen fifties, short back and sides with a parting. He was in a blue pinstripe with waistcoat and striped tie. A doorstep evangelist, maybe.

He was Burton Sands, taking a day from his annual holiday allowance in the hope of discovering more about Otis Joy's relations with women. He was confident that a history of philandering was behind the appointment of Rachel Jansen as PCC treasurer. So the visit wasn't about evangelism, but it was a mission. His grudge against the rector of Foxford filled his mind. He had no clear idea at this stage how he would use any information he acquired. He just needed it like some people need affection.

'Nice day,' he said to no one in particular.

'Anything to eat, sir?' asked Ben, the landlord. 'The specials are on the board.'

'Eat? I don't think so.'

'Pies are good,' said a bearded man known locally as Nelson through some small seafaring experience he'd once unwisely revealed to this sarcastic bunch. 'Mary in the kitchen is famous for her pies.'

'Just the lemonade, thank you.'

It was becoming clear that this stranger to the pub was good value. Nelson said, 'You shouldn't drink on an empty stomach.' He could be just as sarcastic as the rest. 'Got far to go, have you?'

'I'm from Foxford.'

'Foxford down Warminster way?' said Ben. 'Our last vicar went there, didn't he?'

Someone confirmed it.

'Popular young chap,' added Ben. 'Name of Joy.'

Burton couldn't have wished for a better lead-in. 'The

Reverend Joy. Yes, I know him. He's quite popular in Foxford,' he said as if he couldn't fully understand the reason.

'Church was full here when he were vicar,' said Nelson. 'Are you a church-goer, young man?'

'Yes, I am.'

'I thought so. You'll pardon me for saying so, but you have the look of one of the faithful.'

'I don't know how you tell,' said Burton naively, ignoring the sly smiles and wanting to get the conversation back to Otis Joy. 'He's an excellent preacher.'

'Helped my business on a Sunday lunchtime,' said Ben the landlord. 'They came here after the service, thirsty from singing all the hymns.'

'Different story now,' said Nelson. 'The new bloke is a dead loss.'

'Your loss is our gain, then,' Burton commented, keeping them on the subject, and wittily, he thought. Then he dangled some tasty bait. 'He's well liked, specially by the ladies.'

Disappointingly, no one was interested.

He was compelled to add, 'I suppose he would be, with his good looks.'

No response.

'And his lively personality, of course.'

He was not good at this. They started talking among themselves about last night's football on the television. Personally, he knew nothing about football. He tried to get the landlord back on track. 'Of course, you'd have seen another side of the man. He was married while he was here, was he not?'

A nod.

'She died, I heard. His wife.'

'Correct.' There was a guarded note in the voice that

told Burton he wasn't going to get much more from this
source.

'How very sad.'

'Yes.'

'She must have been quite young.'

'True,' said the landlord. Then, addressing the others:
'That was never a goal, that third one. It should never have
been allowed.'

Burton Sands picked up his lemonade and took it to a
table. After ten minutes he got up and left.

He walked up the street in the thin October sunshine
and paused to watch a squirrel tightroping across a power
cable with a nut in its teeth. Halfway over, it spotted Sands
and froze for a second before completing the crossing,
when it transferred to a tree and streaked upwards and
out of sight. That squirrel seemed to sum up Old Mordern.
Burton already disliked the place. It had darker stonework
and less thatch than Foxford. The church at the top of the
street was obviously Victorian, the tower topped by an ugly
saddleback roof and a square stair-turret.

He strolled as far as the church gate. Nobody should
object if he wandered among the gravestones; in these
days when so many people were researching their family
histories it was nothing unusual for strangers to walk up
and down churchyards studying every inscription.

The stone that interested him didn't take long to find. It
was close to the church building on the west side, a simple
memorial:

Claudine Joy

1975–1998

Beloved wife of Rev. Otis Joy

Vicar of this Parish

He did the mental arithmetic, worked out that she had

been younger than he was now, and moved on, into St Saviour's.

His first impression was of the cold interior. Then of another sort of bleakness, a sense of neglect, or at least austerity. The velvet curtains that were meant to act as a draught excluder over the door had lost the nap in patches where hands had drawn them across. He was standing on a strip of plain cord matting worn thin by years of use and fraying in places. It linked with another strip along the length of the aisle. He was puzzled. Lively, well-supported churches replace fabrics when they get shabby. Even the altar cloth wanted replacing. The linen looked clean, yet it had obviously been laundered a few times too many. In structure this was a fine church with some strikingly beautiful stained windows. All it wanted was some redecoration and some money spent on the soft fabrics. True, there were some nicely worked kneelers hanging under the pews, but they would have been donated by the women who made them. The things that were the responsibility of the parish council were crying out for replacement.

He heard a movement. A woman was at work arranging white and yellow chrysanthemums in a large, chipped vase below the pulpit.

She spoke a greeting and Burton responded and offered to turn on the lights. The chance of a civilised conversation about the former vicar was surely better here than in the pub. He wished he'd thought of it earlier. Of course he couldn't have relied on anyone being inside.

'You should have seen it last weekend when we had the Harvest Festival,' the woman said. 'It looked a lot more homely then.' She was tall and slim, in her sixties, and wearing a green apron and gardening gloves. 'Do you know the church?'

'My first time,' answered Burton.

'It doesn't have much of a history compared to some in the area, but we like it to be seen at its best.'

'You've lived here some time?'

'Over twenty years. We came from London originally. You can probably tell I'm not local.'

'Seen some vicars come and go, then?' This was the height of subtlety by Burton's standards.

'That's for sure. They're listed on the board by the door. I've known four different ones in my time here.'

He walked over to the board and said aloud, 'Otis Joy. There's a fine name.' This time, he was going to pretend he hadn't even heard of the man. He would learn more that way. The people in the pub might have said more if he hadn't revealed that he was from Joy's present parish.

'A fine man, too,' said the flower-arranger. 'He had charisma in abundance. Like that President Kennedy.'

Another notorious womaniser, thought Burton. Was that significant? 'I happened to notice the name Joy outside on one of the headstones.'

'That would be his wife's grave, poor soul. She was French, a charming young lady with a kind word for everyone, and always beautifully turned out.'

'What happened?'

'It was dreadful. One of those chance events that bring tragedy when you least expect it. She was stung by a bee.'

'And it killed her?'

'Very quickly. Some people are allergic to bee-stings, apparently, and she was one of them. The rector found her dead in the shower. When they did the post mortem they found this bee-sting. The pathologist said a bee must have got into the shower-compartment and been trapped somehow and attacked Mrs Joy when she stepped inside.'

'Strange.'

'Not really. You see, there was a lavender hedge all

round the rectory, close to the walls, and the bees are really drawn to lavender, if you've ever noticed. They come to it in hundreds on a sunny day. It was hot and the shower-room window was open. A combination of things.'

'Why would a bee go in the shower?' said Burton, deeply suspicious.

'I don't know. Perhaps she had some scented soap in there.'

'I never heard of bees being interested in soap.'

'Lavender soap.'

'When did this thing happen?'

'Shortly before Otis moved away. We were sorry to see him go, but we all said it was a good thing he went. Too many unhappy associations in that vicarage for him.'

'Yes, it's understandable.' Burton made a huge effort to sound sympathetic.

'The Church of England put in another shower for the new vicar. There was nothing wrong with the old one, but they changed it, just the same.'

'Very considerate.'

'Speaking for myself,' she said, 'I wouldn't take a shower there now, knowing what happened. Showers frighten me, anyway, ever since I saw that Hitchcock film. Oh, what was it called?'

'Why would you take a shower in the vicarage?'

She frowned, thrown by his way of taking every statement literally. 'I'm not speaking personally. I don't visit there. I was just putting myself in the position of the new vicar or his wife.'

'You said it happened shortly before he left. Was he due to leave anyway?'

'No, he could have stayed on for years. We liked him. It was his wife's death that caused him to ask the Church for a move. The people here did their best to help him through the bereavement, cooking for him, and so forth, but it's difficult.'

'Why?

'I mean for ladies wanting to help out. Tongues wag, you know.'

'Why?' asked Burton, interested.

'If you're seen calling too often at the vicarage.'

'What do you mean?'

'It's obvious, isn't it? The young, good-looking vicar suddenly alone in the world. There's always the suspicion that someone who bakes him a pie has an ulterior motive.'

'Flirting?'

'Or something like it.'

'Was Otis Joy a flirt?'

She looked uncomfortable with the word. 'I'm sure he wasn't. He was always open-hearted and outgoing and ready with a joke and that could be mistaken for encouragement, I suppose. But no, he never overstepped the mark, and I'm sure it never crossed his mind. Certain women hover around vicars, buttering them up, always have and always will.'

'Even married vicars?'

'You must have seen it going on. It means nothing usually.'

This was becoming frustrating for Burton Sands. He said with some impatience, 'Is he a ladies' man, or isn't he? You said he was charismatic, like Kennedy.'

'Oh I see.' She blushed. 'No, I didn't mean anything like that.'

This was not so productive as he had hoped. 'What did you mean, then? Good-looking?'

'I meant charming and friendly, but that doesn't imply

that he misbehaved. I never heard a whisper of anything like that.'

'But if women found him attractive . . .'

'I can't answer for other women.' She blushed deeply. 'This is becoming rather distasteful.'

'It's not meant to be.'

She went back to her flower-arranging. 'I don't like talking this way about the poor man. It's unfair. He moved to another parish after his wife died and I hope he's happy there. I really do.'

If her little speech was meant to draw a line under the conversation, it failed. Doggedly, Burton pressed his case. 'Let's suppose he found someone else. You wouldn't mind?'

'That's his business entirely. He's still young. Why shouldn't he marry again in time? I think a vicar should have a wife supporting him if possible.'

'Some don't,' said Burton. He moved towards the altar, his hand curving over the padding on the communion rail. 'This wants replacing.'

'So does everything else if you look closely,' she said, pleased to change the subject. 'Unfortunately the funds won't run to it. We're rather a poor parish.'

'I can't think why. You said it was well-supported when the Reverend Joy was here.'

'Yes, but the upkeep is too much for a small community like ours. We never had any left over for jobs like that, and we lost our sexton, Mr Skidmore. He was very good at keeping the church in good order.'

'Lost him?'

'Quite literally. It's a mystery. He disappeared one day and nothing has been heard of him since.'

Burton felt a prickling of excitement. 'When did this happen?'

'About two years ago.'

'In the Reverend Joy's time?'

'It was. He was a crusty old character, Fred, a bit sharp with visitors. He dug the graves and polished the communion vessels and cut the grass and brushed the path. He's officially a missing person, but most of us think he must be dead. He had no life outside the village. His cottage is still just as he left it, boarded up now. I suppose they'll do something about it in time.'

'How does someone disappear?' said Burton.

'That's the mystery. Time goes on, and no one does anything about it. They ought to look in the reservoir, in my opinion. He could have drowned.'

'He'd come to the surface.'

'Well, I can't think where else he could be. Perhaps his mind went, and he wandered off. He was a bit strange at times.'

'You won't be paying his wages any more,' Burton pointed out. 'You could get someone else.'

'I don't think we could afford it any more. I know, because my husband is on the PCC. We had such a shortfall – is that the word? – that the bishop took a personal interest in our finances earlier this year.'

'Really? The bishop?'

'Bishop Marcus.'

'The one who died in the quarry.'

'You heard about that?'

'He was our bishop, too.' Burton was silent for a moment, digesting all the information he'd learned. 'So the bishop asked to see the books?'

'He came here personally and made copies of everything. We were hoping it would lead to a reduction in our quota, but we haven't heard anything. I don't suppose we will now.'

'I can't think why you're short of funds,' said Burton, thinking professionally now. 'Otis Joy was a popular vicar, you said? He must have had good congregations.'

'The best I can remember.'

'Then the collections must have been healthy enough. That's your regular source of income.'

'I suppose it's just that people aren't particularly generous here.'

'You ought to have a fabric fund.'

'I wouldn't know about that.'

'I'm an accountant. I can tell you, you ought to have a fabric fund. By that, I don't mean curtains and things. I mean a fund for upkeep of the building generally.'

'Quite a lot is done by volunteers,' she said.

'Not enough,' said Burton tartly. 'You've got to manage these things on a businesslike footing. Who's your treasurer?'

'Old Mr Vincent. Perhaps that's the trouble,' she said thoughtfully. 'He's been in the job for years and years. He's nearly ninety now.'

'Is he competent to do the job at that age?'

'It's not for me to say.'

'Someone ought to ask the question. You'd better mention it to your husband if he's on the PCC.' Burton was working himself up to quite a lather of indignation, reminded painfully of his own grievance. 'That's half the trouble with the modern church, well-meaning people doing jobs incompetently, and everyone too well-behaved to speak out. What did you say your name is?'

'I didn't say it.' The flower-arranging lady wished she had never started this.

'Well, whoever you are, madam, I tell you this: it's up to the lay people like you and me to ask questions and blow whistles if necessary, or the clergy get away with murder.'

She nodded, doing her best to humour him. She had not seen such intensity in a young man before.

15

Rachel took a phone call from Otis one Thursday morning in November. He asked how she was.

Heart pumping at the sound of his voice, she said with all the calm she could dredge up, 'So-so. I'm trying to get on with things. No sense in feeling sorry for myself.' As she spoke, she was thinking *but I wouldn't mind some sympathy from you.*

'I'm sure you're right. Are people helping out?'

'Some are.'

He was quick to say, 'Some aren't, you mean?'

'Some find me scary now.'

'*Scary?*'

'I've been touched by death. It's some primitive fear that I'll spread the bad luck to them.'

'It can't be that, Rachel. They're stuck for the right words, that's all. Hang in there. They'll lighten up.'

Hang in there. She smiled at the phrase, from a clergyman. Shouldn't he have been telling her about the patience of Job?

He told her, 'I was about to invite myself for coffee and a chat. How are you placed?'

How was she placed? Over the moon, now. 'Come whenever you like.'

'Tomorrow morning?'

Twenty-four hours away. She had an urge to say, 'Why

not now?' but she stopped herself. No doubt he had his day filled with choir practice and hospital visits and ecumenical meetings.

He was saying, 'A simple cup of instant, right? That's what I drink all the time. I don't want you going to any trouble.'

She managed to sound casual and light-hearted. 'All right. Instant, in a chipped mug.'

'And not so much as a digestive biscuit.'

The first sign of the festive season, winking lights on the fir tree outside the Foxford Arms at the end of November, was not widely welcomed. It came too soon for most villagers. The shops and streets of Frome and Warminster had been decorated since the beginning of the month; out here, people liked to believe they didn't need to rush things.

'It's all about the cash register,' Owen Cumberbatch said in the bar, where he held forth nightly. 'Pack the customers in at all costs.'

'No, it isn't, not here it isn't,' insisted the publican, Joe Jackson. 'It's no busier here tonight than any other day. It's about bringing a little joy into the village. Lord knows, we've had an unhappy few months, what with poor old Stanley passing on, and then that fellow Gary Jansen. Let's try and cheer ourselves up.'

A voice from the outer reaches called out, 'Well said, Joe.'

'Did I hear you say drinks on the house, dear boy?' said Owen.

'No, you didn't. I've got a living to make like everyone else. You'll get your glass of punch on the carol-singing evening, if you go round the village with the choir, that is.'

'When's that?'

Sometimes people forgot how recent an arrival Owen was. He seemed to have been telling his stories for ever.

'About ten days before Christmas. They go round the houses collecting money for the church.'

'And mince pies,' added PC George Mitchell from his seat by the fire, 'and the odd glass of something warm. It's a good evening.'

'You can count on me, then,' said Owen. 'I've sung with the best.'

'The Three Tenors?'

Owen disregarded that. 'My good friend Sir Geraint Evans wanted me to go professional, but I had other plans at the time. I can still hit top C when I want to.'

'We don't want any of that. You'll frighten the livestock,' said Joe Jackson. 'You'll be better off carrying one of the lanterns.'

The friend of the famous found it difficult to comprehend why people failed to warm to him in this village. He shifted the focus of the discussion. 'I expect OJ joins the carol-singers?'

'OJ?'

'The rector.'

At one of the three tables grandiosely called the dining area, Burton Sands paused over the microwaved steak pie he was quietly consuming. Burton's week had been thrown into disarray by his visit to Old Mordern. He'd come to the pub because he hadn't been shopping for food. At the mention of the rector he put down his knife and fork and leaned back in his chair so as not to miss a word.

'Wouldn't surprise me if he turns it into another jam session,' Owen went on.

'Get away!' said someone.

'He's not one to be troubled by tradition. You've seen it for yourself. Anyone who can turn a funeral into the

Twelfth Street Rag isn't going to think twice about trampling on people's feelings.'

'That wasn't his doing,' said George Mitchell. 'That was the widow wanted that.'

'Bollocks, dear boy. She'd never have thought of that in her state of grief. Typical Otis Joy, that was.'

'What do you know about it?'

The buzz of conversation around the bar stopped suddenly, enabling Burton Sands to overhear every scrap of gossip about the rector.

Owen Cumberbatch claimed smugly, 'I happen to know the way the man works, his *modus operandi*. He's a master of deception. If you or I had something dodgy to cover up, we'd do it quietly when no one was around. Not that fellow. He does it with a bloody fanfare. Everyone cheers and says what a great bloke he is. Showmanship, dear boy.'

'What's he got to hide?' said Joe Jackson.

'There you go,' said Owen, snapping his fingers. 'You're blind, you lot. I knew a fellow once – a very good friend of mine – called Borra. He was the world's greatest pickpocket. This was in my circus days.'

'Here we go,' some voice said from the dark.

'When I was no more than a lad,' Owen went on, unfazed. 'Borra was doing it legitimately, as an act. He'd invite several of the audience into the ring and sit them on chairs in full view, under the spotlights, and not only empty their pockets, but remove ties, wristwatches, braces, even, and the poor suckers wouldn't feel a thing, wouldn't know it had been done. That's what OJ is doing to you lot, and you're the mugs who can't see it, because he distracts you with all the razzmatazz.'

'What's he up to?'

Owen spread his hands and smiled.

'Come on,' said Jackson. 'We're waiting to hear.'

Over in the dining area, Burton Sands was so eager to hear that he'd abandoned his pie and turned right round in his chair.

Owen shook his head and picked up his drink. 'There's none so blind as those that will not see.'

It was out of character, but he refused to say any more. Normal conversation was restored.

Presently, Burton Sands materialised at Owen's elbow and offered him a drink, a fateful moment, this coming together of bombast and calculation, for Owen was happy to say in private what he'd been unwilling to tell the whole pub. Mostly, Burton listened, trying not to betray his amazement at the litany of wickedness Owen was only too happy to repeat for him. Not merely fiddling the funds, not just philandering with the ladies of the parish, but murder, serial murder. Burton's festering suspicions of Otis Joy were justified, according to this man. His head reeled. A clergyman who killed his own wife, a sexton, a PCC treasurer, and maybe others?

'And you seriously think he kills people when they find out about his embezzlement?'

'Without a doubt, dear boy.'

Burton hesitated on the brink of the chasm of evil that had just opened up. 'I heard a rumour that prior to Bishop Marcus's death, he was investigating Joy.'

Up to this moment Owen hadn't made any connection between Otis Joy and the death of the bishop. However, no one was his equal at claiming other people's gossip as his own. 'Spot on. I heard it, too. And you wonder if he had anything to do with the bishop's death? You bet your life he did.'

'It isn't far from here, that quarry,' Burton said, more to himself than Owen.

Owen was thinking fast. 'Easy enough to dress it up as a suicide.'

Burton was appalled. In a wicked, wicked world, surely this was beyond all.

He left the pub soon after with eyes as wide as a bushbaby's.

Twenty minutes later, Owen got off the stool and collected his coat and Russian fur hat – the last relic, he liked to tell people, of his days as an undercover servant of the Queen – without noticing PC George Mitchell leave his place by the fire and follow him out. The first he was aware of it was a firm grip on his upper arm outside the pub door.

'A quiet word, Owen.'

'Here?' Owen's face was turning strange colours in the lights of the Christmas tree.

'I'll walk with you.'

They started along the road.

'Normally I don't take much notice of things said in pubs,' Mitchell told him, 'but you went overboard in there tonight. It was close to slander.'

'Slander?' said Owen. 'Not me. I'm a truth-teller, through and through.'

'You know who I am?'

'I do, indeed.'

'With me, you'd better stick to facts.'

'I intend to.'

'What is it about the rector, then? What were you getting at?'

Owen was less fluent at this point of the evening. 'The rector? You mean . . . ? What *do* you mean?'

'You were saying the jazz at Gary Jansen's funeral was his doing.'

'In a way, in a way,' Owen hedged.

'As if he had some ulterior motive.'

'Did I?'

'You talked about a *modus operandi*.'

'Well, yes.'

'As if he was up to something criminal.'

'I can't *prove* anything.'

'You made it up, because you don't like the man.'

'No, no. I wouldn't do that.'

'So you do know something.'

'Things I pick up here and there, that's all.'

'Such as?'

Owen sighed heavily. There was no pleasure in giving up his scant information this way. 'Well, I knew him before, in his former parish. No one can deny that wherever Otis Joy goes, sudden deaths take place. His young wife. The sexton. He comes here and what happens? The church treasurer drops dead.'

'People die unexpectedly every day,' said George.

'Yes, but they aren't all closely connected with one man. Then Gary Jansen goes.'

'You can't link Gary Jansen with these others. He didn't even go to church.'

'His widow does. She's the new treasurer.'

George hesitated, weighing what had just been said. 'What are you saying? That it has to do with money?'

'I don't honestly know. All I can tell you is that I saw Gary Jansen on the day he died talking to the rector outside the village shop and it didn't look to me as if they were on about the weather, or the state of the world. Serious things were being said.'

'By Gary?'

'Oh, yes. He was doing most of the talking. And the rector didn't like what he was hearing.'

'Is that it?' said George. 'That's your case against the rector? You saw him talking to Jansen?'

'On the day he died,' Owen repeated.

'Meaning what?'

'Meaning they weren't unknown to each other, those two, just because Gary wasn't a church-goer. Gary said something that got up Joy's nose. I don't know what it was. But just suppose he found out a couple of things about Joy's past. Wouldn't Joy want him out of the way, and quickly?'

'Owen, this is a crock of shit.'

'Do you mind?'

George stopped and grabbed Owen's coat-front and pulled him almost nose to nose. 'And if you go on repeating it, people are going to get stroppy with you and I'm not going to guarantee your safety. Do you follow me? So cut the crap.'

Rachel made scones for Otis and the whole cottage filled with the smell of baking. She was sure from her visit to the rectory kitchen that he was no cook himself. The shelves had looked bare except for tins and cereal packets. No doubt he lived on convenience foods. Impressing a man with her cooking might not do much for her feminist credentials, but she was sure she could make a real difference to his quality of life. She wondered if his wife – the one who had died so tragically – had been a good cook. It wasn't certain. The French make a big deal of their culinary skills, but they often go out to eat.

The right way was to be subtle about it. Let the scones make their own suggestion.

He arrived on time, buoyant as usual, saying it was a peach of a day for the time of year. Rachel thought he was overplaying the heartiness a bit, probably to gloss over what happened the last time he came. To avoid more embarrassment on the sofa, she asked if he minded coffee in the kitchen, and he was in there like a terrier scenting rabbit.

They faced each other across the kitchen table, formal as privy councillors. 'We agreed instant coffee,' he reminded her as she reached for the cafetière.

'That was a joke.'

'I'm glad to hear it.'

'You secretly wanted real coffee?'

'No, I mean if you can joke at a time like this, you're winning. Here's one you may not have heard: the first pair ate the first apple. Geddit?'

She managed a smile, but she didn't want this to be a laugh-in. She said straight out, 'There wasn't any love between Gary and me. I'd be lying if I said there was.'

He shifted awkwardly on his chair.

She had to say more now she had started. 'You must have realised. But it's still a shock, becoming a widow, I mean. Well, you understand. You lost your wife suddenly, didn't you?'

He looked even more uncomfortable. He was bound to respond seriously. 'It wasn't so much the way I felt in myself. There was grief, but I could handle that. It was the reaction of other people – like you told me on the phone. They cut you. They don't know what to say, most of them, so they stay clear.'

She nodded. 'You feel as if you've got the plague.'

'It doesn't last long. Do the things you normally would and they'll be more relaxed with you. Christmas is coming up. Make a point of joining in things, the carol concert, the midnight service. Parties, if you want.'

'So soon?'

'We've left the Victorian age behind. I mean, you don't have to overdo it. I wouldn't walk around waving a sprig of mistletoe.'

'Not *this* Christmas,' she said.

She hoped for a positive response. Certainly his eyes opened wider. Too wide. He looked startled. Otis Joy was shockable.

'These are great,' he said, holding up a piece of scone, but Rachel wasn't to be sidetracked. She was more in control than when he last came here. Disposing of Gary had strengthened her.

'It must have been different for you, losing your wife.'

He looked away. All too obviously, he didn't like talking about his wife. 'How do you mean?'

'I expect you were very close. Gary and I weren't. You know how he went off to America for three weeks.'

He seized the chance to talk about Gary. 'It was important to him, wasn't it – the jazz? Chance of a lifetime?'

'And I thought I was going to share it with him,' Rachel said, 'but it turned out to be a guys-only trip. Actually I realised while he was away that I was happier without him around.'

'You feel guilty about that?'

'Now that he's dead? No. Why should I?'

'Right,' he said without much conviction. 'You gave him a wonderful send-off.'

'I couldn't have done it without your support, Otis.'

He blinked at the mention of his name. 'It raised a few eyebrows among the clergy, but they know me by now. And so what? There was reverence in what we did. I think the Lord approved, even if the Lord Bishops didn't.'

'Did you get into trouble over it?'

'No, thanks to good timing. We don't have a bish until the new one is enthroned. Marcus Glastonbury wouldn't have been too thrilled, I have to say.'

She smiled. 'You mean he wasn't a jazz man?'

He grinned back, avoiding the cheap quip about the kind of man the bishop was. 'Still, you must be pleased that Gary got to New Orleans.'

'Yes – and it wasn't a letdown, as it could easily have been. They had a terrific time. Met lots of other jazz fanatics.' She paused, pacing the conversation, fascinated to see how he would react to the next statement. 'Wasn't that strange about the Canadian Otis Joy who was training to be a priest?'

He said quite smoothly, 'Curious, yes. I've got some sympathy for anyone else with a name like mine who goes in for the Church.'

'This man must have been about your age, too.'

'Is that so?' He was trying to sound casual about it.

'I wondered if he could have been you – if you were ordained in Canada.'

He shook his head. 'Boring old Church of England, I'm afraid. I spent some time in Canada, but my college was in Brighton.'

'There's nothing boring about you,' she told him. 'You don't mind me asking? I'd love to know more about you, where you were born, that kind of thing.'

He took a moment to butter the second half of his scone, spreading it evenly. 'Well, it wasn't Canada. I'm from Norfolk originally.'

'And your parents died?'

'Did I tell you about that? A car crash. I was seven at the time.'

'That's terrible.'

'I'm over it now.'

'But losing your parents at that age . . .'

'I survived. No thanks to the nuns. They were Catholics, my parents, so I was sent to Ireland, to this orphanage run by the Sisters of Mercy. Not well named. The scripture was beaten into us. And I went to a Jesuit school where the principal teacher was the strap.'

'Poor Otis. You've had more than your share of hardship.'

'Slings and arrows,' he said dismissively. 'We all face them at some time in our lives. Some poor beggars take more hits than others. No sense in complaining. They gave me a wonderful grounding in the Bible. I can argue theology with anyone.'

Something in his tone made her say, 'But there's more to life than theology.'

'It was a narrow education, yes. Knowing the Beatitudes by heart wasn't going to make me into a brain surgeon. After quitting school I found it very hard settling to anything.'

'Then you went to that wedding you told me about?'

'Right, and turned my back on the Church of Rome.'

'Revenge?'

He laughed. 'These days I get along fine with the good Fathers.'

'Losing your parents like that must have traumatised you.'

'Kids are resilient. It helps me understand how my parishioners feel when they lose someone.'

'You've been there, done that, yes?'

'Got the T-shirt.'

'Read the book, seen the video.'

'As the Reverend Sydney Smith once put it, "I have, alas, only one illusion left, and that is the Archbishop of Canterbury."'

'How do you remember all these wicked quotes?'

'Self-preservation. Clergymen shouldn't take themselves too seriously.'

'But you're brilliant at the job. You may be the

Archbishop yourself one day. You deserve to be. You're doing so much for the church in this village.'

'Running a parish is all I want, Rachel. It's a great high. You wouldn't believe the buzz I get from it. I don't want to be a bishop.'

'But you must have some ambition to rise in the Church.'

'I'm there,' he told her with a conviction in his eyes and voice that she couldn't mistake for anything but the truth. 'I've made it. I've moved mountains to get where I am, and nothing is going to shift me. Nobody had better try. This is all I could desire from life – or nearly all.'

'What else?'

'I'd like to travel one day.'

She'd hoped he would say he wanted to marry again, or start a family. Just a hint that he was of the same mind as she was. Was that too much to ask?

The missionary zeal had shifted from his face and all his attention was on her, and her hopes flickered again. 'There's something I want to ask you, Rachel. I don't know if this is too soon to mention it.'

'Yes?'

'Are you happy to carry on doing the parish accounts?'

16

John Neary, washing his car outside the house on Saturday afternoon, was surprised to see Burton Sands coming across the street as if to speak. They knew each other from the confirmation classes, and never usually exchanged a word outside. Neary had only to look at Burton in his flat cap and anorak to want to turn the other way. No doubt about it: the village bore was making a beeline for him.

'Did you hear? They've picked the new bishop,' Burton said as if it was as vital to the nation as the choice of England striker.

'Have they?'

'He's from Radstock.'

'Is he?' Neary carried on hosing his hub caps in the expectation that the man would soon go away.

'When I say "they", I mean the Dean and Chapter. They'll shortly announce a date for the Consecration.' Sands was one of those irritating church-goers who took pride in knowing all the ecclesiastical terminology. 'Then he'll be enthroned at Glastonbury and take possession of his see.'

John Neary didn't even look up.

Burton wasn't discouraged. 'It should be early next year. So things will soon be back to normal.'

Neary couldn't think of any way his life had been made

abnormal by the church politics at Glastonbury. He didn't care what was happening there.

Burton came to the point. 'The new bishop will be able to confirm us. We'll all be going back to the rectory to brush up on the service. The rector promised us one more meeting.'

'See you there, then,' said Neary, spotting a chance to end the dialogue.

'Yes. Early January, I expect, if he remembers. Do you think we ought to remind him?'

Neary was beginning to think the only way to get rid of Burton Sands was to turn the hose on him.

'Someone should,' continued Burton. 'He'll have plenty on his plate over Christmas.'

'Mm.'

'And I'm not talking about turkey.'

Neary lifted an eyebrow. Had he heard right? Was Sands making a joke?

Still he lingered.

'The bees hibernate at this time of year, do they?'

'What?' Neary was wholly thrown by this new avenue of conversation.

'Your bees. You still keep bees, don't you?'

The five hives in the back garden meant more to Neary than the garden itself, his house, his car, or – it has to be said – his confirmation. He pulled the hose from the car and let the water gush downwards in a stream that spread quickly along the street. When people mentioned his bees, it was usually to complain. Two of the hives had swarmed at the end of the summer. 'What have my bees got to do with the new bishop?'

'Nothing,' said Burton.

'How do you know about them?'

'The honey's got your label. I get it sometimes in the shop. It's good. Really good.'

A rapid reassessment took place. Neary decided he may have misjudged Burton. If the man was a satisfied customer, he wasn't such a pain after all. 'Last summer's crop was better than usual. We had some good dry spells.'

'The bees don't like the damp?'

'A certain amount of water is necessary. You'll see them drinking at puddles in the spring. They carry the water back to the hive. But the sort of rain we get most summers isn't helpful.'

'What happens in the winter? Do you leave some honey in the hives?'

'Certainly. They need it now. All through the winter they cluster on the combs inside the hive and live off their reserves.'

'Sometimes if it's sunny in the winter, you see bees outside.'

'They go out for a shit.'

Burton gave him a long look. He'd been caught before by people taking advantage of his willingness to believe every statement.

'Call of nature, if you want it in polite language,' Neary explained in all seriousness. 'They don't like soiling the hive.'

'You seem to know a lot about it.'

'You have to, or you lose them.'

'Any chance of seeing inside one of your hives?'

'No chance,' said Neary. 'Nothing personal, but you don't disturb them in the winter months. Are you thinking of taking it up?'

'Just interested,' said Burton. 'Do you get stung much?'

'You get a few when you start. Bees aren't usually aggressive unless you do something to upset them.'

'You wear protective clothing?'

'Of course. And you have a smoke gun. It keeps them off you. They get a whiff of that and they panic a bit and eat their fill from the honey cells in the hive. Then they're docile.'

'Some people are allergic to bee-stings,' said Burton.

Neary said with caution, 'True.'

'It can be fatal.'

'In rare cases. Fortunately, I'm not one of them. Bee-keepers become immune after a while.'

'It's called anaphylactic shock,' Burton persisted doggedly with this rather negative line on beekeeping. 'The air passages get constricted. The throat tightens. A single sting in the region of the throat can cause suffocation and unconsciousness in just a few minutes. I've been reading about it.'

Neary went back to hosing the car again. Sooner or later people who talked to him about bees always got around to their nuisance value.

'People who know they're in danger from bee-stings keep anti-histamine ready just in case,' Burton added.

'For God's sake. It's about a one in a million chance,' Neary pointed out. 'Bees don't attack people for no reason at all.'

'I understand that,' said Burton, following him around the car as he worked, without realising the risk he was exposed to from the hose. 'But just suppose an evil-minded person wanted to kill someone else – someone they knew was allergic to bee-stings. Is there any way they could arrange for a bee to attack someone?'

'*Arrange* it?'

'Yes.'

'Murder them, you mean? You're talking a load of cobblers, Burton.'

'It's unlikely, I know, but could it be done?'

'No way. Bees have their own agenda. They don't sting to order.'

Burton wasn't satisfied. 'Suppose you trapped some inside a house. In a room – a bathroom, for instance – and this person with the allergy went in there to take a shower.'

'Trapped bees wouldn't stay around the shower. They'd fly to the window. Why are you asking this?'

'Doesn't matter.'

'It's a non-starter. If you're aiming to do away with someone, choose a more reliable weapon than a honey bee.'

'I'm not aiming to do anything so wicked,' said Burton in an offended tone. 'It isn't me.'

'Well, it wouldn't work anyway. Even if a bee was trapped, it would be trying to get away and someone with an allergy isn't going to go anywhere near it.'

Still he persisted. 'You can't think of any way it could be done?'

'I told you, no.' John Neary was firm. Even if he could come up with some freakish theory, he didn't want bees getting a bad name in Foxford.

Burton reluctantly gave up. 'I'll see you at that confirmation rehearsal, then.' He moved off, unsatisfied, frowning.

Rachel, too, was far from satisfied. Her 'comfort' from Otis had not amounted to as much as she had hoped. His latest visit had disappointed her. The freshly baked scones hadn't worked any charm at all. It was too soon after Gary's death to expect a proposal of marriage, she kept telling herself, but she felt entitled to *some* show of affection behind closed doors. He'd only looked like relaxing when he got up to leave. And he'd made no arrangement to call again. She hadn't asked if he would. That would have been too humiliating.

Besides, he would need to see her from time to time about the accounts. And that was odd. He'd told her his aim would be to trouble her as little as possible. He had used his contingency fund to bank the surplus from the harvest supper and he could deal with various other amounts that were coming in.

Was it his reputation as a man of God that bothered him? Maybe. She had to keep reminding herself that priests can't behave like other men. There would be turmoil going on in his mind, the tug of loyalties between his faith and his animal passion. God, she hoped animal passion would win, and soon.

She wasn't helped by a visit later in the day from Cynthia, keen to know exactly what had happened. Cyn started on the uneaten scones as if she meant to clear the plate, whilst debriefing her with the thoroughness of a spymaster. 'You're not telling me you didn't cry on his shoulder and get a cuddle? How did you pass the time, then? Not saying prayers, I bet.'

'We drank coffee and talked about the way people find it difficult to approach a widow. It was all terribly serious.'

'And totally boring, by the sound of it. What's bugging Otis? He fancies you something rotten, I know he does.'

'Come off it, Cyn.'

'If it didn't sound vulgar, I'd say it stands out.'

Rachel sighed and tried to smile.

'It doesn't? You don't think so?' said Cynthia in disbelief.

'He's a clergyman.'

'That doesn't make him frigid.'

'He still behaved like a clergyman.'

Cynthia paused, and flicked back some hair from her face. 'Well, if he doesn't go for you, I'm revising my game-plan.'

'What do you mean?'

'I was sure I didn't stand a snowball's, but I may think again now. We got on quite well at the harvest supper.' She widened her eyes, watching Rachel for her reaction. 'I'd say we clicked, actually. Has he ever said anything to you about me?'

'Not that I remember.'

Cynthia looked away from Rachel, making calculations. 'It must be getting on for two years since his wife died. He ought to be up for it by now. Someone's going to land him, so why not me?'

Cynthia, riding roughshod as usual, with no regard for anyone's feelings.

'It's up to you,' said Rachel, feigning indifference. She didn't seriously rate Cynthia as a rival.

'There isn't anyone else, is there?' Cynthia said. 'I'd like to know where he goes on his day off. Do you think it's a woman?'

'Your mind, Cynthia! I keep telling you he's a clergyman.'

She put out her tongue and blew a loud raspberry. 'First and foremost, he's a bloke, ducky.'

'Well, I don't think he'd behave like that.' Not with anyone except me, Rachel thought privately, and not with me, yet awhile, she thought bleakly.

'Some people say he's not above a bit of sinning. And I mean worse things than a bit of parallel parking,' Cynthia pointed out. 'They say he's a serial murderer.'

'Stupid. Owen Cumberbatch is a disgrace, spreading stories like that.'

'Remember I told you it wouldn't be long before he

accused Otis of having something to do with Gary's death? Well, it happened. He was dropping hints about it in the pub last week. More than hints, I'm told. He was saying your New Orleans-style funeral – not your funeral, Rach, know what I mean? – was put on to divert attention from what really happened.'

Rachel's cheeks burned. She wanted to stop this dangerous talk, but she didn't know how.

Instead, Cynthia trundled on like a ten-ton tank. 'The way it was done was typical Otis Joy, according to Owen. His *modus operandi* – did I say that right?'

Rachel shrugged, trying to keep her poise.

Cynthia explained, 'It's a term the police use for the way a criminal goes to work. They know certain villains use Semtex, or sawn-off shotguns, or something.'

'This was a *funeral*, for Heaven's sake,' Rachel succeeded in saying.

'Yes, but what a funeral. Otis covers his crimes by making such a song and dance about the victim that you couldn't possibly suspect him. The big scene in church. The funeral oration that has everyone reaching for their Kleenex. That's the theory, anyway.'

'It's bullshit. The jazz funeral was my suggestion. Otis didn't think of it.'

'I know, darling. Do you think I'd be making a play for a serial murderer? I'd have to be out of my tiny mind. We both know Owen is full of wind and piss.'

'The trouble is not everyone knows that. Throw enough mud, and some will stick.'

For some time after Cynthia left, Rachel sat biting her fingernails, reflecting on the truth of her own words. If that detestable man Cumberbatch was putting it around that Otis had murdered Gary, people didn't have to believe the gossip before they started speculating on a possible motive. There was only one: Gary had to be removed so that Otis could marry her.

Had the story reached Otis's ears? It would explain why he was being ultra-cautious.

Mud sticks.

Yes.

Everything was clearer. He was protecting her reputation. Now that she viewed his actions in this light, she loved him more than ever. She understood. He was playing a long game, and she would have to play it the same way.

He was back.

Incredibly, Burton Sands was standing on John Neary's doorstep at eight-thirty in the evening like a Jehovah's Witness trying to save one more sinner before bedtime.

'What is it now?'

'I've thought of something else.'

'I'm quite busy, actually.'

'Mind if I come in. It won't take long.'

Neary would have liked to slam the door in Burton's face, but you don't do that sort of thing in a village, particularly to a fellow member of the confirmation class. He had little option but to do the Christian thing and miss the rest of the TV programme he'd been watching. He made way for Burton to step in.

Reluctantly, Neary pressed the mute button on the remote control.

'It's about the bees,' said Burton.

'My bees?' He was ready to defend them.

'No. Any bees. They always have their queen, don't they? It all revolves around her, doesn't it? The hive, the honey, collecting the nectar?'

'It's Saturday night, Burton. Surely you haven't come round here for a lesson on beekeeping?'

'I'm right about the queen, aren't I?'

Neary sighed. 'Pretty well. She exists to lay eggs. Thousands of them. None of the other bees can do that unless they're made into queens.'

The brown eyes gleamed. 'This is the point, then. What happens if you remove the queen from the hive and put her somewhere else? They're bound to go looking for her, aren't they?'

'What are you driving at? You're still on about using bees to kill someone?'

'If you took the queen into a house, and the bees came looking for her—'

'Ain't necessarily so, Burton.'

'Why not?'

'They can replace a queen very easily. When the queen dies, or leaves the hive, they make an emergency queen cell by enlarging a worker cell. The lava in there migrates into the bigger space and is specially fed with royal jelly – you've heard of that? – and turns into a queen. So there's an in-built procedure. They don't "go looking", as you put it. They make a new queen.'

Burton looked unconvinced. 'What about when they swarm?'

'That's usually when the colony outgrows the space in the hive. They rear a new queen, and the old queen leaves with a portion of the colony and they find a new place to nest. They have the queen with them. They're not swarming in search of her.'

'Could you lure a swarm into a house, through a bathroom window, say?'

Neary was becoming impatient. 'What's this about, Burton? Are you wanting to do away with a rich aunt? Because there are easier ways than persuading bees to do it for you.'

Sands twitched at the suggestion and then said in his earnest manner, 'This is confidential, but I heard about a case of a woman who was stung by a bee while taking a shower. She was allergic to them, and she died. It's possible that the husband wanted her out of the way. He's said by some people to be a murderer, but no one knows for sure. He's very clever.'

'He'd have to be, to do it with bees. Is he a bee-keeper?'

'Not to my knowledge.'

'Forget it, then. He's innocent.'

But he would not forget it. 'Isn't there a substance that attracts bees?'

'Pheromone. It's produced by the bees, by the Nasonov, or scent gland. They fan their wings to disperse it and attract other workers, for example when they find the entrance to a new nest.'

'Is it used by beekeepers?'

'You mean to attract the colony to a new hive?'

'Yes.'

'It can be. I believe it's produced synthetically and sold.'

'And if an evil-minded person obtained some and smeared it around a bathroom, would it bring some bees there?'

'Could do. But you still have to persuade them to sting, and that's not guaranteed. A bee that stings a person is going to leave behind its sting mechanism and part of its viscera. That kills the bee inside twenty-four hours. They don't sting for the hell of it. Not usually.'

'There are exceptions?'

'You do get aggressive colonies sometimes.'

'Killer bees?'

'They're something else. African. We don't get killer bees here.'

'But you just said—'

'All I'm saying is that certain strains are more likely to sting than others. It's to do with their genetic make-up, but they're also made more angry when the nectar isn't flowing due to bad weather. And some crops such as oil-seed rape have an effect when they work them in isolation.'

'If you knew of a colony like that, and you had some of that synthetic stuff—'

Neary was unwilling to join in Burton's theory. 'Listen, if I wanted someone to get stung I wouldn't fiddle about trying to attract the bees to the scene of the crime.'

'What would you do?'

'Use a jam jar.'

'What?'

'To catch some. Then I'd take them up to the bathroom and hold the open end against my victim's flesh. If she's taking a shower, as you suggest, and I'm married to her, she'd be an easy target. They'll sting, all right, being trapped. If she's allergic, she's not going to stay conscious for long. Much simpler.'

'That certainly is,' said Burton with admiration. 'I don't know why I didn't think of it. The murderer needn't be a beekeeper at all. He's only got to go out to the garden and catch a bee in a jar.'

'He'd have to be a right bastard to do that to his wife.'

Burton agreed. 'He would.'

17

During the week a notice typical of the rector appeared on the board outside the church: 'BEAT THE CHRISTMAS RUSH. SEE YOU HERE ON SUNDAY'. And at Morning Service, he gave good value as usual, telling of the small boy who got the words of the Lord's Prayer muddled and said, 'Forgive us our Christmases, as we forgive those that Christmas against us.' In a sense the boy got it right, he said, 'Because it's not a bad idea to ask God to forgive us our Christmases. And maybe he will if we've taken time out to worship him – which is my cue to appeal for the best turn-out ever for the carol singing around the village in aid of church funds. You don't have to be a good singer. Everyone can give it a belt, and if you really have no voice at all just knock on doors and rattle a tin. This is when we show the rest of the village how to have a good time celebrating the true meaning of Christmas. If we do it in the right spirit, some will surely get the message and think, "Hey, that lot aren't so po-faced after all. I might give church a try."'

After the service, Rachel managed once again to slip out unseen, squeezing behind a couple who were telling Otis about their trip to the Holy Land. She couldn't bear the formality of shaking hands when she really wanted to be hugged and kissed.

She didn't escape Cynthia, who caught her before the lychgate.

'I saw you giving him the go-by. What is it between you two – have you crossed him off your visiting list?'

'He was talking to the Cartwrights.'

'Come off it, darling. You didn't even give a wave as you went by. Listen, if you don't watch out some of us are going to throw our hats in the ring – or something more intimate.'

'I'm not stopping you,' Rachel said.

'Beg pardon?'

'I said I'm not stopping you. It's a free country.'

'Don't be like that. I was only kidding. Are you turning out for the carols?'

'I may give it a miss this year.'

'Better not. It's much better if you get back in the swing of things.'

She recalled Otis saying much the same thing.

Cynthia was saying, 'It's always a fun evening.'

'You're going?'

'Out in the dark with Otis? Try and keep me away. You never know who you might bump into.'

She warmed to Cynthia's hearty optimism. 'All right, I'll come – if only to see how you make out.'

'Brill. Let's have tidings of comfort and joy. You can have the comfort . . .'

There was an overnight peppering of snow and the old Cortina was reluctant to start this morning. Too many short trips on parochial duties: the battery was weak. Otis Joy tried the starter a third time, and got the motor stuttering into action. One day he might get something better than this old runabout. Unlike most men, he'd never taken much interest in cars. He knew of a more exciting way to spend money. Anyway, the long drive to come would recharge the battery nicely. Yours and mine, old friend, he thought.

He cruised out of the rectory gates humming 'The Holly and the Ivy', enjoying being awake at an hour when most people hadn't even thought of getting out of bed. It would be an hour or more before he could turn off the headlamps. So he wasn't aware of the smart blue Renault that followed him out of the village and along the A350 keeping at a distance. It was just a pair of lights in the rear-view mirror.

After his usual treat of a cooked breakfast at the café in Blandford Forum and a few more miles of driving in daylight, he did notice one blue vehicle steadily fifty yards behind. Nothing to worry about, he decided. On this narrow stretch between Blandford and the coast everyone drove in convoy or risked death.

The further he got towards the coast, the better he felt. The carols got livelier. 'God rest ye, merry gentlemen' – what he could remember of the words – kept him going for a while, followed by a quick-tempo version of 'I saw three ships come sailing in'. This was Tuesday, his own day to spend as he liked – or at least until the carol-singing round the village. He didn't think of what he was doing as an escape, but simply a precious blank page in his diary, a chance to relax. Happily he had never regarded his church duties as drudgery. They were his purpose in life, uniquely satisfying. But he needed a break once a week doing something else. Six days shalt thou labour and do all thy work.

The blue car remained behind him after the roundabout linking with the A35, and he still didn't attach any importance to it. He couldn't see who the driver was because the sun was up with that silvery light you get in winter and everyone had their sun shields down. So he drove all the way to Hamworthy and his usual spot beside Holes Bay without suspecting anyone had tracked him here. And when a boat man gets to the coast, he doesn't spend time looking around the car park. Cobb's Marina was not so swanky as the Poole Harbour Yacht Club at Salterns, yet some fine boats were berthed here, valued in big bucks, and his own craft was one of the most admired.

A fellow owner greeted him as soon as he opened the car door. 'Nice day, Bill.'

'A bit fresh, Terry,' he responded, reaching behind for his crew cap. He was well known here from his regular visits, but not as the Reverend Otis Joy. To the yachting crowd he was Bill Beggarstaff. If you're going for an assumed name, don't choose Smith or Jones. People are readier to accept you if the name is memorable.

'Not so choppy, though,' said Terry. 'Thinking of taking her out?'

'I doubt it. I don't have much time today.'

'But you'll fit in a beer at lunch?'

'I expect so.'

'Not long to Christmas. Are you coming down then?'

'Christmas is a busy time for me.'

He gathered a few things from the car and carried them across to the marina and out along the pontoon where the love of his life, his sports cruiser, was moored with the largest boats.

The *Revelation* was a gleaming white forty-footer, Italian-made, only two years old, in immaculate condition, with radar arch and an echo sounder. In his black quilted blouson, canvas pants and boots, 'Bill Beggarstaff' was a familiar figure here each Tuesday keeping his property spruce and seaworthy.

After a check to see that everything was as he'd left it –
apart from a few seagull-droppings that he wiped off – he
went aboard and below to the saloon. Some heat would be
a good idea, and then coffee. He had just switched on the
air system when he heard steps above. Someone had come
aboard.

He assumed it was Terry. You don't board other people's
boats unannounced, but as they'd just had the snatch of
conversation it was excusable.

This wasn't Terry. A woman opened the saloon door and
came down the steps, bold as the first crocus. Otis had so
fully disengaged himself from Foxford that he needed a
moment to register who she was.

Cynthia Haydenhall.

His two worlds collided horribly.

The last time he'd spoken to Mrs Haydenhall was at the
harvest supper, when she was all sparkle and cleavage. This
morning she was in a striped sweater and jeans, but she
had the same predatory look.

'Morning, Rector.'

He said, 'I don't understand.'

'Nor me,' she said, her big blue eyes swivelling at the
luxury of the surroundings. 'I wondered how you spent
your days off, but I never pictured this.'

'Mrs Haydenhall—'

'Cynthia.'

'How did you . . . ?'

'I watched you get out of your car and walk across to
the marina. I was certain it was you, so . . .' She stopped,
sighed, and said, 'No, I'd better come clean. I followed
you from Foxford.'

'The blue car?'

'Yes. The Renault. You spotted me, then. It's a damned
liberty. Nothing can excuse it.'

'You got up early, specially to follow me?'

'Absolutely. May I sit down?' She sank onto one of the shaped leather cushions. 'I don't want you thinking I'm a stalker, Otis. Being furtive isn't my style at all. My curiosity got the better of me, so I thought what the hell, I'll trail him all the way and find out where he goes each Tuesday. And now that I know, I can't creep away without even saying hello.'

Otis didn't give a toss for the social niceties. He was livid with himself for being so careless. Too angry even to plan his next move. 'Coffee?'

She flashed a wide, gratified smile. 'Please. I had to sit in my car and wait when you stopped for breakfast in Blandford.'

Trying to keep his fury in check, he stepped into the galley, switched on the kettle and spooned coffee into two mugs. 'And is the curiosity satisfied now?' He sounded calm, even though he had this electric storm in his head.

'Not yet, if you want the truth,' said Cynthia candidly. 'If you don't mind me asking, do you own this?'

'She's mine, yes.'

'Must have cost a bomb.'

'All my savings and a bit more.'

'Wow!'

'That's my choice. I like boats.'

'You never mention it in the village.'

'No reason to.'

'It's your bolt-hole?'

'My home, actually. The rectory belongs to the Church.'

'I can't get over it – a country clergyman with a gorgeous boat like this, or do I call it a ship? I mean, boats this size are made for millionaires, or the mafia.'

He laughed.

'Do they know you down here?'

'By a different name. I don't parade around in the dog-collar. Milk and sugar?'

'Black, please. No sugar.'

His brain was in overdrive. He had to deal with this emergency. Get a grip, Otis, he told himself. 'Did you, er, tell anyone you were planning to follow me this morning?'

'Certainly not,' she said with injured virtue. 'I can be very discreet. I wouldn't dream of giving you away, Otis, if that's what you're thinking.'

That's what I'm thinking, he chanted in his mind like a response to the litany.

She drew a line along the table with her fingertip, looking down. 'I'll be only too happy to share your secret. I thought when we sat together at the harvest supper that we were on a wave-length. Didn't you feel the same?'

She was making a pitch. God, how blind he'd been. 'It was fun, great fun, but I didn't expect it . . .'

'. . . to lead to anything?' She eagerly completed the sentence for him. 'Well, I didn't either, but I've thought a lot about you since. Too much. I didn't want to force the pace. Maybe you were only being sociable?'

He handed her the mug. 'Friendly.'

Unhappy with the word, her eyes narrowed. 'Friendly, yes, you were.' She hesitated, and shot him a look that conveyed some apprehension. 'You might be offended at this question. Do you have a friend down here in Poole?'

He frowned. 'What gives you that idea?'

She added, 'I thought, with the boat, you might . . .'

'You're right,' he said, and watched her face fall.

'There *is* someone?'

'No, but I am offended.'

'Oh.'

'I don't have a secret lover.'

A sigh of satisfaction escaped her and she babbled on tactlessly, 'Because there's no end of village gossip about your days off.'

'I'm sure,' he said without giving anything away. 'And if you were seen aboard my boat, they'd have more to get their tongues wagging, wouldn't they?'

'No one's going to see us down here.'

That 'us' activated him like a switch. If he gave this woman the least encouragement she'd soon be tearing off her clothes or his. Far worse, she'd carry the tale back to Foxford. He took a long sip of coffee and said, 'How would you like a sea trip?'

'Whee!' piped Cynthia. 'I'd adore it.'

'Just out into Poole Bay and back. I don't have too much time today. Must get back for the carols.'

'Me, too.'

'You'll need warmer clothes unless you want to stay below.'

'I've got a thick coat in the car.'

'Right. While you collect it, I'll start her up. Ever done any crewing?'

'You're joking.'

He went up to the cockpit and watched her go to the car park and across to the blue Renault he hadn't looked for when he parked his own car. Nobody could have seen her except possibly Terry, and he'd gone off to his own boat, an Ocean 38 berthed at the other end of the pontoon. Nobody else was about. These cold December days deterred all but the hardiest of sailors.

He knew what he must do. He started the twin engines – so much more responsive than his old car – and looked at the time. The one drawback about this marina was that you had to co-ordinate times with the opening of Poole Bridge every two hours. The next slot was within the half-hour.

She came aboard again in a long fur coat wholly unsuitable for sea cruising.

'That may get wet if you go aft,' he warned.

'It's only a cheap thing,' she told him. 'You didn't think it was real?'

'Want to sit in the captain's seat, then?'

He showed her the two seats in front of the controls in the covered cockpit. She pulled the coat off her shoulders. 'It's really warm in here. This is *so* exciting, Otis.' She brandished a silver hipflask. 'I keep this in the car for emergencies and men I fancy.'

He went down to loosen the mooring lines, then cast off and rejoined her. The *Revelation* got under way in a stately exit from the marina and into the Back Water Channel, well marked by stakes and leading to Poole Harbour. Approaching the lifting bridge, he gave three toots.

'Would that be Poole on our left?' Cynthia asked, getting his attention with her hand on his arm.

'To port.'

'You're really up with this sailoring lark, darling. The only port I know is Sandeman's.'

He pretended he hadn't heard. 'You'll see the customs steps and the Town Quay presently. Oyster Bank Beacon up ahead marks the edge of the mud we don't want to visit.'

She offered him the hipflask. 'It's Courvoisier.'

'No thanks.'

'I hope you don't mind me asking, but isn't it expensive running a boat this size on your stipend?'

'Iniquitous,' he agreed. 'The berthing fees alone would horrify you.'

After some thought she said with a strong note of doubt, 'I suppose if this is the only thing you spend your money on . . .'

'Right.'

He steered into the Main Channel with its wide curve around the east side of Brownsea Island.

'I had no idea it was such an enormous harbour.'

'Second biggest in the world.'

'You must have some private income. You'd never do this otherwise.'

'Bit nosy, aren't you?'

'Anyone would be, I should think.'

'The boat cost two hundred grand.'

'Well, I'll be . . .'

He smiled. 'The Good Book tells us that the Lord will provide, and he did.'

'As much as that?'

'After my wife died there was a lump sum in insurance.'

'Oh.'

There was an interval not of silence, but of the hum of the turbines and the sputter of water.

Eventually Cynthia said, 'I bet she'd rather you spent it on a boat than another woman. I would.'

He let that pass and pointed out more landmarks. 'The race platform for Parkstone Yacht Club. Poole Harbour Yacht Club beyond, with the marina. All very civilised now, but in bygone days these waters were thick with smugglers and pirates. The French and Spanish merchantmen went in terror of the local Blackbeard, a ruthless character they called "Arripay".'

'Come again?'

'"Arripay." Round here, he was just Harry Page.'

She giggled at that. 'Wouldn't you like to be a pirate? All girls dream of being captured by one.'

'Pirates weren't romantic at all.'

'Doesn't matter. You could be one and get away with it.

No one knows who you really are – well, no one except me, and I'm your prisoner now. At your mercy, on your pirate vessel.'

'What am I supposed to do? Make you walk the plank?'

'Lord, no. I can't swim. But you could have your wicked way with me. A Jolly Roger.'

'That's a flag.'

'Not in my phrasebook, darling.' Quickly, she added, 'Pure fantasy, of course.'

'I hope so.'

'That's not very gallant, Otis.'

He concentrated on his helmsmanship. The streams can be strong at the harbour exit between Sandbanks and South Haven Point. Lining up the beacon at the end of the training bank, he took them into Poole Bay by the route known as Swash Channel. 'We'll open up a bit now.'

'Us – or the engines?' asked Cynthia, laughing. She was steadily knocking back cognac.

'She'll do thirty-five knots.'

'What's that to a landlubber like me?'

'About forty. Doesn't sound much, but on water . . .'

'Go on, then. Scare me.'

He gave the pair of 660-horsepower engines more power and the five-bladed propellors fairly whipped the big boat over the water. It was reasonably calm today and he could motor into the waves without too much of a pounding.

'Brilliant!' shouted Cynthia.

He knew these waters well, the overfalls from Handfast Point down to Anvil, and the tide race off Old Harry on the ebb. Often he would steer a challenging course along the coast and test the boat in onshore winds. Today, he headed resolutely out to sea. After a while he eased the throttle imperceptibly – enough for easier conversation.

'Keep a look out for dolphins.'

'Really?' she said. 'I've never seen one outside an aquarium.'

'You could get lucky.'

Over to the east, they got a clear view of the Needles in sunlight off the Isle of Wight. He pointed them out. 'I'd like to take you closer, but this is a south-west wind and it can be tricky.'

'Better safe than sorry,' she said. 'Can we stop?'

'Heave to, you mean. If you like.'

'It's not as if we're in anyone's way. I'd like to enjoy the scenery.'

Suits me, he thought as he cut to dead-slow.

She offered the hipflask again. He shook his head.

'So what do you think of me?' she asked. 'I know I shouldn't have been so nosy, following you this morning, but can I be forgiven? I won't tell a soul. Promise.'

'You'll tell anyone who wants to know,' he said. He was in a candid what-the-hell frame of mind. 'I don't blame you. I thought I was safe using another name all this way from the village.'

'Does it matter if they find out?'

'Yes. It matters. Come on, you know the score. They'll ask how I can afford a motor cruiser. They're suspicious of me already, some of them.'

'How *do* you afford it?'

'By diverting church funds.'

A gasp. 'Oh, my God – you're kidding.'

'No. As you said, my stipend wouldn't pay for it.'

She stared at him, saucer-eyed. 'Let me get this clear. Are you telling me you're a crooked vicar?'

'That's a bit harsh, but yes. I take a cut of the parish income.'

'In expenses?'

He laughed. 'This is some expense.'

'Jesus. How do you square it with your conscience?'

'No problem. It's money we'd pay the diocese to keep the bishop's wine cellar stocked.'

'How do you square it with God, then?'

'He hasn't raised it with me, so I don't trouble him.'

Cynthia stared at him for a moment and then shook her head. 'Half the time I don't know whether to believe you. Isn't it one of the Ten Commandments: Thou shalt not steal?'

He gazed out to sea. 'Yes, I'm not too strong on the Commandments. I can truly say I've never coveted my neighbour's ox, but as for the rest . . .'

She wagged a finger. 'Otis, you're a wicked boy. Someone ought to teach you a lesson.'

She couldn't have picked a worse thing to say. Muscles were twitching in his face.

Her hand grabbed his wrist. 'Well, if you don't fancy playing the pirate chief, maybe I should. After what you just told me, sailor, I think you should feel the cat o'nine tails across your flanks.'

'Leave it, Cynthia.' He turned to glare at her and twisted his arm free.

'Cyn, if you like, since we're on the subject.' She must have used that joke before. Her mouth was curved into a seductive smile. 'If you can't take the cat, you'll have to settle for a spanking.'

'I'll pass on that.'

'I thought that was why men bought these huge boats, to have fun with their girlfriends. I wouldn't hurt you – much.'

She was giving enough openings for an orgy, only he had a different agenda.

'Why don't you put it on autopilot?' she suggested.

At last he sounded more enthusiastic. 'Top idea. Would you like to come up to the flybridge?'

'Naughty. What are you suggesting?'

'The deck above. Out in the open. Better view.'

'All right.'

'You'll need your coat.' He could have added, 'And a life jacket,' but he didn't.

18

After the build-up he'd given the carol singing, there was puzzlement when the rector failed to appear on Tuesday evening. Almost everyone else was there in warm clothes, some carrying lanterns, some their musical instruments. For twenty minutes they waited in the crisp evening air outside the church door. 'Happen he's not well,' somebody suggested, so Peggy Winner offered to knock at the rectory door. She got no reply. The place was in darkness. Then George Mitchell remembered that this was normally the rector's day off.

'I expect he's gone off for the day and forgotten,' said Peggy.

'Not our rector,' said George, who had become a staunch supporter through the Scrabble sessions. 'He's not the forgetful sort. I reckon he's held up somewhere. Trouble with the car, most like.' People tended to believe George because he was a policeman.

'Where would he have gone?' a woman asked.

Nobody could say.

'He gets up very early on his days off,' Burton Sands said as if early rising was suspicious behaviour. 'He could be miles away.'

'Disposing of another one,' murmured Owen Cumberbatch.

'What did you say?' said George Mitchell.

'Nothing at all, old boy. Not a word.'

They decided to start without the rector. If he turned up late, he would hear the singing and know where to look for them. They walked to the first group of houses and started with a good rallying carol, 'O Come, all ye faithful'.

'Knowing Otis and his flare for the dramatic, this is all set up for a huge surprise,' Peggy confided to Rachel after the last chorus was sung and the boxes rattled at the doorsteps. 'He's going to come up the street in a minute dressed as Santa Claus.'

'I doubt it,' said Rachel. 'Santa isn't part of the real Christmas story.'

'The Angel of the Lord, then,' said Peggy, laughing. 'With plastic wings and a ruddy great halo.'

Rachel didn't smile. Otis's absence worried her. And she was also puzzled as to why Cynthia hadn't turned out. She'd promised to be there.

During the walk from the first carol-stop to the second, and aided by the hipflasks being passed around, a subtle change took place. The singers, representing at least three-quarters of those who filled the church on Sundays, started to chat with a frankness they never managed after service, and much of the chat was critical of the rector.

'It's bad of him to let us down,' Peggy remarked to Rachel. 'He's such a card normally. We need him to keep us cheerful.'

'I expect he'll turn up,' Rachel said. 'He never misses church events.'

'Well, he shouldn't, should he?' Peggy said. 'It's his job. Where *does* he go on his days off?'

'Don't ask me,' said Rachel.

'Do you think he's got a woman tucked away somewhere?'

The question was beneath contempt. Rachel clicked her tongue and looked away.

'No offence, love. It's just that you've seen a little more of him than some of us – through doing the accounts, I mean – and I wondered if he gave any clues.'

'We don't talk about personal matters.'

Norman Gregor, the churchwarden, at the head of the group with Geoff Elliott, was saying, 'This isn't very good. He should have phoned.'

'It's no disaster, Norman,' said Elliott. 'It's not like a service. We can cope.'

And Burton Sands said in confidence to Mitchell, 'When there's an opportunity, I'd like to talk to you about the rector. I think he ought to be investigated.'

'Have you been talking to Owen by any chance?' said George.

They had reached one of the farms along the route. Picking their way with the help of torches, they trudged along the track to the house. The dim shapes of silent, seated sheep could just be seen over the drystone walls.

'We get a mince pie here,' Norman Gregor reminded the others.

'What do you think – "While shepherds watched"?' suggested Geoff Elliott, who had assumed the role of choirmaster.

It seemed appropriate, so the brass section played the opening bars.

After five minutes of lusty singing and fifteen consuming the farmer's wife's heated mince pies, they moved on. Owen Cumberbatch had a fresh theory about the rector's absence, and was happy to tell anyone who would listen except George Mitchell. 'Detained by the police, "helping them with their inquiries", as they charmingly put it. They had to catch up with him eventually, didn't they? You can't go on eliminating innocent people and expect to get away with it.'

Peggy would have none of it. 'He's a man of God, Owen. They don't go in for murder.'

'Plenty of it in the Bible, dear,' said Owen.

Rachel wished someone would murder Owen.

They moved on steadily through their repertoire, stopping at all the traditional points, and still the rector hadn't joined them. Almost two hours after the start they ended up at the Foxford Arms.

'He's probably sitting inside with a smile on his face,' said Peggy.

'He'll owe us a drink if he is,' said Norman Gregor.

But he was not in the pub. Unkind things might have been said at this end of the evening if Joe Jackson had not been standing just inside the door behind a steaming punchbowl. Normally a solemn figure, he was wearing reindeer horns and an apron made to look as if he was wearing a corset. He ladled generous glasses for everyone except the children, who were given their own non-alcoholic concoction. And there were more mince pies that most people passed by.

The singing started up again. Not carols. 'Nellie Dean', because everyone knew the words. Then Joe Jackson, who had a good bass voice and hadn't used it singing carols, gave them an old gallows song, 'Salisbury Plain', followed by 'Barbara Allen', the ballad of the fair maid who ignored the man who died of love for her, and then, full of remorse, died herself.

'Lovely tunes, but such morbid songs,' said Peggy Winner. 'Can't you give us something more cheerful? Rachel's slipped off home already. I'm sure it was the singing put her off.'

Joe said in a huff, 'If it's something cheerful you want, ask George for "The Laughing Policeman".'

Sarcasm often misses the mark. Peggy took Joe at his word. 'Would you, George?'

George Mitchell pretended to need persuading, but everyone knew that once asked he would get up and give his party piece. Nobody minded that he wasn't much of a singer. It was a treat to hear the law making an ass of itself.

It wasn't Joe Jackson's choice of songs that drove Rachel away. She'd left feeling strangely dissatisfied because the evening had lacked the two people who had urged her to join in. She was mystified why Cynthia hadn't turned out, and decided to call on her before it got too late. But when she got to Primrose Cottage the place was in darkness. Cynthia couldn't have gone to bed ill because the bedroom curtains weren't drawn. Odd. The silly woman had been so gung-ho and joky about going around in the dark with Otis Joy. What could have cropped up that was more of an attraction?

Feeling let down, she returned up the street to her own cottage.

Just before reaching the village shop she was dazzled by headlights. She stepped aside in case the driver hadn't seen her. The car was coming at a speed that was downright dangerous at night in a village. She thought it was going straight through, but the brakes screeched and it came to a halt outside the pub. A male figure got out and went inside as if desperate for a drink before the place closed. He need not have hurried. On the carol-singing night the Foxford Arms always remained open long after the official closing time.

When she got closer she saw that the car was Otis's Cortina. So he'd only just got back.

Curious as she was to know where he'd been, she didn't go back into the pub.

*   *   *

She would have heard Otis Joy telling the carollers, 'I don't know how to face you all. I let you down badly. One of those things you can't possibly predict. A woman dropped dead in front of me. You can't walk away from that, can you, whoever you are? And if you happen to be a minister of the Church, well . . . It was very sudden. Mercifully she didn't know much about it, poor soul, but the sight of her could have been upsetting for others. You do what you can to cope with an emergency like that, and of course it takes longer than you can spare. And I wasn't near a phone. I suppose I ought to get one of those mobiles, and you can bet if I do I won't find another occasion to use it. Anyway, I do apologise to you all. How did it go?'

They told him the singing had been well received and people had been generous all round the village. Geoff Elliott had just counted the money and bagged it up – over two hundred pounds.

'I'd like to put in a fiver myself,' said Otis at once. 'Where's Geoff?'

Elliott waved from across the room. Otis went over, produced a five-pound note and offered to take care of the money overnight. 'I don't see our treasurer here.'

'Rachel? She left earlier. She was with us for the carols.'

'Good. I'm glad she's getting involved in village life again.'

He left soon after, cashbags in hand. It had been a harrowing day, he said, and he was due at the school to take class six for scripture in the morning.

The story of the woman who had dropped dead put a premature end to the singsong. It would have been insensitive to start again. Many of the carol party were getting up to leave, among them PC George Mitchell.

'So when can we talk?' Burton Sands pressed him.

'What about?' said George as if he hadn't heard Burton's earlier approach.

'You know . . .' Burton's eyes shifted to the door. The rector was outside starting his car.

George said slowly, spacing his words, 'If it's anything more than tittle-tattle, come and see me at the station tomorrow. If not, I suggest you forget about the whole thing.'

Burton reddened and reached for his coat.

Before daylight Rachel took a walk to the other end of the village and saw that Cynthia's curtains were still pulled back as if she hadn't slept there. No lights showed in Primrose Cottage. The morning paper had been delivered and was half sticking out of the letterbox.

She went back and tried phoning. Cynthia's voice on the answerphone told her to wait for the signal and then leave a message.

'It's not like her to go off without telling anyone,' she said later in the shop.

'Some family crisis, I expect,' said Davy Todd in his unflustered way. When the Day of Judgement arrived, Davy would still open the shop and put out the newspapers.

'She could have gone away for Christmas,' said the girl who helped in the mornings.

'She'd have cancelled the papers,' Davy pointed out. 'She's very well organised, is Mrs Haydenhall. I reckon she'll be back some time today. We thought the rector was missing yesterday, and he came back.'

Quick to follow up, Rachel asked what explanation Otis had given and was told about the woman dropping dead and throwing his plans into confusion. It was such an original excuse that it had to be true.

'Did he say where this happened?'

'No one asked him,' said Davy. 'So we still don't know where he goes on Tuesdays. He's entitled to some privacy, I say, same as the rest of us.'

'Of course,' said Rachel.

Her concern about Cynthia increased after hearing about the woman who dropped dead. Suppose she'd collapsed in the house and nobody knew. Poor Stanley Burrows had lain dead in his cottage for at least two days before anyone thought to look inside.

'Burton,' said George Mitchell after listening impassively to the list of appalling crimes laid at the door of the rectory, 'this is not respectful.'

He was with Burton Sands in one of the interview rooms at Warminster Police Station. Sometimes people called at George's cottage in Foxford to report things, but this was the official place, and Burton was determined to do things by the book.

'He's not entitled to respect if he did these things,' the dour young man insisted.

'Ah, but he is until proved guilty, and we're a long, long way from that. What's your motive?'

'Mine? It's not *my* motive you should be questioning. I'm doing what a responsible citizen should, informing you what I know.'

George gave it to him straight. 'Nothing. That's what you know. There's plenty you suspect, but I can't arrest a man on suspicions alone. A man of the cloth.'

'That's the real objection, isn't it?' said Burton, flushing all over his freckled skin. 'He's a clergyman, so he must be innocent.'

'I never heard of one who murdered people.'

'So he gets away with it, time and again.'

'You're just repeating yourself,' said George. 'Where's

the evidence? The Crown Prosecution Service would fall about laughing at what you've told me so far.'

'The evidence is in the parish accounts,' said Burton obdurately. 'If I could get hold of the books and do an audit I'd prove he's an embezzler. He robbed the last parish he was in, and he's robbing this one.'

'You don't know that.'

'But I do. They had such a shortfall at Old Mordern that the bishop personally investigated.'

'While the Reverend Joy was vicar there?'

'No, after he left.'

'Could have been the new vicar, then. And if it was investigated, why wasn't he charged with fiddling the books – if he did?'

'Because Bishop Marcus died – or was killed – before it came out.'

'Who told you this, about the bishop investigating?'

'One of the congregation there.'

'Owen Cumberbatch?'

'No, a woman I met there. She was arranging flowers the day I visited.'

George let his breath out slowly. 'You've actually been to his last parish checking up?'

'I knew nobody else would,' Burton said with a red-eyed stare.

'Don't sling mud in my direction, laddie,' George checked him. 'What did this woman tell you?'

'She said Bishop Marcus personally inspected the Old Mordern books before he died. And made copies of everything.'

'What for?'

'She thought it was because they asked for a reduction in their quota – the money the diocese gets – but I know better. It was because the bishop was on to the Reverend Joy.'

'Next you'll be telling me he murdered the bishop.'

Burton looked the policeman up and down and decided the homicide of a bishop, on top of the other killings, might throw some doubt on his thesis. 'He may have murdered his wife.'

'Oh, come on.'

Burton related the story of the fatal bee-sting and said how simple it would be to kill someone allergic to bees by using some trapped in a jam jar.

'I never heard anything so far-fetched in my life,' said George. 'Why would he want to murder his young wife, for God's sake?'

'If she found out too much about him . . .'

'So now we have three murders pinned on the Reverend Joy: the sexton of Old Mordern, the late Mrs Joy and Stanley Burrows.'

'And another.'

'Who's that?'

'Gary Jansen.'

George shook his head. 'Lord love us, Burton, you're away with the fairies. How is he supposed to have murdered Gary? The man died of heart failure. I've seen the death certificate.'

'You can induce heart failure if you know about poisons.'

'Poison, was it, this time? Are you certain it wasn't the killer bees?'

'You don't have to be sarcastic,' said Burton. 'You ought to be making notes. Stanley Burrows was poisoned – he swallowed some sort of drug, didn't he? – and I say Gary Jansen went the same way. The rector was seen with him on the day he died.'

'Where?'

'In the street, outside the shop.'

'By Owen Cumberbatch, you mean? Now *there's* an impartial witness.'

'And, more important, Jansen went up to the rectory that afternoon.'

'I didn't think they knew each other,' said George.

'He was seen going through the gates by Ann Porter, one of the communion class. Joy could easily have slipped something in his drink.'

'Poison, you mean?'

'Of course.'

George Mitchell said in a tone that showed his tolerance was strained, 'And why would the rector wish to do away with Gary Jansen?'

'Because Gary found something out.'

'Ah.' George gave an ironic nod that was lost on Burton.

'I'm not sure what it was, but they had strong words about it in the street and my guess is that they continued the argument up at the rectory.'

'You're not sure what it was,' said George with contempt, 'but you're willing to guess. You're willing to destroy a good man's reputation on guesswork. Well, it doesn't cut ice with me, Burton. You've told me very little I don't know, and not a shred of substance.'

'You could look at the parish accounts.'

'We did.'

'You did?'

'In connection with Stanley's suicide, and we found nothing wrong.'

For a short interval Burton brooded on that. 'It's what doesn't go through the books that you have to worry about,' he said presently. 'Did you notice how he grabbed the carol-singing money last night? Do you think that will appear in the accounts, every penny of it?'

George said in the same tone as before, conceding

nothing, 'This is all speculation, Burton, and it does you no credit. Let's lay our cards on the table. Everyone knows you're bitter about being passed over for treasurer. Why don't you let it rest?'

Burton's pale skin flushed bright pink. 'Cards on the table, is it? All right, everyone knows you're in Joy's pocket. You're up to the rectory every Monday playing Scrabble with him.'

'You'd better get out,' said George.

'You shouldn't be dealing with this. I want to speak to someone else.'

George stepped to the door and opened it. 'Out.'

19

Two days after Cynthia went missing, Rachel asked George Mitchell if anything was being done to find her.

'She's a grown-up,' George answered in his easy-going style. 'She's at liberty to go off for a few days. Don't fret, my dear.'

The patronising words enraged her. 'I'm *not* fretting. I'm telling you something is wrong. It's totally out of character. Someone should look inside the house just in case—'

He stopped her. 'Not much point, my dear. I looked in her garage and her car isn't inside. She's gone away for sure.'

So he *had* taken some interest.

'I still think you should do something,' she said, realising how lame it sounded. There was nothing anyone could do except wait for news of Cynthia.

A week from Christmas she felt none of the so-called festive spirit that harangued her every time she looked at the television or turned on the radio. Several people had already asked if she was spending Christmas Day in company and she said she preferred to be alone this year, which was not quite true. She had no desire to join in anyone's family party, but she was pretty certain Cynthia would have invited her up to Primrose Cottage. Cyn had been so supportive since Gary went, and she'd never spoken of her own family, so Rachel had assumed they would spend at least part of the holiday together.

Now she had to think again.

If only it could be managed without the rest of Foxford knowing, her ideal Christmas would be shared with Otis, after he'd finished his duties at the church. She didn't know his plans yet and she felt she couldn't ask.

Burton Sands was one of those dogged individuals who will not be put off. The meeting with George Mitchell had achieved little, but it had got him thinking. Maybe the policeman was right to say that clergymen didn't ever commit murder. It would make a mockery of their faith. Yet this didn't discourage Burton. Instead, it started him on a new tack, a brilliant one that would explain so much. What if Joy wasn't a clergyman at all, but a con-man who had somehow convinced the diocese he was ordained?

Lunchtime on Thursday found him in the reference section at Warminster Library, leafing through back numbers of the *Wiltshire Times*, trawling for information on Joy's background. Something must have appeared in the paper when the new incumbent arrived at Foxford. He found it quite soon, with an insufferably saintlike photo.

NEW RECTOR FOR FOXFORD

The new Rector of Foxford is to be the Rev. Otis Joy, the diocese announced this week. The Rev. Joy has been vicar of Old Mordern, near Chippenham, since 1998. He is 28, and a widower. After training at St Cyriac's Theological College, Brighton, he was ordained in 1994, and served as curate at Old Mordern until the retirement of the incumbent, when he became the youngest vicar in the diocese.

'I am delighted to be coming to Foxford,' the Rev.

Joy said this week. 'St Bartholomew's is a church
rich in history in a beautiful village. I look forward
eagerly to carrying on the excellent ministry of my
predecessor, Henry Sandford.'

'And milking the funds,' Burton said aloud and got an
anxious glance from a woman at an adjacent table.

The mention of a theological college was a setback to
his latest theory, unless Joy had made it up. Unfortunately
there was something about Brighton that sounded possible. A man like Joy *would* choose a college in a popular
seaside resort.

He looked up St Cyriac's in the phone book, went to
a payphone and called them. The term had finished and
the students had gone down, he was told by someone
who didn't sound very important in the college set-up.
He explained that he just wanted a word with the archi-
vist, or whoever looked after the records of former students. The young woman on the phone was cagy. The
college wouldn't let anyone look at personal records,
she said. Burton explained in the most convincing tone
he could manage that he wasn't interested in personal
details. It was only a matter of confirming things that
were in the public domain, dates, and so on. Politely
she said she didn't have a copy of the college regis-
ters. However, the librarian would be there on Saturday
morning doing the annual stocktake and might be willing
to help.

St Cyriac's wasn't really in Brighton. It was a Victorian
mock gothic building sited high on the South Downs north
of the town, right on the edge of the Devil's Dyke (Burton
noted with grim satisfaction).

On the long drive from Foxford, he'd decided on his

strategy. Evidently St Cyriac's were hot on data protection, so he needed a compelling story.

The librarian was a canny, silver-haired Scottish lady, and Burton's confidence dipped when she began by saying, 'I was advised that you were coming, and I'm afraid you've wasted your time. I'm not at liberty to divulge information about former students.'

Burton said truthfully, 'I've driven a hundred miles,' and untruthfully, 'and nobody told me this.'

'That is unfortunate,' she admitted, without actually giving an inch.

'I don't want to know anything confidential.'

'Everything in student records is confidential.'

'It's for a surprise party for our rector,' he said with fine conviction for a man who usually told the truth. 'You must have seen that television programme *This is Your Life*. Well, we're planning something like that for his thirtieth birthday.'

Unmoved, she said, 'I can't help.'

'He's such a popular priest,' said Burton, at the limit of his imagination to keep this going. 'He preaches a fine sermon. So different in style from our last rector. Should have been an entertainer, really. He has a great fund of jokes, always in good taste and to the point.'

Curiosity got the better of her. 'What's his name?'

'Joy. Otis Joy.'

Her expression miraculously softened. 'I remember Otis Joy.'

'You do?'

'He was a saucy birkie, as we say north of the border, very popular. We all had a soft spot for Otis.'

'So you were here when he was?'

'Yes, indeed. And is he really coming up to thirty soon?'

'Next year, if we've got it right.'

She slid out a computer keyboard from a recess under her desktop. By a strange twist, Joy's charming ways had come to Burton's aid. 'You're right,' she said, staring at her monitor. 'I think of him as no more than a lad. He was younger than the average when he entered college. Most of our entrants have had work experience in other careers, but Otis had more confidence than any of his year.'

'Hadn't he been in work?'

'Apparently not. He came to us from Canada, and he'd done some training for the ministry over there, according to this. He knew his Bible better than any student of his year. But I don't think he's Canadian by birth. He didn't have any accent that I recall, though it wouldn't surprise me if he was Irish. He had a touch of the blarney, for sure. No, it says here he was born in Norwich.'

'When?'

'You know that,' she told him sharply. 'The seventeenth of March, nineteen seventy.'

'Of course.'

'I wonder what took him to Canada,' she mused aloud, forgetting all about confidentiality. 'He was at Milton Davidson Memorial College, Toronto, until ninety-three. Was he only with us a year, then? I can picture him more clearly than some who stayed for three.'

'When was he ordained?' Burton asked.

'Nineteen ninety-four.'

'That's certain, is it? The ordination?'

'Absolutely certain. I was there, praying for them all.' She frowned at the question and another of Burton's theories went out of the window.

Christmas crept up quickly, ambushing everyone, and Rachel found herself at midnight mass, the service nobody wanted to miss, in her usual pew, shoehorned between young men with beer on their breath. All the extra chairs from the parish hall were brought in, and still some people stood at the back. The youngest choirboy, singing 'Away in a manger', was impossible to see as he threaded his way up the narrow aisle between chairs at the ends of the pews. Behind the choristers, Otis sported the glittering hand-worked cope that always came out on this holy night.

The carol ended and he started speaking the time-honoured words of the liturgy without any amplification. His voice resonating through the church made Rachel feel very emotional. When her favourite carol, 'O little town of Bethlehem' was sung, and she reached that line about the hopes and fears of all the years, her eyes moistened and there was a lump in her throat. She knew far too much about hopes and fears.

After everyone filed out at the end, Otis stood in the porch as usual shaking hands, making a point of not missing anyone. Short of sneaking out through the vestry, there was no escape, and when Rachel's turn came he clasped her right hand between both of his and said, 'Ah, Rachel, shall I see you at Morning Service tomorrow?'

She hadn't intended going, because it was a family service and she would feel conspicuous. He must have seen the hesitation in her eyes when he added, 'Wearing your treasurer's hat.'

She took a moment to fathom what he meant. She was thinking of hats, literally. 'If you want.'

'Please.'

She moved on, still without fully understanding. Surely he didn't want to hand over the offertories from the spate of Christmas collections. The money would be more secure in the church safe until the banks reopened.

Outside, under a starry sky, the beginnings of a frost

glistened on the headstones. People lingered on the path, wishing each other Christmases happy, merry, peaceful, great and wonderful. But what can you wish someone who has recently buried her husband? Rachel slipped past them all and went home. She was dreaming of a Joyful Christmas and she didn't think it was likely.

She was in church as requested on Christmas morning and heard Otis give a short and surprising sermon pitched mainly at the children. 'Some of you are asking if there really is a Father Christmas, and I don't have to tell you boys and girls, today of all days, that of course there is. Of course! And can anyone tell me his real name?'

There was a chorus of answers, some of them correct.

Otis raised his thumbs. 'Right. Santa Claus. Or Saint Nicholas, to say it in full. Saint Nicholas was a very kind bishop who lived an awfully long time ago, and we are told he was one of the wise members of the Council of Nicaea who met to write down what Christians believe. There was a man called Arius who was trying to put about some ideas that were wrong, and the story goes that Bishop Nicholas socked him on the jaw. I don't know if that's true, but I do know that Nicholas helped to write the Creed that we said this morning. Who can tell me the first words of the Creed?'

The Sunday school teachers must have done a good job because 'I believe in God the Father' was clearly audible in the mix of replies.

'Yes, and the Creed is still used by Christians everywhere, and not just in the Church of England. So whether you are Protestant, Roman Catholic or Eastern Orthodox, you speak the words that Santa Claus approved each time you come to church. That's a good enough reason to believe in him, isn't it? Because he was so wise and generous, he became the children's saint, your special saint, and it is an ancient custom in some countries for someone to dress up as a bishop, as Santa Claus, around Christmas time, and give small presents to good children. It's the custom we adopted, and long may it continue. Happy Christmas, Santa. Happy Christmas to you all.'

At the end, Rachel waited in her pew and was the last to leave except for Geoff Elliott, who was right out of earshot, collecting hymnbooks from the lady chapel. Otis smiled when she reached him. 'Glad you came,' he said.

She smiled. 'So am I. I loved the sermon.'

He looked thoughtful. 'When I was a little kid in the children's home, we had a visit each Christmas from a guy dressed up as St Nick. He wore a mitre and a false beard and carried a crook and each of us was given a present that we had to share with the others. I got the same thing two years running, *Bible Stories for Little Folk*. Didn't matter, because we had to give them in at the end of the day to be used in the reading class.'

'Not much of a Christmas.'

'The nuns enjoyed it. A noggin with old Nick. How are you spending today? Quietly?'

She nodded.

'Alone, I mean?'

'Yes.'

'Then you won't mind if I call about tea-time?'

Elated, she said, 'I'd love to see you. Come earlier if you can.'

'I have some other visits to make. People who've had a rough time of late. Some of the old folk. The kids in hospital. I guess I'll be with you about four-thirty to five.'

'Poor you.'

'Not poor at all,' he said. 'This is the best day of the year. I'm privileged.' And he obviously meant it.

'Will you get a Christmas lunch?'

'Lunches all the way if I could eat them.' He held up his hands. 'No, Rachel. I know my limits.'

Every pulse in her body pounding, she moved on air all the way back to the cottage, planning what she would cook, wear, do with her hair. She had come alive again and Otis was forgiven for being so distant in recent days. The remark about the treasurer's hat must have been just a blind in case people overheard. He'd chosen to see her, of all the people in the parish, on this of all days. Ah, the transforming magic of Christmas!

The time went amazingly fast. So much had to be packed in: tidying up, dusting, lighting a wood fire, showering, shampooing, ironing her silk top, dressing, defrosting cakes, adjusting the lighting, rearranging the Christmas decorations, choosing the right CDs, putting away the photos of her mother and father. There it was – four-thirty – and she was just about ready in her black leather pants and crimson top, with her hair loose and the lights winking on the little Christmas tree and the fire glowing nicely.

It was closer to five-fifteen when he came, still in his clerical shirt and dark suit. 'My,' he said when he saw her. 'I should have changed.'

She'd been over her first words many times. 'I expect you're awash with tea so I thought you'd go for a small scotch.'

He showed how small, with his thumb and forefinger almost touching.

'I'm not going to force any food on you, but there's blackcurrant mousse or raspberry cheesecake, or something savoury if you prefer.'

He was frowning slightly. 'Don't get me wrong, Rachel. I just came for a quiet chat.'

'Didn't anyone tell you it's Christmas Day, Otis?'

The even teeth flashed and the man of the world in him said, 'Nice one. Back of the net.'

'I mean you can relax. Duty done.'

'Just about.'

'This isn't duty, is it – cheering up the lonely widow?' She poured two generous whiskies and handed him his. 'Once again, happy Christmas.'

He took the drink to the armchair, rather than the high-risk settee. 'I *would* like to talk shop for a moment.'

She settled opposite him, seated on the shaggy rug in front of the hearth, enjoying the way the firelight picked out his high, sharp cheekbones. 'Go ahead.'

'I'm told I've lost the confidence of some people in the parish.'

Feeling a chill run through her, she said, 'You don't mean me?'

'No, no. Others. Only one or two, but they talk to one or two more, and so it spreads.'

Shocked that he knew so much of what was going on, she started to say, 'I don't think—'

'Let's face it,' he said. 'I let everyone down on the night of the carol-singing.'

'Otis, it couldn't be helped.'

'Maybe, but I know some of the things that were said. Wide of the mark, actually. The problem is that once questions are asked, they don't go away. Drip, drip. Sooner or later someone is going to start digging for dirt. They may want to go through the accounts.'

'They've no right.'

'I think you'll find they have the right.'

'Everything's in order.'

'I'm sure, but you know what people are like where money is concerned.'

She said, 'We're talking about Burton Sands.'

No observable reaction came from Otis. 'That's one name I was given. Burton is still smarting because I didn't ask him to be our treasurer. Understandable. I'm sure he can do double-entry book-keeping with the best of them. But the PCC chose you.'

'To my amazement,' Rachel admitted.

'And we're mighty glad we did.' He raised his glass in tribute. 'If Burton or anyone else asks for a sight of the books, you can say you're currently working on them. The end of the year is upon us. They have to be audited in January ready for the February meeting of the PCC. You can't be parted from them at this busy time – which must be true.'

'It is.'

'You don't mind me mentioning it?'

'Of course not.' She gave a nervous laugh and, trying too hard to be sympathetic, came out with something she immediately regretted. 'Some of the things being said about you are so ridiculous you wouldn't credit them.'

He smiled faintly. 'About me knocking off my parishioners left, right and centre?'

He knew. She couldn't think where to look, she was so mortified at bringing this up.

Otis appeared unfazed. 'Dear old Owen has been putting that one around as long as I've known him – and that was at my previous parish. Talk about dwindling congregations. I wouldn't have any left at all by his count.'

She insisted firmly, 'Nobody takes him seriously.'

'That isn't quite true,' he said. 'Burton is half convinced already. In the end, people do begin to have their doubts. The old drip, drip. It could force me to leave.'

Stricken, she blurted out, 'Oh, no! But if it's untrue . . .'

Otis closed her down. 'What are you doing on the third of January, Rachel? I'm giving a rave-up at the rectory for

the confirmation candidates. One or two of the Parish
Council will be there. Can you make it?'

She was reeling from what she had just been told. He
couldn't *leave*. She loved him. She'd committed murder
for him.

'It's a Monday,' he added.

Floundering, she said tonelessly, 'I'd love to come.'
Then, with passion, 'You can't let gossips drive you out
with lies.'

'It's a fragile job, mine. I can't stay in it without the
confidence of my parish,' he explained with a steadiness
that showed he'd thought it through. 'If the back-stabbing
gets worse, I'm history. Out of here.'

'No!' She moved across the rug to his side, grabbed his
hand and gripped it tightly. 'Don't. I'll die.'

He tensed, clearly surprised by the force of her reaction.
'Rachel, what is this?'

'I love you, that's what,' she said, tears streaming down
her cheeks. 'I couldn't bear you to go away.' She pressed
her face into the curve of his neck and shoulder, afraid
of her own impulsiveness, mentally pleading with him to
hold onto her, and forever.

'Rachel,' he said and then repeated her name as if he
couldn't think what else to say.

She clung to him, sobbing, squeezing his hand.

Finally he found some words. 'That evening I was here
before, I shouldn't have—'

'Don't say that,' she cried out. 'It was beautiful. You
made me feel wanted.'

'No, it was wrong,' he insisted. 'I'm in holy orders.'

She drew away enough to look at him through the blur
of her tears. 'I'm not asking you to do anything wrong.
Marry me.'

Silence.

He was some removes away in thoughts of his own. Eventually he sighed and still said nothing, and Rachel waited for an answer until she knew he wasn't going to give one, this word-spinner who could enthral a church full of people with his eloquence. Her emotions seesawed. This man she worshipped hadn't come here to make love to her, or propose marriage. He wanted to make sure the bloody account books didn't get into the wrong hands.

And she'd poisoned Gary thinking she would free herself for Otis. What an idiot she was.

She pushed herself away from him, got up and ran out of the room.

A little later he followed her into the kitchen and said he couldn't walk out of the house without saying anything. He made coffee for her, and talked, while she was mainly silent. The church wasn't just a job, he explained, or just a section of his life. It was his whole existence. Through it, he came alive. It was more potent and powerful than sex, or relationships, music, sport or anything that drove most men. He liked to interact with people, but through his work as a priest, rather than on a personal level.

Rachel said, 'But how can you be a good priest if you don't share the same experiences as other people?'

He understood the point immediately. 'My wife used to say the same thing. It's a dilemma. I focus everything on the ministry, you see. I'm wedded to my job. I know I do it well, and I know I couldn't do anything else. I'm not a good Christian – I mean that, I'm damaged spiritually – but I can be an effective priest and I take enormous satisfaction from that. Claudine called it monomania, and I suppose she was right. She felt excluded. I failed as a husband.'

She started to say, 'It doesn't mean—'

'But it does, it does!' he told her with the passion he

usually kept for the pulpit. 'I can't tell you the risks I've taken to get to this point in my life. There's no compromise, Rachel.'

Soon after, he left.

20

T hree days after Christmas, a Renault car with an R registration was examined by the Bournemouth police. It had stood in a minor road near the bus station for about ten days according to people living there. Nobody remembered seeing it arrive. The police checked the national computer records and found the owner was Mrs Cynthia Haydenhall, of Primrose Cottage, Foxford, Wiltshire.

The local police were informed. After checking once more that no one was inside Primrose Cottage, PC George Mitchell reported Cynthia to Police Headquarters as a missing person.

The news spread rapidly. No one knew of any connection Cynthia had with Bournemouth. She didn't particularly like the sea and it was a long way to go Christmas shopping. Out of season Bournemouth is best known for its conference centre and its concerts, but there had been no conference in the week preceding Christmas, and the only events at the Pavilion were children's shows.

A search operation was mounted in the Bournemouth area. Empty buildings, wasteland, woodland and the beaches were checked. Posters were put up. The local press were informed. Nothing of substance was discovered.

Back in Foxford, there were fears for Cynthia's safety. The fact that she hadn't cancelled her newspaper was taken seriously at last. She wasn't the kind of person who would take off for weeks on end without letting anyone know.

George Mitchell and three officers from Warminster made house-to-house inquiries. It was difficult. Normally ten days is not an over-long period in people's memories, but with Christmas intervening it was like asking about some event that happened six weeks before.

'I wish you'd listened to me,' Rachel reminded George when he knocked on her door. 'I knew something was wrong when she didn't turn up for the carol evening. She told me she'd be there. She really looked forward to it.'

George noticed how pale Rachel was looking, worse, he thought, than when her husband died. He supposed she and Mrs Haydenhall were closer friends than he'd imagined. 'We've got a lot of men and women working on this in Bournemouth,' he told her. 'Don't give up hope.'

Burton Sands had tried repeatedly to get through to Milton Davidson College, Toronto. All over the world everything stopped for Christmas, it seemed. And then for the New Year. It was not until January 3rd that someone picked up a phone.

Usefully for Burton, the most senior staff have to come into college during holidays to deal with urgent business. He was put through to the Deputy Principal. This time he dropped the *This is Your Life* ploy for something simpler. 'I'm checking the records of clergy who came to Britain from abroad,' he said as if this was part of a larger project. 'I have a name here and I wonder if you'd confirm that he was with you until nineteen ninety-three. Otis Joy.'

'I'll bet it is,' said the voice on the line. 'I don't envy you.'

Burton was forced to explain that Otis Joy was someone's name, not a cynical aside.

'You say he came to Britain?'

'Right.'

'Wrong – if you mean our guy. We had a student of that name, but he didn't go to England. He didn't go anywhere.'

'Why?'

'He died.'

Burton gripped the phone and pressed it harder to his ear. 'Did you say "*died*"?'

'Sure. In nineteen ninety-three, the year you mentioned. He drove his car off a mountain road when he was on vacation in Vancouver. A sheer drop. No chance.'

'This is Otis Joy?'

'It's not a name you forget, specially in a theological college. He was the only student of that name we had on our books, or ever had.'

'Did you know him personally?'

'Otis? Sure. I've been here fifteen years. He was in my tutor group. Nice guy.'

'Would you mind describing him? There's obviously some confusion in our records.'

'Sounds like it. Let's see. He was short, Afro-Caribbean, rather overweight—'

Burton blurted out his reaction. 'A black man?'

'Are we at cross purposes here?'

'We must be. The man I know is white.'

'We're wasting our time then. These are two different guys.'

'But he claims to have been at your college. It's on his file.'

'I don't think so.'

'I'm telling you,' insisted Burton. 'He finished his training at Brighton. Their records show he attended Milton Davidson College. There is only one college of that name in Toronto, I suppose?'

'In the world.'

As if by consent, they let a moment of hard thinking go by.

'If you had a picture of your Mr Joy,' said the Deputy Principal with a new, suspicious tone, 'I'd be interested to see it.'

'I can supply one.'

'OK. Do you have access to a scanner and e-mail? We could do this today. I'm here until six, our time.'

Burton said he would see to it, and they exchanged e-mail addresses.

That head and shoulders shot in the *Wiltshire Times* would do if he could get hold of a sharper print. They sometimes had the originals on file at the newspaper office in Trowbridge and sold copies. He left work early and drove over there. They had a brown envelope stuffed with pictures of the man from various functions they'd covered. Burton went through it and found the print he wanted. A nice glossy postcard-size mugshot.

On his own computer at home, he scanned the photo and sent it with a short e-mail message to Toronto. Within a couple of minutes his phone rang.

'I don't know this man,' said the Deputy Principal. 'He never attended this college.'

'Did the picture come over cleanly?' Burton asked.

'It's very clear. I know my students, and this man was never one of them. I also rechecked at our alumni office and there was only one Otis Joy in attendance here in the past twenty years. If someone of that name is claiming affiliation with our college, he's an impostor.'

Burton put down the phone and experienced a pleasurable sensation of power amounting almost to rapture. 'Got you, you bastard,' he said aloud.

He looked at his watch. Twenty minutes to get showered and dressed for the last confirmation class, followed by the rector's party.

Watching the man behind his great desk in the rectory, with the books of sermons behind him and *The Light of the World* to his left, listening to his confident and lucid interpretation of the Order of Confirmation, Burton still found it difficult to credit that this was a bogus priest.

'And when the moment comes and the bishop lays his hand on your head, you will hear some of the most comforting words in our liturgy: "Defend, O Lord, this thy Servant, with thy heavenly grace, that he may continue thine for ever." *Defend* – it's a word we find throughout the *Book of Common Prayer*. "Defend us thy humble servants in all assaults of our enemies."' Joy curved his hand over the glass paperweight of St Paul's Cathedral. '". . . and by thy great mercy defend us from all perils and dangers of this night." Some people have told me they felt strengthened by God at this moment, and of course they are.'

Burton had spoken to nobody of his sensational discovery. This evening he felt detached from the confirmation candidates, watching them listen respectfully to the man he would soon expose. They were in for a shock, but not yet. He would choose his moment. This evening gave him the chance to settle the business beyond reasonable doubt. This was a high-risk plan, but he had right on his side, and if you can't rely on God's protection in a Church of England property, it's a poor lookout for mankind. There was another 'defend' in the Prayer Book that Joy had not chosen to mention: Psalm 42. 'Give sentence with me, O

God, and defend my cause against the ungodly people: O deliver me from the deceitful and wicked man.'

The spiel was coming to an end. 'And then, of course, there follows a communion, your first, and we went through the service last time. Simple, beautiful, comforting.' Joy's eyebrows formed the shape of a Norman arch as he closed his prayer book. 'If any of you have last-minute questions, or concerns, I'm here to help. I'll be with you at the service, and should you feel nervous just imagine how the new bishop will be feeling. Let's not forget that it may be your confirmation, but it's his baptism.'

The doorbell rang and Joy got up. 'I asked the parish council to join us and all of them are coming except Rachel Jansen, who sends her regrets. This kind of get-together is difficult for her so soon after Gary's death.' He went off to receive his first guests.

'Where's it happening?' asked John Neary.

'In that big room, for sure,' said Ann Porter. 'Shall we go through?'

'You carry on,' said Burton casually. 'I'll join you presently.'

'Didn't know you were a smoker,' said Neary.

'I'm not. I need a few minutes to myself.'

'Says you.'

The minute the others were out of the room, Burton crossed to the filing cabinet by the door. Joy would be busy with his guests for some time, a perfect opportunity.

It wasn't locked. The top drawer was stuffed with bulging files that turned out to be circulars from the diocesan office at Glastonbury. He tried the next. Letters, hundreds of them. Local societies wanting a speaker. People researching their family history. And quite a batch about brass-rubbing. Useless. With hope ebbing away, he pulled out the third and last drawer. Agendas and minutes of parish council meetings. Orders of service from years back. Sermons. But no personal papers.

The doorbell rang at least three times while he was still in the office. Sudden noises weren't good for his nerves.

He tried the drawers of Joy's great mahogany desk. Blank stationery, stamps, paperclips and a stapler. A wire basket on the windowsill excited him briefly. It was stacked high with paper. Catalogues of religious books.

This was not so simple as he'd hoped.

The two box files on the bookshelf were the only possibilities left. One was filled with church music, and when he opened the other dozens of communion wafers scattered across the floor. He used valuable time picking them up.

Outside the office he stood in the hall for a moment listening to the voices in the front room. They sounded well launched into conversation about how they'd celebrated the new year. With luck, he wouldn't be missed for a while.

This, after all, was the last opportunity he would get to search the rectory for evidence of the man's real identity. But which room? Apart from the drawing room where everyone was, and the kitchen, dining room and cloakroom – unlikely places to keep private documents – there was only the upper floor. Was it worth the risk? Fainter hearts than Burton's might have abandoned the search. He braced himself and crept upstairs. Joy's bedroom was as likely a place as any.

The stairs creaked horribly. If the front-room door was flung open and Joy demanded to know where he was going he'd say he needed the bathroom. How was he to know there was a cloakroom downstairs?

He'd reached the landing halfway up when the doorbell went once more and Joy came out into the hall. Burton backed out of sight and waited.

Peggy Winner, downstairs, said, 'Am I the last?'

Joy told her, 'Don't worry, Peggy. We're still missing someone, but I can't think who it is.'

He took her coat and hung it in the hall and they went back to the others.

Burton climbed the rest of the stairs. He'd have to be quick now. Tiptoed along the upstairs passage, opening doors. Found the bathroom and a guest room bare of everything except the bed and a wardrobe.

The next room had to be Joy's.

It wasn't how he imagined a rector's bedroom might be. No crucifix, Bible or embroidered text. A music centre, portable TV and double bed with a quilt covered in a Mondrian design. Two shelves of fat paperbacks. Every sea story Patrick O'Brian had written. Quite a few Hornblowers.

He looked around for the kind of box or briefcase that might contain personal papers. Nothing. Looked into the wardrobe, the chest of drawers and the bedside cupboard. Felt on top of the wardrobe and among the shoes at the bottom.

Then the bedroom door opened and a voice said, 'What the fuck are you doing?'

He swung around guiltily.

It wasn't Joy, thank God. It was John Neary.

'Poking around,' he answered.

'What for?'

'You'll find out soon enough.'

'Bloody hell. I was sent to collect you from the study. He thinks you're overcome with shyness, or something. I heard you moving about up here, so I came up.'

'You don't have to tell anyone,' said Burton.

'What's up with you – creeping around up here?' demanded Neary.

'Just don't say anything to him please. I'll come down.'

'Bloody weirdo.'

Sheepishly, Burton followed him downstairs. In the room where the party was, Ann said loudly, 'Here he is. Where were you all this time?'

'Bit of a headache,' was the best Burton could think to answer.

'Do you want something for it?' Joy asked.

Burton shook his head.

Neary rolled his eyes upwards and said nothing, and the talk started up again. Peggy Winner was asking if the rector minded sleeping alone in this old building.

'Is that an offer, Peg?' said Geoff Elliott, chuckling over his fourth gin and tonic.

'No problem. The rectory has a good atmosphere,' said Joy.

'Everyone said it was haunted when I was a kiddie,' said Peggy.

'If it is, the ghost has got to be one of my predecessors in the job,' said Joy, 'so it doesn't bother me. A blue lady or a knight in armour might give me the jitters, but not a humble cleric. There are some I'd definitely like to meet.'

'Waldo Wallace?' suggested Norman Gregor.

'Top of the list.'

'And what would you ask him?'

Joy held out his hands expansively. 'There'd be no need to ask him anything. The man was unstoppable, full of good stories, like the one about Archbishop Tait at a dinner party. The old Archbishop was sitting next to the Duchess of Sutherland and suddenly went white as a sheet, turned to her and said confidentially, "It's come to pass as I feared. I dreaded this. I think I'm having a stroke." The Duchess said without even looking his way, "Relax, your Grace, it's *my* leg you're pinching, not your own."'

Everyone liked the story. 'He sounds like a man after your own heart,' Gregor said. 'Some of your stories aren't so bad, Rector.'

'The best ones I borrowed from Waldo. He threw better parties than me, too. His home brew was a legend in the parish.'

'Where was it brewed?'

'Underneath us, in the cellar. Unfortunately some tee-total rector removed it all early this century, but you can still see traces of the kegs on the floor.'

'What do you use it for?'

'The cellar? All the furniture I don't want. Someone who comes after me may find a need for a Victorian commode or a wind-up gramophone, but I get by without them.'

'Things like that could be valuable,' said Peggy.

'Oh, I sold the Chippendale chairs.'

'I never know when you're serious,' she said.

Burton stood with Ann Porter near the door, saying little, listening to the man in his element, the centre of attention, charming an audience. Inwardly Burton was fuming that for all the risk he'd taken, no evidence had come to light. But the mention of a cellar had not escaped him. 'Which way is the cloakroom?' he asked Ann.

After she'd told him, he nodded, as if asking her to cover for him, and stepped outside again. Surely that cellar was worth looking into.

He guessed there might be access somewhere towards the rear of the house, through the kitchen, and he was right. There was a door in the scullery, to the left of the old leaded sink. The key was in the lock. He let himself in, located a light-switch and went down some whitewashed steps.

The cellar was in a respectable state, as if some effort had been made to keep it free from dust and cobwebs. Plenty of old furniture was stored down here, just as Joy had claimed. Otherwise all he could see were newspapers and magazines in tidy stacks. He stepped around an old coat-stand, checking the furniture, trying to miss nothing, hopeful of locating another filing cabinet. You can tell when a place has been untouched for years, and this was not it.

Then he saw the display cabinet, an unappealing mid-Victorian piece in some dark wood, without legs, and with three glass doors. What caught his eye was the array of white boxes and small brown bottles, an unlikely collection to be housed here. He opened one of the doors. The interior was in use as a medicine cabinet.

Odd, he thought. Why keep your medicines down here when most people want them handy in the bathroom, or at least in the house? He looked more closely. These weren't the sorts of medicines you keep for emergencies. There were no Band-Aids, aspirins, Alka-Seltzers or Vaseline. Neither were they prescription drugs. They had labels, certainly, but they were hand-written, with just the names of the contents, and nothing about dosage. Burton was not well up on pharmacy, but he was intrigued by this lot. Insulin, hyoscine, morphine, dextromoramide, aconite, digoxin, antimony. Even with his limited knowledge he could tell there were poisons here, lethal poisons. What was a village rector doing with a collection like this hidden in his cellar?

It shocked Burton to the core. He'd harboured suspicions of malpractice, impersonation, even the taking of life. None of it had prepared him for this. For all the evidence to the contrary, he couldn't shake off the thought of Joy as a man of God.

What now? Here was the proof that the man was evil. He hesitated, dry-mouthed with stress, raking his fingers through his hair and tugging at it.

21

Frustration for Burton Sands: PC George Mitchell wasn't at home. 'You'd be better off waiting till tomorrow, my dear,' said Mrs Mitchell, echoing her husband's laid-back style of speech and raising Burton's blood pressure by several points. 'He won't be back till late. He had to drive all the way to Lymington to look at a body they took from the sea at Milford. I'm not supposed to say, but they think it could be poor Mrs Haydenhall.'

Burton didn't fully take this in. He hadn't extricated his thoughts from that cellar. 'What time do you expect him?'

'Well, he didn't leave till six, and 'tis a two-hour drive, easy. He'll need a bite to eat, if he can stomach anything after a gruesome duty like that. Corpses don't look nice after some days in the water. I'll be surprised to see him before midnight. Why don't you come back in the morning, dear?'

'Did you say the body in the water is Mrs Haydenhall?'

Dorothy Mitchell pressed a finger to her lips as if she'd said too much already. ''Tis not certain yet. That's why George has gone.'

'What was she doing in the sea?'

'Who could possibly say, my dear? Keep it to yourself, won't you?'

Burton looked at his watch. 'This can't wait till tomorrow.'

'My George won't be wanting to talk.'

'I haven't come for a chat. I've got evidence of a major crime. I'd better phone Warminster.'

'If 'tis village, I wouldn't,' she said mildly, but with a look that was not mild. 'George always deals with Foxford matters. They'll give the job to him anyway.'

'Does he have a mobile?'

'George?' She smiled at the notion.

'Can you get him to phone me when he gets in, whatever time it is?'

'I can ask him. If he's not of a mind to pick up the phone, he won't.'

'It's very urgent.'

Burton returned to his cottage. He'd left the party at the rectory before it looked like coming to an end, saying his headache wouldn't shift. Joy had professed concern and again offered a painkiller. The audacity of the man! Knowing what was in that cellar, Burton wouldn't accept a glass of water from Otis Joy, let alone a pill.

He sat close to the phone, primed. On the table in front of him was a small brown pill-bottle labelled Atropine. He'd taken the risk of removing it from the cellar knowing he wouldn't be believed otherwise. With any luck, Joy wouldn't notice it was gone.

How could anyone have acquired such a collection of poisons without working in a pharmacy? Burton was lost for an explanation. It would be up to the police to find out. All he could do was tell them what he'd seen, show them the bottle and his copy of the newspaper report linking the rector with the college in Canada. They could get a search warrant and raid the rectory. Then maybe they'd find the personal papers that his own search had failed to turn up – and discover the real identity of 'Otis Joy'.

He kept looking at the time. He had his front-room

curtain pulled back in case he saw the police car drive up the street. Several went by at eleven, when the pub closed. George would come from the opposite direction.

It was ten to midnight when he spotted the white Renault with the police stripes along the side. He snatched up the bottle and was out of the cottage and across the street before George Mitchell opened his car door.

'Bugger off, Burton, I haven't got time for you.'

It wasn't the reception Burton felt he was entitled to.

'It's important. It's about the rector. I've been waiting hours for you.'

'Is he dead?'

'No.'

'Standing on the church tower and about to jump off?'

'No.'

'Wait some more, then. I'll see you in the morning.'

Burton said in a hard, tight voice, 'No, that isn't good enough. If you don't take this seriously, I'll go straight home and dial nine-nine-nine.'

'Come in, then,' George said wearily. And to his wife, as he entered, 'Yes, it was her.'

'Poor creature, God rest her soul,' said Mrs Mitchell.

Next morning at Warminster Police Station, George outlined the case against the rector to Chief Inspector Doug Somerville, the senior CID man, one of the new breed of detectives, brash, unbelievably young and with a low opinion of village bobbies.

'Fantastic,' was Somerville's first comment, and it was said without admiration.

'That's been my feeling all along,' George admitted, 'but the evidence is stacking up.'

'What evidence? This?' Somerville tapped the pill-bottle with his finger, knocking it over.

'It says atropine. That's a poison, isn't it?'

'It's a medicine.'

'What for?'

'Bellyache.' Somerville took a textbook from the shelf behind him, leafed through the pages, and started reading. '"Medicinal uses: the relief of gastrointestinal spasm and biliary and renal colic. Prescribed orally in doses of five hundred micrograms three times a day, increasing if required to up to two milligrams daily."'

'I reckon if you take enough, it's poison,' George said.

'Take enough of anything and it's poison. It depends on the dose.'

'What about the hyoscine? There was hyoscine there. That's a killer, I know. Crippen killed his wife with it.'

Somerville turned a few more pages and read out, '"Hyoscine, also known as scopolamine. Widely used in the treatment of travel sickness."' He shut the book. 'Your Mr Sands found the rector's medical supplies.'

George shot him a rebellious look. 'I don't think so.'

Somerville sighed and glanced up at the clock. 'Listen. What have we got on this jerk? He calls himself Otis Joy, and it may not be his real name. So what? People are allowed to change their names.'

'But the real Otis Joy died in a car accident in Canada and the rector claims he was at the same college, Milton Davidson Memorial. It's here.' George picked up the copy of the *Wiltshire Times* report.

'So he borrowed the name to buff up his image. He's a cool clergyman.'

'The point is, they don't recognise his picture at Milton Davidson.'

'So?'

'I don't think he studied there. He's a fraud. He took over the identity of a theological student who died and used his papers to get into a British college.'

'To become a vicar?'

'Yes.'

'Why?'

'Who can say?' said George. 'Something in his past? They wouldn't take someone with a prison record, would they?'

'You're guessing now, George.'

'If he really wanted to enter the church, and if he had a . . . what's the word?'

'Vocation?'

'Right. It's not like other jobs. It's a call from God, or that's what they believe. Nothing is going to stand in his way.'

'You can't have it both ways. If he's that committed to religion, he's not going to murder people.'

'I thought the same as you until I found out these things,' said George. 'I've had time to think about him. I reckon I know what makes him tick, and it isn't faith in God. It's the attraction of being a priest. He gets his kick from standing up in the pulpit telling us how to live our lives. Doesn't matter if he doesn't practise what he preaches. It's power. Respect. It's the best job in the world to him, and he's going to keep it. He got it by trickery and he's going to hang on to it, come what may.'

Somerville was still unmoved. 'It's not the profile of your average serial killer.'

'He's not average in any way.'

'I don't buy it, George.'

'Are you saying we just ignore all these deaths?'

'They're unrelated.'

George was stung by this sweeping dismissal of everything he'd said. Personally he bore no malice against Joy;
in fact, he got on well with the man. With a sense of
duty he'd put friendship aside and tipped off CID, and
now he was being treated like a time-waster. 'When they
mount up like this, they ought to be taken seriously,'
he said. 'I know I haven't got a lot of evidence, but
the man hasn't been investigated. We could easily turn
something up.'

'Where's the link?' demanded Somerville.

'It's him. He's the link.'

'What's the MO, then? You've got a sexton who disappeared into thin air, a Frenchwoman stung by a bee, a
bishop who jumps, or was pushed, into a quarry, a church
treasurer who swallows amylobarbitone and a jazz freak
with a heart attack. Serial killers don't keep changing
their MO.'

'Maybe this one is the exception. He's clever.'

'He'd need to be.'

'When every murder is different, you don't connect
them.'

'You're telling me. And even if you *could* link Otis Joy
to each of them—'

'Which I can,' put in George.

'Even if these were unlawful killings with his fingerprints
all over them, you've still got to work out why. What's his
motive?'

'I couldn't tell you that.' admitted George, and added
sarcastically. 'I'm not in CID.'

Somerville's eyes narrowed.

George added rapidly, 'But if I was, I'd also be interested
in Cynthia Haydenhall's death.' It was his last card and not
a trump, but worth playing. 'She's the woman I identified
last night. Missing since a week before Christmas. Went

off without telling anyone and didn't turn up for the carol-singing round the village, which she'd told people she'd do. This was Joy's day off. He missed the carol-singing, too. Got back to the village late.'

'And her body turns up in the sea?'

'Washed up at Milford early yesterday.'

'Signs of violence?'

'Nothing obvious.'

'Who was she? A church-goer?'

'Very much so. A regular. Organised the harvest supper. Divorced, with money. Nice cottage. Bit of a busybody, but not unpopular.'

'Suicidal?'

'Not the type.'

For the first time, Somerville seemed to be wavering. He picked up the little bottle of tablets and stood it where it had been on the desk. 'It's another sudden death, I grant you. We'll get nowhere with this woman if no marks are showing.'

George remained silent, willing to let the process happen in its own time.

Somerville rubbed the side of his face as if checking whether he'd shaved. 'Joy got back late on the day the woman disappeared, you say?'

'Between ten and eleven. It's his day off from his church duties.'

'That's all you've got on him? I don't buy it.'

'Her car was abandoned in Bournemouth. We can check it for prints.'

'His prints? If he's as smart as you say, he won't have left any.'

Even George's patience was over-stretched. 'Basically, sir, are you saying don't bother?'

'I'm saying if we want to make a case against Joy,

we pick a stronger one than this. Is she the only body
we have?'

'Most of them disappeared, or were disposed of.'

'Cremated?'

'There's the jazz man, Gary Jansen. He was buried.'

'The heart case?'

'Supposedly heart. It was diagnosed by a GP who should
have retired five years ago.'

'What was the link with Joy?'

'Gary Jansen was the husband of the new treasurer, the
one who replaced Stanley Burrows – after *he* died suddenly.
Gary visited the rectory on the afternoon of his death. It's
possible Joy slipped him something that induced the heart
attack.'

'Why?'

George held out his hands in appeal. 'I can't answer that.
Jansen may have found something out. I told you there are
suspicions that Joy fiddles the books.'

'It's a big jump from embezzlement to murder.'

'His living was at stake. He wouldn't survive in the
church if he was caught.'

'I thought you said Jansen was just back from New
Orleans. Have you ever flown the Atlantic, George? On
your first day back you're in no shape to check account
books.'

'Some other thing triggered it, then. He could have
heard the rumours that Joy slept with his wife.'

'For crying out loud. So this rector is a fornicator, as
well as an embezzler and a killer?' Sarcasm returned, with
interest.

'Rumours, I said. Jansen comes back from the States
to find his wife is treasurer when she hasn't any experience of book-keeping.' George could almost hear Burton
prompting him.

'So Jansen goes up to the rectory to sort out Joy and dies of a heart attack the same night?'

George leaned back in his chair, sensing that this could be a turning point. Appearing to take an interest in the veins on the back of his left hand he said without looking directly at Somerville, 'If he was given a poisonous substance, there's a way of finding out.'

'An exhumation?'

'Of all these suspicious deaths, it's the only one where Joy could have made a mistake,' said George. 'He should have made sure Jansen was cremated.'

'What stopped him? Had Jansen left instructions?'

'No.'

'Joy could have persuaded the widow, if he was having her.'

'Lost his nerve, I reckon,' said George. 'You need a second doctor's opinion before a cremation can take place. It was a risk. Some other doctor might have asked the questions old Dr Perkins didn't.'

'Joy doesn't strike me as a man who loses his nerve,' said Somerville. 'If he really is a serial killer, he's very cool indeed.'

George nodded, willing to concede the point. He was making headway at last, the way Somerville was talking.

'It's more likely he took a calculated risk,' Somerville went on. 'He weighed up the odds and decided it was simpler and safer to go for a burial. You're the coroner's officer, George. Do you think you can swing an exhumation order on the case we have?'

'I can try.'

22

T he finding of Cynthia's body devastated Rachel. You can tell yourself a thousand times that a missing person must be gone for ever, but no amount of reasoning can spare you from cold certainty. The thought of poor Cyn being washed up on the tide with the driftwood was horrible. She kept picturing her, mauled by the sea, lying at the water's edge with seaweed clinging to her and little white crabs crawling over her dead flesh. She couldn't understand how such a tragedy had happened. Cyn never mentioned the sea. And she wasn't suicidal; there were few people Rachel knew with a stronger grip on life. She was always positive, always planning her next project. She'd even convinced herself she stood a chance with Otis.

An accident, then? It had to be, but how? Surely she hadn't fallen off a boat. She had no connection with boats that Rachel knew of. Anyway, why would anyone except a deep-sea fisherman want to go on a boat in freezing December?

People were saying the inquest would provide some answers. Maybe clues had been found. Maybe someone remembered seeing Cynthia at Milford on Sea. It was a long way from home, so she may have been staying at a guesthouse, wanting some quiet days alone (though that didn't sound like Cynthia). And it would have been a swift turn-about from her promise to be at the carol-singing.

These thoughts were still tormenting her when PC George Mitchell opened her garden gate and marched up to her front door in businesslike fashion. He wants me as a witness for the inquest, she thought.

'I don't know how best to say this, Rachel,' he began when he had lowered himself, far from relaxed, deep into the cushions of her vast settee. 'There's no way I can put it without giving you a shock.'

'If it's about Cynthia, I know already.'

'Cynthia?'

'Mrs Haydenhall.'

'Er, no. I've not come about that.' He flattened his palms against the upholstery as if he felt it might swallow him altogether.

'What is it, then?'

'You probably know I have another job on top of my police duties. I'm the coroner's officer, and that's why I'm here.'

'Something to do with the coroner?'

'A problem – a complication, let's say – has come up. New information. The possibility that things may not have been so straightforward as they appeared at the time.'

She tensed. 'What are you trying to tell me?'

'We've applied for an exhumation order for Gary. When I say "we", I mean the police.'

Her worst nightmare. 'You're going to dig him up?'

'Believe me, Rachel, we don't disturb the dead without good reason. A thing like this is new in my own experience. But I'll make sure it's all carried out with proper respect. They fetch out the coffin at first light, when village people aren't about. Then he'll be taken to a mortuary and examined. When it's all done, he'll be reburied. Are you all right? Shall I get you some water?'

She shook her head. He'd plunged her into molten terror and now he was offering a glass of water.

'Why? Why are they doing this?'

'Suspicions that a mistake may have been made by the doctor – in good faith, I'm sure.'

She heard herself saying things she'd rehearsed in her head for this worst of all scenarios. 'Gary died of a heart attack. He was being treated for heart disease.'

'No question of that. It's all on record. But we have to be certain of the diagnosis, and this is the only way.'

'I don't follow this at all.' Torn between fear and denial, she was trying to recover some poise. 'Suspicions, you said. What do you mean – *suspicions*?'

'It's part of a larger inquiry into a number of recent deaths.'

'What?' Horrified, she played the words over to herself.

'Sorry, but I can't go into detail.'

She took short, shallow breaths, her brain racing. What did they think – that she'd killed others, as well as Gary? 'And what if I don't give permission?'

'It's out of your hands, Rachel. The coroner has jurisdiction here. If he's satisfied that a mistake may have been made, he can authorise it.'

Her head throbbed and she wondered if she *was* going to faint. 'When?'

'All the evidence is on his desk now. You can take it he won't turn down the application. Things could happen quite soon. We'll have a top man for the post mortem. If it was just heart failure, he'll know.'

It seemed to Rachel that George expected her to break down and confess. She had enough self-control, just, to deny him that triumph.

Long after the wretched man had extricated himself from

the sofa and gone, she stood with her arms tightly across her chest, trying to stop the convulsive shaking. The image in her brain was no longer of Cynthia's beached body, but herself handcuffed and with a blanket over her head being led to a police car. Neighbours shouting abuse. The hand on her head guiding her into the back seat. Questions at the police station. The charge. The cell. The magistrates' court. God, what a fool she'd been. If only Gary had been cremated, this couldn't have happened. If only she hadn't killed him at all . . .

Panicky thoughts continued to stream through her brain. In the dock at the Central Criminal Court, being sentenced to life imprisonment and taken down by the warders.

There was no way out of this now. It was naive to hope that they wouldn't find traces of aconitine. It may have been the undetectable poison in Victorian times but you could bet modern science had ways of testing for it. A top pathologist was going to find traces in Gary's organs. She could hear him giving evidence for the prosecution. Hear the neighbours saying a huge clump of monkshood grew in her garden before she dug it up.

Black despair gripped her. She'd tried to get away with it and failed. Would she get a lighter sentence if she confessed before they did the exhumation? Or was it already too late to make any difference?

Mentally she put herself in the dock again and tried pleading diminished responsibility. She'd been desperately unhappy with Gary. He'd neglected her, taken separate holidays. Beaten her; yes, she'd need to say he was a wife-beater, and so he had been . . . almost. He had come close to hitting her more than once and she could play up the violence without fear of contradiction. He'd accused her falsely of being unfaithful. Caused her acute embarrassment by going up to the rectory to brand Otis as an adulterer.

Otis.

He was a major player in this tragedy.

Would he vouch for her in court? Could she depend on him to say there wasn't an iota of truth in Gary's wild imaginings?

If she couldn't bank on Otis, there was no hope left in the world.

She needed him to speak up for her with all the dignity and authority of his position as parish priest. That, she told herself, would massively strengthen her case and win sympathy. If he was firm in denying that anything happened between them, then Gary's charge of immorality would be seen as manifestly unfair. Was one fumbled clinch on the sofa going to trouble his Christian conscience? He'd ruin his own reputation if he said anything about it.

The court would accept that she had been provoked beyond endurance. She'd heard of several cases of battered wives being treated leniently by the courts after confessing to killing their brutal husbands under extreme provocation. '*It is the view of this court that you have already suffered enough, Mrs Jansen. You are no danger to the public, and a long term of detention would serve no purpose. In view of the extreme provocation you were under, and taking into account your full and frank confession to unlawful killing, I am directing the jury not to convict on the charge of murder. They will instead decide whether you are guilty of the lesser charge of voluntary manslaughter, for which the law allows me to exercise discretion over sentencing.*'

Would that it were true!

Impulsively she snatched up the phone and called Otis, praying she wouldn't hear an answerphone message.

'Joy.'

He was there, thank God.

'Otis, it's Rachel. I'm in the most awful trouble. Can I see you urgently?'

'What's up?'

'I'd rather not say on the phone.'

'Can you come to the rectory?'

'Now?'

'Give me twenty minutes.'

She gave him ten. On the way up there she saw two people she wished she hadn't, Owen Cumberbatch and his sister. Miss Cumberbatch waved in a friendly way. Owen – the village snoop – just stared, curious to see where she was heading. She didn't turn round after passing them, but she was sure he watched every pace she took towards the rectory.

Otis opened the door before she needed to knock and she hurried inside and blurted out the news that the police were going to exhume Gary.

He looked surprised and genuinely concerned. 'Whatever for?'

'They think I poisoned him, and, God forgive me, I did.' Without any more warning than that, she threw herself on his mercy. She had to be totally open with him.

His hand went to the strip of white across his throat as if to check that it was there. 'Rachel, this can't be true.'

'I dug up some roots from the garden and added them to his curry. That's what killed him. The doctor said it was heart failure, but he didn't arrive until Gary was too far gone to speak.'

He shaped his mouth to respond and nothing came out. This silver-tongued man was totally at a loss.

'I used aconite.'

He stared, frowning.

'From a plant called monkshood.'

Miraculously, his expression softened. 'Aconite?' he repeated in a tone she'd never heard from him before. It sounded oddly like reverence. He might have been chanting the name of one of the Old Testament prophets.

'It's extremely poisonous,' she said.

'Deadly,' he agreed in the same awed tone.

Weird. She felt no disapproval from him; almost the reverse. 'It's supposed to have been undetectable once, but I'm sure it isn't these days. Otis, I don't expect anyone to forgive me, but I'm telling you because you're the only person I want to confide in. My marriage was hell. You could see that, couldn't you?'

'What?' His thoughts hadn't moved on from the mention of aconite.

'Gary and I. A disaster area.'

'You told me you weren't very close, but—'

'He was out to humiliate me – and you as well. He thought you and I had . . . had made love while he was in America.'

He said evenly, 'I know that.'

'Yes, and you told me he came here – ready to start a fight or something – and you defused it.'

'I told him it was untrue, which it was.'

She made a little moaning sound. 'How I wish I'd known you would handle him so well. I should have had the sense to see, but I couldn't think straight, I was in such a state. With me the same day he was full of threats. He frightened me, pushed me around. I can't take violence, Otis.'

'So you poisoned his food?' he said without even a hint of censure. She must have been deluded, but once more she thought she heard admiration in his tone.

'He'd already complained of chest pains and called the doctor.'

'Wasn't that the poison?'

'No! I'm talking about earlier in the week, just after he got back from America. The pain was angina, Dr Perkins said. He gave him a tablet and it worked. He slept well. The next day, on the Wednesday, he was better, back to his old self, running me down, running everything down. America was marvellous and everything about Britain was third-rate. It wasn't until later in the week he noticed the wine stain on the carpet and wanted to know how it got there.'

'And you told him?'

'Not everything. I just said you came with the account books, but he assumed it was ... much more than it was. Well, he was like that, practically paranoid about anything I do. He called me horrible names. Pushed me against a wall and threatened me. And he was hell-bent on making trouble with you. Said he'd beat the truth out of you. Then almost in the same breath said he wanted a curry. I know I was wicked to do it, but all I could see ahead of me was misery and humiliation. The curry gave me a chance to do something about it. I'm like that. Giddy Girl, my mother used to call me. Ninety-nine per cent of the time I act normally and then something triggers me to do a crazy thing that gets me into terrible trouble.'

He nodded. 'I've noticed.'

'I'm desperate.'

'And you think I can help?'

Her voice faltered. She sobbed, and said in a rush, 'Otis, I'm scared out of my skin and you're the only person in this world I trust. The police think I killed other people as well.'

He said tight-lipped, offended. 'That isn't true.' He had turned quite pink at the suggestion, a development that Rachel took as support. 'They can't fit you up with all their unsolved crimes just because you're under suspicion of killing your husband.'

'They're trying to scare me into confessing, I suppose.'

'You could be right about that. Who else do they say you killed?'

'George didn't say. I've been trying to work it out and I think they must mean Stanley, for one. I suppose they think I gave that poison to Stanley – whatever it was he took . . .'

'Amylobarbitone.'

'. . . because I was after his job as treasurer, just to be able to cosy up to you.'

'They're way off beam there,' he said firmly, too firmly for Rachel's bruised emotions, but she didn't let it show. 'You know what village gossip is like.'

'Gossip is one thing. The police are supposed to deal in facts.'

'They can get things wrong. I'm the village Jezebel according to some people. They could believe I'm responsible for Cynthia's death as well.'

'*Cynthia?* Why?'

'Because she was a rival. She was always telling people she fancied you.'

He shook his head. 'Silly woman. I'm a clergyman, not a sex object. What exactly did George Mitchell say? What were his precise words?'

'Something like "it's just part of a larger inquiry into a number of deaths". He must have meant Stanley and Cynthia. Who else is there?'

'God knows,' said Otis, and the mild blasphemy slipped casually from his tongue as though he were operating at another level.

She was praying that he was, that he would come up with some brilliant suggestion that would save her. If anyone could work miracles, Otis was the one. But for the moment he was locked in thoughts of his own.

The entire dialogue had taken place in the hall. Now he pushed open his office door and gestured to her to go in. It was warmer in there and smelt reassuringly of him. She sat down in the chair in front of the desk. 'What am I going to do, Otis? I'm terrified.'

He perched himself on the edge of the desk and asked, 'How much have you admitted to George Mitchell?'

'Nothing. You're the only one I told.'

'You're certain?'

'I swear.'

'Then say nothing.'

'You don't think I should confess?'

He pulled a face at the suggestion, then thought better of it. 'To God, yes.'

'But not to the police?'

Firmly he told her, 'Not to anyone else. We don't know what they'll find when they exhume Gary. You're assuming they'll find traces of aconite, but it may not be so simple. I know a little about – em – chemistry, and I can tell you that you picked a beauty.'

She looked at him in amazement.

He said quickly, 'I'm speaking scientifically now. Alkaloid poisons like aconite are not easy to detect, even with spectrometry and so on, particularly so long after death as this. Unless you tell the police yourself, they won't know what they're looking for. He died of cardiac failure, and that will be confirmed, but the cause is far less obvious. It's not so simple as looking for arsenic.'

'I thought if I confessed I might get a lighter sentence.'

He shook his head. 'Rachel, you're making all kinds of assumptions. Can you be sure you poisoned Gary?'

'Positive. I wouldn't lie about it.'

'You cut up monkshood root and added it to the curry?'

'Yes.'

'But you can't be totally sure it killed him.'

'Oh, but I can.'

His eyes closed and he raised his palm to cut off her flow of self-recrimination. 'Listen, Rachel. I'm trying to help you. In the week before your husband died, he saw the doctor because of a heart problem, is that right?'

'Angina.'

'That's what old Dr Perkins believed, but he may have misread the symptoms. Gary had a chest pain, you say?'

'Yes.'

'That could have been more serious, a mild heart attack. And he had a second attack, the one that killed him, on the night he died. Was it caused by what he ate, or was it always going to happen? You don't know for sure.'

Without fully believing, she stared ahead, at the unexpected escape route he was showing her. 'I'd never thought of that.'

'It's time you did. Do you know the fatal dose for aconite?'

'No. I just chopped some up and put it in the pot.'

'Well, then.'

'Quite a lot, actually,' she admitted.

'But did he eat it all?'

'Most of it. I threw some away.'

'And he had a history of heart problems?'

'Yes!' The exit opened wider. Only Otis could have thought of it. The man was a genius. She stood up and embraced him.

He allowed her to hold him without returning the embrace. He was deep in his own thoughts again. In a moment he said, 'It would be sensible if you got away from the village while this is going on. People are going to comment on it. You know how sensitive you are to village opinion. You don't want to be goaded into saying anything the police could use against you.'

'Won't that look suspicious?'

'It's understandable to want to be somewhere else when they're digging up your husband.'

She had to make a mental effort to grasp her new role as the innocent widow. He was right. She was in such emotional turmoil that she could easily give herself away with an unguarded remark. And she didn't want more questions from the police, either. 'But I don't know where to go.'

'I do. Can you be ready to leave early tomorrow, say around six?'

'With you?' Her eyes moistened. She *was* emotional.

'I'll drive you there. It's my day off. Pack for a holiday. Clothes, money, cards, chequebook. Have you got anything in a building society?'

'A bit.'

'Bring your passbook, then. Don't leave anything of value in the house. You'd better bring the parish books as well.'

'Where are we going?'

'A secret. If you're going into retreat, it's better nobody knows.'

She trusted him totally.

They were at sea by nine next morning. A green, choppy sea with flecks of foam catching the light under a white January sky. Amazed that Otis owned a boat, and at a loss to account for the size and luxury of the *Revelation*, Rachel sat beside him in the cockpit waiting to see what other surprises this wonderman had in store. 'It's my indulgence,' he said as if that explained everything.

'Isn't that a religious word?'

He laughed. 'I hadn't thought of that.'

'What exactly is an indulgence?'

'Remission of punishment for our sins. It's Roman Catholic doctrine. You confess to the good father and he acts as God's spokesman and decides if the offence can be pardoned.'

'Nothing to do with expensive boats, then?'

'No, bribing the priest with a motor-cruiser is definitely discouraged. Anyway, we Protestants are dead against indulgences. It was the sale of them that led to the Reformation.'

'So you bought this yourself?'

He nodded and looked ahead, tacitly inviting her to drop the subject.

She didn't. 'How do you answer someone who says a priest shouldn't live like this?'

'With Ecclesiastes, Seven, Fourteen: "In the day of prosperity, be joyful." Tuesday is my day of prosperity.'

'I'm not going to get a serious answer, then.'

'All right. I'll try and explain. There's this restless part of me that needs to break out sometimes.'

'Snap,' said Rachel. 'I'm like that, except I do the most appalling things in moments of madness. Well, you know.'

'Giddy Girl.'

'Exactly.'

'So do I.'

'Do wicked things?'

He turned and their eyes met briefly and for the first time since that evening he had brought the account books to her cottage she basked in his warmth. She *knew* he was over the awkwardness that had blighted their friendship. He told her, 'You shared your secret with me. I appreciate that.'

'Unloaded my fear, you mean.'

'It took courage to do what you did.'

'Poisoning my husband? Nine parts fear to one part courage.'

He laughed. 'You improve with practice.'

'I hope not.' She smiled back.

'You do. I've got better at it.'

She heard him, failed to understand, played his words over in her brain, looked ahead for some time, and finally said, 'Got better at what?'

'Murder.' He gazed out at the ocean while her thoughts went through a series of convulsions. 'We're two of a kind, Rachel.'

The hackneyed phrase did nothing to lessen the shock.

He went on, 'You were honest with me, so I'll come clean with you. The stories doing the rounds are slightly exaggerated. I didn't murder my wife. She died by a tragic accident, from a bee-sting. But I own up to four others.'

Inside, she was rigid. 'Please say you made that up.'

'Wish I could.'

Their dialogue stopped as suddenly as if someone had switched off a radio.

She thought she was going to pass out.

Finally, after searching his face for a vestige of amusement and finding none, she asked, 'How could you?'

'But you know. Desperation drives us to it. Each of them threatened my living. I could have been found out.'

She hesitated. 'What was there to find out?'

'That I misuse parish funds. You suspected as much, didn't you, but you kept quiet?'

'The contingency fund?'

'Right.' He patted the steering wheel with something between pride and affection. 'This is the contingency.'

'And you killed people for this? You – a priest?'

'People who found out.'

'I can't believe this.'

'It isn't just the boat. It's my whole existence.'

She waited. They were down to the wire now.

'Underneath it all, I'm a coward,' he said, 'frightened to face the world. I think I do a good job as a priest. It's the only job I can do. I was raised in religion, force-fed it morning, noon and night when I was a kid.'

'In the children's home?'

'Yes. From the nuns, and later, at school, the Jesuits. I'm very well grounded in the Bible. Through it I've achieved the outward signs of self-respect, status, confidence. The church is the obvious life for me. Second nature. But deep inside there's a stunted creature who couldn't cope with any other way of life.'

'Never. You're so confident. You inspire people. You speak with such sincerity.'

'Echoing the stuff I've heard a million times. In this game, Rachel, you're lost if you admit to anyone that you have doubts, or committed a sin. I learned about survival the hard way. Stealing from the kitchen in the orphanage when I was hungry and being naive enough to own up. The so-called Sisters of Mercy had me on my knees in the chapel for three hours asking God to punish me and then bared my butt in front of everyone at supper-time and answered my prayers. And no supper. I was eight years old. It didn't stop me stealing, only I got smart and avoided the canings – except when I was stupid enough to boast to other kids about it and they grassed me up. Another hard lesson. Another beating. And Sister Carmel had a strong right arm. Good preparation for my secondary education with the Jesuits, except they used the strap and had even stronger arms. Taught me the Bible, I must say – and turned me right off the Roman Church.'

In spite of the shock he'd given her, she was moved by the story. 'It would have put me off religion altogether.'

'No, at the end of my schooling when they threw me overboard I clung to it – as the only thing I was any good at. Too scared to let go. The bravest thing I could manage was a sideways move, to the Church of England. Joining them was a huge act of rebellion for me – revenge on the Pope and his minions. I knew my Bible so well that I swanned through theological college. Did three years' training in one. I love it, being a priest, doing everything a priest does and doing it with energy and imagination.'

'But not behaving like one.'

He sighed.

'I understand what you've told me about your child-hood,' Rachel said. 'Anyone would sympathise, but it can't excuse what you told me a moment ago.'

'About the killings? I wasn't justifying them. I'm simply saying it's the way I am, Rachel. I act as I always have. I steal from the church, and I cover my tracks.'

'But you stole from the orphanage because you were hungry.'

'Fair point,' he admitted with a faint smile. 'Once a thief . . .' He stopped himself. 'No, that's too flip by half. It runs deep, this need to have an escape route. As a kid, I couldn't run away. I tried, more than once, and got dragged back and punished. If I'd had the boat then . . .'

'Four, you said.' Her voice shook as she spoke.

'A man you wouldn't know called Fred Skidmore, the sexton at my last parish, a full-time snoop who threatened me with blackmail. He's down a mineshaft on Exmoor now. Then Marcus Glastonbury.'

'The bishop!'

'Left me no option. Told me I had to resign the living.'

'But he jumped off—'

'Was dropped,' he corrected her gently. 'I killed him in my study, cracked him over the head with a glass paperweight and disposed of him later in the quarry.' Some seconds elapsed while he concentrated on steering a true course through a choppy stretch. 'You want to know who else, but don't like to ask? Stanley Burrows, of course. Nice man, but a stubborn old cuss. He was going to hand over anyway, only he wanted to do it on his terms, showing everything to the new treasurer, including my building society accounts. He wouldn't be budged. I couldn't allow that. Slipped him a powder with his whisky.'

She hesitated. It seemed only fitting to allow a moment's silence out of respect for Stanley before asking the question she could scarcely bring herself to speak. 'Who was . . . ?'

'The fourth?' He pointed out of the window. 'Do you see the headland with Hurst Castle out there? The beach further round to port is Milford on Sea, where she was washed up.'

She could only whisper, 'Cynthia?'

'She ambushed me. Caught me right off guard. She turned up at the marina one morning, having trailed me all the way from Foxford. You know what Cynthia was like. There was no way she would keep a secret.'

After another long silence, Rachel said, 'Cynthia was very good to me.'

'I know. I could have told you she slipped over the side by accident, but I want to be as honest with you as you were with me.'

'She was on this boat?'

'I think she enjoyed her last hour alive. She was terrific company, as you know.'

A defining moment had come in Rachel's dealings with

Otis. Outraged for poor Cyn, she said, 'How can you be so unfeeling?'

'Haven't you been listening?'

'But Cynthia – of all people.'

He assessed her with a look. Something new crept into his voice, a tone he had not used before. 'She expected me to have sex with her.'

She dismissed it as mischievous, a blatant attempt to turn her against her friend. 'That was Cynthia. All bluster. She'd have run a mile.'

'In this cabin? She wasn't fooling, Rachel, believe me.'

With a casual air that didn't hide her true concern, she asked, 'So did you?'

'What?'

'Do it with her?'

'Come on! We had nothing in common except a laugh or two.'

'But that isn't why you killed her? Because she made a pass, and you weren't interested?'

'I told you the reason she had to go. I couldn't trust her to keep her mouth shut. If she'd lived, it would have been all over Wiltshire and all over for me.'

She stared ahead at the sea. 'I didn't know you were so cold-blooded.'

'Of course you didn't. Nobody knows until it's too late.'

If that was a veiled threat, it passed Rachel by. The grief she felt for Cynthia blotted out everything. She could picture her sitting beside him in this cockpit flirting in her cheerful, outrageous way without dreaming what was on his mind. How could he live with the knowledge of what he had done?

As if he was reading her thoughts, he said, 'You won't know this, but she had a kink about beating men. She wanted me to go along with it. She couldn't have asked me anything more certain to make me flip.'

It rang true. Poor, misguided Cynthia.

He said, 'There's a line in *Macbeth* when he says he's stepped in blood so far that there's no return.'

'At least Macbeth had a conscience.'

'At least I've told you the truth.'

She felt sick to the stomach. 'Would you take me back now?'

'Weren't you listening, Rachel? There's no going back once you've stepped in blood. Let's go up to the flybridge and get some air.'

23

Rachel was not seen again in Foxford. But her absence caused no concern at all for the first week, particularly after word got round that Gary's body had been exhumed early on Wednesday morning. It was no wonder she didn't wish to be at home when the press came knocking at her door. And there was no suggestion that she was running from the law; the police had no suspicion that she had murdered Gary.

They were waiting for the post mortem evidence that would nail Otis Joy. Meanwhile inquiries with the Toronto police confirmed Burton Sands's information. A theology student called Otis Joy had died in a car crash in Vancouver in 1993. It was also confirmed that someone of the same name was ordained into the Church of England in Brighton in September, 1994.

The person glorying in that name continued his parish duties with unflagging enthusiasm, a charming Baptism on Saturday (babies never cried when he held them), the usual Sunday services and an ecumenical meeting on Monday evening. Even by his own dynamic standards, his energy in these first days of the new year was remarkable. The sermons were inspired, delivered with passion and humanity and not without the touches of humour that were his trademark. He increased his visits to the lonely and the sick; the schools; the hospitals; the clubs and societies. It was almost as if he knew his days in Foxford were numbered.

PC George Mitchell and DCI Somerville were in attendance – standing well back – at the post mortem examination of Gary Jansen's remains. If they expected results, they were disappointed. 'There's nothing in the naked-eye findings to challenge the doctor's diagnosis,' the pathologist summed up, as he peeled off the gloves. 'Nothing inconsistent with simple cardiac failure. If you're looking for signs of a poisoning, I can't help you with what's here. It's going to be up to the forensic lab. I've taken all the samples I can, and we'll see what a toxicologist finds, if anything. I wouldn't put money on it.'

George Mitchell was horrified. Outside he said to Somerville, 'What if the results don't show anything? He could get away with serial murder and still be preaching to the village on Sundays.'

'George,' said Somerville, 'get real, will you?'

'What?'

'Some bastards do get away with it. We know they're guilty, but we don't have enough to convict.'

George said forlornly, 'We pinned everything on this. This was our best hope of getting the evidence.'

'Right. Let's be positive. They'll test for all the poisons in the book. You can be sure of that. Let's see what they come up with.'

'And meanwhile . . . ?'

'Don't let him know he's in the frame.'

'Do I go on playing Scrabble with him on Monday nights?'

Somerville laughed. 'That's up to you, but I wouldn't drink the coffee.'

'It's no joke. He's murdered people.'

'Conjecture.'

'We know he's a phoney. He changed his name.'

'So did St Paul.'

George sighed heavily.

Sensing, perhaps, that a senior CID man should be more upbeat, Somerville said, 'While we wait for these results, we'll beaver away, collecting statements from other crucial witnesses. I want to interview the woman, the widow, Mrs Jansen.'

'Rachel? She's not at home.'

'Where's she gone?'

'Don't know. Could be on holiday.'

'That's a pain. If any of this has truth in it, her dealings with the rector could be crucial. Can you find out where she went?'

'I'll try.'

'She's the parish treasurer, isn't she?'

George nodded.

'We'll need the account books to see if the rumours about Joy milking the funds have any basis. I suppose they're in her house?'

'That's where I'd expect them to be.'

'You don't think she's covering up for him?'

'For the rector? I hadn't thought of it.'

'If there *was* an affair going on . . .'

'Village gossip. I wouldn't pin too much on that. He's got his faults, God knows, but I don't think he's after the women.'

'She's got to be interviewed soon. Find her.'

She was not found, that week or the next. George asked around and discovered nothing. Rachel had told no one of her plans, just as Cynthia Haydenhall had gone off before Christmas without a word to anyone. A horrid possibility crept into George's mind.

*   *   *

Burton Sands called on George one evening and asked why the rector had not been arrested yet.

'It's out of my hands,' said George.

'It's disgraceful,' said Burton. 'I gave you enough evidence to put him away for the rest of his life. He's still at liberty.'

'They're working on it. You know Gary Jansen was exhumed,' said George.

'That was ten days ago.'

'It can't be hurried.'

'He'll get away if you don't arrest him.'

'He hasn't gone,' George pointed out. 'He could have gone, and he hasn't.'

'Bluffing it out.'

'That's why we have to make sure of everything.'

'Did they find any poison in the body?'

'We don't know yet.'

The test results came in from the Home Office Forensic Science Laboratory at Chepstow on a Friday morning two weeks after the autopsy. Tissue samples taken from Gary Jansen's body showed a minute trace of aconitine, one of the most virulent poisons known.

DCI Somerville called the lab to find out more.

'You might well ask,' said the toxicologist on the end of the phone. 'We don't know of a case in Britain since eighteen eighty-one. We were very excited when the gas-chromatographic screen picked it up. It's an alkaloid, a plant poison, derived from monkshood. The stuff grows wild in shady, moist places all over Europe and North America. You've probably got some near you. There's a cultivated variety as well. Usually it's purple in colour, but you can get it in white, pale blue and reddish-blue. Are you a gardener?'

'Some chance.'

'It was common at one time, flavour of the month, but you have to go a long way back. "Stepmothers' poison", the Greeks called it. And the Romans used it so much that the Emperor Trajan banned them from growing it in their gardens. Right through the Middle Ages people were poisoning their rich uncles with it. It fell out of favour in modern times because the neuropathy is so obvious. Tingling and numbness in the mouth, throat, hands and limbs. Severe stomach pains, nausea and vomiting. Diarrhoea. Want me to go on?'

'Be my guest.'

'OK. Loss of power in the limbs, giddiness, deafness and impairment of vision, indistinct speech, loss of consciousness and convulsions. Didn't the GP pick up on any of this?'

'He wasn't called till late.'

'Who called him – the patient?'

'The wife.'

'She must have seen him suffering.'

For a moment the case against Otis Joy teetered slightly. Then Somerville remembered. 'No. She was out all evening. Got back late.'

'Poor sod – having to endure all that on his own. Horrible symptoms.'

'When she got back he was too far gone to talk. The diagnosis was a heart attack.'

'Correct, in a sense. The ultimate cause of death is cardiac or respiratory failure from paralysis of the brain. Why wasn't there a PM at the time?'

'The GP had been treating him for a heart problem.'

'Even so.'

'Perkins is one of the old school. Ought to be retired.'

'He will be, if this comes to court.'

Somerville thanked him and said they were sure to be in touch again. He phoned George Mitchell and told him the news.

George said, 'I'm punching the air, sir. We've got him at last!'

'Can you get over here fast?'

'You bet I can.'

At the main police station, Warminster's CID team was setting up an incident room and Somerville was calling himself the SIO – senior investigating officer. George was shown into an office where three senior detectives waited.

'I can tell you about monkshood,' George offered. He was more of a countryman than any of these clever dicks. 'The leaves look a little like parsley, except this grows at least a metre high. It grows wild in the woods round here, down by the River Wylye. Purple flowers. You don't come across it so much as when I was a lad. Farmers get rid of it as soon as it appears because it's just as deadly for animals as it is for humans. The "monk's hood" is the shape of the flower.'

'There's a garden variety,' Somerville said.

'Yes, you can get it in other colours if you want. Looks nice enough in your herbaceous border if you put it in a shady position.'

'Does it come with a health warning?' one of the detectives asked.

'Certainly ought to.'

'George, you know what I'm going to ask next?' said Somerville.

'If it grows in the rectory garden? I couldn't tell you. It's a wilderness, that garden. The rector doesn't have time to look after it.'

Somerville didn't like being so predictable. 'Did I say anything about his garden? If the plant occurs locally, it doesn't have to be grown at the rectory. Come to that, he could have used pure aconitine in powder form. If that tosspot Sands is right, Joy has a fine collection of poisons.'

'Where would he get the pure poison?'

'God knows.'

'A pharmacy?'

'Unlikely. It says in the book it was formerly used in low concentrations as a liniment for rheumatism, but that was many years back. It went into a cure for toothache, too, applied as a tincture.'

'Dodgy,' said George. 'Personally, I'd rather put up with the toothache.'

Somerville saw no humour in the situation. 'If the Crown Prosecution Service are going to take this on board we have to give them more than we've got so far.'

'Proof of poisoning,' George said. 'You've got that.'

'Big deal. And now all we have to prove is that Otis Joy administered it, and how, and why.'

'Gary Jansen was seen going into the rectory on the afternoon of his death,' said George. 'Ann Porter was a witness to that.'

One of the others asked, 'How long does this stuff take to kick in?'

'Up to an hour,' said Somerville. 'You get the tingling and numbness in the mouth first, and the other symptoms follow on. Death can take anything up to several hours.'

'Well, then.'

'A sighting of the victim going into the rectory won't be enough for the CPS,' said Somerville with a glare. 'They want the lot, full chain of evidence. A poisoning has to go to the Central Criminal Court. There's sure to be massive public interest.'

There was a moment for reflection while the senior detectives imagined the sensation of a clergyman on trial for a series of murders. Warminster had not seen anything like it since the spate of flying saucer stories in the sixties.

'When this breaks, we're going to be under siege,' said Somerville.

'He's got to be questioned,' one of the others pointed out.

'So do we nick him now?' said another.

Somerville vibrated his lips. He didn't want the press and television muscling in at this delicate stage of the enquiry. 'George, you know the guy. Would he come in and make a voluntary statement? He won't want the media crawling all over him any more than we do.'

'Are you asking my advice, Mr Somerville, or do you want me to fetch him in?'

'Both.'

'But I'm not CID.'

'You're the man who visits his house for the Scrabble. Persuade him – gently. Low key, right?'

'I can try.'

'You don't sound optimistic.'

'With Otis, you can't be. Just when I think I'm way ahead of him, he comes up with a seven-letter word.'

'Like murder?'

'That's six.'

24

George was uneasy with the assignment he'd been given. Even allowing that Otis Joy was probably a wicked and dangerous man, it was a kind of betrayal to trade on their friendship to bring him in. He wished he'd never mentioned the Scrabble evenings to Somerville. 'Low key', they'd blithely told him, as if it was a routine matter to ask a man in holy orders to accompany you to the police station and make a voluntary statement.

So when he rang twice at the rectory door and got no response he was mightily relieved. He decided the rector was out in the parish somewhere doing his pastoral duties, sensible man.

He went home for lunch.

After lunch, he thought he'd better try again.

No one was there. A seed of uncertainty was sown. Had Otis done a runner?

He called at the shop and asked Davy Todd if he'd seen the rector.

Davy said, 'Well, he'll be at Warminster by now, won't he?'

'Will he?' George said more cheerfully, assuming that CID had come to their senses and sent someone else to pick him up.

'That's where half the village has gone today. For the confirmation service at All Hallows.'

George sighed.

'If you went to church regular, you'd know what's going on,' added Todd.

'What time is the service?'

'Three. You could get there if you want.'

George weighed his options. It was still down to him to round up the suspect. He couldn't interrupt a church service, but if he caught Otis coming out, it would be a short walk to the nick, which was just across the street from All Hallows. He was in duty bound to make the attempt.

He went back for the car.

The confirmation candidates stood in groups near the west door of All Hallows, the largest, though not the most attractive, church in Warminster. The old building had suffered badly from modern restorers, whose aim seemed to have been to remove all traces of the Norman origins, all the arches, scallops and mouldings, all the mellow local stone, and replace it with faced blocks the colour of margarine. However, it was roomy inside, which was why it had been chosen for today's service.

George spotted the Foxford group – not quite half the village, but getting on for forty of them, including families. He went over and asked Ann Porter if she'd seen the rector. She said he'd arrived and gone into the church to get into his robes.

The question must have been overheard by Burton Sands, because he came over and said, 'Are you going to arrest him?'

'What for?' said Ann in surprise.

George raised his chin a little and said, 'That isn't the way we do things, Burton.'

'You don't do anything,' said Burton.

'What's this about?' demanded Ann, already hyped up for the occasion. 'Has our rector been up to naughties?'

George moved away, but Burton came with him. 'You know Rachel Jansen has gone? That's another one. You've got to act before he wipes out the rest of us.'

'Don't push it, Burton. Things are happening,' said George.

'Like what? You exhumed Gary Jansen and no one has heard a thing. That was over two weeks ago.'

'We had to wait for the tests,' muttered George. 'Why don't you go back to the others now?'

'"Had to wait for the tests,"' Burton taunted him. 'No action at all. I gave you enough information to put him away for the rest of his life and nothing has happened except he's claimed another victim.'

'Why don't you get your mind on what you're here for?' George told him. 'Think some Christian thoughts.'

'How can I, when he's going to join in the service? You could arrest him now.'

'I'm going to speak to him when it's over.'

'Really?'

George shouldn't have said more, but it was nice to take the wind out of Burton's sails, and the temptation was great. 'The test results came in this morning. They found a trace of poison in the body.'

People were entering the church now, and John Neary had his hand in the air, beckoning to Burton to rejoin the Foxford group.

'What poison?'

'A deadly one,' said George. 'Look, they're going in.'

He decided to go into the service and sit at the back. Why stand outside on a January afternoon when they had the heating on? He wasn't a regular church-goer, but he'd been confirmed in his teens, by the unfortunate Marcus

Glastonbury, fated to be remembered as the Bend Over Bishop. George listened to the mighty organ and tried not to think about the late bishop.

The candidates from six local churches were seated in the front pews, and many relatives attended in support, so the nave was packed. Latecomers had to find places in the crosswise seating in the transepts. The clergy, when they entered behind the bishop in their glittering vestments, sat in the choirstalls. George spotted Joy looking devout and untroubled in a cream chasuble with a green and gold cross motif. In this sanctified place it was more than George could do to credit the dreadful crimes the man was supposed to have committed. It took the single-mindedness of Burton Sands to hold onto the conviction that a murderer was in their midst.

The service began with a few words of welcome from the new bishop, a short, stout man with horn-rimmed spectacles, wearing a crimson mitre. His voice was amplified, so he must have had a microphone cunningly secreted in the robes. Briefly he explained what would happen, and its significance, and that afterwards there would be tea and cakes for everyone in the parish rooms. A hymn followed, and then the bishop spoke the words of the preface in a clear, brisk, business-like fashion. No one would doze off while he was leading a service. Quite soon he had reached the main part, the questions and responses leading up to the moment when each candidate in turn went forward to kneel before him and be admitted to full membership by the hand placed on the head.

George watched the Foxford people go forward, the children first, and then the adults, including Sands, Neary and Ann Porter.

It all progressed seamlessly into the communion service when the candidates were to receive the sacrament for the first time. After the parish priests had knelt in front of the bishop and received their wafers and wine, they helped him administer it to the new communicants, who approached the altar rail. Later, the rest of the congregation would be invited to come forward.

At the back of the church, George had decided he would not join in this time. He would have felt self-conscious going up to the front in his uniform. Instead, he watched and waited, trying to work out what he would say to the rector. It would have to be over the tea and cakes. 'We're trying to clarify a few matters, Otis, and we think you could help us.' No, better still: '. . . we'd welcome your advice.' How about 'expert advice'? That would be overdoing it. '. . . welcome your input'? Perhaps not. 'We're trying to make sense of a few things and we'd welcome your advice.' Nonchalantly he would add, 'Just across the street at the police station.'

Sorted.

He sat back in the pew and submitted to the solemnity of what was going on, listening to the soft strains of the organ playing a communion interlude, doing his best to be respectful and forget he was a policeman on duty. So it was remarkable that a terrible thought popped into his brain just as Otis Joy was moving along the altar rail with the chalice in one hand and the napkin in the other.

One of the other priests had already administered the wafers to the Foxford candidates. Joy was following, quietly intoning the words of the service.

George felt compelled to act. The congregation at large hadn't moved yet, but he did. By chance he had a place at the end of the pew and he stood up and strode up the aisle, his regulation shoes clattering on the paved floor. Presently he broke into a run. It had to be a real emergency for George to run. People turned to stare. Clearly he wasn't racing to be first in line at the altar rail. Probably if he had not been in uniform someone would have tried to stop him. Even the bishop looked up.

George continued running, as unstoppable as the Athenian who brought news of the victory at Marathon. Otis Joy was one of the few who didn't look up. He was absorbed in what he was doing.

Unluckily George was not built for speed. He wasn't in time to stop Joy administering the wine to Burton Sands. Burton got off his knees, took a pace back from the rail, turned, put his hand to his throat and collapsed like a felled tree.

Joy didn't give him a glance. He had already moved on and was offering the chalice to the next communicant, Ann Porter. Ann, of course, was a crucial witness in the case, the person who had seen Gary Jansen visit the rectory on the day he was poisoned.

George yelled, 'Ann, don't drink it!'

This time Joy looked up.

Everyone looked up. Even the people kneeling to receive the sacrament turned to see what was going on. They saw the burly policeman leap over Burton's lifeless body and dash the chalice from Joy's hands.

The bishop said, 'Christ Almighty!' into his amplifying system and was heard all over the church. He could have said something worse.

25

'If that was your idea of "low key", what happens when you pull out all the stops?'

George Mitchell tried to let Somerville's sarcasm pass him by. Silence was the best option.

'You dash up the aisle like a demented bride and knock the communion wine out of the priest's hand, assuming it was poisoned? Is that discreet policing? What were you doing in the church in the first place? Don't answer that. I don't wish to know.' Somerville turned to one of his team. 'What's the latest on Mr Sands?'

'He's fine, sir. Gone home.'

'Fully recovered, then?'

'He fainted.'

'I don't blame him. I would have fainted if I'd seen this buffalo bearing down on me.'

'He says he thought he must have swallowed poison. He passed out with the shock.'

Somerville turned back to George. 'So having created mayhem, stopped the service, splashed wine over the bishop's hand-embroidered vestments – a laundry bill that puts us over budget for this year and the next – you charge the Rector of Foxford with attempted murder and march him over here in cuffs and hand him to the custody sergeant. Not what I asked you to do, was it? Jesus Christ, what a foul-up.'

George could have said he had perceived a real danger to the lives of two crucial witnesses, but he knew there was no defence after the bear garden he'd made of the communion service. He just thanked his stars he was uniform branch, not CID. Somerville could rant to kingdom come. The fact remained that he'd asked a uniformed officer to do a job that should have gone to a detective.

Somerville raked a hand through his hair and groaned. 'So how do we unscramble this mess?'

There was an uncomfortable silence in the major incident room. Finally he said to George, 'When you arrested him on suspicion of murder, did you mention which murder?'

George thought about it and shook his head. At the time, he'd thought Burton was dead. He would have given Burton's name if he had given any, but he had not.

'That's a small mercy, then. You'd better leave us while you're riding high.'

George left.

Somerville looked at his watch. 'Let's go to work on this tosspot. We've had him in the cells for an hour already.'

Otis Joy sat behind the table in the interview room looking as you would expect a priest mistakenly arrested to look: puzzled, troubled and innocent. He was no longer in his church robes, but he had the air of a Christian martyr.

Somerville couldn't help being affected by it. 'This isn't the way we wanted this to be, Rector,' he admitted humbly once the taping procedures had been explained. 'It's been triggered by events beyond my control. PC Mitchell – the officer in the church – exceeded his brief. He shouldn't have been there.'

'It was sacrilege,' said Joy, seizing the high ground.

'Possibly.'

'No, Chief Inspector. Not possibly. Certainly.'

'All right, have it your way.'

'If the bishop is worth his salt, he'll demand an enquiry from the Chief Constable.'

'We'll see.'

'About what happened in the church and what's happened to me since.'

'Have you suffered any violence?'

'To my reputation, yes. Three hundred people saw me handcuffed in church.'

'Not without cause.'

'The man fainted. He wasn't poisoned with the blessed sacrament. It's a revolting idea.'

'I said PC Mitchell made a mistake.'

'Is that where the buck stops? With George Mitchell?'

Somerville had no answer.

Joy went on, 'I know him pretty well. He respects the church. He must have been under orders.'

'He was supposed to invite you here to help us with our enquiries into a suspicious death.'

'He arrested me for murder.'

'If you want to make an issue of this,' said Somerville, 'you *are* here on a murder rap. We exhumed the body of Gary Jansen. The results of the forensic tests came in today and traces of poison were found.'

'That doesn't surprise me,' said Joy – and he didn't appear surprised either.

'You *know* he was poisoned?'

'Oh, yes.'

At first it seemed Somerville hadn't heard, but after a moment's delay he exchanged a triumphant glance with the detective inspector sitting beside him, turned back to Joy and said, 'How do you know?'

'Sorry. Can't say.'

'Why not?'

'I don't betray a confidence.'

'What do you mean – someone confessed to you?'

'No, no. We don't go in for confessions in the Church of England, except in the General Confession. "We have done those things which we ought not to have done."'

'If you know someone poisoned this man, it's your duty to inform us.'

'I'm not taking lessons from you about my duty.'

'You're bullshitting, Rector. You know about this because you poisoned Gary Jansen yourself.'

'Is that the reason I'm here? You believe I murdered Gary?'

'Yes.'

'Then you'd better release me. I didn't.'

'We've obtained a search warrant. We'll go through the rectory until we find that poison.'

'I'd say, "Be my guest," but in the circumstances . . .'

'Don't come it, with me, Rector. You're going to go down for this one. We have the proof.'

If they did, it made no impact on Joy in the next twenty minutes. They fired questions at him and nothing of substance emerged before the door of the interview room opened and Somerville was asked by one of his team to step outside. 'This had better be important,' he said.

It was.

A man called Terry Rye had contacted Bournemouth Police after recognising a picture in the *Daily Mail* of a woman reported drowned. She was named as Cynthia Haydenhall. Terry Rye remembered seeing the same woman at Cobb's Marina in Holes Bay, Poole, shortly before Christmas. She'd visited one of the boat owners, a man called Bill Beggarstaff, and gone aboard his motor-cruiser, the *Revelation,* which was a state-of-the-art job, a forty-footer, one of the biggest in the marina. The boat had left the marina the same morning and not returned since.

Somerville was chastened. 'I was bloody sure Cynthia was one of Joy's victims.'

'Could it be another alias?' said the sergeant, trying to be upbeat.

'Beggarstaff? If you believe that, you've got to believe the Rector of Foxford owns a motor-cruiser worth a couple of hundred grand. On his stipend, he couldn't pay the mooring fees, let alone the price of a boat.'

'So it's someone else?'

'Someone she thought was her sugar-daddy, I expect. Some rich crook who had what he wanted from her and dumped her overboard.'

'If she boarded the boat in Poole, why did her car turn up in Bournemouth?'

'Beggarstaff must have moved it there. Are Bournemouth going to pick him up?'

'When they find him, sir.'

'Fat chance. By now he'll be on the Costa del Sol with all the other ex-pat villains.'

He went back to Otis Joy and bluffed. 'Things are not looking good for you, Rector.'

'Really?'

'We're closing in. But let's concentrate on Gary Jansen, shall we? We have a witness who saw him going into your rectory a matter of hours before he died.'

'That's no big deal,' said Joy. 'Gary asked to come. He had some idea that his wife and I were over-friendly. I put him right and he went on his way.'

'You weren't friendly with her?'

'I said "over-friendly". You know what I mean. I'm

friendly with everyone in the parish, or try to be. I'm not so daft as to start relationships.'

'Did he eat or drink anything while he was with you?'

'No.'

'You say you put him right. Was there a fight?'

Joy closed his eyes. 'I'm a man of God, Chief Inspector. I don't fight. It was a civilised chat.'

'This "man of God" stuff wants examining. You claim to be an ordained priest.'

'I am.'

'You went through a service, yes.'

'I went through theological college.'

'St Cyriac's?'

'Yes.'

'For about a year. According to their records you were at a Canadian college before that.'

'Is that a crime?'

'There's no record of you at the Canadian college. Someone else with a similar name was killed in a car crash. You took over his name and came to England claiming to be trained.'

'It's official – the change of name. It appealed to me when I read it somewhere. It is allowed, you know.'

'What were you called before that?'

'Brown. John Brown. Otis Joy has a better ring to it, you must agree.'

'Where did you study before you started at St Cyriac's?'

'This is sounding more and more like an interview for a job. I was in Canada. I had private tuition from one of the staff at Milton Davidson. That's why you won't find my name in the register.'

Somerville knew nothing about training for the priesthood. He was floundering. He terminated the interview and had Joy returned to the cells.

Under PACE, the Police and Criminal Evidence Act, he was required to review Joy's detention after six hours. In theory, they could keep him for up to thirty-six before applying to a magistrate for an extension, but it had to be justified. There had to be some prospect of formally charging the man.

The whole thing had been set in motion too soon. He had George bloody Mitchell to thank for that.

'The search of the rectory had better turn up something we can pin on him,' he said to his sergeant. 'When did they go in? Two hours ago?'

'Roughly.'

'Contact them. See what they've got.'

The sergeant called the team at Foxford. He reported back to Somerville: 'Sod all, so far. It's a big building, but they've done all the obvious stuff already.'

'The poisons in the cellar?'

'There were a few harmless things in a wooden cabinet: some aspirin, indigestion tablets, a cure for mouth ulcers, ointment for athlete's foot, Alka-Seltzer.'

'The bugger's changed it all over.'

'Very likely. He's way above us plods.'

'We're not going to stick anything on him,' said Somerville, all his confidence drained. 'We can strap him all day and all night about crimes he won't admit, and he'll never roll over.'

'Can't we get him on the embezzlement?'

'That's a job for the fraud squad. It takes months – and you can bet the bloody books have disappeared with Rachel Jansen.'

'So a murderer walks free?'

'We're in the real world, sergeant.'

Otis Joy was released from custody at nine fifteen that

evening. In a philosophical mood, he returned to the rectory and found it ravaged by the search team. He packed a few things into a rucksack and put his Moulton bike in the boot of the Cortina and drove out of Foxford for ever.

26

P artings are painful and this one needed to be violent. At around 5.30 a.m., Joy drove into a breaker's yard three miles out of Lymington, ripped the number plates and the tax-disc from the old Cortina and smashed the windscreen and slashed two of the tyres, before abandoning it among scores of other unwanted cars. With just the rucksack as baggage, he got on his fold-up bike, pedalled into the town and caught the first ferry crossing to the Isle of Wight.

Yarmouth, on the quiet side of the island, will never rival Cowes as a sailing resort, but it has a good harbour once you have negotiated the treacherous waters of the Narrows. Here, Otis Joy had berthed the *Revelation* some weeks earlier.

He was pleased, as always, to get the first sight of his motor-cruiser, white sides dappled with reflections in rare February sunlight. The harbour authority had recently upgraded the moorings with new pontoons. Yachtsmen preferred them to the old fore-and-aft moorings because the boats stayed static.

He wheeled the bike along the pontoon and lifted everything aboard and took stock of his boat. On his instruction, the name had been painted over. It was now the *Catatonia*. The superstructure had been cleaned, he was pleased to find. He opened the saloon door and said, 'Anyone aboard?'

A voice from the cabin called, 'Otis?'

'Who else?'

Rachel came up the steps, dressed for the maritime life in a fleece windstopper and jeans. She had been living here – holed up, as she thought of it – for almost three weeks, at Joy's invitation.

She gave him a questioning look. They didn't embrace.

'You've kept her shipshape,' he complimented her. 'How are you taking to life on the water?'

'It's OK.' Anxiously she asked, 'What's going on in Foxford?'

'Too much. Time to move on.'

'Do they know about me?'

'No.'

'Thank God for that.' She eyed the rucksack. 'You look as if you've come to stay.'

'There are two cabins,' he said. 'Of course if you don't feel comfortable with me aboard . . .'

'It's your boat. I'll do whatever you decide,' she said stiffly, hands together, twisting her fingers.

'Let's make coffee and talk it over.'

They went down to the saloon.

'We're two of a kind, aren't we?' he said when the mugs were on the table.

'Notorious?'

'You're not. No one suspects you. As a matter of fact, they tried to stitch me up for Gary's murder.'

Nervous of him, she tried to make light of it. 'Get away! That would have been ironic.'

'Yes, I might have been starting a life sentence in Parkhurst thinking of you only ten miles up the road living in my boat.'

'I would have looked after it.'

'I can see.'

'And instead?'

'I need a new parish.'

She laughed with more confidence. That *had* to be one of his jokes.

But he went on solemnly, 'I was thinking about New Zealand. I doubt if I'll be welcome in the Church of England any more.'

'You want to remain a priest?'

'Passionately. I must.'

'After all that's happened?'

'It's what I do. By now, you know what drives me.'

'Won't they know about you in New Zealand? It's a small world these days.'

'I'll change my name, of course. I was thinking of Wilby. How does that grab you?'

'Wilby? It's unusual.'

'Wilby Good. Not bad for a reverend.'

She still didn't know how much of this was meant to amuse. After a pause, she said, 'That's a long voyage.'

'We can do it in stages, stopping along the way.'

'*We?*'

'I said we're two of a kind.'

'It doesn't mean you're stuck with me,' said Rachel.

Otis shook his head. He didn't think of it like that. He saw her in a wholly different light since she had shared her secret with him. She was interesting now. Attractive. Desirable in a way that had been impossible before. 'Rachel, I'm asking you to come with me if you will. We know the worst about each other, and that can be a basis for trust. Before you took me into your confidence about what happened with Gary, I wouldn't have told a living soul the things I've done. We can be open with each other.'

She said, 'I want to forget the past.'

'So would you consider being Mrs Good?'

She coloured deeply. 'You mean pretend?'

'No. For real.'

'I don't know.' She was too surprised to give an answer. 'I don't have to decide today?'

'Not for months,' he said. 'See if I live up to my new name.'

They left Yarmouth on the high tide.

Later in the day, they berthed at St Peter Port in Guernsey and picked up some stores. They had supper ashore. When they returned to the boat, he took out a black velvet bag.

'What's that?' she asked.

He rattled the tiles inside. 'You *do* play Scrabble?'

Towards the end of the game, he made a seven-letter word.

Getaway.

CRIME AND THRILLER FAN?

CHECK OUT THECRIMEVAULT.COM

The online home of
exceptional crime fiction

KEEP YOURSELF
IN SUSPENSE

Sign up to our newsletter for regular recommendations,
competitions and exclusives at www.thecrimevault.com/connect

Follow us on twitter for all the latest news @TheCrimeVault

1

D. Bilbrough
Copyright © 1977 Thankyou Music

Abba Father, let me be
Yours and Yours alone.
May my will for ever be
Evermore Your own.
Never let my heart grow cold,
Never let me go,
Abba Father, let me be
Yours and Yours alone.

KT-514-174

2   Henry Francis Lyte, 1793–1847

Abide with me; fast falls the eventide;
The darkness deepens; Lord, with me abide
When other helpers fail, and comforts flee,
Help of the helpless, O abide with me.

Swift to its close ebbs out life's little day;
Earth's joys grow dim, its glories pass away;
Change and decay in all around I see:
O Thou who changest not, abide with me!

I need Thy presence every passing hour;
What but Thy grace can foil the tempter's
    power?
Who like Thyself my guide and stay can be?
Through cloud and sunshine, O abide with me.

I fear no foe, with Thee at hand to bless;
Ills have no weight, and tears no bitterness;
Where is death's sting? where, grave thy
    victory?
I triumph still, if Thou abide with me.

Hold Thou Thy Cross before my closing eyes,
Shine through the gloom, and point me to the
    skies;
Heaven's morning breaks, and earth's vain
    shadows flee:
In life, in death, O Lord, abide with me!

3

All hail King Jesus
All hail Emmanuel
King of Kings,
Lord of Lords, bright morning star,
Ev'ry day you give me breath
I'll sing your praises
And I'll reign with you throughout eternity.

In His presence daily live.

I surrender all,
I surrender all,
All to Thee, my blessed Saviour,
I surrender all,

All to Jesus I surrender,
Humbly at His feet I bow,
Worldly pleasures all forsaken,
Take me, Jesus, take me now.

All to Jesus I surrender,
Make me, Saviour, wholly Thine;
Let me feel the Holy Spirit,
Truly know that Thou art mine.

All to Jesus I surrender,
Lord, I give myself to Thee;
Fill me with Thy love and power,
Let Thy blessing fall on me.

All to Jesus I surrender,
Now I feel the sacred flame;
Oh, the joy of full salvation!
Glory, glory to His name!

5   Edward Perronet, 1726–92
       John Rippon, 1751–1836

All hail the power of Jesus' name!
Let angels prostrate fall;
Bring forth the royal diadem,
And crown Him Lord of all.

Crown Him, ye martyrs of our God,
Who from His altar call;
Extol the stem of Jesse's rod
And crown Him Lord of all.

Ye seed of Israel's chosen race,
And ransomed from the fall,
Hail Him who saves you by His grace,
And crown Him Lord of all.

Let every kindred, every tribe,
On this terrestrial ball,
To Him all majesty ascribe,
And crown Him Lord of all.

O that with yonder sacred throng
We at His feet may fall,
Join in the everlasting song,
And crown Him Lord of all!

6 William Kethe, 1520–94

All people that on earth do dwell,
Sing to the Lord with cheerful voice:
Him serve with mirth, His praise forth tell;
Come ye before Him and rejoice.

The Lord, ye know, is God indeed;
Without our aid He did us make:
We are His folk, He doth us feed;
And for His sheep He doth us take.

O enter then His gates with praise;
Approach with joy His courts unto;
Praise, laud, and bless His name always,
For it is seemly so to do.

For why? The Lord our God is good;
His mercy is for ever sure;
His truth at all times firmly stood,
And shall from age to age endure.

7 Anon

1. **Alleluia** (*repeat seven times*)

2. How I love Him

3. Blessed Jesus

4. My Redeemer

5. Jesus is Lord

6. Alleluia

8 Copyright © 1975
Celebration Services (International) Ltd.

All the riches of His grace,
All the fulness of His blessings,
All the sweetness of His love
He gives to you, He gives to me.

Oh, the blood of Jesus, (*repeat twice*)
It washes white as snow.

Oh, the word of Jesus, (*repeat twice*)
It cleanses white as snow.

Oh, the love of Jesus, (*repeat twice*)
It makes His body whole.

Oh, the blood of Jesus, (repeat twice)
It washes white as snow.

9 Copyright © 1973 Donald Fishel The Word of God

Alleluia, alleluia,
Give thanks to the risen Lord,
Alleluia, alleluia,
Give praise to His name.

Jesus is Lord of all the earth
He is the King of creation

Spread the good news o'er all the earth
Jesus has died and has risen.

We have been crucified with Christ.
Now we shall live for ever.

God has proclaimed the just reward,
Life for all men, alleluia.

Come let us praise the living God,
Joyfully sing to our Saviour.

10 John Newton 1725–1807

Amazing grace! How sweet the sound
That saved a wretch like me.
I once was lost, but now am found,
Was blind, but now I see.

'Twas grace that taught my heart to fear,
And grace my fears relieved.
How precious did that grace appear
The hour I first believed.

Through many dangers, toils and snares
I have already come;
'Tis grace hath brought me safe thus far
And grace will lead me home.

When we've been there ten thousand years
Bright shining as the sun,
We've no less days to sing God's praise
Than when we've first begun.

11 Charles Wesley, 1707–88

And can it be that I should gain
An interest in the Saviour's blood?
Died He for me, who caused his pain?
For me, who Him to death pursued?
Amazing love! How can it be
That Thou, my God, shouldst die for me!

'Tis mystery all! The Immortal dies:
Who can explore His strange design?
In vain the first-born seraph tries
To sound the depths of love divine.
'Tis mercy all! Let earth adore,
Let angel minds inquire no more.

He left His Father's throne above –
So free, so infinite His grace –
Emptied Himself of all but love,
And bled for Adam's helpless race.
'Tis mercy all, immense and free;
For, O my God, it found out me!

Long my imprisoned spirit lay
Fast bound in sin and nature's night;
Thine eye diffused a quickening ray –
I woke, the dungeon flamed with light;
My chains fell off, my heart was free,
I rose, went forth, and followed Thee.

No condemnation now I dread;
Jesus, and all in Him, is mine!
Alive in Him, my living Head,
And clothed in righteousness divine,
Bold I approach the eternal throne,
And claim the crown, through Christ, my own.

12 Gordon V. Thompson – Canada
Copyright © 1974 by Eric Glass

Behold, the darkness shall cover the earth,
And gross darkness the people;
But the Lord shall arise upon thee,
And His glory shall be seen upon thee.

Arise, shine; for thy light is come,
And the glory of the Lord is risen.
Oh, arise, shine; for thy light is come,
And the glory of the Lord is upon thee.

The gentiles shall come to thy light,
And kings to the brightness of thy rising.
And they shall call thee the city of the Lord,
The Zion of the Holy One of Israel.

Lift up thine eyes round about and see,
They gather themselves together.
And they shall come, thy sons from afar,
And thy daughters shall be nursed at thy side.

Then shalt thou see and flow together,
And thy heart shall be enlarged;
The abundance of the sea is converted unto
    thee,
And the nations shall come unto thee.

The sun shall no more go down, neither
Shall the moon withdraw itself;
But the Lord shall be thine everlasting light,
And the days of thy mourning shall be ended.

13 Copyright © 1979 Word Music (UK)

As we are gathered, Jesus is here,
One with each other, Jesus is here,
Joined by the Spirit, washed in the blood,
Part of the body, the church of God,
As we are gathered, Jesus is here.
One with each other, Jesus is here.

14 Copyright Control

Ascribe greatness to our God the rock,
His work is perfect and all His ways are just
    Repeat 2 lines
A God of faithfulness and without injustice,
Good and upright is He.
    Repeat 2 lines

15 Caroline Noel, 1817–77

At the name of Jesus
Every knee shall bow,
Every tongue confess Him
King of glory now.
'Tis the Father's pleasure
We should call Him Lord,
Who from the beginning
Was the mighty Word:

Mighty and mysterious
In the highest height,
God from everlasting,
Very light of light.
In the Father's bosom,
With the Spirit blest,
Love, in love eternal,
Rest, in perfect rest.

Humbled for a season,
To receive a name
From the lips of sinners
Unto whom He came,
Faithfully He bore it
Spotless to the last,
Brought it back victorious,
When from death He passed;

Bore it up triumphant
With its human light,
Through all ranks of creatures,
To the central height;
To the throne of Godhead,
To the Father's breast,
Filled it with the glory
Of that perfect rest.

In your hearts enthrone Him;
There let Him subdue
All that is not holy,
All that is not true:
Crown Him as your captain
In temptation's hour,
Let His will enfold you
In its light and power.

Brothers, this Lord Jesus
Shall return again,
With His Father's glory,
With His angel-train;
For all wreaths of empire
Meet upon His brow,
And our hearts confess Him
King of glory now.

16

Be still and know that I am God (*repeat twice*).

17
Ancient Irish
tr. by Mary Elizabeth Byrne, 1880–1931
Versified by Eleanor Henrietta Hull

Be Thou my vision, O Lord of my heart;
Naught be all else to me, save that Thou art –
Thou my best thought, by day or by night,
Waking or sleeping, Thy presence my light.

Be Thou my Wisdom, Thou my true Word;
I ever with Thee, Thou with me, Lord;
Thou my great Father, I Thy true son;
Thou in me dwelling, and I with Thee one.

Be Thou my battle-shield, sword for the fight,
Be Thou my dignity, Thou my delight.
Thou my soul's shelter, Thou my high tower:
Raise Thou me heavenward,
  O Power of my power.

Riches I heed not, nor man's empty praise,
Thou mine inheritance, now and always:
Thou and Thou only, first in my heart,
High King of heaven, my treasure Thou art.

High King of heaven, after victory won,
May I reach heaven's joys,
  O bright heaven's Sun!
Heart of my own heart, whatever befall,
Still be my Vision, O Ruler of all.

18
Gloria & William J. Gaither
Copyright © 1971 by William J. Gaither
Coronation Music

God sent His Son, they called Him Jesus;
He came to love, heal, and forgive;
He lived and died to buy my pardon,
An empty grave is there to prove my Saviour
  lives.

  Because He lives I can face tomorrow;
  Because He lives all fear is gone;
  Because I know He holds the future,
  And life is worth the living just because He
    lives.

How sweet to hold a new-born baby,
And feel the pride, and joy he gives;
But greater still the calm assurance,
This child can face uncertain days because He
  lives.

And then one day I'll cross the river;
I'll fight life's final war with pain;
And then as death gives way to vict'ry,
I'll see the lights of glory and I'll know He lives.

19
Phil Potter
Copyright © 1981 Thankyou Music

Because your love is better than life,
With my lips I will glorify you,
I will praise you as long as I live,
In your name I lift my hands.

Because your Son has given me life,
With my lips I will glorify you,
I will praise you as long as I live,
In your name I lift my hands.

Because your Spirit is filling my life,
With my lips I will glorify you,
I will praise you as long as I live,
In your name I lift my hands.

Because your love is better than life,
With my lips I will glorify you,
I will praise you as long as I live,
In your name I lift my hands.

20
Elizabeth Cecilia Clephane, 1836–69

Beneath the Cross of Jesus
I fain would take my stand –
The shadow of a mighty rock
Within a weary land;
A home within a wilderness,
A rest upon the way,
From the burning of the noontide heat
And the burden of the day.

Upon that Cross of Jesus
Mine eye at times can see
The very dying form of One
Who suffered there for me.
And from my stricken heart, with tears,
Two wonders I confess –
The wonders of redeeming love,
And my own worthlessness.

I take, O Cross, thy shadow,
For my abiding-place!
I ask no other sunshine than
The sunshine of His face;
Content to let the world go by,
To know no gain or loss –
My sinful self my only shame,
My glory all – the Cross.

21 B. Gillman
Copyright © 1977 Thankyou Music

Bind us together Lord,
Bind us together
With cords that cannot be broken;
Bind us together Lord,
Bind us together
O bind us together with love

There is only one God,
There is only one King,
There is only one Body
That is why we sing:

Made for the glory of God,
Purchased by His precious Son.
Born with the right to be clean,
For Jesus the victory has won. . . .

You are the family of God.
You are the promise divine.
You are God's chosen desire.
You are the glorious new wine. . . .

Alternative words are at end of this book

22 Frances van Alstyne, 1820–1915

Blessed assurance, Jesus is mine:
O what a foretaste of glory divine!
Heir of salvation, purchase of God;
Born of His Spirit, washed in His blood.
This is my story, this is my song,
Praising my Saviour all the day long.

Perfect submission, perfect delight,
Visions of rapture burst on my sight;
Angels descending, bring from above
Echoes of mercy, whispers of love.

Perfect submission, all is at rest,
I in my Saviour am happy and blest;
Watching and waiting, looking above,
Filled with His goodness, lost in His love.

23 Anon

Break forth into joy O my soul; (*repeat*)
In the presence of the Lord
There is joy for evermore;
Break forth, break forth into joy.

24 Psalm 103

Bless the Lord, O my soul,
And all that is within me,
Bless His holy Name.
He has done great things, (*repeat twice*)
Bless His holy Name.
Bless the Lord, O my soul,
And all that is within me,
Bless His holy Name.

25 Edwin Hatch, 1835–89

Breathe on me, Breath of God;
Fill me with life anew.
That I may love what Thou dost love,
And do what Thou wouldst do.

Breathe on me, Breath of God,
Until my heart is pure,
Until with Thee I will one will,
To do and to endure.

Breathe on me, Breath of God,
Till I am wholly Thine,
Until this earthly part of me
Glows with Thy fire divine.

Breathe on me, Breath of God;
So shall I never die,
But live with Thee the perfect life
Of Thine eternity.

26 Psalm 103

Bless the Lord, O my soul, (*repeat*)
And all that is within me
Bless His holy Name,
Bless the Lord, O my Soul, (*repeat*)
And all that is within me
Bless His holy Name,
King of Kings (for ever and ever)
Lord of Lords (for ever and ever)
King of Kings (for ever and ever)
King of Kings and Lord of lords,
Bless the Lord, O my soul, (*repeat*)
And all that is within me
Bless His holy Name,
Bless the Lord, O my soul (*repeat*)
And all that is within me
Bless His Holy Name.

27 from the Latin (c. seventh century)
J. M. Neale, 1818–1866
© Jubilee Hymns

Christ is made the sure foundation,
Christ the head and corner-stone
Chosen of the Lord and precious,
Binding all the Church in one;
Holy Zion's help for ever,
And her confidence alone.

All within that holy city
Dearly loved of God on high,
In exultant jubilation
Sing, in perfect harmony;
God the One-in-Three adoring
In glad hymns eternally.

We as living stones invoke you:
Come among us, Lord, today!
With your gracious loving-kindness
Hear your children as we pray;
And the fulness of your blessing
In our fellowship display.

Here entrust to all your servants
What we long from you to gain –
That on earth and in the heavens
We one people shall remain,
Till united in your glory
Evermore with you we reign.

Praise and honour to the Father,
Praise and honour to the Son,
Praise and honour to the Spirit,
Ever Three and ever One;
One in power and one in glory
While eternal ages run.

28 Copyright © Michael Saward (1932–)

Christ triumphant ever reigning,
Saviour, Master, King,
Lord of heav'n, our lives sustaining,
Hear us as we sing:

Yours the glory and the crown,
The high renown,
The eternal name.

Word incarnate, truth revealing,
Son of Man on earth!
Power and majesty concealing
By your humble birth:

Suffering servant, scorned, ill-treated,
Victim crucified!
Death is through the cross defeated,
Sinners justified:

Priestly king, enthroned for ever
High in heaven above!
Sin and death and hell shall never
Stifle hymns of love:

So, our hearts and voices raising
Through the ages long,
Ceaselessly upon you gazing,
This shall be our song.

29 T. W. Maltby
Copyright © 1943 Salvationist
Publishing & Supplies, Ltd.

Christ is the answer to my ev'ry need;
Christ is the answer, He is my friend indeed,
Problems of life my spirit may assail,
With Christ my Saviour I need never fail,
For Christ is the answer to my need.

30 R. Hudson Pope
Copyright © Scripture Gift Mission

Cleanse me from my sin, Lord,
Put Thy pow'r within, Lord,
Take me as I am, Lord,
And make me all Thine own.
Keep me day by day, Lord,
Underneath Thy sway, Lord,
Make my heart Thy palace,
And Thy royal throne.

31 A. Carter
Copyright © 1977 Thankyou Music

Come and praise Him, royal priesthood,
Come and worship, holy nation,
Worship Jesus, our Redeemer,
He is precious, King of glory.

32 Anon

Come bless the Lord,
All ye servants of the Lord,
Who stand by night
In the house of the Lord,
Lift up your hands
In the holy place,
Come bless the Lord. (*repeat*)

33 Copyright © Christopher Idle (1938–)
from Revelation 4–5 etc.

Come and see the shining hope that Christ's
apostle saw;
On the earth, confusion, but in heaven an open
door,
Where the living creatures praise the Lamb for
evermore:
Love has the victory for ever!

Amen, he comes! to bring his own reward!
Amen, praise God! for justice now restored;
Kingdoms of the world become the
    kingdoms of the Lord:
Love has the victory for ever!.

All the gifts you send us, Lord, are faithful,
    good, and true;
Holiness and righteousness are shown in all
    you do;
Who can see your greatest Gift and fail to
    worship you?
Love has the victory for ever!

Power and salvation all belong to God on high!
So the mighty multitudes of heaven make their
    cry,
Singing Alleluia! where the echoes never die:
Love has the victory for ever!

34 Bianco da Siena, d. 1434;
tr. by Richard Frederick Littledale, 1833–90

Come down, O Love Divine,
Seek Thou this soul of mine,
And visit it with Thine own ardour glowing;
O Comforter, draw near,
Within my heart appear
And kindle it Thy holy flame bestowing.

O let it freely burn,
Till earthly passions turn
To dust and ashes, in its heat consuming;
And let Thy glorious light
Shine ever on my sight,
And clothe me round, the while my path
    illuming.

Let holy charity
Mine outward vesture be,
And lowliness become mine inner clothing;
True lowliness of heart,
Which takes the humbler part,
And o'er its own shortcomings weeps with
    loathing.

And so the yearning strong,
With which the soul will long,
Shall far outpass the power of human telling;
For none can guess its grace,
Till he become the place
Wherein the Holy Spirit makes His dwelling.

35 Robert Walmsley, 1831–1905

Come let us sing of a wonderful love,
Tender and true;
Out of the heart of the Father above,

Streaming to me and to you:
Wonderful love
Dwells in the heart of the Father above.

Jesus, the Saviour, this gospel to tell,
Joyfully came;
Came with the helpless and hopeless to dwell,
Sharing their sorrow and shame;
Seeking the lost,
Saving, redeeming at measureless cost.

Jesus is seeking the wanderers yet;
Why do they roam?
Love only waits to forgive and forget;
Home! weary wanderers, home!
Wonderful love
Dwells in the heart of the Father above.

Come to my heart, O Thou wonderful love,
Come and abide,
Lifting my life till it rises above
Envy and falsehood and pride;
Seeking to be
Lowly and humble, a learner of Thee.

36 Anon, 9th or 10th cent.:
tr. by John Cosin, 1594–1672

Come, Holy Ghost, our souls inspire,
And lighten with celestial fire;
Thou the anointing Spirit art,
Who dost Thy sevenfold gifts impart:

Thy blessed unction from above
Is comfort, life, and fire of love;
Enable with perpetual light
The dullness of our blinded sight:

Anoint and cheer our soiled face
With the abundance of Thy grace:
Keep far our foes, give peace at home;
Where Thou art Guide no ill can come.

Teach us to know the Father, Son,
and Thee, of both, to be but One;
That through the ages all along
This, this may be our endless song:

Praise to Thy eternal merit,
Father, Son, and Holy Spirit!

37 Isaac Watts, 1674–1748

Come, let us join our cheerful songs
With angels round the throne;
Ten thousand thousand are their tongues,
But all their joys are one.

"Worthy the Lamb that died!" they cry,
"To be exalted thus";
"Worthy the Lamb!" our lips reply,
"For He was slain for us."

Jesus is worthy to receive
Honour and power divine;
And blessings more than we can give
Be, Lord, for ever Thine.

Let all that dwell above the sky,
And air, and earth, and seas,
Conspire to lift Thy glories high,
And speak Thine endless praise.

The whole creation join in one,
To bless the sacred name
Of Him that sits upon the throne,
And to adore the Lamb.

38 Jodi Page
Copyright © 1975 Celebration Services
(International) Ltd.

Come to the waters
And I will give you rest
Come to the waters
And you will be refreshed.

Jesus said, Come unto me
All ye weary, heavy laden.'

Jesus said, of the waters that he gave,
He who drinks shall never thirst again.

Jesus said, 'He who believes in me
Out of him shall flow living waters.'

So with joy ye shall draw water
Out of wells of salvation.

39 Matthew Bridges, 1800–94
Godfrey Thring, 1823–1903

Crown Him with many crowns,
The Lamb upon His throne;
Hark! how the heavenly anthem drowns
All music but its own:
Awake, my soul, and sing
Of Him who died for thee,
And hail Him as thy chosen King
Through all eternity.

Crown Him the Son of God
Before the worlds began;
And ye who tread where He had trod,
Crown Him the Son of Man,
Who every grief hath known
That wrings the human breast,
And takes and bears them for His own,
That all in Him may rest.

Crown Him the Lord of life,
Who triumphed o'er the grave,
And rose victorious in the strife,
For those He came to save:
His glories now we sing,
Who died and rose on high,
Who died eternal life to bring,
And lives that death may die.

Crown Him the Lord of heaven,
Enthroned in worlds above;
Crown Him the King to whom is given
The wondrous name of love:
All hail, Redeemer, hail!
For Thou hast died for me;
Thy praise shall never, never fail
Throughout eternity.

40 John Greenleaf Whittier, 1807–82

Dear Lord and Father of mankind,
Forgive our foolish ways;
Re-clothe us in our rightful mind;
In purer lives Thy service find,
In deeper reverence, praise.

In simple trust like theirs who heard,
Beside the Syrian sea,
The gracious calling of the Lord,
Let us, like them, without a word
Rise up and follow Thee.

O Sabbath rest by Galilee!
O calm of hills above,
Where Jesus knelt to share with Thee
The silence of eternity,
Interpreted by love!

With that deep hush subduing all
Our words and works that drown
The tender whisper of Thy call,
As noiseless let Thy blessing fall
As fell Thy manna down.

Drop Thy still dews of quietness,
Till all our strivings cease;
Take from our souls the strain and stress,
And let our ordered lives confess
The beauty of Thy peace.

Breathe through the heats of our desire
Thy coolness and Thy balm;
Let sense be dumb, let flesh retire;
Speak through the earthquake, wind and fire,
O still small voice of calm!

41 Gerald Markland
Copyright © 1978 Kevin Mayhew Ltd.

Do not be afraid, *for I have redeemed you.*
I have called you by your name; you are
mine.

When you walk through the waters I'll be with
you.
You will never sink beneath the waves.

When the fire is burning all around you,
You will never be consumed by the flames.

When the fear of loneliness is looming,
Then remember I am at your side.

When you dwell in the exile of the stranger,
Remember you are precious in my eyes.

You are mine, O my child; I am your Father,
And I love you with a perfect love.

42 John 14:1–6
Copyright © 1980 Bible Society

Do not be worried and upset.
Believe in God, believe also in me,
There are many rooms in my Father's house,
And I'm going to prepare a place,
Prepare a place for you.

I am the way, the truth and the life;
No one goes to the Father except by me.
I am the way, the truth and the life,
And I'm going to prepare a place,
Prepare a place for you.

After I go and prepare a place for you,
I will come back and take you to myself,
So that you may come and be where I am.
And I'm going to prepare a place,
Prepare a place for you.

I am the way, the truth and the life;
No one goes to the Father except by me.
I am the way, the truth and the life,
And I'm going to prepare a place,
Prepare a place for you.
And I'm going to prepare a place,
Prepare a place for you.

43 Love Maria Willis, 1824–1908

Father, hear the prayer we offer:
Not for ease that prayer shall be,
But for strength, that we may ever
Live our lives courageously.

Not for ever in green pastures
Do we ask our way to be:
But by steep and rugged pathways
Would we strive to climb to Thee.

Not for ever by still waters
Would we idly quiet stay;
But would smite the living fountains
From the rocks along our way.

Be our strength in hours of weakness,
In our wanderings be our guide;
Through endeavour, failure, danger,
Father, be Thou at our side.

Let our path be bright or dreary,
Storm or sunshine be our share;
May our souls, in hope unweary,
Make Thy work our ceaseless prayer.

44 Terrye Coelho
Copyright © 1972 Maranatha Music
Word Music (UK)

Father, we adore you,
Lay our lives before you:
How we love you!

Jesus, we adore you,
Lay our lives before you:
How we love you!

Spirit, we adore you,
Lay our lives before you:
How we love you!

45 J. Hewer
Copyright © 1975 Thankyou Music

Father, I place into your hands
The things that I can't do.
Father, I place into your hands
The times that I've been through.
Father, I place into your hands
The way that I should go,
For I know I always can trust you.

Father, I place into your hands
My friends and family.
Father, I place into your hands
The things that trouble me.
Father, I place into your hands
The person I would be,
For I know I always can trust you.

Father, we love to seek your face,
We love to hear your voice.
Father, we love to sing your praise,
And in your name rejoice.
Father, we love to walk with you
And in your presence rest,
For we know we always can trust you.

Father, I want to be with you
And do the things you do.
Father, I want to speak the words
That you are speaking too.
Father, I want to love the ones
That you will draw to you,
For I know that I am one with you.

46
Donna Adkins
Copyright © 1976, 1981 Word Music (UK)

Father, we love You,
We worship and adore You,
Glorify Your name
In all the earth.
Glorify Your name, (*repeat twice*)
In all the earth.

Jesus, we love You,
We worship and adore You,
Glorify Your name,
In all the earth.
Glorify Your name (*repeat twice*)
In all the earth.

Spirit, we love You,
We worship and adore You,
Glorify Your name
In all the earth.
Glorify Your name, (*repeat twice*)
In all the earth.

47
Priscilla Wright
Copyright © 1971, 1975 Celebration Services
(International) Ltd.

Fear not, rejoice and be glad,
The Lord hath done a great thing;
Hath poured out His Spirit on all mankind,
On those who confess His name.

The fig tree is budding, the vine beareth fruit,
The wheat fields are golden with grain.
Thrust in the sickle, the harvest is ripe,
The Lord has given us rain.

Ye shall eat in plenty and be satisfied,
The mountains will drip with sweet wine.
My children shall drink of the fountain of life,
My children will know they are mine.

My people shall know that I am the Lord,
Their shame I have taken away.
My Spirit will lead them together again,
My Spirit will show them the way.

My children shall dwell in a body of love,
A light to the world they will be.
Life shall come forth from the Father above,
My body will set mankind free.

48
Horatius Bonar, 1808–82

Fill Thou my life, O Lord my God,
In every part with praise,
That my whole being may proclaim
Thy being and Thy ways.

Not for the lip of praise alone,
Nor e'en the praising heart,
I ask, but for a life made up
Of praise in every part:

Praise in the common things of life,
Its goings out and in;
Praise in each duty and each deed,
However small and mean.

Fill every part of me with praise;
Let all my being speak
Of Thee and of Thy love, O lord,
Poor though I be and weak.

So shalt Thou, Lord from me, e'en me,
Receive the glory due;
And so shall I begin on earth
The song for ever new.

So shall no part of day or night
From sacredness be free;
But all my life, in every step,
Be fellowship with Thee.

49
John Samuel Bewley Monsell, 1811–75

Fight the good fight with all thy might;
Christ is thy strength, and Christ thy right;
Lay hold on life, and it shall be
Thy joy and crown eternally.

Run the straight race through God's good
    grace;
Lift up thine eyes, and seek His face,
Life with its path before thee lies;
Christ is the way, and Christ the prize.

Cast care aside, lean on thy Guide,
His boundless mercy will provide;
Lean, and thy trusting soul shall prove,
Christ is thy life, and Christ thy love.

Faint not, nor fear, His arm is near,
He changeth not, and thou art dear,
Only believe, and thou shalt see
That Christ is all in all to thee.

50

D. Richards
Copyright © 1977 Thankyou Music

For I'm building a people of power
And I'm making a people of praise,
That will move thro' this land by My Spirit,
And will glorify My precious Name.
Build your Church, Lord,
Make us strong, Lord,
Join our hearts, Lord, through Your Son
Make us one, Lord, in Your Body,
In the Kingdom of Your Son.

51

William Walsham How, 1823–97

For all the saints who from their labours rest,
Who Thee by faith before the world confessed,
Thy name, O Jesu, be for ever blest.
Alleluia!

Thou wast their Rock, their Fortress, and their
   Might;
Thou, Lord, their Captain in the well fought
   fight;
Thou in the darkness drear their one true Light.
Alleluia!

O may Thy soldiers, faithful, true, and bold,
Fight as the saints who nobly fought of old,
And win, with them, the victor's crown of gold!
Alleluia!

O blest communion, fellowship divine!
We feebly struggle; they in glory shine,
Yet all are one in Thee, for all are Thine.
Alleluia!

And when the strife is fierce, the warfare long,
Steals on the ear the distant triumph song,
And hearts are brave again, and arms are
   strong.
Alleluia!

The golden evening brightens in the west;
Soon, soon to faithful warriors cometh rest;
Sweet is the calm of paradise the blest.
Alleluia!

But lo! there breaks a yet more glorious day:
The saints triumphant rise in bright array;
The King of Glory passes on His way.
Alleluia!

From earth's wide bounds, from ocean's
   farthest coast,
Through gates of pearl streams in the countless
   host,
Singing to Father, Son and Holy Ghost:
Alleluia!

52

F. Pratt Green 1903–
Copyright © Stainer & Bell

For the fruits of his creation,
Thanks be to God!
For his gifts to every nation,
Thanks be to God!
For the ploughing, sowing, reaping,
Silent growth while we are sleeping;
Future needs in earth's safe seeking,
Thanks be to God!

In the just reward of labour,
God's will is done;
In the help we give our neighbour,
God's will is done;
In our worldwide task of caring
For the hungry and despairing;
In the harvests we are sharing,
God's will is done.

For the harvests of the Spirit
Thanks be to God!
For the good we all inherit,
Thanks be to God!
For the wonders that astound us,
For the truths that still confound us;
Most of all, that love has found us,
Thanks be to God!

53

Pete Sanchez Jr.
Copyright © 1977 Pete Sanchez Jr.

For thou, O Lord,
Art high above all the earth,
Thou art exalted far above all gods
For thou, O Lord,
Art high above all the earth,
Thou art exalted far above all gods.
I exalt Thee, I exalt Thee,
I exalt Thee O Lord,
I exalt Thee, I exalt Thee,
I exalt Thee O Lord.

54

Psalm 113: 3.1.2.

From the rising of the sun
To the going down of the same
The Lord's name is to be praised.
From the rising of the sun
To the going down of the same
The Lord's name is to be praised.
Praise ye the Lord,
Praise Him O ye servants of the Lord,
Praise the name of the Lord,
Blessed be the name of the Lord
From this time forth,
And for evermore.

55 Charles Wesley, 1707–88

Forth in Thy name, O Lord, I go,
My daily labour to pursue,
Thee, only Thee, resolved to know
In all I think, or speak, or do.

The task Thy wisdom hath assigned
O let me cheerfully fulfil,
In all my works Thy presence find,
And prove Thy acceptable will.

Thee may I set at my right hand,
Whose eyes my inmost substance see,
And labour on at Thy command,
And offer all my works to Thee.

Give me to bear Thy easy yoke,
And every moment watch and pray,
And still to things eternal look,
And hasten to Thy glorious day:

For Thee delightfully employ
Whate'er Thy bounteous grace hath given,
And run my course with even joy,
And closely walk with Thee to heaven.

56 Joan Robinson

Father God, I love you (*repeat twice*)
Come into my life.

Jesus, I love you (*repeat twice*)
Come into my life.

Spirit, I love you (*repeat twice*)
Come into my life.

Alleluia, alleluia,
Alleluia, alleluia.

57 Katherine Agnes May Kelly, 1869–1942
Copyright © National Young Life Campaign

Give me a sight, O Saviour,
Of Thy wondrous love to me,
Of the love that brought Thee down to earth,
To die on Calvary.

O make me understand it,
Help me to take it in,
What it meant to Thee,
The Holy One,
To bear away my sin.

Was it the nails, O Saviour,
That bound Thee to the tree?
Nay, 'twas Thine everlasting love,
Thy love for me, for me.

O wonder of all wonders,
That through Thy death for me
My open sins, my secret sins,
Can all forgiven be!

Then melt my heart, O Saviour,
Bend me, yes, break me down,
Until I own Thee Conqueror,
And Lord and Sovereign crown.

58 Anon

Give me oil in my lamp, keep me burning.
Give me oil in my lamp, I pray.
Give me oil in my lamp, keep me burning,
Keep me burning 'til the break of day.

Sing hosanna, Sing hosanna,
Sing hosanna to the King of Kings!
Sing hosanna, Sing hosanna, Sing hosanna
To the King.

Make me a fisher of men, keep me seeking.
Make me a fisher of men, I pray.
Make me a fisher of men, keep me seeking,
Keep me seeking 'til the break of day.

Give me joy in my heart, keep me singing.
Give me joy in my heart, I pray.
Give me joy in my heart, keep me singing,
Keep me singing 'til the break of day.

Give me love in my heart, keep me serving.
Give me love in my heart, I pray.
Give me love in my heart, keep me serving,
Keep me serving 'til the break of day.

59 John Newton, 1725–1807

Glorious things of thee are spoken,
Zion, city of our God;
He, whose word cannot be broken,
Formed thee for His own abode.
On the Rock of Ages founded,
What can shake thy sure repose?
With salvation's walls surrounded,
Thou may'st smile at all thy foes.

See, the streams of living waters,
Springing from eternal love,
Well supply thy sons and daughters
And all fear of want remove;
Who can faint, while such a river
Ever flows their thirst to assuage?
Grace which, like the Lord, the Giver
Never fails from age to age.

Saviour, if of Zion's city
I, through grace, a member am,

Let the world deride or pity,
I will glory in Thy name:
Fading is the worldling's pleasure,
All his boasted pomp and show:
Solid joys and lasting treasure
None but Zion's children know.

60 Carol Owens
Copyright © 1972 Lexicon Music Inc.
Word Music (UK)

God forgave my sin in Jesus' name.
I've been born again in Jesus' name.
And in Jesus' name I come to you
To share his love as he told me to.

He said, 'Freely,
Freely you have received;
Freely, freely give.
Go in my name and because you believe,
Others will know that I live.'

All pow'r is giv'n in Jesus' name.
In earth and heav'n in Jesus' name.
And in Jesus' name I come to you
To share his pow'r as he told me to.

61 © James E. Seddon 1915–

Go forth and tell! O Church of God, awake!
God's saving news to all the nations take:
Proclaim Christ Jesus, saviour, Lord, and king,
That all the world his worthy praise may sing.

Go forth and tell God's love embraces all;
He will in grace respond to all who call:
How shall they call if they have never heard
The gracious invitation of his word?

Go forth and tell! Men still in darkness lie;
In wealth or want, in sin they live and die:
Give us, O Lord, concern of heart and mind,
A love like yours which cares for all mankind.

Go forth and tell! The doors are open wide:
Share God's good gifts – let no one be denied;
Live out your life as Christ your Lord shall
choose,
Your ransomed powers for his sole glory use.

Go forth and tell! O church of God, arise!
Go in the strength which Christ your Lord
supplies;
Go till all nations his great name adore
And serve him, Lord and king for evermore.

62 T. O. Chisholm, 1866–1960
Copyright © 1923/1951 Hope Publishing

Great is Thy faithfulness, O God my Father,
There is no shadow of turning with Thee;

Thou changest not, Thy compassions they fail
not,
As Thou hast been Thou for ever wilt be.

Great is Thy faithfulness!
Great is Thy faithfulness!
Morning by morning new mercies I see;
All I have needed Thy hand hath provided, -
Great is Thy faithfulness, Lord, unto me!

Summer and winter, and spring-time and
harvest,
Sun, moon and stars in their courses above,
Join with all nature in manifold witness
To Thy great faithfulness, mercy and love.

Pardon for sin and a peace that endureth,
Thine own dear presence to cheer and to
guide;
Strength for today and bright hope for
tomorrow,
Blessings all mine, with ten thousand beside!

63 William Williams, 1717–91, altd.

Guide me, O Thou great Jehovah,
Pilgrim through this barren land;
I am weak, but Thou art mighty;
Hold me with Thy powerful hand:
Bread of heaven,
Feed me now and evermore.

Open now the crystal fountain,
Whence the healing stream doth flow;
Let the fiery, cloudy pillar
Lead me all my journey through:
Strong deliverer,
Be Thou still my strength and shield.

When I tread the verge of Jordan,
Bid my anxious fears subside:
Death of death, and hell's destruction,
Land me safe on Canaan's side:
Songs of praises
I will ever give to Thee.

64 James Montgomery, 1771–1854

Hail to the Lord's Anointed;
Great David's greater Son!
Hail, in the time appointed
His reign on earth begun!
He comes to break oppression,
To set the captive free,
To take away transgression,
And rule in equity.

He comes, with succour speedy,
To those who suffer wrong;
To help the poor and needy,
And bid the weak be strong:
To give them songs for sighing,
Their darkness turn to light,
Whose souls, condemned and dying,
Were precious in His sight.

He shall come down like showers
Upon the fruitful earth:
Love, joy, and hope, like flowers,
Spring in His path to birth:
Before Him, on the mountains,
Shall peace the herald go;
And righteousness in fountains,
From hill to valley flow.

Kings shall fall down before Him,
And gold and incense bring;
All nations shall adore Him,
His praise all people sing;
To Him shall prayer unceasing
And daily vows ascend;
His kingdom still increasing,
A kingdom without end.

O'er every foe victorious,
He on His throne shall rest;
From age to age more glorious,
All-blessing and all-blest.
The tide of time shall never
His covenant remove;
His name shall stand for ever
His changeless name of Love.

65 Copyright © 1972 Scripture in Song

**Hallelujah! for the Lord our God the
Almighty reigns.** (repeat)
Let us rejoice and be glad and give the glory
unto Him.
Hallelujah! for the Lord our God the Almighty
reigns.

66 Tim Cullen
Copyright © 1975 Celebration Services
(International) Ltd.

Hallelujah, my Father,
For giving us your Son;
Sending him in to the world
To be given up for men,
Knowing we would bruise him
And smite him from the earth.
Hallelujah, my Father,
In his death is my birth.
Hallelujah, my Father,
In his life is my life.

67 W. C. Dix, 1837–98, altd.

Hallelujah! sing to Jesus,
His the sceptre, His the throne;
Hallelujah! His the triumph,
His the victory alone;
Hark! the songs of peaceful Sion
Thunder like a mighty flood;
Jesus out of every nation
Hath redeemed us by His blood.

Hallelujah! not as orphans
Are we left in sorrow now;
Hallelujah! He is near us,
Faith believes, nor questions how:
Though the cloud from sight received Him
When the forty days were o'er,
Shall our hearts forget His promise,
"I am with you evermore"?

Hallelujah! bread of angels,
Thou on earth our food, our stay;
Hallelujah! here the sinful
Flee to Thee from day to day;
Intercessor, friend of sinners,
Earth's Redeemer, plead for me,
Where the songs of all the sinless
Sweep across the crystal sea.

Hallelujah! Hallelujah!
Glory be to God on high;
To the Father, and the Saviour,
Who has gained the victory;
Glory to the Holy Spirit,
Fount of love and sanctity.
Hallelujah! Hallelujah!
To the triune Majesty.

68 Jimmy Owens
Copyright © Lexicon Music Inc.
Word Music (UK)

He is here, He is here,
He is moving among us;
He is here, He is here,
As we gather in His name!
He is here, He is here,
And He wants to work a wonder;
He is here as we gather in His name.

He is Lord, He is Lord,
Let us worship before Him;
He is Lord, He is Lord,
As we gather in His name!
He is Lord, He is Lord,
Let us praise and adore Him
Yesterday and today and for evermore the
same.

69 Anon

He is Lord. He is Lord.
He is risen from the dead,
And He is Lord.
Ev'ry knee shall bow,
Ev'ry tongue confess
That Jesus Christ is Lord.

70 D. Wood

**His Hands were pierced, the Hands that
made**
The mountain range and everglade;
That washed the stains of sin away
And changed earth's darkness into day.

His Feet were pierced, the Feet that trod
The furthest shining star of God;
And left their imprint deep and clear
On ev'ry winding pathway here.

His Heart was pierced, the Heart that burned
To comfort every heart that yearned!
And from it came a cleansing flood,
The river of redeeming Blood.

His Hands and Feet and Heart, all three
Were pierced for me on Calvary,
And here and now, to Him I bring
My hands, feet, heart, an offering.

71 Anon

His name is higher than any other,
His name is Jesus, His name is Lord.
His name is Wonderful, His name is Counsellor,
His name is Prince of Peace, the mighty God.
His name is higher than any other,
His name is Jesus, His name is Lord.

72 Audrey Mieir
Copyright © 1959 Manna Music Inc.

His name is wonderful, (*repeat twice*)
Jesus my Lord.
He is the mighty king,
Master of everything,
His name is wonderful,
Jesus my Lord.
He's the great shepherd,
The rock of all ages,
Almighty God is He;
Bow down before Him,
Love and adore Him,
His name is wonderful,
Jesus my Lord!

73 Reginald Heber, 1783–1826

Holy, holy, holy, Lord God almighty!
Early in the morning our song shall rise to Thee;
Holy, holy, holy, merciful and mighty,
God in three Persons, blessed Trinity!

Holy, holy, holy! all the saints adore Thee,
Casting down their golden crowns around the
    glassy sea;
Cherubim and seraphim falling down before
    Thee,
Who wast, and art, and evermore shall be.

Holy, holy, holy! though the darkness hide
    Thee,
Though the eye of sinful man Thy glory may
    not see,
Only Thou art holy; there is none beside Thee,
Perfect in power, in love, and purity.

Holy, holy, holy, Lord God almighty!
All Thy works shall praise Thy name, in earth,
    and sky, and sea:
Holy, holy, holy, merciful and mighty,
God in three Persons, blessed Trinity!

74 Anon

Holy, holy, holy is the Lord;
Holy is the Lord God almighty!
Holy, holy, holy is the Lord;
Holy is the Lord God almighty!
Who was, and is, and is to come;
Holy, holy, holy is the Lord!

Jesus, Jesus, Jesus is the Lord;
Jesus is the Lord God almighty;
Jesus, Jesus, Jesus is the Lord;
Jesus is the Lord God almighty,
Who was, and is, and is to come:
Holy, holy, holy is the Lord!

Worthy, worthy, worthy is the Lord;
Worthy is the Lord God almighty!
Worthy, worthy, worthy is the Lord;
Worthy is the Lord God almighty!
Who was, and is, and is to come:
Holy, holy, holy is the Lord!

Glory, glory, glory to the Lord;
Glory to the Lord God almighty,
Glory, glory, glory to the Lord;
Glory to the Lord God almighty,
Who was, and is, and is to come:
Holy, holy, holy is the Lord!

75
Jimmy Owens
Copyright © 1972 Lexicon Music Inc.
Word Music (UK)

Holy, holy, holy, holy,
Holy, holy, Lord God almighty!
And we lift our hearts before you
As a token of our love:
Holy, holy, holy, holy.

Gracious Father, gracious Father,
We're so glad to be your children, gracious
    Father;
And we lift our heads before you
As a token of our love,
Gracious Father, gracious Father.

Precious Jesus, precious Jesus,
We're so glad that you've redeemed us,
    precious Jesus;
And we lift our hands before you
As a token of our love,
Precious Jesus, precious Jesus.

Holy Spirit, Holy Spirit,
Come and fill our hearts anew, Holy Spirit! –
And we lift our voice before you
As a token of our love,
Holy Spirit, Holy Spirit.

Hallelujah, hallelujah,
Hallelujah, hallelujah –
And we lift our hearts before you
As a token of our love
Hallelujah, hallelujah.

76   "K" in Rippon's *selection*, 1787, *altd.*

How firm a foundation, ye saints of the Lord,
Is laid for your faith in His excellent word:
What more can He say than to you He hath
    said,
You who unto Jesus for refuge have fled?

Fear not, He is with thee, O be not dismayed;
For He is thy God, and will still give thee aid;
He'll strengthen thee, help thee, and cause thee
    to stand,
Upheld by His righteous, omnipotent hand.

In every condition, in sickness, in health,
In poverty's vale, or abounding in wealth;
At home and abroad, on the land, on the sea,
As thy days may demand shall thy strength
    ever be.

When through the deep waters He calls thee
    to go,
The rivers of grief shall not thee overflow;
For He will be with thee in trouble to bless,
And sanctify to thee thy deepest distress.

When through fiery trials thy pathway shall lie,
His grace all-sufficient shall be thy supply;
The flame shall not hurt thee, His only design
Thy dross to consume and thy gold to refine.

The soul that on Jesus has leaned for repose
He will not, He will not, desert to its foes;
That soul, though all hell should endeavour to
    shake,
He'll never, no never, no never forsake.

77   J. Hart, 1712–1768

How good is the God we adore!
Our faithful, unchangeable friend:
His love is as great as his power
And knows neither measure nor end.

For Christ is the first and the last;
His Spirit will guide us safe home:
We'll praise him for all that is past
And trust him for all that's to come.

78   John Newton, 1725–1807, altd.

How sweet the name of Jesus sounds
In a believer's ear!
It soothes his sorrows, heals his wounds,
And drives away his fear.

It makes the wounded spirit whole.
And calms the troubled breast;
'Tis manna to the hungry soul,
And to the weary rest.

Dear name! the rock on which I build,
My shield and hiding-place,
My never-failing treasury, filled
With boundless stores of grace.

Jesus! my shepherd, brother, friend,
My prophet, priest, and king;
My lord, my life, my way, my end,
Accept the praise I bring.

Weak is the effort of my heart,
And cold my warmest thought;
But when I see Thee as Thou art,
I'll praise Thee as I ought.

Till then I would Thy love proclaim
With every fleeting breath;
And may the music of Thy name
Refresh my soul in death!

79

L. E. Smith Jnr
Copyright © 1974/1978 Thankyou Music

How lovely on the mountains are the feet of Him
Who brings good news, good news,
Proclaiming peace, announcing news of
    happiness,
Our God reigns, our God reigns, (*repeat twice*)

Popular Version

You watchmen lift your voices joyfully as one,
Shout for your King, your King.
See eye to eye the Lord restoring Zion:
Your God reigns, your God reigns!

Waste places of Jerusalem break forth with
    joy,
We are redeemed, redeemed.
The Lord has saved and comforted His people:
Your God reigns, your God reigns!

Ends of the earth, see the salvation of your God,
Jesus is Lord, is Lord.
Before the nations He has bared His holy arm:
Your God reigns, your God reigns!

Original Version

He had no stately form, He had no majesty,
That we should be – drawn to Him.
He was despised and we took no account of
    Him,
Yet now He reigns – with the Most High.
    Now He reigns (repeat three times)
    With the Most High!

It was our sin and guilt that bruised and
    wounded Him,
It was our sin – that brought Him down.
When we like sheep had gone astray, our
    Shepherd came
And on His shoulders – bore our shame.
    On His shoulders (repeat three times)
    He bore our shame.

Meek as a lamb that's led out to the
    slaughterhouse,
Dumb as a sheep – before its shearer,
His life ran down upon the ground like pouring
    rain,
That we might be – born again.
    That we might be (repeat three times)
    Born again.

Out from the tomb He came with grace and
    majesty,
He is alive – He is alive.
God loves us so – see here His hands, His feet,
    His side,
Yes, we know – He is alive.
    He is alive! (repeat four times)

How lovely on the mountains are the feet of
    Him
Who brings good news, good news,
Announcing peace, proclaiming news of
    happiness:
Our God reigns, our God reigns.
    Our God reigns (repeat four times)

80

S. Suzanne Toolan
Copyright © 1971 by G. I. A. Publications, Inc.

I am the bread of life;
He who comes to me shall not hunger;
He who believes in me shall not thirst.
No-one can come to me unless the Father draw
    him.

    And I will raise him up,
    And I will raise him up,
    And I will raise him up
    On the last day.

The bread that I will give
Is my flesh for the life of the world
And he who eats of this bread,
He shall live for ever, he shall live for ever.

Unless you eat
Of the flesh of the Son of man
And drink of his blood,
And drink of his blood you shall not have life
    within you.

I am the resurrection,
I am the life.
He who believes in me,
Even if he die, he shall live for ever.

Yes, Lord, we believe
That you are the Christ,
The Son of God,
Who has come into the world.

81

Frances Ridley Havergal, 1836–79

I am trusting Thee, Lord Jesus,
Trusting only Thee;
Trusting Thee for full salvation, Great and free.

I am trusting Thee for pardon,
At Thy feet I bow;
For Thy grace and tender mercy, Trusting now.

I am trusting Thee for cleansing
In the crimson flood;
Trusting Thee to make me holy By Thy blood.

I am trusting Thee to guide me;
Thou alone shalt lead,
Every day and hour supplying All my need.

I am trusting Thee for power,
Thine can never fail;
Words which Thou Thyself shalt give me. Must prevail.

I am trusting Thee, Lord Jesus;
Never let me fall;
I am trusting Thee for ever, And for all.

82 Anon

I am weak but Thou art strong;
Jesus keep me from all wrong
I'll be satisfied as long
As I walk, let me walk, close with Thee.

Just a closer walk with Thee
Grant it, Jesus, this my plea
Daily walking close with Thee
Let it be, dear Lord, let it be.

Through this world of toils and snares,
If I falter, Lord, who cares?
Who with me my burden shares?
None but Thee, dear Lord, none but Thee.

When my feeble life is o'er,
Time for me will be no more,
Guide me gently, safely home,
To Thy Kingdom's shore, to Thy shore.

83 William Young Fullerton, 1857–1932

I cannot tell why He, whom angels worship,
Should set His love upon the sons of men,
Or why, as Shepherd, He should seek the wanderers,
To bring them back, they know not how or when.
But this I know, that He was born of Mary,
When Bethlehem's manger was His only home,
And that He lived at Nazareth and laboured,
And so the Saviour, Saviour of the world, is come.

I cannot tell how silently He suffered,
As with His peace He graced this place of tears,
Or how His heart upon the Cross was broken,
The crown of pain to three and thirty years.
But this I know, He heals the broken-hearted,

And stays our sin, and calms our lurking fear,
And lifts the burden from the heavy laden,
For yet the Saviour, Saviour of the world, is here.

I cannot tell how He will win the nations,
How He will claim His earthly heritage,
How satisfy the needs and aspirations
Of east and West, of sinner and of sage.
But this I know, all flesh shall see His glory,
And He shall reap the harvest He has sown,
And some glad day His sun shall shine in splendour
When He the Saviour, Saviour of the world, is known.

I cannot tell how all the lands shall worship,
When, at His bidding, every storm is stilled,
Or who can say how great the jubilation
When all the hearts of men with love are filled.
But this I know, the skies will thrill with rapture,
And myriad, myriad human voices sing,
And earth to heaven, and heaven to earth, will answer:
At last the Saviour, Saviour of the world, is King!

84

I have decided to follow Jesus, (*repeat twice*)
No turning back, no turning back.

The world behind me, the cross before me,
(*repeat twice*)
No turning back, no turning back.

Tho' none go with me, I still will follow, (*repeat twice*)
No turning back, no turning back.

Will you decide now to follow Jesus? (*repeat twice*)
No turning back, no turning back.

85 Horatius Bonar, 1808–89

I heard the voice of Jesus say:
Come unto Me and rest;
Lay down, thou weary one, lay down
Thy head upon My breast!
I came to Jesus as I was,
Weary, and worn, and sad;
I found in Him a resting-place,
And He has made me glad.

I heard the voice of Jesus say:
Behold, I freely give
The living water; thirsty one,
Stoop down and drink, and live!

I came to Jesus, and I drank
Of that life-giving stream;
My thirst was quenched, my soul revived,
And now I live in Him.

I heard the voice of Jesus say:
I am this dark world's Light;
Look unto Me, thy morn shall rise,
And all thy day be bright!
I looked to Jesus and I found
In Him my star, my sun;
And in that light of life I'll walk
Till travelling days are done.

86
Samuel Medley, 1738–99

I know that my Redeemer lives!
What joy the blest assurance gives!
He lives, He lives, who once was dead;
He lives, my everlasting Head!

He lives, to bless me with His love;
He lives, to plead for me above;
He lives, my hungry soul to feed;
He lives, to help in time of need.

He lives, and grants me daily breath;
He lives, and I shall conquer death;
He lives, my mansion to prepare;
He lives, to lead me safely there.

He lives, all glory to His name;
He lives, my Saviour, still the same;
What joy the blest assurance gives!;
I know that my Redeemer lives!

87
Laurie Klein
Copyright © 1978 Word Music (UK)

I love You, Lord,
And I lift my voice
To worship You,
O my soul rejoice.
Take joy, my King,
In what You hear,
May it be a sweet,
Sweet sound in Your ear.

88
R. Wilson
Copyright © 1978 Thankyou Music

**I hear the sound of rustling in the leaves of
the trees,**
The Spirit of the Lord has come down on the
earth.
The Church that seemed in slumber has now
risen from its knees
And dry bones are responding with the fruits
of new birth.
Oh this is now a time for declaration,

The word will go to all men ev'rywhere,
The Church is here for healing of the nations,
Behold the day of Jesus drawing near.

*My tongue will be the pen of a ready writer,
And what the Father gives to me I'll sing,
I only want to be His breath,
I only want to glorify the King.*

And all around the world the body waits
expectantly,
The promise of the Father is now ready to fall.
The watchmen on the tower all exhort us to
prepare.
And the church responds – a people who will
answer the call.
And this is not a phase which is passing,
It's the start of an age that is to come.
And where is the wise man and the scoffer?
Before the face of Jesus they are dumb.

A body now prepared by God and ready for
war,
The prompting of the Spirit is our word of
command.
We rise, a mighty army, at the bidding of the
Lord,
The devils see and fear, for their time is at
hand.
And children of the Lord hear our commission
That we should love and serve our God as one.
The Spirit won't be hindered by division
In the perfect work that Jesus has begun.

89
D. W. Whittle, 1840–1901

I know not why God's wondrous grace
To me has been made known;
Nor why – unworthy as I am –
He claimed me for His own.

*But "I know whom I have believed; and
am persuaded that He is able to keep that
which I've committed unto Him against
that day."*

I know not how this saving faith
To me He did impart;
Or how believing in His word
Wrought peace within my heart.

I know not how the Spirit moves,
Convincing men of sin;
Revealing Jesus through the word,
Creating faith in Him.

I know not what of good or ill
May be reserved for me –
Of weary ways or golden days
Before His face I see.

90 Copyright © J. M. Barnes

I love my Lord because He heard my voice.
My God, He listens to my prayer.
Because He hears me when I call on Him,
Through all my days I shall pray.

My soul was saved from death; my eyes from
tears;
My feet now walk before the Lord;
Yet in despair I thought my end was near
My faith in life disappeared.

What can I do to thank God for His love –
For all His benefits to me?
I will lift up salvation's cup on high
And call on Him by His Name.

My vows to Him I promise to fulfil,
To Him I sacrifice my life.
He freed me from the servitude of sin
And now I serve as His slave.

Unite in praise, great family of God,
His children, bring to Him your thanks.
City of Peace, where God has made His home
With one accord, praise His Name!

91 Kathleen Thomerson
Copyright © 1970, 1975 Celebration
Services (International) Ltd

I love the name of Jesus,
King of my heart,
He is ev'rything to me.
I bless the name of Jesus,
Reign in my life,
Show the Father's love so free.
Spirit of love,
Spirit of power,
Shine through eternity.
I love the name of Jesus,
Light of the world,
Let me walk each day with thee.

I love the name of Jesus,
Risen above,
And he loves and prays for me.
I bless the name of Jesus,
Ruling on high
With a glorious majesty.
Spirit of love,
Spirit of power,
Shine through eterntity.
I praise the name of Jesus,
Lord of my life,
For he died to set me free.

I love the name of Jesus,
Splendour of God,
And his face I long to see.
I bless the name of Jesus,

Shepherd of men;
By his side I now can be.
Spirit of love,
Spirit of power,
Shine through eternity.
I praise the name of Jesus,
For he is love,
And that love he gives to me.

92 Annie Sherwood Hawks, 1835–1918

I need Thee ev'ry hour,
Most gracious Lord;
No tender voice like Thine
Can peace afford.

I need Thee, O I need Thee!
Ev'ry hour I need Thee:
O bless me, now, my Saviour!
I come to Thee.

I need Thee ev'ry hour,
Stay Thou near by;
Temptations lose their pow'r
When Thou art nigh.

I need Thee ev'ry hour,
In joy or pain;
Come quickly and abide
Or life is vain.

I need Thee ev'ry hour,
Teach me Thy will;
And Thy rich promises
In me fulfil.

I need Thee ev'ry hour,
Most Holy One;
O make me Thine indeed,
Thou blessed Son!

93 Anon

**I want to worship the Lord with all of my
heart,**
Give him my all and not just a part.
Lift up my hands to the King of Kings,
Praise him in everything.

94 A. H. Ackley
Copyright © 1933 by Homer A. Rodeheaver
Word Music (UK)

I serve a risen Saviour,
He's in the world today;
I know that He is living,
Whatever men may say;
I see His hand of mercy,
I hear His voice of cheer.
And just the time I need Him
He's always near.

He lives, He lives,
Christ Jesus lives today!
He walks with me and talks with me
Along life's narrow way.
He lives, He lives,
Salvation to impart!
You ask me how I know He lives?
He lives within my heart.

In all the world around me
I see His loving care,
And tho' my heart grows weary
I never will despair;
I know that He is leading,
Thro' all the stormy blast,
The day of His appearing
Will come at last.

Rejoice, rejoice, O Christian,
Lift up your voice and sing
Eternal hallelujahs
To Jesus Christ the King!
The Hope of all who seek Him,
The Help of all who find,
None other is so loving,
So good and kind.

95
M. Warrington
Copyright © 1972 Youth With A
Mission, Inc.

I trust in thee, O Lord.
I say, 'Thou art my God.'
My times are in thy hand. (*repeat*)

Blessed be the Lord,
For He has wondrously shown
His steadfast love to me (*repeat*)

96
Rich Cook
Copyright © Control

I will call upon the Lord,
Who is worthy to be praised.
So shall I be saved from my enemies
The Lord liveth and blessed be my rock
And may the God of my salvation be exalted.

97
Leona Vonbrethorst
Copyright © 1976 Word Music (UK)

**I will enter His gates with thanksgiving in
my heart,**
I will enter His courts with praise,
I will say this is the day that the Lord has made,
I will rejoice for He has made me glad.
He has made me glad, He has made me glad.
I will rejoice for He has made me glad.
Repeat last 2 lines

98
Brent Chambers
© 1977 Scripture in Song

**I will give thanks to Thee, O Lord, among
the peoples,**
I will sing praises to Thee among the nations.
For Thy steadfast love is great, is great to the
heavens,
And Thy faithfulness, Thy faithfulness, to the
clouds.
Be exalted, O God, above the heavens,
Let Thy glory be over all the earth!
Be exalted, O God, above the heavens,
Let Thy glory, let Thy glory,
Let Thy glory be over all the earth!

99
Max Dyer
Copyright © 1974, 1975 Celebration
Services (International) Ltd.

I will sing, I will sing a song unto the Lord.
(*repeat twice*)
Alleluia, glory to the Lord
Alleluia, alleluia, glory to the Lord (repeat
twice)
Alleluia, glory to the Lord

We will come, we will come as one before the
Lord (*repeat twice*)
Alleluia, glory to the Lord.

If the Son, if the Son shall make you free (*repeat*
twice)
You shall be free indeed.

They that sow in tears shall reap in joy. (*repeat*
twice)
Alleluia, glory to the Lord.

Ev'ry knee shall bow and ev'ry tongue confess
(*repeat twice*)
That Jesus Christ is Lord

In his name, in his name we have the victory.
(*repeat twice*)
Alleluia, glory to the Lord.

100
Isaac Watts 1674–1748

I'm not ashamed to own my Lord,
Or to defend His cause,
Maintain the honour of His Word,
The glory of His cross.

Jesus, my God! I know His name,
His Name is all my trust;
Nor will He put my soul to shame,
Nor let my hope be lost.

Firm as His throne His promise stands,
And He can well secure
What I've committed to His hands,
Till the decisive hour.

Then will He own my worthless name
Before His Father's face;
And, in the New Jerusalem,
Appoint my soul a place.

101 F. H. Rawley, 1854–1952
Copyright © M.M.S.

I will sing the wondrous story
Of the Christ who died for me, –
How He left the realms of glory
For the cross on Calvary.
Yes, I'll sing the wondrous story
Of the Christ who died for me, –
Sing it with His saints in glory,
Gathered by the crystal sea.

I was lost: but Jesus found me,
Found the sheep that went astray,
Raised me up and gently led me
Back into the narrow way.
Days of darkness still may meet me,
Sorrow's path I oft may tread;
But His presence still is with me,
By His guiding hand I'm led.

He will keep me till the river
Rolls its waters at my feet:
Then He'll bear me safely over,
Made by grace for glory meet.
Yes, I'll sing the wondrous story
Of the Christ who died for me, –
Sing it with His saints in glory,
Gathered by the crystal sea.

102 Donya Brockway
© 1972 His Eye Music/
Cherry Blossom Music
Word Music (UK)

I will sing unto the Lord as long as I live,
I will sing praise to my God while I have my
  being,
My meditation of Him shall be sweet,
I will be glad, I will be glad in the Lord.
Bless thou the Lord, O my soul,
Praise ye the Lord,
  Repeat last 2 lines three times

103 Walter Chalmers Smith, 1824–1908.

Immortal, invisible, God only wise,
In light inaccessible hid from our eyes,
Most blessed, most glorious, the Ancient of
  Days,
Almighty, victorious, Thy great name we
  praise.

Unresting, unhasting, and silent as light,
Nor wanting, nor wasting, Thou rulest in might;
Thy justice like mountains high soaring above,
Thy clouds which are fountains of goodness
  and love.

To all life Thou givest – to both great and small;
In all life Thou livest, the true life of all;
We blossom and flourish as leaves on the tree,
And wither and perish – but nought changeth
  Thee.

Great Father of Glory, pure Father of Light,
Thine angels adore Thee, all veiling their sight;
All laud we would render; O help us to see:
'Tis only the splendour of light hideth Thee.

Immortal, invisible, God only wise,
In light inaccessible hid from our eyes,
Most blessed, most glorious, the Ancient of
  Days,
Almighty, victorious, Thy great name we
  praise.

104 Frances Ridley Havergal, 1836–79

In full and glad surrender
I give myself to Thee,
Thine utterly and only
And evermore to be.

O Son of God, Who lov'st me,
I will be Thine alone;
And all I have and am, Lord,
Shall henceforth be Thine own!

Reign over me, Lord Jesus;
O make my heart Thy throne;
It shall be Thine, dear Saviour,
It shall be Thine alone.

O come and reign, Lord Jesus;
Rule over everything!
And keep me always loyal,
And true to Thee, my King.

105 Bob Kilpatrick
Copyright © Prism Tree Music

In my life Lord, be glorified, be glorified;
In my life Lord, be glorified today.

In your church, Lord, be glorified, be glorified;
In your church, Lord, be glorified today.

106 Anna Laetitia Waring 1820–1910

In heavenly love abiding,
No change my heart shall fear;
And safe is such confiding
For nothing changes here:
The storm may roar without me,
My heart may low be laid;
But God is round about me,
And can I be dismayed?

Wherever He may guide me,
No want shall turn me back;
My Shepherd is beside me,
And nothing can I lack;
His wisdom ever waketh,
His sight is never dim;
He knows the way He taketh,
And I will walk with Him.

Green pastures are before me,
Which yet I have not seen;
Bright skies will soon be o'er me,
Where the dark clouds have been:
My hope I cannot measure,
My path to life is free;
My Saviour has my treasure,
And He will walk with me.

107 John Bowring, 1792–1872

In the cross of Christ I glory,
Towering o'er the wrecks of time;
All the light of sacred story
Gathers round its head sublime,

When the woes of life o'ertake me,
Hopes deceive, and fears annoy,
Never shall the cross forsake me;
Lo! it glows with peace and joy.

When the sun of bliss is beaming
Light and love upon my way,
From the cross the radiance streaming
Adds more lustre to the day.

Bane and blessing, pain and pleasure,
By the cross are sanctified;
Peace is there that knows no measure,
Joys that through all time abide.

In the cross of Christ I glory,
Towering o'er the wrecks of time:
All the light of sacred story
Gathers round its head sublime.

108 Psalm 22: 3, 25.

**In the presence of your people I will praise
your name**
For alone you are holy, enthroned on the
praises of Israel.
Let us celebrate your goodness and your
steadfast love.
May your name be exalted here on earth and
in heav'n above.

109 Anon

In the name of Jesus, (*repeat*)
We have the victory.
In the name of Jesus, (*repeat*)
Demons will have to flee.
Who can tell what God can do?
Who can tell of his love for you?
In the name of Jesus, Jesus,
We have the victory.

110 William Walsham How 1823–97

It is a thing most wonderful,
Almost too wonderful to be,
That God's own Son should come from heaven,
And die to save a child like me.

And yet I know that it is true;
He chose a poor and humble lot,
And wept and toiled and mourned and died,
For love of those who loved Him not.

I sometimes think about the Cross,
And shut my eyes and try to see
The cruel nails and crown of thorns,
And Jesus crucified for me.

But even could I see Him die,
I could but see a little part
Of that great love which like a fire
Is always burning in His heart.

I cannot tell how He could love
A child so weak and full of sin;
His love must be most wonderful,
If He could die my love to win.

It is most wonderful to know
His love for me so free and sure;
But 'tis more wonderful to see
My love for Him so faint and poor.

And yet I want to love Thee, Lord;
O light the flame within my heart,
And I will love Thee more and more,
Until I see Thee as Thou art.

111 Kurt Kaiser
Copyright © 1969 Lexicon Music Inc.
Word Music (UK)

It only takes a spark to get a fire going
And soon all those around can warm up in its
glowing;
That's how it is with God's love, once you've
experienced it
You spread His love to everyone;
You want to pass it on.

What a wondrous time is spring when all the
trees are budding
The birds begin to sing; the flowers start their
blooming;
That's how it is with God's love, once you've
experienced it you want to sing,
It's fresh like spring; you want to pass it on.

I wish for you, my friend, this happiness, that
I've found
You can depend on Him, It matters not where
you're bound;
I'll shout it from the mountain top, I want my
world to know;
The Lord of love has come to me, I want to
pass it on.

112 Mary Shekleton, 1827–83

**It passeth knowledge, that dear love of
Thine,**
My Saviour, Jesus! Yet this soul of mine
Would of Thy love, in all its breadth and length,
Its height and depth, and everlasting strength,
Know more and more.

It passeth telling, that dear love of Thine,
My Saviour, Jesus! Yet these lips of mine
Would fain proclaim to sinners far and near
A love which can remove all guilty fear,
And love beget.

It passeth praises, that dear love of Thine,
My Saviour, Jesus! Yet this heart of mine
Would sing that love, so full, so rich, so free.
Which brings a rebel sinner, such as me,
Nigh unto God.

O fill me, Saviour, Jesus, with Thy love!
Lead, lead me to the living fount above;
Thither may I, in simple faith, draw nigh,
And never to another fountain fly,
But unto Thee.

And then, when Jesus face to face I see,
When at His lofty throne I bow the knee,
Then of His love, in all its breadth and length,
Its height and depth, its everlasting strength,
My soul shall sing.

113 James Grindlay Small 1817–88

I've found a friend; O such a friend!
He loved me ere I knew Him;
He drew me with the cords of love,
And thus He bound me;
And round my heart still closely twine
Those ties which nought can sever;
For I am His, and He is mine,
For ever and for ever.

I've found a friend; O such a Friend!
He bled, He died to save me;
And not alone the gift of life,
But His own self He gave me.
Nought that I have mine own I call,
I hold it for the Giver:
My heart, my strength, my life, my all
Are His, and His for ever.

I've found a Friend; O such a Friend!
All power to Him is given,
To guard me on my onward course
And bring me safe to heaven.
Eternal glories gleam afar,
To nerve my faint endeavour;
So now to watch, to work, to war,
And then to rest for ever.

I've found a Friend; O such a Friend,
So kind, and true, and tender!
So wise a Counsellor and Guide,
So mighty a Defender!
From Him who loves me now so well
What power my soul shall sever?
Shall life or death? shall earth or hell?
No! I am His for ever.

114 Anon

I've got peace like a river, peace like a river,
I've got peace like a river, in my soul,
I've got peace like a river, peace like a river,
I've got peace like a river, in my soul.

115 Betty Pulkingham
Copyright © 1974, 1975 Celebration
Services (International) Ltd.

Jesus, Lamb of God,
Have mercy on us.
Jesus, bearer of our sins,
Have mercy on us.
Jesus, redeemer of the world,
Give us your peace. (*repeat*)

116 Cecil Frances Alexander 1818–95

Jesus call us; o'er the tumult
Of our life's wild restless sea,
Day by day His voice is sounding,
Saying, "Christian, follow me";

As, of old, apostles heard it
By the Galilean lake,
Turned from home, and toil, and kindred,
Leaving all for His dear sake.

Jesus calls us from the worship
Of the vain world's golden store,
From each idol that would keep us,
Saying, "Christian, love Me more."

In our joys and in our sorrows
Days of toil and hours of ease,
Still He calls, in cares and pleasures,
"Christian, love Me more than these."

Jesus calls us! By Thy mercies,
Saviour, may we hear Thy call,
Give our hearts to Thine obedience,
Serve and love Thee best of all.

117 Anon

Jesus Christ is alive today,
I know, I know it's true.
Sov'reign of the Universe,
I give him homage due.
Seated there at God's right hand,
I am with him in the promised land.
Jesus lives and reigns in me,
That's how I know it's true.

118
David Bolton
Copyright © 1975 Thankyou Music

Jesus, how lovely you are!
You are so gentle so pure and kind,
You shine like the morning star:
Jesus, how lovely you are.

Alleluia, Jesus is my Lord and King
Alleluia, Jesus is my everything.

Alleluia, Jesus died and rose again;
Alleluia, Jesus forgave all my sin.

Alleluia, Jesus is meek and lowly;
Alleluia, Jesus is pure and holy.

Alleluia, Jesus is the bridegroom;
Alleluia, Jesus will take his bride soon.

119
David J Mansell
Copyright © 1980 Springtide/Word
Music (UK)

Jesus is Lord! Creation's voice proclaims it,
For by his power each tree and flower was
    planned and made.
Jesus is Lord! The universe declares it.
Sun, moon and stars in heaven cry Jesus is Lord!

Jesus is Lord! Jesus is Lord!
Praise him with 'Hallelujahs' for Jesus is Lord!

Jesus is Lord! Yet from his throne eternal
In flesh he came to die in pain on Calv'ry's tree.
Jesus is Lord! From him all life proceeding,
Yet gave his life a ransom thus setting us free.

Jesus is Lord! O'er sin the mighty conqueror,
From death he rose and all his foes shall own
    his name.
Jesus is Lord! God sends his Holy Spirit
To show by works of power that Jesus is Lord.

120 Charles Wesley 1707–88, altd.

Jesus, lover of my soul,
Let me to Thy bosom fly,
While the nearer waters roll,
While the tempest still is high:
Hide me, O my Saviour, hide,
Till the storm of life is past;
Safe into the haven guide;
O receive my soul at last!

Other refuge have I none,
Hangs my helpless soul on Thee;
Leave, ah! leave me not alone,
Still support and comfort me:
All my trust on Thee is stayed;
All my help from Thee I bring;
Cover my defenceless head
With the shadow of Thy wing.

Thou, O Christ, art all I want;
More than all in Thee I find;
Raise the fallen, cheer the faint,
Heal the sick, and lead the blind.
Just and holy is Thy name,
I am all unrighteousness;
False, and full of sin I am,
Thou art full of truth and grace.

Plenteous grace with Thee is found,
Grace to cover all my sin;
Let the healing streams abound,
Make and keep me pure within.
Thou of life the fountain art,
Freely let me take of Thee;
Spring Thou up within my heart,
Rise to all eternity.

121
N. J. Clayton
Copyright © 1938, 1943 by Norman
J. Clayton Word Music (UK)

Jesus my Lord will love me for ever,
From Him no pow'r of evil can sever,
He gave His life to ransom my soul,
Now I belong to Him:

Now I belong to Jesus,
Jesus belongs to me,
Not for the years of time alone,
But for eternity.

Once I was lost in sin's degradation,
Jesus came down to bring me salvation,
Lifted me up from sorrow and shame,
Now I belong to Him:

Joy floods my soul for Jesus has saved me,
Freed me from sin that long had enslaved me,
His precious blood He gave to redeem,
Now I belong to Him.

122 Nada Hearn
Copyright © 1974/1978 Scripture in Song

Jesus, Name above all names.
Beautiful Saviour, glorious Lord,
Emmanuel, God is with us,
Blessed Redeemer, Living Word.

123 Isaac Watts 1674–1748

Jesus shall reign where'er the sun
Does His successive journeys run;
His kingdom stretch from shore to shore
Till moons shall rise and set no more.

To Him shall endless prayer be made,
And princes throng to crown His head;
His name like sweet perfume shall rise
With every morning sacrifice.

People and realms of every tongue
Dwell on his love with sweetest song;
And infant voices shall proclaim
Their early blessings on His name.

Blessings abound where'er He reigns;
The prisoner leaps to lose his chains,
The weary find eternal rest,
And all the sons of want are bless'd.

Let every creature rise and bring
The highest honours to our King;
Angels descend with songs again;
And earth repeats the loud Amen.

124 G. Kendrick
Copyright © 1977 Thankyou Music

Jesus, stand among us at the meeting of our
lives,
Be our sweet agreement at the meeting of our
eyes;
O, Jesus, we love You, so we gather here,
Join our hearts in unity and take away our fear.

So to You we're gathering out of each and every
land,
Christ the love between us at the joining of our
hands;
O, Jesus, we love You, so we gather here,
Join our hearts in unity and take away our fear.

125 William Pennefather 1816–73

Jesus, stand among us
In Thy risen power;
Let this time of worship
Be a hallowed hour.

Breathe the Holy Spirit
Into every heart;
Bid the fears and sorrows
From each soul depart.

Thus with quickened footsteps
We'll pursue our way,
Watching for the dawning
Of eternal day.

126 Charles Wesley, 1708–88

Jesus, the name high over all,
In hell, or earth, or sky:
Angels and men before it fall,
And devils fear and fly. (*repeat*)

Jesus, the name to sinners dear,
The name to sinners giv'n;
It scatters all their guilty fear,
It turns their hell to heav'n. (*repeat*)

Jesus the prisoner's fetters breaks,
And bruises Satan's head;
Pow'r into strengthless souls He speaks,
And life into the dead. (*repeat*)

Oh, that the world might taste and see.
The riches of His grace!
The arms of love that compass me,
Would all mankind embrace. (*repeat*)

His only righteousness I show,
His saving truth proclaim:
'Tis all my business here below,
To cry, "Behold the Lamb!" (*repeat*)

Happy, if with my latest breath
I may but gasp His name:
Preach Him to all and cry in death,
"Behold, behold the Lamb!" (*repeat*)

127
D. Bryant
Copyright © 1978 Thankyou Music

Jesus take me as I am,
I can come no other way.
Take me deeper into You,
Make my flesh life melt away.
Make me like a precious stone,
Crystal clear and finely honed.
Life of Jesus shining through,
Giving glory back to You.

128
from the Latin (twelfth century)
R. Palmer 1808–87

Jesus, the joy of loving hearts,
True source of life, and light of men;
From the best bliss that earth imparts
We turn unfilled to you again.

Your truth unchanged has ever stood,
You rescue those who on you call;
To those yet seeking, you are good –
To those who find you, all-in-all.

We taste of you, the living bread,
And long to feast upon you still;
We drink from you, the fountain-head,
Our thirsty souls from you we fill.

Our restless spirits long for you,
Whichever way our lot is cast,
Glad when your gracious smile we view,
Blessed when our faith can hold you fast.

Jesus, for ever with us stay,
Make all our moments calm and bright;
Chase the dark night of sin away,
Spread through the world your holy light.

129
Bernard of Clairvaux, 1091–1153
Tr. by Edward Caswall, 1814–78

Jesus, the very thought of Thee
With sweetness fills the breast;
But sweeter far Thy face to see,
And in Thy presence rest.

Nor voice can sing, nor heart can frame,
Nor can the mem'ry find,
A sweeter sound than Thy blest name,
O Saviour of mankind!

O Hope of ev'ry contrite heart,
O Joy of all the meek,
To those who ask, how kind Thou art!
How good to those who seek!

But what to those who find! Ah, this
Nor tongue nor pen can show:
The love of Jesus, what it is,
None but His loved ones know.

Jesus, our only joy be Thou,
As Thou our prize wilt be;
In Thee be all our glory now,
And thro' eternity.

130
Fred Dunn © Thankyou Music
Psalm 100

Jubilate, ev'rybody,
Serve the Lord in all your ways,
And come before his presence singing;
Enter now his courts with praise.
For the Lord our God is gracious,
And his mercy everlasting.
Jubilate, jubilate,
Jubilate deo!

131
P. Kyle
Copyright © 1980 Thankyou Music

Jesus we enthrone You
We proclaim You our King.
Standing here in the midst of us
We raise You up with our praise,
And as we worship build a throne, (*repeat twice*)
Come Lord Jesus and take Your place.

132
Charlotte Elliott 1789–1871

Just as I am, without one plea,
But that Thy blood was shed for me,
And that Thou bidd'st me come to Thee,
O Lamb of God, I come! I come!

Just as I am, and waiting not
To rid my soul of one dark blot,
To Thee, whose blood can cleanse each spot,
O Lamb of God, I come! I come!

Just as I am, tho' tossed about
With many a conflict, many a doubt,
Fightings within, and fears without,
O Lamb of God, I come! I come!

Just as I am, poor, wretched, blind,
Sight, riches, healing of the mind,
Yea, all I need, in Thee to find,
O Lamb of God, I come! I come!

Just as I am, Thou wilt receive,
Wilt welcome, pardon, cleanse, relieve;
Because Thy promise I believe,
O Lamb of God, I come! I come!

Just as I am, Thy love unknown
Hath broken ev'ry barrier down
Now, to be Thine, yea, Thine alone,
O Lamb of God, I come! I come!

133 Copyright © 1963 Melvin Harrell
Gospel Publishing House

Let all that is within me cry, 'Holy'. (*repeat*)
Holy, Holy, Holy is the Lamb that was slain.

Let all that is within me cry, 'Worthy' . . . 'Jesus'
. . . 'glory' . . .

134 G. Kendrick
Copyright © 1977 Thankyou Music

Let Me have My way among you.
Do not strive, do not strive, (*repeat*)
For Mine is the power and the glory
For ever and ever the same.
Let Me have My way among you,
Do not strive, do not strive.

We'll let You have Your way among us,
We'll not strive, we'll not strive (*repeat*)
For Yours is the power and the glory
For ever and ever the same.
We'll let You have Your way among us,
We'll not strive, we'll not strive.

Let My peace rule within your hearts,
Do not strive, do not strive (*repeat*)
For Mine is the power and the glory
For ever and ever the same.
Let My peace rule within your hearts,
Do not strive, do not strive.

We'll let Your peace rule within our hearts,
We'll not strive, we'll not strive (*repeat*)
For Yours. . . etc.

135 George Herbert 1593–1633

Let all the world in every corner sing
"My God and King!"
The heavens are not too high;
His praise may thither fly:
The earth is not too low;
His praises there may grow.
Let all the world in every corner sing
"My God and King!"

Let all the world in every corner sing
"My God and King!"
The Church with psalms must shout,
No door can keep them out:
But, above all, the heart
Must bear the longest part.
Let all the world in every corner sing
"My God and King!"

136 Albert Orsborn

Let the beauty of Jesus be seen in me,
All His wondrous compassion and purity,
Oh, Thou Spirit Divine,
All my nature refine,
Till the beauty of Jesus be seen in me.

137 D. Bilbrough
Copyright © 1979 Thankyou Music

Let there be love shared among us,
Let there be love in our eyes,
May now Your love sweep this nation,
Cause us O Lord to arise,
Give us a fresh understanding
Of brotherly love that is real,
Let there be love shared among us,
Let there be love.

138 Gloria Gaither and William J. Gaither
Copyright © 1972 by William J. Gaither
Coronation Music

Let's just praise the Lord!
Praise the Lord!
Let's just lift our hearts* to heaven
And praise the Lord;
Let's just praise the Lord!
Praise the Lord!
Let's just lift our hearts* to heaven
And Praise the Lord!

*Alternate lyrics, "voices", "hands".

139 G. W. Kitchen 1827–1912
and M. R. Newbolt 1874–1956
© Hymns Ancient & Modern,
Jubilate Hymns

***Lift high the cross**, the love of Christ
proclaim
Till all the world adores his sacred name!*

Come, Christians, follow where the captain
trod,
The king victorious, Christ the Son of God:

Each new-born soldier of the crucified
Bears on his brow the seal of him who died:

This is the sign that Satan's armies fear
And angels veil their faces to revere:

Saved by the cross on which their Lord was
slain,
See Adam's children their lost home regain:

From north and south, from east and west they
raise
In growing unison their songs of praise:

Let every race and every language tell
Of him who saves our souls from death and
hell!

O Lord, once lifted on the tree of pain,
Draw all the world to seek you once again:

Set up your throne, that earth's despair may
cease
Beneath the shadow of its healing peace:

140 Frances Ridley Havergal, 1836–79

Like a river, glorious
Is God's perfect peace,
Over all victorious
In its bright increase;
Perfect, yet it floweth
Fuller every day,
Perfect, yet it groweth
Deeper all the way.

Stayed upon Jehovah,
Hearts are fully blest;
Finding, as He promised,
Perfect peace and rest.

Hidden in the hollow
Of His blessed hand,
Never foe can follow
Never traitor stand;
Not a surge of worry,
Not a shade of care,
Not a blast of hurry
Touch the Spirit there.

Every joy or trial
Falleth from above,
Traced upon our dial
By the Sun of love.
We may trust Him fully
All for us to do;
They who trust Him wholly
Find Him wholly true.

141 Charles Wesley, 1707–88

Lo! He comes with clouds descending,
Once for favoured sinners slain;
Thousand thousand saints attending,
Swell the triumph of His train;
Hallelujah!
God appears on earth to reign.

Every eye shall now behold Him
Robed in dreadful majesty;
Those who set at nought and sold Him,
Pierced and nailed Him to the tree,
Deeply wailing,
Shall the true Messiah see.

Now redemption, long expected,
See in solemn pomp appear!
All His saints, by man rejected,
Now shall meet Him in the air.
Hallelujah!
See the day of God appear.

Yea, Amen! Let all adore Thee,
High on Thy eternal throne;
Saviour, take the power and glory,
Claim the kingdom of Thine own;
Hallelujah!
Everlasting God, come down!

142 Timothy Dudley-Smith 1926–
Copyright ©

Lord, for the years your love has kept and
guided,
Urged and inspired us, cheered us on our way,
Sought us and saved us, pardoned and
provided:
Lord of the years, we bring our thanks today.

Lord, for that Word, the Word of life which
fires us,
Speaks to our hearts and sets our souls ablaze,
Teaches and trains, rebukes us and inspires us:
Lord of the Word, receive your people's praise.

Lord, for our land, in this our generation,
Spirits oppressed by pleasure, wealth and care:
For young and old, for commonwealth and
nation,
Lord of our land, be pleased to hear our prayer.

Lord, for our world, where men disown and
doubt you,
Loveless in strength, and comfortless in pain,
Hungry and helpless, lost indeed without you:
Lord of the world, we pray that Christ may
reign.

Lord for ourselves; in living power remake us –
Self on the cross and Christ upon the throne,
Past put behind us, for the future take us:
Lord of our lives, to live for Christ alone.

143 William Tidd Matson 1833–99

Lord, I was blind! I could not see
In Thy marred visage any grace:
But now the beauty of Thy face
In radiant vision dawns on me.

Lord, I was deaf! I could not hear
The thrilling music of Thy voice;
But now I hear Thee and rejoice,
And all Thine uttered words are dear.

Lord, I was dumb! I could not speak
The grace and glory of Thy name;
But now, as touched with living flame,
My lips Thine eager praises wake.

Lord, I was dead! I could not stir
My lifeless soul to come to Thee;
But now, since Thou has quickened me,
I rise from sin's dark sepulchre.

For Thou hast made the blind to see,
The deaf to hear, the dumb to speak,
The dead to live; and lo, I break
The chains of my captivity!

144 T. Hatton

Lord, make me an instrument,
An instrument of worship,
I lift up my hands in Thy name,
Lord, make me an instrument,
An instrument of worship,
I lift up my hands in Thy name.

I'll sing you a love song,
A love song of worship;
I lift up my hands in Thy name.
I'll sing you a love song.
A love song to Jesus;
I lift up my hands in Thy name.

Lord, make us a symphony,
A symphony of worship;
We lift up our hands in Thy name,
Lord, make us a symphony,
A symphony of worship;
We lift up our hands in Thy name.

145 Copyright © Michael Perry, 1942–

Like a mighty river flowing,
Like a flower in beauty growing,
Far beyond all human knowing
Is the perfect peace of God.

Like the hills serene and even,
Like the coursing clouds of heaven,
Like the heart that's been forgiven,
Is the perfect peace of God.

Like the summer breezes playing,
Like the tall trees softly swaying,
Like the lips of silent praying
Is the perfect peace of God.

Like the morning sun ascended,
Like the scents of evening blended,
Like a friendship never ended
Is the perfect peace of God.

Like the azure ocean swelling,
Like the jewel all-excelling,
Far beyond our human telling
Is the perfect peace of God.

146 Copyright © Christopher Porteous 1935–

Lord may we see your hands and side
Touch you and feel your presence near
Lord could our eyes behold those clouds
And watch you rising disappear,
Help us to pray for your return
To watch until you come to reign
And be your witness through the world
To speak and glorify your name.

Lord unto you we lift our eyes
Help us to live as you desire
Bring down upon us power to win
Through tongues of Holy Spirit fire.
Lord breathe upon us to receive
The grace and love your Spirit gives
And may we know you with us now
Because in us your Spirit lives.

147 Copyright © Michael Saward 1932–

Lord of the cross of shame,
Set my cold heart aflame
With love for you, my saviour and my master;
Who on that lonely day
Bore all my sins away,
And saved me from the judgement and
    disaster.

Lord of the empty tomb,
Born of a virgin's womb,
Triumphant over death, its power defeated;
How gladly now I sing
Your praise, my risen king,
And worship you, in heaven's splendour
    seated.

Lord of my life today,
Teach me to live and pray
As one who knows the joy of sins forgiven;
So may I ever be,
Now and eternally,
One with my fellow-citizens in heaven.

148 Frances Ridley Havergal 1836–79

Lord, speak to me, that I may speak
In living echoes of Thy tone;
As Thou hast sought, so let me seek
Thy erring children lost and lone.

O lead me, Lord, that I may lead
The wandering and the wavering feet;
O feed me, Lord, that I may feed
Thy hungering ones with manna sweet.

O strengthen me, that, while I stand
Firm on the rock, and strong in Thee,
I may stretch out a loving hand
To wrestlers with the troubled sea.

O teach me, Lord, that I may teach
The precious things Thou dost impart;
And wing my words, that they may reach
The hidden depths of many a heart.

O give Thine own sweet rest to me,
That I may speak with soothing power
A word in season, as from Thee,
To weary ones in needful hour.

O fill me with Thy fullness, Lord,
Until my very heart o'erflow
In kindling thought and glowing word,
Thy love to tell, Thy praise to show.

O use me, Lord, use even me,
Just as Thou wilt, and when, and where,
Until Thy blessed face I see,
Thy rest, Thy joy, Thy glory share.

149 Charles Wesley 1707–88

Love divine, all loves excelling,
Joy of heaven, to earth come down,
Fix in us Thy humble dwelling,
All Thy faithful mercies crown:
Jesus, Thou art all compassion,
Pure, unbounded love Thou art;
Visit us with Thy salvation,
Enter every trembling heart.

Breathe, O breathe Thy loving Spirit
Into every troubled breast;
Let us all in Thee inherit,
Let us find Thy promised rest;
Take away the love of sinning,
Alpha and omega be;
End of faith, as its beginning,
Set our hearts at liberty.

Come, almighty to deliver,
Let us all Thy grace receive;
Suddenly return, and never,
Never more Thy temples leave.
Thee we would be always blessing,
Serve Thee as Thy hosts above,
Pray, and praise Thee without ceasing,
Glory in Thy perfect love.

Finish, then, Thy new creation:
Pure and spotless let us be;
Let us see Thy great salvation,
Perfectly restored in Thee,
Changed from glory into glory,
Till in heaven we take our place,
Till we cast our crowns before Thee,
Lost in wonder, love, and praise.

150 Robert Lowry 1826–99

Low in the grave He lay,
Jesus, my Saviour;
Waiting the coming day,
Jesus, my Lord.

Up from the grave He arose,
With a mighty triumph o'er His foes;
He arose a Victor from the dark domain,
And he lives for ever with His saints to reign:
He arose! He arose! Hallelujah! Christ arose!

Vainly they watch His bed,
Jesus, my Saviour;
Vainly they seal the dead,
Jesus, my Lord.

Death cannot keep his prey,
Jesus, my Saviour,
He tore the bars away,
Jesus, my Lord

151 Jack W. Hayford
Copyright © 1981 Rocksmith Music

Majesty, worship His Majesty;
Unto Jesus be glory, honour and praise.
Majesty, kingdom authority, flows from His
    throne
Unto His own, His anthem raise.
So exalt, lift up on high the name of Jesus
Magnify, come glorify, Christ Jesus the King.
Majesty, worship His Majesty,
Jesus who died, now glorified, King of all Kings.

152 George Matheson 1842–1906

Make me a captive, Lord,
And then I shall be free;
Force me to render up my sword,
And I shall conqueror be.
I sink in life's alarms
When by myself I stand;
Imprison me within Thine arms,
And strong shall be my hand.

My heart is weak and poor
Until it master find;
It has no spring of action sure –
It varies with the wind.
It cannot freely move,
Till Thou has wrought its chain;
Enslave it with Thy matchless love,
And deathless it shall reign.

My power is faint and low
Till I have learned to serve;
It wants the needed fire to glow,
It wants the breeze to nerve;
It cannot drive the world,
Until itself be driven;
Its flag can only be unfurled
When Thou shalt breathe from heaven.

My will is not my own
Till Thou has made it Thine;
If it would reach a monarch's throne
It must its crown resign;
It only stands unbent,
Amid the clashing strife,
When on Thy bosom it has leant
And found in Thee its life.

153 Sebastian Temple
Copyright © 1967 Franciscan Communications

Make me a channel of your peace.
Where there is hatred let me bring your love;
Where there is injury, your pardon, Lord;
And where there's doubt, true faith in you.

Oh, master, grant that I may never seek
So much to be consoled as to console;
To be understood as to understand;
To be loved, as to love with all my soul.

Make me a channel of your peace.
Where there's despair in life let me bring hope;
Where there is darkness, only light;
And where there's sadness, ever joy.

Make me a channel of your peace.
It is in pardoning that we are pardoned,
In giving to all men that we receive;
And in dying that we're born to eternal life.

154 Philipp Bliss 1838–76

Man of Sorrows! What a name
For the Son of God, who came
Ruined sinners to reclaim!
Hallelujah! what a Saviour!

Bearing shame and scoffing rude,
In my place condemned He stood;
Sealed my pardon with His blood;
Hallelujah, what a Saviour!

Guilty, vile and helpless we;
Spotless Lamb of God was He:
Full atonement – can it be?
Hallelujah! what a Saviour!

Lifted up was He to die.
It is finished! was His cry;
Now in heaven exalted high;
Hallelujah! what a Saviour!

When He comes, our glorious King,
All His ransomed home to bring,
Then anew this song we'll sing:
Hallelujah! what a Saviour!

155 Frances Ridley Havergal 1836–79

Master, speak! Thy servant heareth,
Waiting for Thy gracious word,
Longing for Thy voice that cheereth;
Master, let it now be heard,
I am listening, Lord, for Thee;
What hast Thou to say to me?

Speak to me by name, O Master!
Let me know it is to me;
Speak, that I may follow faster,
With a step more firm and free,
Where the Shepherd leads the flock
In the shadow of the rock.

Master, speak! though least and lowest,
Let me not unheard depart;
Master, speak! for O Thou knowest
All the yearning of my heart;
Knowest all its truest need;
Speak, and make me blest indeed.

Master, speak! and make me ready,
When Thy voice is truly heard,
With obedience glad and steady
Still to follow every word,
I am listening, Lord, for Thee;
Master, speak, O speak to me!

156 Cliff Barrows
Copyright © 1982 by Cliff Barrows

May God's blessing surround you each day
As you trust Him and walk in His way,
May His presence within guard and keep you
  from sin,
Go in peace, go in joy, go in love.

157 Kate B. Wilkinson 1859–1928

May the mind of Christ my Saviour
Live in me from day to day,
By His love and power controlling
All I do and say.

May the Word of God dwell richly
In my heart from hour to hour,
So that all may see I triumph
Only through his power.

May the peace of God my Father
Rule my life in everything,
That I may be calm to comfort
Sick and sorrowing.

May the love of Jesus fill me,
As the waters fill the sea;
Him exalting, self abasing,
This is victory.

May I run the race before me,
Strong and brave to face the foe,
Looking only unto Jesus,
As I onward go.

158 Ray Palmer 1808–87

My faith looks up to Thee,
Thou Lamb of Calvary,
Saviour divine:
Now hear me while I pray;
Take all my guilt away;
O let me from this day
Be wholly Thine.

May Thy rich grace impart
Strength to my fainting heart,
My zeal inspire.
As Thou hast died for me,
O may my love to Thee
Pure, warm, and changeless be,
A living fire.

While life's dark maze I tread,
And griefs around me spread,
Be Thou my guide;
Bid darkness turn to day,
Wipe sorrow's tears away,
Nor let me ever stray
From Thee aside

When ends life's transient dream,
When death's co!d sullen stream
Shall o'er me roll,
Blest Saviour, then in love,
Fear and distrust remove;
O bear me safe above,
A ransomed soul.

159 Luke I: 46–47, 49

My soul doth magnify the Lord,
And my spirit hath rejoiced in God my Saviour
For he that is mighty hath done great things,
And holy is his name.
My soul doth magnify the Lord, (*repeat*)
And my Spirit hath rejoiced in God my Saviour
For he that is mighty hath done great things,
And holy is his name.
My soul doth magnify the Lord, (*repeat*)
And my spirit hath rejoiced in God my saviour
For he that is mighty hath done great things,
And holy is his name.

160 Samuel Crossman c. 1624–83

My song is love unknown;
My Saviour's love to me;
Love to the loveless shown,
That they may lovely be.
O who am I,
That for my sake,
My Lord should take
Frail flesh, and die?

He came from His blest Throne,
Salvation to bestow;
But men made strange, and none
The longed-for Christ would know.
But O my friend!
My Friend indeed,
Who at my need
His life did spend.

Sometimes they strew His way,
And His sweet praises sing;
Resounding all the day,
Hosannas to their King.
Then: 'Crucify!'
Is all their breath,
And for His death
They thirst and cry.

Why, what hath my Lord done?
What makes this rage and spite?
He made the lame to run,
He gave the blind their sight.
Sweet injuries!
Yet they at these
Themselves displease,
And 'gainst Him rise.

They rise and needs will have
My dear Lord made away:
A murderer they save;
The Prince of life they slay.

Yet cheerful He
To suffering goes,
That He His foes
From thence might free.

In life, no house, no home
My Lord on earth might have;
In death, no friendly tomb
But what a stranger gave.
What may I say?
Heav'n was His home;
But mine the tomb
Wherein He lay.

Here might I stay and sing,
No story so divine;
Never was love, dear King,
Never was grief like Thine.
This is my Friend,
In whose sweet praise
I all my days
Could gladly spend.

161 J. Keble 1792–1866

New every morning is the love
Our waking and uprising prove:
Through sleep and darkness safely brought,
Restored to life and power and thought.

New mercies, each returning day,
Surround your people as they pray:
New dangers past, new sins forgiven,
New thoughts of God, new hopes of heaven.

If in our daily life our mind
Be set to honour all we find,
New treasures still, of countless price,
God will provide for sacrifice.

The trivial round, the common task,
Will give us all we ought to ask:
Room to deny ourselves, a road
To bring us daily nearer God.

Prepare us, Lord, in your dear love
For perfect rest with you above,
And help us, this and every day,
To grow more like you as we pray.

162 E. Mote 1797–1874
Words © in this version Jubilate Hymns

My hope is built on nothing less
Than Jesus' blood and righteousness;
No merit of my own I claim,
But wholly trust in Jesus' name.
On Christ, the solid rock, I stand –
All other ground is sinking sand.

When weary in this earthly race,
I rest on his unchanging grace;
In every wild and stormy gale
My anchor holds and will not fail.

His vow, his covenant and blood
Are my defence against the flood;
When earthly hopes are swept away
He will uphold me on that day.

When the last trumpet's voice shall sound,
O may I then in him be found!
Clothed in his righteousness alone,
Faultless to stand before his throne.

163 Martin Rinkart 1586–1649
tr. by Catherine Winkworth 1829–78

Now thank we all our God,
With hearts, and hands, and voices;
Who wondrous things hath done,
In whom His world rejoices;
Who, from our mothers' arms,
Hath blessed us on our way
With countless gifts of love,
And still is ours today.

O may this bounteous God
Through all our life be near us,
With ever-joyful hearts
And blessed peace to cheer us,
And keep us in His grace,
And guide us when perplexed,
And free us from all ills
In this world and the next.

All praise and thanks to God
The Father now be given,
The Son, and Him who reigns
With Them in highest heaven:
The one, eternal God,
Whom earth and heaven adore;
For thus it was, is now,
And shall be evermore.

164 Elizabeth A. P. Head, 1850–1936
Copyright © Control

O Breath of life, come sweeping through us,
Revive your church with life and power;
O Breath of life, come, cleanse, renew us
And fit your church to meet this hour.

O Breath of love, come breathe within us,
Renewing thought and will and heart;
Come, love of Christ, afresh to win us,
Revive your church in every part!

O Wind of God, come bend us, break us
Till humbly we confess our need;
Then, in your tenderness remake us,
Revive, restore – for this we plead.

165 J. Wade c. 1711–86

O come let us adore Him, (*repeat twice*)
Christ the Lord.

166 William Cowper 1731–1800

O for a closer walk with God,
A calm and heavenly frame,
A light to shine upon the road
That leads me to the Lamb.

Where is the blessedness I knew
When first I saw the Lord?
Where is that soul-refreshing view
Of Jesus and His word?

What peaceful hours I once enjoyed!
How sweet their memory still!
But they have left an aching void
The world can never fill.

Return, O holy dove! return,
Sweet messenger of rest!
I hate the sins that made Thee mourn,
And drove Thee from my breast.

The dearest idol I have known,
Whate'er that idol be,
Help me to tear it from Thy throne,
And worship only Thee.

So shall my walk be close with God,
Calm and serene my frame;
So purer light shall mark the road
That leads me to the Lamb.

167 Charles Wesley 1707–88

O for a heart to praise my God,
A heart from sin set free,
A heart that always feels Thy blood
So freely shed for me.

A heart resigned, submissive, meek,
My great Redeemer's throne,
Where only Christ is heard to speak,
Where Jesus reigns alone:

A humble, lowly, contrite heart,
Believing, true, and clean;
Which neither life nor death can part
From Him that dwells within:

A heart in every thought renewed,
And full of love divine;
Perfect, and right, and pure, and good,
A copy, Lord, of Thine.

Thy nature, gracious Lord, impart;
Come quickly from above,
Write Thy new name upon my heart,
Thy new, best name of love.

168 Charles Wesley 1707–88, altd.

O for a thousand tongues to sing
My great Redeemer's praise,
The glories of my God and King,
The triumphs of His grace!

Jesus! The name that charms our fears,
That bids our sorrows cease;
'Tis music in the sinner's ears,
'Tis life, and health, and peace.

He breaks the power of cancelled sin,
He sets the prisoner free;
His blood can make the foulest clean;
His blood availed for me.

He speaks, and, listening to His voice,
New life the dead receive,
The mournful, broken hearts rejoice,
The humble poor believe.

Hear Him, ye deaf; His praise, ye dumb,
Your loosened tongues employ:
Ye blind, behold your Saviour come;
And leap, ye lame, for joy.

My gracious Master and my God,
Assist me to proclaim,
To spread through all the earth abroad,
The honours of Thy name.

169 P. Doddridge 1702–1751

O happy day! that fixed my choice
On Thee, my Saviour and my God!
Well may this glowing heart rejoice,
And tell its raptures all abroad.

O happy day! O happy day!
When Jesus washed my sins away;
He taught me how to watch and pray,
And live rejoicing ev'ry day;
O happy day! O happy day!
When Jesus wash'd my sins away.

'Tis done, the great transaction's done!
I am my Lord's, and He is mine!
He drew me, and I followed on,
Charmed to confess the voice divine.

Now rest, my long divided heart,
Fixed on this blissful centre, rest;
Nor ever from thy Lord depart,
With Him of ev'ry good possessed.

High heav'n, that heard the solemn vow,
That vow renewed shall daily hear;
Till in life's latest hour I bow,
And bless in death a bond so dear.

170 Norman Warren
Copyright © Norman Warren, 1980

O Holy Spirit breathe on me, (*repeat*)
And cleanse away my sin,
Fill me with love within:
O Holy Spirit breathe on me!

O Holy Spirit fill my life, (*repeat*)
Take all my pride from me,
Give me humility:
O Holy Spirit breathe on me!

O Holy Spirit make me new, (*repeat*)
Make Jesus real to me,
Give me his purity:
O Holy Spirit breathe on me!

O Holy Spirit wind of God, (*repeat*)
Give me your power today,
To live for you always:
O Holy Spirit breathe on me!

171 George Matheson 1842–1906

O Love that wilt not let me go,
I rest my weary soul in Thee;
I give Thee back the life I owe,
That in Thine ocean depths its flow
May richer, fuller be.

O Light that followest all my way,
I yield my flickering torch to Thee;
My heart restores its borrowed ray,
That in Thy sunshine's blaze its day
May brighter, fairer be.

O Joy that seekest me through pain,
I cannot close my heart to Thee;
I trace the rainbow through the rain,
And feel the promise is not vain
That morn shall tearless be.

O Cross that liftest up my head,
I dare not ask to fly from Thee;
I lay in dust life's glory dead,
And from the ground there blossoms red
Life that shall endless be.

172 J. E. Bode 1816–74

O Jesus, I have promised
To serve Thee to the end;
Be Thou for ever near me,
My master and my friend;
I shall not fear the battle
If Thou art by my side,
Nor wander from the pathway
If Thou wilt be my guide.

O let me feel Thee near me;
The world is ever near;
I see the sights that dazzle,
The tempting sounds I hear;
My foes are ever near me,
Around me and within;
But, Jesus, draw Thou nearer,
And shield my soul from sin.

O let me hear Thee speaking
In accents clear and still,
Above the storms of passion,
The murmurs of self-will;
O speak to reassure me,
To hasten or control;
O speak, and make me listen,
Thou guardian of my soul.

O Jesus, Thou hast promised,
To all who follow Thee,
That where Thou art in glory
There shall Thy servant be;
And, Jesus, I have promised
To serve Thee to the end;
O give me grace to follow
My master and my friend.

O let me see Thy footmarks,
And in them plant mine own;
My hope to follow duly
Is in Thy strength alone;
O guide me, call me, draw me,
Uphold me to the end;
And then in heaven receive me,
My Saviour and my friend!

173 Translated from the Russian by
Stuart K. Hine © 1953

O Lord my God! When I in awesome wonder
Consider all the works Thy hand hath made,
I see the stars, I hear the mighty thunder,
Thy power throughout the universe displayed;

Then sings my soul, my Saviour God, to Thee,
How great Thou art! How great Thou art!
Then sings my soul, my Saviour God, to Thee,
How great Thou art! How great Thou art!

When through the woods and forest glades I
wander
And hear the birds sing sweetly in the trees;
When I look down from lofty mountain
grandeur,
And hear the brook, and feel the gentle breeze;

And when I think that God His Son not sparing,
Sent Him to die – I scarce can take it in.
That on the cross my burden gladly bearing,
He bled and died to take away my sin:

When Christ shall come with shout of
acclamation
And take me home – what joy shall fill my heart!
Then shall I bow in humble adoration
And there proclaim, my God, how great Thou
art!

174   Charles Wesley 1707–88

O Thou who camest from above
The pure, celestial fire to impart,
Kindle a flame of sacred love
On the mean altar of my heart.

There let it for Thy glory burn,
With inextinguishable blaze;
And, trembling, to its source return
In humble love and fervent praise.

Jesus, confirm my heart's desire
To work and speak and think for Thee;
Still let me guard the holy fire,
And still stir up Thy gift in me;

Ready for all Thy perfect will,
My acts of faith and love repeat,
Till death Thine endless mercies seal,
And make the sacrifice complete.

175
Copyright © 1913
Rev. George Bennard
Rodeheaver/Word Music (UK)

On a hill far away stood an old rugged cross,
The emblem of suffering and shame;
And I love that old cross where the dearest
and best
For a world of lost sinners was slain.

So I'll cherish the old rugged cross
Till my trophies at last I lay down;
I will cling to the old rugged cross
And exchange it someday for a crown.

O, the old rugged cross, so despised by the
world,
Has a wondrous attraction for me;
For the dear Lamb of God left his glory above
To bear it to dark Calvary.

In the old rugged cross, stained with blood so
divine,
A wondrous beauty I see;
For 'twas on that old cross Jesus suffered and
died
To pardon and sanctify me.

To the old rugged cross I will ever be true,
Its shame and reproach gladly bear;
Then He'll call me someday to my home far
away,
When his glory for ever I'll share.

176
Pat Uhl Howard
Copyright © 1967, 1970, 1978, 1979 by the
American Catholic Press

O what a gift! What a wonderful gift!
Who can tell the wonders of the Lord?
Let us open our eyes, our ears, and our
hearts;
It is Christ the Lord, it is He!

In the stillness of the night
When the world was asleep,
The Almighty Word leapt out.
He came to Mary. He came to us.
Christ came to the land of Galilee.
Christ our Lord and our King!

On the night before He died
It was Passover night,
And He gathered His friends together,
He broke the bread, He blessed the wine;
It was the gift of His love and His life.
Christ our Lord and our King!

On the hill of Calvary
The world held its breath
For there, for the world to see,
God gave His Son, His very own Son
For the love of you and me.
Christ our Lord and our King!

Early on that morning
When the world was sleeping,
Back to life came He!
He conquered death, He conquered sin,
But the vict'ry He gave to you and me!
Christ our Lord and our King!

Some day with the saints
We will come before our Father
And then we will shout and dance and sing.
For in our midst for our eyes to see
Will be Christ our Lord and our King.
Christ our Lord and our King!

177 W. W. How 1823–97

O Word of God incarnate,
O wisdom from on high,
O truth unchanged, unchanging,
O light of our dark sky,
We praise Thee for the radiance,
That from the hallowed page,
A lantern to our footsteps,
Shines on from age to age.

The Church from her dear Master
Received the gift divine,
And still that light she lifteth
O'er all the earth to shine:
It is the golden casket
Where gems of truth are stored;
It is the heaven-drawn picture
Of Christ, the living Word.

It floateth like a banner
Before God's host unfurled
It shineth like a beacon
Above the darkling world:
It is the chart and compass
That o'er life's surging sea,
Mid mists and rocks and quicksands
Still guide, O Christ, to Thee.

O make Thy Church, dear Saviour,
A lamp of burnished gold,
To bear before the nations
Thy true light as of old;
O teach Thy wandering pilgrims
By this their path to trace,
Till, clouds and darkness ended,
They see Thee face to face!

178 Robert Grant 1779–1838

O worship the King,
All-glorious above;
O gratefully sing
His power and His love;
Our shield and defender,
The ancient of days,
Pavilioned in splendour,
And girded with praise.

O tell of His might,
O sing of His grace
Whose robe is the light,
Whose canopy, space;
His chariots of wrath
The deep thunder-clouds form,
And dark is His path
On the wings of the storm.

The earth, with its store
Of wonders untold,
Almighty, Thy power
Hath founded of old:
Hath stablished it fast
By a changeless decree,
And round it hath cast
Like a mantle, the sea.

Thy bountiful care
What tongue can recite?
It breathes in the air,
It shines in the light,
It streams from the hills,
It descends to the plain,
And sweetly distils
In the dew and the rain.

Frail children of dust,
And feeble as frail,
In Thee do we trust,
Nor find Thee to fail:
Thy mercies, how tender,
How firm to the end,
Our maker, defender,
Redeemer and friend!

O Lord of all might,
How boundless Thy love!
While angels delight
To hymn Thee above,
The humbler creation,
Though feeble their lays,
With true adoration
Shall sing to Thy praise.

179 John Samuel Bewley Monsell 1811–75

O worship the Lord in the beauty of holiness!
Bow down before Him, His glory proclaim;
With gold of obedience and incense of
        lowliness,
Kneel and adore Him, the Lord is His name.

Low at His feet lay thy burden of carefulness,
High in His heart He will bear it for thee,
Comfort thy sorrows, and answer thy
        prayerfulness,
Guiding thy steps as may best for thee be.

Fear not to enter His courts in the slenderness
Of the poor wealth thou wouldst reckon as
thine:
Truth in its beauty and love in its tenderness:
These are the offerings to lay on His shrine.

These, though we bring them in trembling and
fearfulness,
He will accept for the name that is dear;
Mornings of joy give for evenings of
tearfulness,
Trust for our trembling, and hope for our fear.

O worship the Lord in the beauty of holiness!
Bow down before Him, His glory proclaim;
With gold of obedience and incense of
lowliness,
Kneel and adore Him, the Lord is His name.

180 J. Wilbur Chapman 1859–1918

**One day when heaven was filled with His
praises,**
One day when sin was as black as could be,
Jesus came forth to be born of a virgin,
Dwelt amongst men, my example is He!

Living, He lov'd me; dying, He sav'd me;
Buried, He carried my sins far away,
Rising, He justified freely for ever:
One day He's coming O glorious day.

One day they led Him up Calvary's mountain,
One day they nailed Him to die on the tree;
Suffering anguish, despised and rejected;
Bearing our sins, my Redeemer is He!

One day they left Him alone in the garden,
One day He rested, from suffering free;
Angels came down o'er His tomb to keep vigil;
Hope of the hopeless, my Saviour is He!

One day the grave could conceal Him no
longer,
One day the stone rolled away from the door;
Then He arose, over death He had conquered;
Now is ascended, my Lord evermore!

One day the trumpet will sound for His coming,
One day the skies with His glory will shine;
Wonderful day, my beloved ones bringing;
Glorious Saviour, this Jesus is mine!

181 Robert Cure
© 1976 Maranatha Music/Word Music (UK)

Open our eyes, Lord,
We want to see Jesus,
To reach out and touch Him
And say that we love Him;
Open our ears Lord,
And help us to listen:
O open our eyes, Lord,
We want to see Jesus!

182 Joanne Pond
Copyright © 1980 Thankyou Music

O give thanks to the Lord, all you His people,
O give thanks to the Lord, for He is good.
Let us praise, let us thank, let us celebrate and
dance;
O give thanks to the Lord, for He is good.

183 Copyright Control

Peace is flowing like a river,
Flowing out through you and me,
Spreading out in to the desert,
Setting all the captives free.

Love is flowing. . .Joy. . .Faith. . .Hope etc. . .

184 Edward Henry Bickersteth 1825–1906

**Peace, perfect peace, in this dark world of
sin?**
The blood of Jesus whispers peace within.

Peace, perfect peace, by thronging duties
pressed?
To do the will of Jesus, this is rest.

Peace, perfect peace, with sorrows surging
round?
In Jesus' presence nought but calm is found.

Peace, perfect peace, with loved ones far
away?
In Jesus' keeping we are safe, and they.

Peace, perfect peace, our future all unknown?
Jesus we know, and He is on the throne.

Peace, perfect peace, death shadowing us and
ours?
Jesus has vanquished death and all its powers.

It is enough: earth's struggles soon shall cease,
And Jesus call us to heaven's perfect peace.

185

Praise God from whom all blessings flow;
Praise Him all creatures here below.
Praise Him above ye heavenly hosts;
Praise Father, Son, and Holy Ghost.

186 Frances van Alstyne 1820–1915

Praise Him! praise Him! Jesus, our blessed Redeemer!
Sing, O earth – His wonderful love proclaim!
Hail Him! hail Him! highest archangels in glory;
Strength and honour give to His holy name!
Like a shepherd, Jesus will guard His children,
In His arms He carries them all day long.

Praise Him! praise Him! tell of His excellent
greatness;
Praise Him! praise Him ever in joyful song!

Praise Him! praise Him! Jesus, our blessed
Redeemer!
For our sins He suffered, and bled, and died;
He – our rock, our hope of eternal salvation,
Hail Him! hail Him! Jesus, the Crucified!
Sound His praises – Jesus who bore our
sorrows,
Love unbounded, wonderful, deep, and strong.

Praise Him! praise Him! Jesus, our blessed
Redeemer!
Heavenly portals, loud with hosannas ring!
Jesus, Saviour, reigneth for ever and ever:
Crown Him! crown Him! prophet, and priest,
and king!
Christ is coming, over the world victorious,
Power and glory unto the Lord belong.

187 H. F. Lyte 1793–1847

Praise, my soul, the King of heaven;
To His feet thy tribute bring;
Ransomed, healed, restored, forgiven,
Who like thee His praise should sing?
Praise Him! praise Him! praise Him! praise Him!
Praise the everlasting King.

Praise Him for His grace and favour
To our fathers, in distress;
Praise Him, still the same for ever,
Slow to chide, and swift to bless:
Praise Him! Praise Him! Praise Him! Praise Him!
Glorious in His faithfulness.

Father-like He tends and spares us;
Well our feeble frame He knows;
In His hands He gently bears us,
Rescues us from all our foes;
Praise Him! Praise Him! Praise Him! Praise Him!
Widely as His mercy flows.

Angels, help us to adore Him!
Ye behold Him face to face;
Sun and moon, bow down before Him;
Dwellers all in time and space.
Praise Him! Praise Him! Praise Him! Praise Him!
Praise with us the God of grace.

188 Psalm 150:1–3
Copyright © Bible Society

Praise the Lord!
Praise Him in His temple!
Praise Him for the mighty things He has done!
Praise the Lord!
Praise Him for His greatness!
Praise Him with trumpets, harps and lyres.
All living creatures, praise! O praise,
O praise, praise the Lord!

189 Roy Hicks
Copyright © 1979 Latter Rain
Music/Word Music (UK)

Praise the name of Jesus (*repeat*)
He's my rock, he's my fortress,
He's my deliverer, in Him will I trust
Praise the name of Jesus.

190 James Montgomery 1771–1854

Prayer is the soul's sincere desire,
Uttered or unexpressed,
The motion of a hidden fire
That trembles in the breast.

Prayer is the burden of a sigh,
The falling of a tear,
The upward glancing of an eye,
When none but God is near.

Prayer is the simplest form of speech
That infant lips can try;
Prayer the sublimest strains that reach
The Majesty on high.

Prayer is the contrite sinner's voice,
Returning from his ways,
While angels in their songs rejoice,
And cry, 'Behold, he prays!'

Prayer is the Christian's vital breath,
The Christian's native air,
His watchword at the gates of death;
He enters heaven with prayer.

No prayer is made on earth alone;
The Holy Spirit pleads;
And Jesus on the eternal throne,
For sinners intercedes.

O Thou by whom we come to God,
The Life, the Truth, the Way,
The path of prayer Thyself hast trod;
Lord, teach us how to pray!

191 John Henry Newman 1801–90

Praise to the Holiest in the height,
And in the depth be praise:
In all His words most wonderful;
Most sure in all His ways.

O loving wisdom of our God!
When all was sin and shame,
A second Adam to the fight
And to the rescue came.

O wisest love! that flesh and blood
Which did in Adam fail,
Should strive afresh against the foe,
Should strive and should prevail.

And that a higher gift than grace
Should flesh and blood refine,
God's presence, and His very self
And essence all-divine.

O generous love! that He, who smote
In man for man the foe,
The double agony in man
For man should undergo.

And in the garden secretly,
And on the Cross on high,
Should teach His brethren, and inspire
To suffer and to die.

Praise to the Holiest in the height,
And in the depth be praise:
In all His words most wonderful;
Most sure in all His ways.

192 Joachim Neander 1650–80
tr. Catherine Winkworth 1829–78, and others

Praise to the Lord, the Almighty, the King of creation;
O my soul, praise Him, for He is thy health and salvation;
All ye who hear
Brothers and sisters, draw near,
Praise Him in glad adoration.

Praise to the Lord, who o'er all things so wondrously reigneth,
Shelters thee under His wings, yea, so gently sustaineth:
Hast thou not seen?
All that is needful hath been
Granted in what He ordaineth.

Praise to the Lord, who doth prosper thy work, and defend thee!
Surely His goodness and mercy here daily attend thee:
Ponder anew
What the Almighty can do,
Who with His love doth befriend thee.

Praise to the Lord! O let all that is in me adore Him!
All that hath life and breath come now with praises before Him!
Let the amen
Sound from His people again:
Gladly for aye we adore Him.

193 Bill Harmon
Copyright © 1958 Gospel Publishing House

Reach out and touch the Lord as He goes by.
You'll find He's not too busy to hear your heart's cry.
He's passing by this moment your needs to supply.
Reach out and touch the Lord as He goes by.

194 Phil. 4.4

Rejoice in the Lord always,
And again I say rejoice (*repeat*),
Rejoice, rejoice, and again I say rejoice
(*repeat*)

195 Charles Wesley 1707–88

Rejoice, the Lord is King!
Your Lord and King adore;
Mortals, give thanks, and sing,
And triumph evermore:

Lift up your heart, lift up your voice;
Rejoice; again I say, Rejoice.

Jesus the Saviour reigns,
The God of truth and love;
When He had purged our stains,
He took His seat above:

His kingdom cannot fail,
He rules o'er earth and heaven;
The keys of death and hell
Are to our Jesus given:

He sits at God's right hand,
Till all His foes submit,
And bow to His command,
And fall beneath His feet:

Rejoice in glorious hope;
Jesus the Judge shall come,
And take His servants up
To their eternal home:

We soon shall hear the archangel's voice;
The trump of God shall sound, Rejoice!

196
Graham Kendrick
Copyright © 1981 Thankyou Music

Restore O Lord
The honour of your name
In works of sovereign power
Come shake the earth again
That men may see
And come with reverent fear
To the Living God
Whose Kingdom shall outlast the years.

Restore O Lord
In all the earth your fame
And in our time revive
The Church that bears your name
And in your anger
Lord remember mercy
Oh Living God
Whose mercy shall outlast the years

Bend us O Lord
Where we are hard and cold
In your refiners fire
Come purify the gold
Though suffering comes
And evil crouches near
Still our Living God
Is reigning he is reigning here

197
A. M. Toplady 1740–78

Rock of Ages, cleft for me,
Let me hide myself in Thee;
Let the water and the blood,
From Thy riven side which flowed,
Be of sin the double cure,
Cleanse me from its guilt and power.

Not the labour of my hands
Can fulfil Thy law's demands;
Could my zeal no respite know,
Could my tears for ever flow,
All for sin could not atone;
Thou must save, and Thou alone.

Nothing in my hand I bring,
Simply to Thy cross I cling;
Naked, come to Thee for dress,
Helpless, look to Thee for grace;
Foul, I to the fountain fly,
Wash me, Saviour, or I die.

While I draw this fleeting breath,
When mine eyes shall close in death,
When I soar through tracts unknown,
See Thee on Thy judgement throne;
Rock of ages, cleft for me,
Let me hide myself in Thee.

198
Albert Midlane 1825–1909

Revive Thy work, O Lord,
Thy mighty arm make bare;
Speak with the voice that wakes the dead
And make Thy people hear.

Revive Thy work, O Lord,
Disturb this sleep of death;
Quicken the smouldering embers now
By Thine almighty breath.

Revive Thy work, O Lord,
Create soul-thirst for Thee;
And hungering for the bread of life
O may our spirits be!

Revive Thy work, O Lord,
Exalt Thy precious name;
And, by the Holy Ghost, our love
For Thee and Thine inflame.

Revive Thy work, O Lord,
Give pentecostal showers;
The glory shall be all Thine own,
The blessing, Lord, be ours.

199
Anon

Peter and John went to pray,
They met a lame man on the way.
He asked for alms and held out his palms,
And this is what Peter did say:

'Silver and gold have I none,
But such as I have give I thee,
In the name of Jesus Christ of Nazareth,
Rise up and walk!'

He went walking and leaping and praising God,
Walking and leaping and praising God.
'In the name of Jesus Christ of Nazareth,
Rise up and walk!'

200 J. Edwin Orr

Search me, O God, and know my heart today;
Try me, O Lord, and know my thoughts I pray:
See if there be some wicked way in me,
Cleanse me from ev'ry sin and set me free.

I praise Thee, Lord, for cleansing me from sin;
Fulfil Thy Word, and make me pure within;
Fill me with fire, where once I burned with
  shame
Grant my desire to magnify Thy name.

Lord, take my life, and make it wholly Thine;
Fill my poor heart with Thy great love divine;
Take all my will, my passion, self and pride;
I now surrender – Lord, in me abide.

O Holy Ghost, revival comes from Thee;
Send a revival – start the work in me:
Thy Word declares Thou wilt supply our need;
For blessing now, O Lord, I humbly plead.

201 Karen Lafferty
Copyright © 1972 Marantha Music/
Word Music (UK)

Seek ye first the kingdom of God,
And His righteousness,
And all these things shall be added unto you.
Alleluiah, Alleluiah.

Man shall not live by bread alone,
But by every word,
That proceeds from the mouth of God.
Alleluiah, Alleluiah.

Ask and it shall be given unto you,
Seek and ye shall find,
Knock and the door shall be opened up to you.
Alleluiah, Alleluiah.

202 Joan Parsons
Copyright © 1978 Thankyou Music

Seek ye the Lord all ye people,
Turn to Him while He is near.
Let the wicked forsake his own way
And call on Him while He may hear.
Ho ev'ryone who is thirsty,
Come to the waters of life,
Come and drink of the milk and the wine,
Come without money and price.

And there is peace like a river
And glory divine,
If you'll come to the water,
If you'll taste of His wine.
There is love ever flowing
And joy ever full
And there's life everlasting
For us all.

203 Copyright © Timothy Dudley-Smith 1926–

Sing a new song to the Lord,
He to whom wonders belong:
Rejoice in his triumph and tell of his power
O sing to the Lord a new song!

Now to the ends of the earth
See his salvation is shown:
And still he remembers his mercy and truth
Unchanging in love to his own.

Sing a new song and rejoice,
Publish his praises abroad:
Let voices in chorus, with trumpet and horn,
Resound for the joy of the Lord!

Join with the hills and the sea
Thunders of praise to prolong:
In judgement and justice he comes to the earth
O sing to the Lord a new song!

204 Verse 1 copyright © 1974 Linda Stassen,
New Song Ministries. Verses 2–4 Anon

Sing alleluia to the Lord, (*repeat*)
Sing alleluia, sing alleluia,
Sing alleluia to the Lord!

Jesus is risen from the dead, (*repeat*)
Jesus is risen, Jesus is risen,
Jesus is risen from the dead!

Jesus is Lord of heaven and earth, (*repeat*)
Jesus is Lord, Jesus is Lord,
Jesus is Lord of heaven and earth.

Jesus is coming for his own, (*repeat*)
Jesus is coming, Jesus is coming,
Jesus is coming for his own.

205 Psalm 119:18

Open Thou mine eyes, that I may behold
Wondrous, wondrous things out of Thy law.

206 C. Sylvester Horne 1865–1914

Sing we the king who is coming to reign,
Glory to Jesus, the lamb that was slain.
Life and salvation His empire shall bring,
Joy to the nation when Jesus is King.

Come let us sing: Praise to our King.
Jesus our King, Jesus our King:
This is our song, who to Jesus belong:
Glory to Jesus, to Jesus our King.

All men shall dwell in His marvellous light,
Races long severed His love shall unite,
Justice and truth from His sceptre shall spring,
Wrong shall be ended when Jesus is King.

All shall be well in His kingdom of peace,
Freedom shall flourish and wisdom increase,
Foe shall be friend when His triumph we sing,
Sword shall be sickle when Jesus is King.

Souls shall be saved from the burden of sin.
Doubt shall not darken his witness within,
Hell hath no terrors, and death hath no sting;
Love is victorious, when Jesus is King.

Kingdom of Christ, for Thy coming we pray,
Hasten, O Father, the dawn of the day
When this new song Thy creation shall sing,
Satan is vanquished and Jesus is King.

207 Charles Wesley, 1707–88

Soldiers of Christ, arise,
And put your armour on,
Strong in the strength which God supplies
Through His eternal Son;
Strong in the Lord of Hosts,
And in His mighty power,
Who in the strength of Jesus trusts
Is more than conqueror.

Stand then in His great might,
With all His strength endued;
But take, to arm you for the fight,
The panoply of God;
That, having all things done,
And all your conflicts passed,
Ye may o'ercome through Christ alone,
And stand entire at last.

Stand then against your foes,
In close and firm array;
Legions of wily fiends oppose
Throughout the evil day:
But meet the sons of night;
But mock their vain design,
Armed in the arms of heavenly light,
Of righteousness divine.

Leave no unguarded place,
No weakness of the soul;
Take every virtue, every grace,
And fortify the whole:
Indissolubly joined,
To battle all proceed;
But arm yourselves with all the mind
That was in Christ, your Head.

208 Andrae Crouch
Copyright © 1978 Lexicon Music Inc.
Word Music (UK)

Soon and very soon we are going to see the
King, (*repeat twice*)
Alleluia, alleluia, we're going to see the King!

No more cryin' there we are going to see the
King, (*repeat twice*)
Alleluia, alleluia, we're going to see the King!

No more dyin' there we are going to see the
King, (*repeat twice*)
Alleluia, alleluia, we're going to see the King!
Alleluia, alleluia, alleluia, alleluia.

Soon and very soon we are going to see the
King, (*repeat twice*)
Alleluia, alleluia, we're going to see the King!
Alleluia, alleluia, alleluia, alleluia.

209 Copyright Control

Spirit of the living God, fall afresh on
me(*repeat*)
Break me, melt me, mould me, fill me;
Spirit of the living God, fall afresh on me.

210 James Montgomery 1771–1854

Stand up and bless the Lord,
Ye people of His choice;
Stand up and bless the Lord your God,
With heart and soul and voice.

Though high above all praise,
Above all blessing high,
Who would not fear His holy name?
And laud and magnify?

O for the living flame
From His own altar brought,
O touch our lips, our minds inspire,
And wing to heaven our thought!

There, with benign regard,
Our hymns He deigns to hear;
Though unrevealed to mortal sense,
Our spirits feel Him near.

God is our strength and song,
And His salvation ours;
Then be His love in Christ proclaimed
With all our ransomed powers.

Stand up and bless the Lord,
The Lord your God adore;
Stand up and bless His glorious name
Henceforth for evermore.

211 George Duffield 1818–88

Stand up! stand up for Jesus!
Ye soldiers of the cross,
Lift high His royal banner;
It must not suffer loss.
From victory unto victory
His army shall He lead,
Till every foe is vanquished
And Christ is Lord indeed.

Stand up! stand up for Jesus!
The trumpet-call obey;
Forth to the mighty conflict
In this His glorious day.
Ye that are men, now serve Him
Against unnumbered foes;
Let courage rise with danger,
And strength to strength oppose.

Stand up! stand up for Jesus!
Stand in His strength alone;
The arm of flesh will fail you,
Ye dare not trust your own.
Put on the gospel armour,
Each piece put on with prayer;
Where duty calls, or danger,
Be never wanting there.

Stand up! stand up for Jesus!
The strife will not be long;
This day the noise of battle,
The next the victor's song.
To him that overcometh
A crown of life shall be;
He with the King of glory
Shall reign eternally.

212 Frances Ridley Havergal 1836–79

Take my life, and let it be
Consecrated, Lord, to Thee;
Take my moments and my days,
Let them flow in ceaseless praise.

Take my hands, and let them move
At the impulse of Thy love;
Take my feet, and let them be
Swift and beautiful for Thee.

Take my voice, and let me sing
Always, only, for my King;
Take my lips, and let them be
Filled with messages from Thee.

Take my silver and my gold,
Not a mite would I withhold;
Take my intellect, and use
Every power as Thou shalt choose.

Take my will, and make it Thine;
It shall be no longer mine:
Take my heart, it is Thine own;
It shall be Thy royal throne.

Take my love; my Lord, I pour
At Thy feet its treasure store:
Take myself, and I will be
Ever, only, all, for Thee.

213 Elizabeth M. Dyke
Copyright © 1982 E. M. Dyke

Teach me to live day by day in your presence, Lord,
Day by day in your presence, Lord, Teach me
to live

Teach me to praise day by day in your Spirit,
Lord *etc.*

Teach me to love day by day in your power,
Lord *etc.*

Teach me to give day by day from my wealth,
O Lord *etc.*

214 W. D. Longstaff 1822–94

Take time to be holy, speak oft with thy Lord;
Abide in Him always, and feed on His Word.
Make friends of God's children, help those who
are weak;
Forgetting in nothing His blessing to seek.

Take time to be holy, the world rushes on;
Spend much time in secret with Jesus alone –
By looking to Jesus, like Him thou shalt be!
Thy friends in thy conduct His likeness shall
see.

Take time to be holy, let Him be thy guide;
And run not before Him, whatever betide;
In joy or in sorrow still follow thy Lord,
And, looking to Jesus, still trust in His Word.

Take time to be holy, be calm in thy soul;
Each thought and each temper beneath His
control;
Thus led by His Spirit to fountains of love,
Thou soon shalt be fitted for service above.

215 Timothy Dudley-Smith 1926–
Copyright © Timothy Dudley-Smith

Tell out, my soul, the greatness of the Lord;
Unnumbered blessings give my spirit voice;
Tender to me the promise of His Word;
In God my Saviour shall my heart rejoice.

Tell out, my soul, the greatness of His Name!
Make known His might, the deeds His arm has
  done;
His mercy sure, from age to age the same;
His Holy Name – the Lord, the Mighty One.

Tell out, my soul, the greatness of His might!
Powers and dominions lay their glory by.
Proud hearts and stubborn wills are put to
  flight,
The hungry fed, the humble lifted high.

Tell out, my soul, the glories of His word!
Firm is His promise, and His mercy sure,
Tell out, my soul, the greatness of the Lord
To children's children and for evermore!

216 A. Huntley
Copyright © 1978 Thankyou Music

Thank you Jesus, thank you Jesus
Thank you Lord for loving me.
  Repeat verse

You went to Calvary, there you died for me,
Thank you Lord for loving me
  Repeat verse

You rose up from the grave, to me new life you
  gave,
Thank you Lord for loving me
  Repeat verse

You're coming back again, and we with you
  shall reign,
Thank you Lord for loving me
  Repeat verse

217 Samuel John Stone, 1839–1900

The Church's one foundation
Is Jesus Christ our Lord:
She is His new creation
By water and the word;
From heaven He came and sought her
To be His holy bride;
With His own blood He bought her,
And for her life He died.

Elect from every nation,
Yet one o'er all the earth,
Her charter of salvation
One Lord, one faith, one birth,
One holy name she blesses,
Partakes one holy food,
And to one hope she presses,
With every grace endued.

Though with a scornful wonder
Men see her sore oppressed,
By schisms rent asunder
By heresies distressed,
Yet saints their watch are keeping,
Their cry goes up: How long?
And soon the night of weeping
Shall be the morn of song.

Mid toil and tribulation,
And tumult of her war,
She waits the consummation
Of peace for evermore,
Till with the vision glorious
Her longing eyes are blest,
And the great Church victorious
Shall be the Church at rest.

Yet she on earth hath union
With God the Three in One,
And mystic sweet communion
With those whose rest is won.
O happy ones and holy!
Lord, give us grace that we,
Like them, the meek and lowly,
On high may dwell with Thee.

218 John Ellerton 1826–93

The day Thou gavest, Lord, is ended,
The darkness falls at Thy behest;
To Thee our morning hymns ascended,
Thy praise shall sanctify our rest.

We thank Thee that Thy Church unsleeping,
While earth rolls onward into light,
Through all the world her watch is keeping,
And rests not now by day or night.

As o'er each continent and island
The dawn leads on another day,
The voice of prayer is never silent,
Nor dies the strain of praise away.

The sun that bids us rest is waking,
Our brethren 'neath the western sky,
And hour by hour fresh lips are making
Thy wondrous doings heard on high.

So be it, Lord; Thy throne shall never,
Like earth's proud empires, pass away;
Thy kingdom stands, and grows for ever,
Till all Thy creatures own Thy sway.

219

Mark Pendergras
Copyright © 1977 Sparrow Song/Candle
Co. Music/World Artist Music Co. Inc.

**The greatest thing in all my life is knowing
you.** (*repeat*)
I want to know you more; I want to know you
more.
The greatest thing in all my life is knowing you.

The greatest thing in all my life is loving you.
(*repeat*)
I want to love you more; I want to love you
more.
The greatest thing in all my life is loving you.

The greatest thing in all my life is serving you.
(*repeat*)
I want to serve you more; I want to serve you
more.
The greatest thing in all my life is serving you.

220 Thomas Kelly 1769–1855

The head that once was crowned with thorns
Is crowned with glory now;
A royal diadem adorns
The mighty victor's brow.

The highest place that heaven affords
Is His by sovereign right,
The King of Kings and Lord of Lords
He reigns in perfect light.

The joy of all who dwell above,
The joy of all below,
To whom He manifests His love,
And grants His name to know.

To them the cross, with all its shame,
With all its grace, is given,
Their name an everlasting name,
Their joy the joy of heaven.

They suffer with their Lord below;
They reign with Him above;
Their profit and their joy, to know
The mystery of His love.

The cross He bore is life and health,
Though shame and death to Him:
His people's hope, His people's wealth,
Their everlasting theme.

221 Henry Williams Baker 1821–1877

The King of love my Shepherd is,
Whose goodness faileth never;
I nothing lack if I am His
And He is mine for ever.

Where streams of living water flow
My ransomed soul He leadeth,
And where the verdant pastures grow
The food celestial feedeth.

Perverse and foolish oft I strayed;
But yet in love He sought me,
And on His shoulder gently laid,
And home rejoicing brought me.

In death's dark vale I fear no ill
With Thee, dear Lord, beside me;
Thy rod and staff my comfort still,
Thy Cross before to guide me.

Thou spread'st a table in my sight;
Thy unction grace bestoweth;
And O what transport of delight
From Thy pure chalice floweth!

And so through all the length of days
Thy goodness faileth never;
Good Shepherd, may I sing Thy praise
Within Thy House for ever!

222 Graham Kendrick
Copyright © 1981 Thankyou Music

The King is among us
His Spirit is here
Lets draw near and worship
Let songs fill the air

He looks down upon us
Delight in his face
Enjoying his childrens' love
Enthralled by our praise

For each child is special
Accepted and loved
A love gift from Jesus
To his Father above

And now he is giving
His gifts to us all
For no one is worthless
And each one is called

The Spirit's anointing
On all flesh comes down
And we shall be channels
For works like his own

We come now believing
Your promise of power
For we are your people
And this is your hour

223 Donald Fishel
Copyright © 1974 Word of God

The light of Christ has come into the
world. (repeat)
(can be sung in two parts)

All men must be born again to see the Kingdom
of God;
The water and the Spirit bring new life in God's
love.

God gave up His only Son out of love for the
world,
So that all men who believe in Him will live for
ever.

The light of God has come to us so that we
might have salvation;
From the darkness of our sins we walk into
glory with Christ Jesus.

224 Diane Davis
Copyright © 1973 by G. I. A.
Publications Inc.

The Lord is a great and mighty king,
Just and gentle with everything.
So with happiness we sing,
And let His praises ring.

We are His voice, we are His song;
Let us praise Him all day long. Alleluia.

We are His body here on earth;
From above He gave us birth. Alleluia.

For our Lord we will stand,
Sent by Him to ev'ry land. Alleluia.

The Lord our God is one,
Father, Spirit and the Son. Alleluia.

225 Roland Fudge
Copyright © 1982 Roland Fudge

The Lord is my strength and my song,
(*repeat*)
And he has become my salvation.
Sing to the Lord, for he has done marvellous
things (*repeat*)
Sing to the Lord, Sing to the Lord,
Sing to the Lord, for he has done marvellous
things
The Lord is my strength and my song, (*repeat*)
And He has become my salvation.

226 Josiah Conder 1789–1855

The Lord is King! Lift up thy voice,
O earth, and all ye heavens rejoice;
From world to world the joy shall ring,
"The Lord omnipotent is King!"

The Lord is King! Who then shall dare
Resist His will, distrust His care,
Or murmur at His wise decree,
Or doubt His royal promises?

The Lord is King! Child of the dust,
The Judge of all the earth is just;
Holy and true are all His ways:
Let every creature speak His praise.

He reigns! Ye saints, exalt your strains;
Your God is King, your Father reigns;
And He is at the Father's side
The man of love, the crucified.

One Lord, one empire, all secures;
He reigns, and life and death are yours,
Through earth and heaven one song shall ring,
The Lord omnipotent is King!

227 Francis Rous, 1579–1659
revised for Scottish Psalter, 1650

The Lord's my shepherd, I'll not want;
He makes me down to lie
In pastures green; He leadeth me
The quiet waters by.

My soul He doth restore again,
And me to walk doth make
Within the paths of righteousness,
E'en for His own name's sake.

Yea, though I walk through death's dark vale,
Yet will I fear none ill;
For Thou art with me, and Thy rod
And staff me comfort still.

My table Thou hast furnished
In presence of my foes;
My head Thou dost with oil anoint,
And my cup overflows.

Goodness and mercy all my life
Shall surely follow me;
And in God's house for evermore
My dwelling-place shall be.

228 Colin Green

Therefore we lift our hearts in praise,
Sing to the living God who saves,
For grace poured out for you and me.

There for ev'ryone to see,
There on the hill at Calvary
Jesus died for you and me.

There for sad and broken men
He rose up from the grave again,
And reigns on high for you and me.

There for such great pain and cost
The Spirit came at Pentecost
And comes in power for you and me.

Therefore we lift our hearts in praise,
Sing to the living God who saves,
For grace poured out for you and me.

229 Edith McNeill
Copyright © 1974/5 Celebration Services (International)

The steadfast love of the Lord never
ceases,
His mercies never come to an end.
They are new ev'ry morning, new ev'ry
morning,
Great is Thy faithfulness, O Lord, Great is
Thy faithfulness.

The Lord is my portion says my soul
Therefore I will hope in Him.

The Lord is good to those who wait for Him,
To the soul that seeks Him.
It is good that we should wait quietly
For the salvation of the Lord.

The Lord will not cast off forever,
But will have compassion.
For he does not willingly afflict
Or grieve the sons of men.

So let us examine all our ways,
And return to the Lord.
Let us lift up our hearts and hands
To God in heav'n.

230 Cecil Frances Alexander 1823–1895

There is a green hill far away
Without a city wall,
Where the dear Lord was crucified
Who died to save us all.

We may not know, we cannot tell
What pains He had to bear;
That we believe it was for us
He hung and suffered there.

He died that we might be forgiven,
He died to make us good,
That we might go at last to heaven
Saved by His precious blood.

There was no other good enough
To pay the price of sin.
He only could unlock the gate
Of heaven, and let us in.

O dearly, dearly has He loved,
And we must love Him too
And trust in His redeeming blood,
And try His works to do.

231 Gary Garrett © 1976/80 Scripture in Song
1 Samuel 2:2

There is none holy as the Lord.
There is none beside Thee.
Neither is there any rock like our God.
There is none holy as the Lord.

232 F. Whitfield
Copyright © 1946 Salvationist Publishing Supplies

There is a Name I love to hear,
I love to speak its worth;
It sounds like music in my ear,
The sweetest name on earth.

O how I love the Saviour's name, (repeat
twice)
The sweetest name on earth.

It tells me of a Saviour's love,
Who died to set me free;
It tells me of His precious blood,
The sinner's perfect plea.

It tells of One whose loving heart
Can feel my deepest woe,
Who in my sorrow bears a part
That none can bear below.

It bids my trembling heart rejoice,
It dries each rising tear;
It tells me in a 'still, small voice'
To trust and never fear.

Jesus, the Name I love so well,
The Name I love to hear!
No saints on earth its worth can tell,
No heart conceive how dear!

233

Tedd Smith
© 1973 Hope Publishing

There's a quiet understanding
When we're gathered in the Spirit,
It's a promise that He gives us,
When we gather in His name.
There's a love we feel in Jesus
There's a manna that He feeds us
It's a promise that He gives us
When we gather in His name.

And we know when we're together,
Sharing love and understanding,
That our brothers and our sisters
Feel the oneness that He brings.
Thank you, thank you, thank you Jesus,
For the way you love and feed us,
For the many ways you lead us,
Thank you, thank you Lord.

234

E. H. Swinstead
Copyright © Control

There's a way back to God from the dark paths of sin;
There's a door that is open and you may go in:
At Calvary's cross is where you begin,
When you come as a sinner to Jesus.

235

Graham Kendrick
Copyright © 1979 Thankyou Music

There's a sound on the wind like a victory song,
Listen now, let it rest on your soul.
It's a song that I learned from a heavenly King,
It's a song of a battle royal.

Come on Heaven's children
The city is in sight.
There will be no sadness
On the other side.

There's a loud shout of victory that leaps from
our hearts
As we wait for our conquering King.
There's a triumph resounding from dark ages
past
To the victory song we now sing.

There'll be the crowns for the conquerors
And white robes to wear,
There'll be no more sorrow or pain.
And the battles of earth shall be lost in the
sight,
Of the glorious Lamb that was slain.

Now the King of the ages approaches the earth,
He will burst through the gates of the sky.
And all men shall bow down to His beautiful
name;
We shall rise with a shout, we shall fly!

236

Michael A. Baughen
Copyright ©

There's no greater name than Jesus,
Name of Him who came to save us
In that saving name of Jesus
Every knee should bow.
Let everything that is 'neath the ground,
Let everything in the world around,
Let everything that's high o'er the sky
Bow at Jesus' Name.
In our minds by faith professing,
In our hearts by inward blessing,
On our tongues by words confessing,
Jesus Christ is Lord.

237

Emily Elizabeth Steele Elliott, 1836–97

Thou didst leave Thy throne
And Thy Kingly crown,
When Thou camest to earth for me;
But in Bethlehem's home
Was there found no room
For Thy holy nativity:
O come to my heart, Lord Jesus;
There is room in my heart for Thee.

Heaven's arches rang
When the angels sang
Proclaiming Thy royal degree;
But of lowly birth
Cam'st Thou, Lord, on earth,
And in great humility:
O come to my heart, Lord Jesus;
There is room in my heart for Thee.

The foxes found rest,
And the birds their nest,
In the shade of the cedar-tree;
But Thy couch was the sod,
O Thou Son of God,
In the deserts of Galilee;
O come to my heart, Lord Jesus,
There is room in my heart for Thee.

Thou camest, O Lord,
With the living word
That should set Thy people free;
But, with mocking scorn
And with crown of thorn,
They bore Thee to Calvary:
O come to my heart, Lord Jesus;
Thy Cross is my only plea.

When heaven's arches ring,
And her choirs shall sing,
At Thy coming to victory
Let Thy voice call me home,
Saying: Yet there is room,
There is room at My side for thee!
And my heart shall rejoice, Lord Jesus,
When Thou comest and callest for me.

238

Edmond Budry 1854–1932
tr. R. Birch Hoyle 1875–1939

Thine be the glory, risen, conquering Son,
Endless is the victory Thou o'er death hast won;
Angels in bright raiment rolled the stone away,
Kept the folded grave-clothes, where Thy body
lay.

Thine be the glory, risen, conquering Son,
Endless is the victory Thou o'er death hast
won.

Lo! Jesus meets us, risen from the tomb;
Lovingly He greets us, scatters fear and gloom;
Let the Church with gladness hymns of triumph
sing,
For her Lord now liveth; death hath lost its
sting.

No more we doubt Thee, glorious Prince of life;
Life is nought without Thee: aid us in our strife;
Make us more than conquerors, through Thy
deathless love:
Bring us safe through Jordan to Thy home
above.

239

This is the day,
This is the day that the Lord has made,
That the Lord has made.
We will rejoice,
We will rejoice and be glad in it,
And be glad in it.
This is the day that the Lord has made,
We will rejoice and be glad in it.
This is the day,
This is the day that the Lord hath made.

This is the day,
This is the day when he rose again,
When he rose again.
We will rejoice,
We will rejoice and be glad in it,
And be glad in it.
This is the day when he rose again.
We will rejoice and be glad in it.
This is the day,
This is the day when he rose again.

This is the day,
This is the day when the Spirit came,
When the Spirit came.
We will rejoice,
We will rejoice and be glad in it,
And be glad in it.
This is the day when the Spirit came.
We will rejoice and be glad in it.
This is the day,
This is the day when the Spirit came.

240

Psalm 118:28,29

Thou art my God and I will praise thee
Thou art my God I will exalt thee.
O give thanks unto the Lord for He is good
For His mercy endureth for ever.

241

Hugh Mitchell
Copyright © 1956/Renewal 1964
Singspiration

Thy loving kindness is better than life,
(*repeat*)
My lips shall praise Thee, thus will I bless Thee,
Thy loving kindness is better than life.

I lift my hands up unto Thy name, (*repeat*)
My lips shall praise Thee, thus will I bless Thee,
Thy loving kindness is better than life.

242

Verse 2 Tom Snail
Rev. 4:11 and 5.9.10
Copyright © 1963 and 1975 Fred Bock Music

Thou art worthy, thou art worthy,
Thou art worthy, O Lord.
Thou art worthy, to receive glory.
Glory and honour and power.
For thou hast created, hast all things created
For thou hast created all things
And for thy pleasure they are created,
Thou art worthy, O Lord.

Thou art worthy, thou art worthy,
Thou art worthy, O Lamb.
Thou art worthy, to receive glory,
And power at the Father's right hand.
For thou hast redeemed us.
Hast ransomed and cleaned us,
By thy blood setting us free.
In white robes arrayed us, kings and priests
made us.
And we are reigning in thee.

243
R. D. Browne 1905–

Thou, Lord, hast given Thyself for our healing;
Poured out Thy life that our souls might be freed.
Love, from the heart of the Father, revealing
Light for our darkness and grace for our need.

Saviour of men, our humanity sharing
Give us a passion for souls that are lost.
Help us to follow, Thy gospel declaring;
Daily to serve Thee and count not the cost.

Pray we for men who today in their blindness
Wander from Thee and Thy kingdom of truth:
Grant them a sight of Thy great loving-
kindness,
Lord of their manhood and guide of their youth.

Come, Holy Spirit, to cleanse and renew us:
Purge us from evil and fill us with power:
Thus shall the waters of healing flow through
us;
So shall revival be born in this hour.

Give to Thy Church, as she tells forth the story,
Strength for her weakness and trust for her
fears;
Make her a channel of grace for Thy glory,
Answer her prayers in the midst of the years.

244
John Marriott 1780–1825

Thou, Whose almighty word
Chaos and darkness heard,
And took their flight;
Hear us, we humbly pray,
And where the Gospel day
Sheds not its glorious ray,
Let there be light.

Thou, Who didst come to bring,
On Thy redeeming wing,
Healing and sight,
Health to the sick in mind,
Sight to the inly blind;
O now to all mankind
Let there be light.

Spirit of truth and love,
Life giving, holy Dove,
Speed forth Thy flight;
Move on the waters' face,
Bearing the lamp of grace,
And in earth's darkest place
Let there be light.

Blessed and holy Three,
Glorious Trinity,
Wisdom, love, might;
Boundless as ocean's tide,
Rolling in fullest pride,
Through the earth, far and wide,
Let there be light.

245
Anon

Thou will keep him in perfect peace (*repeat twice*)
Whose mind is stayed on Thee.

Marvel not that I say unto you (*repeat twice*)
Ye must be born again.

Though your sins as scarlet be (*repeat twice*)
They shall be white as snow.

If the Son shall make you free (*repeat twice*)
Ye shall be free indeed.

They that wait upon the Lord (*repeat twice*)
They shall renew their strength.

Whom shall I send and who will go? (*repeat twice*)
Here I am Lord, send me.

246
Nahum Tate 1652–1715
Nicholas Brady 1639–1726

Through all the changing scenes of life,
In trouble and in joy,
The praises of my God shall still
My heart and tongue employ.

Of His deliverance I will boast,
Till all that are distressed
From my example comfort take,
And charm their griefs to rest.

O magnify the Lord with me,
With me exalt His name;
When in distress to Him I called,
He to my rescue came.

The hosts of God encamp around
The dwellings of the just;
Deliverance He affords to all
Who on His succour trust.

O make but trial of His love;
Experience will decide
How blest they are, and only they,
Who in His truth confide.

Fear Him, ye saints, and you will then
Have nothing else to fear;
Make you His service your delight,
He'll make your wants His care.

247 E. H. Plumptre 1821–91

Thy Hand, O God, has guided
Thy flock from age to age;
The wondrous tale is written,
Full clear, on every page;
Our fathers owned Thy goodness,
And we their deeds record;
And both of this bear witness,
One Church, one Faith, one Lord.

Thy heralds brought glad tidings
To greatest, as to least;
They bade men rise and hasten
To share the great King's feast;
And this was all their teaching,
In every deed and word,
To all alike proclaiming
One Church, One Faith, One Lord.

Through many a day of darkness,
Through many a scene of strife,
The faithful few fought bravely
To guard the nation's life.
Their gospel of redemption,
Sin pardoned, man restored,
Was all in this enfolded,
One Church, one Faith, one Lord.

Thy mercy will not fail us,
Nor leave Thy work undone;
With Thy right hand to help us,
The victory shall be won;
And then, by men and angels,
Thy name shall be adored
And this shall be their anthem,
One Church, one Faith, one Lord.

248 Frances van Alstyne 1820–1915

To God be the glory! Great things He hath done!
So loved He the world that He gave us His Son;
Who yielded His life an atonement for sin,
And opened the life gate that all may go in.
*Praise the Lord! Praise the Lord! Let the earth
hear His voice!*
*Praise the Lord! Praise the Lord! Let the
people rejoice!*
*O come to the Father, through Jesus the Son:
And give Him the glory! Great things He hath
done!*

O perfect redemption, the purchase of blood!
To every believer the promise of God;
The vilest offender who truly believes,
That moment from Jesus a pardon receives.

Great things He hath taught us, great things He
hath done,
And great our rejoicing through Jesus the Son;
But purer, and higher, and greater will be
Our wonder, our rapture, when Jesus we see.

249 Helen H. Lemmell
Copyright © 1922/1950 Singspiration Inc.

O soul are you weary and troubled?
No light in the darkness you see?
There's light for a look at the Saviour
And life more abundant and free!

*Turn your eyes upon Jesus,
Look full in His wonderful face;
And the things of earth will grow strangely
dim
In the light of His glory and grace.*

Through death into life everlasting
He passed and we follow Him there;
Over us sin no more hath dominion
For more than conquerors we are!

His word shall not fail you He promised;
Believe Him, and all will be well:
Then go to a world that is dying
His perfect salvation to tell!

250 Timothy Dudley-Smith 1926–
Copyright © 1970

Timeless love! We sing the story
Praise his wonders, tell his worth;
Love more fair than heaven's glory,
Love more firm than ancient earth!
Tell his faithfulness abroad,
Who is like Him? Praise the Lord!

By His faithfulness surrounded,
North and south His hand proclaim;
Earth and heaven formed and founded,
Skies and seas declare His name!
Wind and storm obey his word,
Who is like Him? Praise the Lord!

Truth and righteousness enthrone Him
Just and equal are his ways;
More than happy, those who own Him,
More than joy, their songs of praise!
Sun and Shield and great Reward
Who is like Him? Praise the Lord!

251 Copyright Control

We are gathering together unto Him (*repeat*)
Unto Him shall the gathering of the people be.
We are gathering together unto Him.

We are offering together unto Him (*repeat*)
Unto Him shall the offering of the people be.
We are offering together unto Him.

We are singing together unto Him (*repeat*)
Unto Him shall the singing of the people be.
We are singing together unto Him.

We are praying together unto Him (*repeat*)
Unto Him shall the praying of the people be.
We are praying together unto Him.

252 Diane Fung
Copyright © 1979 Springtide/Word
Music (UK)

Victory is on our lips and in our lives,
For Jesus has surely been raised from the dead;
And never shall the powers of darkness doubt
  that
Jesus is Lord over all.
Neither shall the powers of darkness triumph,
For Jesus is Lord! Jesus is Lord!
Jesus is Lord over all.

253 Copyright © 1976
Canticle Publications Inc.

We have come into His house
And gathered, in His name   } *Repeat*
To worship Him.
We have come into His house
And gathered in His name to worship Christ
  the Lord,
Worship Him, Christ the Lord.

So forget about yourself
And concentrate on Him   } *Repeat*
  and worship Him
So forget about yourself
And concentrate on Him and worship Christ
  the Lord,
Worship Him, Christ the Lord.

Let us lift up holy hands
And magnify His name   } *Repeat*
  and worship Him.
Let us lift up holy hands
And magnify His name and worship Christ the
  Lord,
Worship Him, Christ the Lord.

254 Song omitted for copyright reasons

255 Priscilla Owens 1829–1907

We have heard a joyful sound:
Jesus saves!
Spread the gladness all around:
Jesus saves!
Bear the news to every land,
Climb the steeps and cross the waves;
Onward! 'tis our Lord's command:
Jesus saves!

Sing above the battle's strife:
Jesus saves!
By His death and endless life,
Jesus saves!
Sing it softly through the gloom,
When the heart for mercy craves;
Sing in triumph o'er the tomb:
Jesus saves!

Give the winds a mighty voice:
Jesus saves!
Let the nations now rejoice:
Jesus saves!
Shout salvation full and free
To every strand that ocean laves –
This our song of victory:
Jesus saves!

256

Ed Baggett
Copyright © 1974, 1975 Celebration
Services (International) Ltd.

We really want to thank you, Lord.
We really want to bless your name.
Hallelujah! Jesus is our king!

We thank you, Lord, for your gift to us,
Your life so rich beyond compare,
The gift of your body here on earth
Of which we sing and share.

We thank you Lord, for our life together,
To live and move in the love of Christ,
Your tenderness which sets us free
To serve you with our lives.

Praise God from whom all blessings flow,
Praise Him all creatures here below.
Praise Him above you heavenly Host,
Praise Father, Son and Holy Ghost.

257

Isaiah 6:1

We see the Lord, *(repeat)*
And he is high and lifted up,
And his train fills the temple.
He is high and lifted up,
And his train fills the temple.
The angels cry, 'Holy', *(repeat)*
The angels cry, 'Holy is the Lord'.

258

Thomas Kelly 1769–1855

We sing the praise of Him who died,
Of Him who died upon the cross;
The sinner's hope let men deride,
For this we count the world but lost.

Inscribed upon the cross we see,
In shining letters, "God is love";
He bears our sins upon the tree,
He brings us mercy from above.

The cross! It takes our guilt away,
It holds the fainting spirit up;
It cheers with hope the gloomy day
And sweetens every bitter cup.

It makes the coward spirit brave,
And nerves the feeble arm for fight;
It takes the terror from the grave,
And gilds the bed of death with light.

The balm of life, the cure of woe,
The measure and the pledge of love;
The sinner's refuge here below,
The angels theme in heaven above.

259

Gordon Brattle
Copyright © Gordon Brattle

We will sing of our Redeemer, He's our King:
All His glory all His praise to you we bring;
With our hearts and with our voices Him we
sing,
We love the Lord, we love His Word. He's our
King.

260

Diane Fung
Copyright © 1978 Springtide/Word Music
(UK)

We'll sing a new song of glorious triumph
For we see the government of God in our lives.
We'll sing a new song of glorious triumph
For we see the government of God in our lives.

He is crowned God of the whole world,
crowned,
King of creation, crowned, ruling the nations
now.
He is crowned God of the whole world,
crowned,
King of creation, crowned, ruling the nations
now.

261

Colin Sterne, 1862–1926

We've a story to tell to the nations,
That shall turn their hearts to the right,
A story of truth and sweetness,
A story of peace and light: *(repeat)*

> *For the darkness shall turn to dawning,*
> *And the dawning to noon-day bright,*
> *And Christ's great kingdom shall come on*
> *earth,*
> *The kingdom of love and light.*

We've a song to be sung to the nations,
That shall lift their hearts to the Lord;
A song that shall conquer evil,
And shatter the spear and sword: *(repeat)*

We've a message to give to the nations,
That the Lord who reigneth above
Hath sent us His Son to save us,
And show us that God is love: *(repeat)*

We've a Saviour to show to the nations,
Who the path of sorrow has trod,
That all of the world's great peoples
Might come to the truth of God: *(repeat)*

262
Joseph Scriven, 1819–86

What a friend we have in Jesus,
All our sins and griefs to bear!
What a privilege to carry
Everything to God in prayer!
O what peace we often forfeit,
O what needless pain we bear –
All because we do not carry
Everything to God in prayer!

Have we trials and temptations?
Is there trouble anywhere?
We should never be discouraged:
Take it to the Lord in prayer!
Can we find a friend so faithful,
Who will all our sorrows share?
Jesus knows our every weakness –
Take it to the Lord in prayer!

Are we weak and heavy-laden,
Cumbered with a load of care?
Jesus only is our refuge,
Take it to the Lord in prayer!
Do thy friends despise, forsake thee?
Take it to the Lord in prayer!
In His arms He'll take and shield thee,
Thou wilt find a solace there.

263
Rufus H. McDaniel

What a wonderful change in my life has been wrought
Since Jesus came into my heart!
I have light in my soul for which long I had sought,
Since Jesus came into my heart!

Since Jesus came into my heart,
Since Jesus came into my heart,
Floods of joy o'er my soul
Like the sea billows roll,
Since Jesus came into my heart.

I'm possessed of a hope that is steadfast and sure,
Since Jesus came into my heart!
And no dark clouds of doubt now my pathway obscure,
Since Jesus came into my heart!

There's a light in the valley of death now for me,
Since Jesus came into my heart!
And the gates of the city beyond I can see,
Since Jesus came into my heart!

I shall go there to dwell in that city, I know,
Since Jesus came into my heart!
And I'm happy, so happy, as onward I go,
Since Jesus came into my heart.

264
Keri Jones/Dave Matthews
Copyright © 1978 Springtime/Word
Music (UK)

When I feel the touch
Of your hand upon my life
It causes me to sing a song
That I love You, Lord.
So from deep within
My spirit singeth unto thee
You are My King,
You are my God,
And I love you, Lord.

265
Isaac Watts, 1674–1748

When I survey the wondrous cross
On which the Prince of glory died,
My richest gain I count but loss,
And pour contempt on all my pride.

Forbid it, Lord, that I should boast,
Save in the death of Christ my God:
All the vain things that charm me most,
I sacrifice them to His blood.

See from His head, His hands, His feet,
Sorrow and love flow mingled down:
Did e'er such love and sorrow meet,
Or thorns compose so rich a crown?

Were the whole realm of nature mine,
That were an offering far too small,
Love so amazing, so divine,
Demands my soul, my life, my all.

266
Anon
tr. by Edward Caswall, 1814–78

When morning gilds the skies,
My heart awaking cries:
May Jesus Christ be praised!
Alike at work and prayer
To Jesus I repair;
May Jesus Christ be praised!

Does sadness fill my mind?
A solace here I find –
May Jesus Christ be praised!
When evil thoughts molest,
With this I shield my breast –
May Jesus Christ be praised!

Be this, when day is past,
Of all my thoughts the last,
May Jesus Christ be praised!
The night becomes as day,
When from the heart we say:
May Jesus Christ be praised!

To God, the Word, on high
The hosts of angels cry,
May Jesus Christ be praised!
Let mortals, too, upraise
Their voice in hymns of praise;
May Jesus Christ be praised!

Let earth's wide circle round
In joyful notes resound:
May Jesus Christ be praised!
Let air, and sea, and sky,
From depth to height, reply:
May Jesus Christ be praised!

Be this while life is mine,
My canticle divine,
May Jesus Christ be praised!
Be this the eternal song
Through all the ages long,
May Jesus Christ be praised!

267 Anon

Wherever I am I'll praise him,
Whenever I can I'll praise him;
For his love surrounds me like a sea;
I'll praise the name of Jesus,
Lift up the name of Jesus,
For the name of Jesus lifted me.

268 James M. Black, 1893–

When the trumpet of the Lord shall sound,
and time shall be no more,
And the morning breaks, eternal, bright, and
fair;
When the saved of earth shall gather over on
the other shore,
And the roll is called up yonder, I'll be there.

When the roll is called up yonder,
(repeat three times)
I'll be there.

On that bright and cloudless morning when the
dead in Christ shall rise,
And the glory of his resurrection share;
When his chosen ones shall gather to their
home beyond the skies,
And the roll is called up yonder, I'll be there.

Let us labour for the Master from the dawn till
setting sun,
Let us talk of all his wond'rous love and care;
Then when all of life is over, and our work on
earth is done.
And the roll is called up yonder, I'll be there.

269 John Henry Sammis 1846–1919

When we walk with the Lord
In the light of His word
What a glory He sheds on our way!
While we do His good will,
He abides with us still,
And with all who will trust and obey.

Trust and obey,
For there's no other way
To be happy in Jesus,
But to trust and obey.

Not a shadow can rise
Not a cloud in the skies,
But His smile quickly drives it away;
Not a doubt nor a fear,
Not a sigh nor a tear,
Can abide while we trust and obey.

Not a burden we bear,
Not a sorry we share,
But our toil He doth richly repay;
Not a grief nor a loss,
Not a frown nor a cross,
But is blest if we trust and obey.

But we never can prove
The delights of His love
Until all on the altar we lay;
For the favour He shows,
And the joy He bestows
Are for them who will trust and obey.

Then in fellowship sweet
We will sit at His feet,
Or we'll walk by His side in the way
What He says we will do
Where He sends we will go
Never fear, only trust and obey.

270 Thoro Harris
Copyright © 1931 Renewed 1959 by
Nazarene Publishing House.

Who can cheer the heart like Jesus,
By His presence all divine?
True and tender, pure and precious,
O how blest to call Him mine!

All that thrills my soul is Jesus,
He is more than life to me; (to me;)
And the fairest of ten thousand,
In my blessed Lord I see.

Love of Christ so freely given,
Grace of God beyond degree,
Mercy higher than the heaven,
Deeper than the deepest sea.

What a wonderful redemption!
Never can a mortal know
How my sin, tho' red like crimson,
Can be whiter than the snow.

Ev'ry need His hand supplying,
Ev'ry good in Him I see;
On His strength divine relying,
He is all in all to me.

By the crystal flowing river
With the ransomed I will sing,
And for ever and for ever
Praise and glorify the King.

271 Benjamin Russell Hanby, 1833–67

Who is He, in yonder stall,
At whose feet the shepherds fall?

'Tis the Lord! O wondrous story!
'Tis the Lord, the King of Glory!
At His feet we humbly fall;
Crown Him, crown Him Lord of all.

Who is He, in yonder cot,
Bending to His toilsome lot?

Who is He, in deep distress,
Fasting in the wilderness?

Who is He that stands and weeps
At the grave where Lazarus sleeps?

Lo, at midnight, who is He
Prays in dark Gethsemane?

Who is He, in Calvary's throes,
Asks for blessings on His foes?

Who is He that from the grave
Comes to heal and help and save?

Who is He that from His throne
Rules through all the worlds alone?

272 Judy Horner Montemayor
Copyright © 1972 Family Crusades Inc.

Who is like unto thee,
O Lord among gods?
Who is like unto thee
Glorious in Holiness
Fearful in praises
Doing wonders
Who is like unto thee.

273 Ruth Dryden
Copyright © 1978 by Genesis Music

Within the veil I now would come,
Into the Holy Place to look upon Thy face.
I see such beauty there, no other can compare,
I worship Thee my Lord within the veil.

274 Frances Ridley Havergal 1836–79

Who is on the Lord's side?
Who will serve the King?
Who will be His helpers
Other lives to bring?
Who will leave the world's side?
Who will face the foe?
Who is on the Lord's side?
Who for Him will go?
By Thy call of mercy,
By Thy grace divine,
We are on the Lord's side;
Saviour, we are Thine.

Not for weight of glory,
Not for crown or palm,
Enter we the army,
Raise the warrior-psalm,
But for love that claimeth
Lives for whom He died
He whom Jesus nameth
Must be on His side.
By Thy love constraining,
By Thy grace divine,
We are on the Lord's side;
Saviour, we are Thine.

Fierce may be the conflict,
Strong may be the foe,
But the King's own army
None can overthrow.
Round His standard ranging,
Victory is secure,
For His truth unchanging
Makes the triumph sure.
Joyfully enlisting,
By Thy grace divine,
We are on the Lord's side;
Saviour, we are Thine.

Chosen to be soldiers
In an alien land,
Chosen, called and faithful,
For our captain's band,
In the service royal
Let us not grow cold;
Let us be right loyal,
Noble, true and bold.
Master, Thou wilt keep us,
By Thy grace divine,
Always on the Lord's side,
Saviour, always Thine.

275 Priscilla Jane Owens, 1829–99

Will your anchor hold in the storms of life,
When the clouds unfold their wings of strife?
When the strong tides lift, and the cables strain,
Will your anchor drift, or firm remain?

We have an anchor that keeps the soul
Steadfast and sure while the billows roll;
Fastened to the rock which cannot move,
Grounded firm and deep in the Saviour's love!

Will your anchor hold in the straits of fear?
When the breakers roar and the reef is near;
While the surges rage, and the wild winds
  blow,
Shall the angry waves then your bark o'erflow?

Will your anchor hold in the floods of death,
When the waters cold chill your latest breath?
On the rising tide you can never fail,
While your anchor holds within the veil.

Will your eyes behold through the morning
  light
The city of gold and the harbour bright?
Will you anchor safe by the heavenly shore,
When life's storms are past for evermore?

276 D. Richards
Copyright © 1980 Thankyou Music

Worthy art Thou, O Lord, our God, of honour
  and power,
For You are reigning now on high, Hallelujah.
Jesus is Lord of all the earth, Hallelujah,
Hallelujah, Hallelujah.

277

Yesterday, today, for ever,
Jesus is the same;
All may change, but Jesus never,
Glory to His Name! (*repeat twice*)
All may change, but Jesus never,
Glory to His Name!

278 Charles Wesley 1707–88, altd.

Ye servants of God,
Your Master proclaim,
And publish abroad
His wonderful name;
The name all-victorious
Of Jesus extol;
His kingdom is glorious,
And rules over all.

God ruleth on high,
Almighty to save;
And still He is nigh,
His presence we have;
The great congregation
His triumph shall sing,
Ascribing salvation
To Jesus our King.

"Salvation to God
Who sits on the throne",
Let all cry aloud,
And honour the Son:
The praises of Jesus
The angels proclaim,
Fall down on their faces,
And worship the Lamb.

Then let us adore,
And give Him His right –
All glory and power,
All wisdom and might:
All honour and blessing,
With angels above;
And thanks never-ceasing,
And infinite love.

279 M. Ford
Copyright © 1978 Springtide/Word
Music (UK)

You are the King of Glory,
You are the Prince of Peace,
You are the Lord of heav'n and earth,
You're the Son of righteousness.
Angels bow down before You,
Worship and adore,
For You have the words of eternal life,
You are Jesus Christ the Lord.
Hosanna to the Son of David!
Hosanna to the King of kings!
Glory in the highest heaven
For Jesus the Messiah reigns!

280 Copyright © Control

Worthy is the Lamb (*repeat three times*)

Holy is the Lamb (*repeat three times*)

Precious is the Lamb (*repeat three times*)

Praises to the Lamb. (*repeat three times*)

Glory to the Lamb. (*repeat three times*)

Jesus is our Lamb. (*repeat three times*)

281 S. Dauermann
Copyright © 1975 by Lillenas Publishing Co.

**You shall go out with joy and be led forth
with peace,**
And the mountains and the hills shall break
forth before you.
There'll be shouts of joy and the trees of the
field
Shall clap, shall clap their hands
And the trees of the field shall clap their hands,
(*repeat twice*)
And you'll go out with joy.

282 Graham Kendrick
Copyright © 1983 Thankyou Music

Led like a lamb
To the slaughter
In silence and shame
There on your back
You carried a world
Of violence and pain
Bleeding, dying (*repeat*)

  You're alive (*repeat*)
  You have risen!
  Alleluia
  And the power
  And the glory
  Is given
  Alleluia
  Jesus to you

At break of dawn
Poor Mary
Still weeping she came
When through her grief
She heard your voice
Now speaking her name
Mary, Master (*repeat*)

At the right hand
Of the Father
Now seated on high
You have begun
Your eternal reign
Of justice and joy
Glory, glory. (*repeat*)

Alternative words for:

21 B. Gillman
Copyright © 1977 Thankyou Music

  Bind us together Lord,
  Bind us together
  With cords that cannot be broken;
  Bind us together Lord,
  Bind us together
  O bind us together with love

There is only one God,
There is only one King,
There is only one Body
That is why we sing:

God has many gifts
Given by his Son –
Building the Body of Christ
Creating a faith that is one;

We are the family of God,
Joined by the Spirit above,
Working together with Christ
Growing and building in love.

Index of First Lines

Titles in italics, where different from the first line.